BAD TO THE BONE

ALSO BY STEPHEN SOLOMITA

A Twist of the Knife
Force of Nature
Forced Entry

BAD
TO THE
BONE

Stephen Solomita

G. P. PUTNAM'S SONS
New York

G. P. Putnam's Sons
Publishers Since 1838
200 Madison Avenue
New York, NY 10016

Library of Congress Cataloging-in-Publication Data
Solomita, Stephen.
    Bad to the bone / Stephen Solomita.
        p.   cm.
    ISBN 0-399-13593-6
    I. Title.
    PS3569.O587B33   1991   90-22611   CIP
    813'.54—dc20

Printed in the United States of America

1   2   3   4   5   6   7   8   9   10

for Susan
my sister, my friend

Have to thank some people. As usual. Ken Inglima for the chemistry lessons and for his patience in the face of willful scientific illiteracy. N. D. Wruble for the info on tox screens. My aunt and uncle, Grace and Al, for the Italian lessons. And Judy Appello, intrepid researcher. Without Judy, I might actually have to work for a living.

This is a work of fiction. Despite the fact that designer drugs have been created in the past and continue to be created. For instance, even though the overall chemical strategy described in this novel is accurate, any actual formula is more likely to make chicken soup than super dope. A word to the wiseguy.

ONE

The afternoon traffic outside the small Eighth Avenue bar, the Blue Rose, where Flo Alamare waited patiently (in direct contrast to the truckers and cabbies out on the street), was backed up from 34th Street down into Chelsea. The root cause of the heavy traffic, on this particular day, lay within Flo Alamare's view—two dozen buses, triple-parked in front of Madison Square Garden, were trying to load a thousand Bronx grammar school students. After three hours of the Ringling Brothers Barnum and Bailey Circus, the kids were enormously excited and the raised voices of exhausted teachers, desperately trying to keep order, complemented the shouts of the children and the blaring horns of frustrated drivers. It was a situation familiar to the teachers, of course, a situation which continually threatened to descend into chaos as some of the more adventurous children cartwheeled down Eighth Avenue.

Inside the Blue Rose bar, the shrieking horns formed a riotous counterpoint to the frenetic salsa pouring from an enormous jukebox. The Blue Rose was a Latino neighborhood bar at night and a haven for local alcoholics during the day. The owner, Henry Martinez, working behind the bar, was used to the horns and the salsa. He understood himself as a businessman and was only interested in filling his customers' needs. The dirt and the noise (he'd decided long ago) was exactly what they needed. Just like they needed the cigarette-scarred bar, the mismatched ashtrays and the dusty bags of pretzels.

He poured an inch of Canadian Club into a small tumbler. Like most bartenders, he knew that his livelihood depended on staying sober enough to collect and count the money coming across the bar. He also knew that his sanity depended on staying just high enough to ignore the depressing, ultimately boring misery that haunted his afternoons. Just high enough to shrug and say "okay" when one of the drunks puked on the floor or pushed a glass into his neighbor's face.

"Bartender?"

Henry Martinez turned to the woman (*la* bitch *blanquita* was the name he'd given her when she first walked through the door) sitting on the stool closest to the window. She presented him with a smooth, white profile framed by shoulder-length black hair, an indifferent profile as cold as her ice-blue suit and white-on-white silk blouse.

"Wha' you wan'?" he asked, glancing toward the other patrons. *La* bitch *blanquita* wasn't the only female in the Blue Rose. Carla Santa Cruz was there, too, all three hundred pounds of her squashed into a booth near the smelly toilet. Carla had been wearing the same clothes for three days and looked more like a pile of wet laundry than a human.

"A Coke." The *blanquita* was looking out the window, as serene and confident as if she'd just stepped up to the bar at the Plaza.

Henry decided to make a joke. "A cocaine?" he asked. "We don' got no cocaine."

"Coca-Cola."

She corrected him without turning her head, and he decided he didn't give a shit whether she was a paying customer or not. He poured her a foamy Coke and took it the length of the bar with every intention of slopping it all over that blue dress. But then she opened her purse to get money to pay him and he looked inside and saw a .38 caliber Smith & Wesson lightweight nestled between her lipstick and her Kleenex.

He was so surprised he stood there with the Coke in his hand, staring into her purse like he couldn't figure out what he was looking at. "Wha'?" he said, then repeated himself. "Wha'?"

He looked up to find *la* bitch *blanquita* offering him a five-dollar bill. Her eyes reached out for his and held him while she communicated her amusement. Her mouth said, "Keep the change," but her eyes were calling him a stupid, insignificant drunk. A man dead to everything except the dirty glasses and human garbage contained by the walls of the Blue Rose.

"*Gracias*," Henry Martinez said, backing toward the register as the woman turned to the window again. "*Gracias*." A few minutes later, as she was leaving, he nodded and whispered it again. *Gracias. Gracias.*

Henry Martinez was wrong about Flo Alamare. She was much too purposeful to bother with Henry Martinez's ego (which was an insult all by itself). She'd only come into the Blue Rose because she needed a clear view of the southwestern corner of Madison Square Garden. That's where the school kids (who got the crummy seats in the upper balcony) would come out. She'd known, of course, that Henry Martinez was about to bust her chops—the smug, male triumph came off him like the stink of the Blue Rose itself. But his discomfort wouldn't feed the source of her power. If there was anything to be learned from the years of submission, it was the relationship between obedience and obligation. They were wound about each other like the two snakes on the caduceus and translated themselves into commitment (not submission) to the will of Davis Craddock.

Flo closed her eyes briefly, enjoying the wave of sensation coursing through her body. The trucks, the horns, the cursing cabbies, the sharp stink of diesel exhaust—the city tingled beneath her skin, as smoothly sensual as a warm ocean breeze. When she opened her eyes to see the little girl with the two red ribbons, she wasn't surprised. She crossed the street quickly, a kind smile pulling up the corners of her mouth, and waved, catching the girl's attention.

"Auntie Flo," the girl, Terry, cried in surprise. "Auntie Flo," she repeated, throwing herself into Flo Alamare's arms.

Marsha Goldstein, Terry Williams' fourth-grade teacher, smiled indulgently. She was standing by the door of Bus 18, counting the kids as they boarded. It was the last important task of a hectic day, and she was anxious to get through it.

"What are you doing here?" Terry asked frankly. All the children had been taught to be direct, and Terry had been one of the brightest.

"Your daddy's going to be a little late," Flo said. "I told him I had an appointment in midtown, and he asked me to pick you up. I'm very glad to see you again."

Flo glanced at Marsha Goldstein (remembering to smile with her eyes as well as her mouth) and the teacher smiled back, nodding her agreement.

"Let's go out for ice cream sodas," Flo said. She stretched out her hand and the child took it without hesitation.

"Why did Daddy make me leave Hanover House? He says I can't go there ever again. Does he really mean it?"

Flo glanced back casually. They were standing at the corner, waiting for the light to change, and she wanted to make sure the teacher hadn't heard. She needn't have worried. Marsha Goldstein, having completed her count, was already stepping onto the bus.

Twenty minutes later, Flo and Terry were driving up Amsterdam Avenue toward 125th Street. Terry lived in the eastern part of the Bronx, in Throgs Neck, a neighborhood of single- and two-family homes with an occasional low-rise apartment building on the main avenues. The houses were not ostentatious, but the blue-collar, mostly Italian whites who dominated the neighborhood worked on their small yards every weekend. Their homes were as important to their collective golden years as their pensions, and neighborly conversations about property value had the same emotional impact as patriotism at a defense plant.

They found a neighborhood candy store on Eastchester Road near

Pelham Parkway and ordered chocolate ice cream sodas. Terry wanted to know everything about her old buddies, especially Flo's son, Michael, who used to be her best friend. She ticked their names off, one after another, and Flo provided the information as best she could. Flo was Terry's bonding mother; she'd been freely chosen from all the women in Hanover House. Hanover House was the place of Terry's birth, the only home she'd ever known until her father pulled her out. Now she was having problems with the neighborhood children.

"The other kids don't like me," she explained seriously. "They only have *one* mother and *one* father, and they hit each other *all* the time. They say I'm a dork."

"Did you tell Billy about it?" Billy was her father's name.

"I used to tell him, but he gets very sad. I think he's having trouble at work." She made a wry face, working her mouth into a thin semicircle. Terry had barely known her father when they were living in Hanover House, but the courts had given him custody after her mother's death. "Do you think Billy means what he says? Do you think he'll let me go back?"

Flo smiled her most loving smile, the one she'd worked years to perfect. She felt a confidence that bordered on ecstasy. Energy surged through her, yet her mind remained clear and serene. "That's just what I want to talk to him about. About sending you for a visit."

They walked back to the small van with Terry beaming at the prospect of seeing her old friends again. Flo returned the child's warmth, thinking how much she really did like little Terry. "Do you want to play a game?" she asked the child.

"Okay."

Flo opened the rear door instead of the passenger's door and hustled the child into the back, climbing in after her. There was only one window in the side of the van, a convex bubble tinted a deep gray. The third row of seats had been removed and a thick lambskin rug lay across the metal floor.

"Let's make Billy a nice surprise," Flo said. "Maybe he'll change his mind, if we give him a nice surprise."

"Okay, what'll we do?"

"Remember how we used to paint clown faces on the kids?"

"When we did the shows?"

"That's right. Do you remember the makeup we used? What was it called?"

"Theatrical makeup." Terry's voice was just a touch contemptuous. How could Auntie Flo think she wouldn't remember something so important? "Are you gonna paint me like a clown? Is that the surprise?"

"I'm going to paint a special design on your forehead. An old Indian sign. It means 'I love you' in Indian sign language. Maybe when Billy sees it, he'll change his mind and let you visit us."

Flo worked quickly. She didn't want Terry to be so late that her father felt obliged to call the police. Billy would know what had happened to his daughter as soon as he spoke to the teacher. It had happened often enough in the past. Children didn't leave Hanover House because children were, after all, the ultimate insurance policies.

Flo drew a large white circle on Terry's forehead and quickly filled it in. A smaller yellow circle followed, at the center of the white circle. Then four lines, two vertical and two horizontal, from the outer edge of the white circle to the outer edge of the yellow. The project took only five minutes to complete and was instantly recognizable for what it was—the crosshairs of a telescopic sight locked onto a bull's eye.

Billy Williams, Terry's father, knew the symbol immediately. His knees buckled when he opened the door to find his daughter standing next to Flo Alamare. "Oh," he whispered, a thin, hopeless cry. "Oh."

"See, Auntie Flo," Terry cried. "I knew he wouldn't like it. He doesn't like anything I do. Please take me back home with you."

Terry began to cry softly, and her father's spirits dropped even further. His shoulders slumped and he lowered his eyes. Flo, who'd been trained to observe the spaces where humans express their real feelings (even when they were *trying* to hide their intentions) had no trouble interpreting Billy's message.

"Why don't you go to your room and let me talk to Billy for a while?" Flo put her arm around the child and pulled her close for a moment. "Don't worry," she said, kissing Terry's forehead. "I think we'll be able to work it out. Okay?"

Flo watched Terry walk into her room, waiting until the door shut before turning back to Billy. "Close the front door and come into the living room."

She knew he'd obey—he was too far down to rebel. Her sharp command was designed to show him that she was aware of his emotional state. He followed dutifully, sitting upright on a straight-backed chair while she settled into a cushioned rocker. The living room was almost barren, a clear indication to Flo of Billy's struggle to establish a new life after a decade at Hanover House.

"I don't believe you'd hurt Terry," Billy protested. He did not raise his eyes to meet Flo's. "You were Terry's bonding mother."

For the first time, Flo felt a slight twinge of anxiety. A gentle reminder of an appointment that would have to be kept. Of what might lie on the other side of ecstasy. "What *I* would or wouldn't do is quite

irrelevant here. Davis makes his own decisions. He's made one already.
He wants Terry back at Hanover House."

"She's my daughter."

"You hardly knew her."

"That wasn't my fault, Flo, I . . ."

"That's the fact, no matter whose fault it was. You hardly knew her
then. You hardly know her now. You want to construct a life for
yourself, but you have no experience at independence. You stayed with
your mommy and daddy until you were thirty, then went directly to
Hanover House. Now you're forty years old and you don't have the
faintest fucking idea how to begin living on your own. That's why you
dragged Terry along when you abandoned us. That's why you spoke to
a lawyer and that's why you're speaking to a writer about doing a
book."

"You know about that?" Billy's voice was filled with wonder. "That
means John Burke told you. John is my best friend."

"Have you picked a title for the book yet?" Flo ignored his comment.
"Maybe *Cult of the Hanoverians*? Or *Davis Craddock Stole My Daughter*?
Yes, by all means put the name of Davis Craddock on the cover. Betray
everything and everybody. You'll probably make a fortune. You'll
probably get rich." She was standing, seeming to tower over Billy
Williams, who held onto the seat of his chair as if he was about to fly
away.

"Flo, I never . . ."

She let her voice go street hard, not bothering with finesse, like a
whaler firing a harpoon into the head of an injured whale. "Don't
bullshit me, Billy. When you left Hanover House, you swore you'd
never betray our way of life to the outside world. You're going to keep
your word, whether you like it or not. First, Terry comes back to us,
where she belongs. You personally deliver her. You knock on the door
and hand her over. Then you go back to your piece-of-shit job, instead
of trying to get rich by betraying Davis Craddock."

"For God's sake, Flo. She's my child. You can't take a child away
from her father. I'll forget the book, but please let me keep my daughter."

He was begging now. There was nothing more to be done. Flo
turned away, delivering her final lines as she walked through the door
and into the street. "No more talk, Billy. Two days is what you've got.
Go take a look at your daughter. Then look in the mirror. See if you've
got the Indian love sign on your *own* forehead."

She was driving alongside the Bruckner Expressway when the need
overcame her. It'd been washing back and forth like a toothache about

to explode since she'd walked into Billy's apartment. She'd hoped that she could make it back to the privacy of Hanover House before she attended to her need, but that was clearly impossible. She pulled the van to the curb, locking the front doors, then opened the glove compartment, reaching inside only to burn the backs of her fingers on the small lightbulb.

"Damn." She sucked at the reddened area absently, then decided that the van must have some kind of an electrical short. Instead of coming on when the glove compartment was opened, the bulb was staying lit all the time. She always kept the van in perfect condition (that was part of overcoming the carelessness that had characterized her life before she'd met Davis Craddock), and she resolved to fix it as soon as she got back to Hanover House. In the meantime, she removed the small bulb, carefully wrapping her fingers in Kleenex tissue before sliding the bulb from its socket. Then she took the syringe, still warm in its black plastic wrapper, and moved to the back of the van.

In some ways, the rush of anticipation was better than the rush of the drug that Davis Craddock called PURE. There was a fear, like a memory, that always managed to push its way into Flo Alamare's consciousness before she injected herself. It whispered of what might follow in a few hours if . . . The fear didn't vanish when she took the full syringe into her hand, but the certainty of relief transformed it into a physical tingling, into what could only be called arousal. Flo felt it in her breasts and her groin as she wrapped her arm with a piece of rubber tubing.

Alternately closing and opening her fingers, pumping the veins up, she examined herself closely. Her arms had remained practically smooth, as Craddock assured her they would. Hanoverian Therapists always used clean syringes and unadulterated drugs, carefully moving the site of their injections *before* veins were damaged. The end result was entirely predictable—whereas street junkies suffered every kind of infection, from a simple abscess to full-blown AIDS, Hanoverians radiated health.

The 25-gauge needle slid easily into the vein running along the outside of Flo Alamare's wrist. With a small sigh, she pulled back on the syringe, drawing a single drop of blood into Davis Craddock's PURE, then pushed down on the plunger. She felt the expected rush of pleasure for a second, but then her universe turned upside down. The ecstasy became a sharp pain which began to burn, hotter and hotter, as it ran through her body. She felt it surge up through her spine and instinctively tried to close her brain off, to confine the agony to her body, to keep her mind alive.

TWO

Jim Tilley was late for the celebration, but neither Jim's wife, Rose, nor their guests, Stanley Moodrow and Betty Haluka, were waiting to begin the party. Jim Tilley was a New York City cop. His time belonged to the NYPD and the two friends sitting comfortably in Rose and Jim's living room were well aware of it.

"It's cop macho," Moodrow explained to Rose and Betty. "Sleeping in the station house. Drinking fifteen cups of coffee a day. Wearing the same clothes. Detectives brag about it in the bars. Even if you *know* it's a lotta crap, you still have to do it. Backing away from a hot investigation is like backing away from a suspect on the street."

"Actually, there isn't any hot investigation," Rose said. "Jim was only supposed to go in for a few hours to prepare some evidence for trial. They've got him doing paperwork."

They went on this way for a long time (well into their second drink) before Jim Tilley made a weary appearance. He managed to greet his stepchildren, Lee and Jeanette, as he came down the hallway into the living room, but then sank into a chair and began to rub at reddened eyes with both fists. Rose, who would have liked a hug, settled for a quick peck on the cheek before heading into the kitchen to give a bowl of Irish stew the three-minute, microwave special. Moodrow had called for the impromptu party (the friends were close enough to call and enjoy spur of the moment parties), but he knew that Tilley would have to unburden himself before the celebration could proceed. He settled back in his chair and took a healthy pull at a glass of Wild Turkey bourbon. Maybe Tilley's story would be a good one.

"Rose told us you were only going in for a short time," Betty said. "If we'd have known you were going to work twelve straight hours, we'd have had our celebration tomorrow night. There's really not that much to making a firm decision *not* to live together, anyway."

Tilley looked up and shrugged. "I should have stayed on patrol. I love the gold shield, but I definitely should've stayed on patrol."

"How'd you get so dirty?" Moodrow asked. "Didn't I teach you to make the uniforms do the dirty work?"

Jim Tilley, much to Betty's surprise, took the question seriously. "The precinct's supposed to be cleaned every night," he responded, "but whatever dirt there is, I was under it all afternoon."

Moodrow looked for a sign that his friend was able to joke about his day, but Jim Tilley was obviously weary. His ordinarily handsome Irish face was pinched and anxious. He looked, to Moodrow, like an aging parish priest. "You wanna take a hit on this before you tell the story?" Moodrow continued. He offered his bourbon, but Tilley drew back in disgust, reaching instead for his wife's bloody mary which he drained at a gulp. Betty, who'd been sipping at her own bloody mary, tried to stop him, but she was on her second drink and just a little too slow. At first Tilley had no reaction, but then a tear began to blossom in the corner of his right eye. It grew until his eye couldn't hold it anymore, then rolled down his cheek, only to be followed by another and another and another.

"Holy shit," he cried, desperately pressing a cocktail napkin against the stream of mucus issuing from both nostrils. "Who made this drink?"

Betty grinned. "I did. Stanley calls them 'Bloody Bettys.' "

"It's very hot. Do you always make it this hot?"

"I use cayenne and horseradish. The horseradish makes it chewy."

"You look like Dracula," Moodrow observed, sipping at his rejected bourbon. "In that movie with Frank Langella. Remember? His eyes got bright red before he bit people."

Tilley had nothing to say in return, but his anxiety was slowly disappearing as the Stolichnaya (almost two ounces) made the jump from his belly to his blood stream. His eyes continued to tear, of course, but he no longer cared.

"I feel like a dumb animal beaten into submission," he declared. "The goddamn job is like being in the army. It's a military organization. The assholes at the top say 'jump,' and if you don't get your feet off the ground, they put you in front of a firing squad."

"This is a shock?" Moodrow asked pleasantly. "Being a cop *is* like being a soldier. So take a lesson. A sergeant in the army knows he can't confront the system head-on, no matter how much he hates it. So he learns to manipulate it. He squeezes it for whatever juice it's got to give."

"Well, today the system squeezed me," Tilley said. "This was supposed to be a nothing day for me and, instead, I got turned into orange juice."

Rose came back into the room, bearing a plate of Irish stew, a fork, a napkin and an unspiced red drink that looked just like a bloody mary. "How did it get so screwed up?"

Having found a sympathetic audience (and a second drink), Tilley began to unburden himself. He and his team were near the end of a year-long attempted-murder investigation involving a crack dealer with a long string of priors. The case was straightforward: the dealer, Ernesto 'Babu' Fariello, identified by a witness, had been arrested an hour after the shooting with a 9mm in his belt. Ballistics, upon comparing the patterns of lands and grooves in slugs found at the scene with slugs fired through Babu's weapon, had sealed Fariello's fate. There was no need for eyewitnesses—they might get a conviction even if the *victim* failed to show up. Nor would witnesses be needed for a second group of felonies that fell into their laps: Tilley and another Detective had tossed Babu's apartment after the arrest and discovered three and a half ounces of cocaine, along with the paraphernalia needed to turn it into crack.

"We're gonna go before the judge tomorrow," Tilley complained, "and the Lieutenant asked me to make sure the chain was intact, which is a sign of favor in the job . . ."

"What chain?" Rose asked.

"The chain of evidence. That's what I'm leading up to. See, the only evidence that matters here is the gun."

"What about the cocaine?"

"No gun, then no probable cause to enter the mutt's apartment, *capisch?*" Tilley noted Betty Haluka's confirming nod. Betty was a Legal Aid lawyer and knew everything there was to know about 'probable cause.' "Mostly it's just a routine job. You trace the route of the evidence, from first contact into the courtroom. First contact was the witness giving us the perp's name. This we have on a sworn statement, which I locate in the file. It's also in the grand jury transcripts. Then me and Joe Baker took the gun off the perp and brought it into the house, so I go back in the file and find the original complaint form and the follow-ups. Both me and my partner, on the day we made the bust, recorded the circumstances in writing, like we're supposed to. The 9mm is in the report, along with a serial number and a note that Joe is gonna take the piece down to the property clerk's room and make a request for a laboratory examination. I go back in the file and find copies of the property clerk's invoice and the lab request form. The ballistic report is also in the file, along with a letter of transmittal from ballistics to the property clerk at the courthouse which means it's up to the district attorney to get the physical gun into the courtroom. Sounds perfect, right?"

"A hundred percent," Betty assured him. "If Fariello was my client, I'd advise him to plead."

Tilley grinned as he lifted his drink to his lips and carefully sipped. "Now there's only one more thing I need to complete the file before I take it over to the district attorney's office where I already have an appointment with an assistant DA. This isn't a trial, by the way. This is a hearing on the evidence and if we don't get the gun admitted, the perp's lawyer will ask for a dismissal and probably get it. So, like I said, there's only one more thing I need to complete the file and seal the mutt's fate and that's the original of the property clerk's invoice, which is why I hustle on down to the property clerk's room and ask the property clerk, Sergeant Joseph Blatt, who happens to be the *only* Jewish alcoholic in the NYPD, for the original. I even give him my receipt with all the numbers right on it."

"And he can't find it," Moodrow said brightly. "Surprise, surprise."

"Shit," Jim shook his head. "You think they screw it up this bad in the real world?"

"How would we know?" Rose observed. "We never worked in the real world. We always worked for the city."

Tilley, his question having been purely rhetorical, ignored her comment. "Well, Blatt doesn't have the property clerk's invoice. Those invoices are numbered consecutively and cross-referenced by complaint number and Blotto Blatt has numbers 55432 and 55434, but no 55433. At first he says he never filled out the form, that I'm crazy, so I remind him that I have the investigator's flimsy in my hand and that he signed it and that if he doesn't cooperate I'm gonna beat the fuck out of him."

"Wrong move," Moodrow observed neutrally. Nourished by the company of his friends and the bourbon in his bloodstream, he could afford to be philosophical. "I worked with Blotto Blatt for twenty-five years. The schmuck's been pushed so far back in the job, he's practically invisible. I got fifty bucks sayin' that he offered to meet you any time, any place."

"That's exactly right."

"Did he mean it?" Betty asked.

Tilley shrugged. He'd been a fighter, professional and amateur, for years. Everybody in the room knew he could tear Blotto Blatt to pieces. "Drunks mean everything they say, but the guy's a wreck. On slow tours, he sneaks into the back of the property room and drinks until he's unconscious. No, there was nothing I could do to the schmuck and by the time I figured it out, he was pissed off and wouldn't help at all. I had to go through every piece of evidence stored in the property room with the lieutenant blowing fire down my neck like a goddamned dragon."

"How could he blame you?" Rose Tilley laid a protective arm across her husband's shoulders, despite the fact that Jim Tilley, finishing his second bloody mary, was feeling no pain whatsoever.

"All the lieutenant knows is that a big collar is going down the toilet and there's no point in blaming Blotto Blatt, because Blatt is too blotto to give a damn. Which leaves me. I swear I went through everything in the goddamned precinct. Boxes, envelopes, bags . . . I saw shit from 1952. I saw bags of dope which aren't even supposed to be kept in a precinct anymore. I found jewelry from burglaries that should have been turned back to the victims. And every inch of it was covered with this fine dusty powder. It came off the crap in clouds and I breathed it until my spit turned black. Then, after I was ninety percent finished and totally filthy, the lieutenant gets a call from the assistant district attorney, a lady named Connie Helprin, who told us hours ago that she'd searched through every scrap of paper in her case file and the original was not in her possession. Now she says she just found it. She says it was stuck to the back of the request for laboratory analysis. Blatt must've sent both over when the gun went to ballistics."

"Did the lieutenant apologize?" Betty asked naively.

"The lieutenant said, 'I knew it had to be somewhere.' Then he went home." Tilley broke out laughing and, after a brief hesitation, his friends joined in.

"I have to admit I'm ashamed," Betty declared. "All these years I've been playing a game called 'pound the paralegals.' That's what lawyers do when something goes wrong with the paperwork."

"Businessmen play 'smack the secretary,' " Rose chimed in. "In fact that's the way the whole world runs. One monkey biting the other."

"It's not the same," Tilley insisted. "A secretary could always quit and find another job."

"So can a cop," Rose quietly observed. Jim had been seriously considering the possibility of leaving the NYPD for more than a year.

"And do what?" Like all cops, Tilley believed that the meaning of the job and a cop's relationship to that meaning, cannot be communicated to civilians. "So tell me, Betty," he changed the subject. "What are we celebrating?"

Betty raised her glass solemnly. "After three weeks of intense cohabitation following the devastating fire in Stanley Moodrow's apartment, Stanley Moodrow and Betty Haluka, for the sake of their loving and tender relationship, have decided to dwell apart. Stanley's going to move out as soon as he can find a place to live."

"Does that mean you're officially homeless?" Rose asked.

"It's not that funny," Moodrow said. "Because a lot of homeless people start off with a burn-out. My building is old, like all the buildings on the Lower East Side, and rats live in the walls, like they do in most tenements. The fire marshall says one of them ate the wiring. He says they got his rat body in a plastic bag. I swear; I'm not bullshitting. His tail is curled up in a little circle. What I think I should've done is leave more garbage around, so the rat wouldn't have had to eat electricity."

"Isn't the landlord going to fix the place up?"

"He says he's gonna make repairs, but nothing happens." Moodrow looked over at Rose and Betty, realizing just how much he loved these women. Rose's face was model-perfect: small bowed mouth; dark, widely spaced eyes; jet-black hair framing soft, milky cheeks. Betty was heavier, with a strong nose and stronger jaw. Her face spoke of character, while Rose seemed every inch the spoiled princess. Of course, reality, as cops inevitably discover, rarely follows appearance. Betty had grown up in the safety of a middle-class home in Forest Hills while Rose had been severely abused for more than a decade. "I tell ya the truth, boys, I'm starting to get a little scared. I know that Betty's right, that we're both crazy and it's important that we should live in different institutions, but the cost of apartments is kicking my butt. I thought I had connections, but the only cheap places (and there aren't many of them) are in buildings that scare the crap out of *me*. The best thing I could find is a sublet in a yuppie co-op for thirteen hundred a month and..."

"This is called *kvetching* in Yiddish," Betty interrupted, squeezing Moodrow's hand. "Until I met Stanley, I didn't think a Gentile could master it."

"Damn," Moodrow complained, "if you can't whine to your friends, who can you whine to?"

"Are you telling me that thirteen hundred's gonna bankrupt you?" Tilley said. "I always thought you were rich."

"Yeah? Up till now I've been payin' five bills a month, rent controlled. Now I gotta cough up thirteen. That comes out to nearly ten thousand dollars a year extra. Plus Betty's Honda went into the tank, and I can't get around by the subway unless I confine my life to Manhattan. You know how much they want for a new car? I'm screwin' around with an old friend of mine who sells cars off the street, but a junker that doesn't wanna start can make your life miserable. Also the second bedroom is a closet. It's not big enough for the work I'm doing and I'm probably gonna have to rent an office. I thought when I got my pension, I was made for life, but everything keeps going up. Including all the crap I lost in the fire. Maybe I can live with my old furniture once the smell disappears, but I gotta replace everything else, including my wardrobe..."

"What about Social Security?" Tilley interrupted, grinning. "That should kick in any day now."

"Stanley's not eligible for Social Security," Betty said.

"Stanley will *never* be eligible for Social Security," Moodrow grunted. "And the next detective third-grade who brings it up is gonna have to have Stanley's size thirteen pulled out of his ass."

"You know what your problem is?" Tilley asked. "You're too sensitive. You need a job."

"You think I'm not working now? I'm out there every day."

"Working for nothing is not the same as working," Rose said. "It doesn't drive you the same way."

Betty nodded in agreement. "Ever since you stopped being a public cop and became a private cop, you've been working for friends and relatives. Being a crusader may be good for the soul, but it's tough on the checkbook. You're gonna have to take some paying jobs."

"And what if the people who need my services can't afford to pay me?"

"Balance it out. Take some *pro bono* work. I've been doing that all through my career." Betty snuggled up close to her lover. It was a warm, dry April evening, a rarity in New York. The windows were open and the sounds of the Lower East Side drifted up to the two couples. One of the things Betty liked about Moodrow was the feeling of safety that went hand in hand with his presence. Nothing could hurt her—not the muggers or the rapists or dealers or the addicts. "Even a crappy lawyer can make more in private practice or in a big law office than I made at Legal Aid, but when I graduated from law school, I wanted to do something good for people. Legal Aid gave me a chance to accomplish my aim without starving."

"Well, I don't know about any Legal Aid for retired cops, but it looks like I'm gonna take a paying job. I got a call this afternoon from a woman named Connie Alamare. You know the Hanoverians, Jim?"

"Down on Ludlow Street, by Canal, right? The cult."

"Yeah, that's them." Moodrow picked absently at a tray of provolone cheese and chunks of Genoa salami rolled in pickled peppers. "What do you hear about them?"

Tilley laughed shortly. "From a police point of view, they couldn't be better. I don't know how many cults we have down here. At least a dozen. Most of them are religious, like the Hare Krishnas or the Transcendental Church of Jesus. I think the Hanoverians are based on some kind of psychology, but I couldn't swear to it. We don't hear much about them down in the Seven."

"That's because they don't recruit on the street. Most of the members are middle class. They come to the Hanoverians for therapy and get sucked in. At least that's what Connie Alamare claims. She says her daughter, Florence, moved into the commune ten years ago, then cut off relations with the family except for an occasional postcard. Connie Alamare kept trying to reach her daughter, but there was nothing until about three years ago. Florence sent Connie a snapshot of a son Connie didn't know about. The kid was about two, and Connie started hoping for a reconciliation. Then the daughter disappeared altogether until six weeks ago when she was found in a lot in the Bronx. She apparently suffered some kind of a stroke and doesn't communicate. Now Connie wants to find out what happened. She says she blames this cult for her daughter's condition and she wants revenge and custody of her grandson. She also says she doesn't care what it costs."

"Stanley, you dog," Betty cried, "you didn't tell me about this."

"I was savin' it for a surprise."

"I know who the Hanoverians are," Rose said. "I remember an article in the *Voice* about the Hanoverians. They were involved in a custody battle and I think there were accusations about threats of violence."

"I'm surprised to hear that," Jim said, "because they have a reputation for being clean. There's more drugs in some of the communes down here than on the street, but the Hanoverians are supposed to be above that."

Moodrow broke in with a smile. "Isn't it interesting that I spent thirty-five years working in this precinct, Rose has been living here for more than a decade, Jim's currently a detective in the Seven, but none of us knows a goddamned thing about a commune with at least two hundred people in it? Now I have another surprise. Ten minutes after I hang up on Connie Alamare, I get a call from Franklyn Goobe."

"The chief of detectives?" Tilley whistled his appreciation. Goobe's nickname, in the job, was 'Silk of All Silks.' He was the ultimate unapproachable, as far removed from the main ranks of detectives as General Eisenhower from G.I. Joe.

"Yeah," Moodrow responded nonchalantly. "That's the way he is now, but I knew Goobe when he was coming up in the job. We never got along. I coulda lived on his monthly bill for hair spray. I think he would've liked to bust me back to patrol, but he was a practical man, like all politicians. He knew I was good and he liked to use me when he had business in the Seven, so he settled for making my life miserable in little ways. Anybody want another drink?"

Moodrow, holding his empty glass aloft, started to get up, but Rose pressed him back into the sofa. "Stay put," she ordered, "and finish the story."

"Well, apparently the cops did some kind of investigation into Florence Alamare's physical condition without turning anything up. The suits are claiming natural causes. A seizure or something like that, but the old lady won't let it rest. She's got a lot of money and she used her lawyer to climb through the ranks until she found the ultimate buck-stopper, Franklyn Goobe. Then she started calling him every day, busting his chops, until he couldn't take it anymore. That's what he said. He called up to congratulate me on my new client and to give me the name of some hairbag in the Four One who's supposed to help me 'coordinate' the investigation."

Nobody said anything for a minute, then Jim Tilley spoke for all of them. "Stanley, are you sure you wanna get involved in this?"

"What am I gonna do? I gotta eat, right? I gotta pay the rent. And the insurance on the car. And all the rest of it. What I'm saying is for the kind of money she's willing to pay, I at least have to go talk to her."

THREE

from *The Autobiography of Davis Craddock*

I remember the day of my liberation—a rainy November afternoon—as if it were yesterday. I was late and wet and Marilyn was telling me, for the umpteenth time, about the uselessness of guilt.

(If she'd known what I had to feel guilty *about*, she might not have been so cavalier, but she liked to interact even then: a matter of ego, take my word for it.)

Suddenly, unexpectedly (and for reasons I've never understood), I simply believed her and the guilt came off like my wet overcoat in the waiting room a few moments before. My sense of it was physical. I *heard* it come off. It fled like a vampire at the approach of day.

Then the session was over and I was walking toward the subway. The rain splattered on my jacket, soaking it (and me) again. I ignored the cold because I knew that underneath the guilt lay freedom. Not, as Marilyn insisted, conscience.

I argued about it with Marilyn later on. I told her that I never had much guilt anyway. What she called guilt, I experienced as confusion. "What you gave me," I told her, "was clarity."

Marilyn thought I was kidding.

The two most significant events of my distinguished career occurred on the same day in November of 1978. First, the news about Jonestown began to come through. Just the death of the congressman and what looked like a massacre, in the beginning. Then, little by little, the *voluntary* nature of the slaughter.

The second event, the catalyst which caused a series of unrelated ideas to coalesce, was a simple nature documentary which I happened to watch on the TV of a chemistry student I was tutoring. The film (I never did get the name of it) was about lions.

For the first twenty minutes, it was a typically humanized narrative. Cubs biting daddies' tails. Mommies nursing cubs. Daddies and mommies courting without actually fucking. Not as deadly as Walt Disney running film backward and forward to make the animals dance, but weak enough, except for the obligatory hunting scene.

The obligatory hunting scene was exceptionally graphic. (In stark contrast to the mating scene.) The filmmaker was attempting to prove that lions kill by strangulation and not by tearing their prey apart, so he ran the kill footage in extreme slow motion.

After a short chase, one lioness anchored a wildebeest by sinking her claws into its hindquarters and pulling downward. A second lioness clamped its jaws around the bottom of the wildebeest's throat. She, too, hung on.

It took a long time for the wildebeest to die. The animal remained standing throughout much of the ordeal. It made occasional running motions with one of its legs, but couldn't move because the lionesses were too heavy. Toward the end of the struggle, the filmmaker zoomed in on the lioness who had her teeth sunk into the wildebeest's throat. Her jaws moved continually as she fought for a deeper hold. In the final moments a trickle of the wildebeest's blood became an unbroken stream—it ran over the jaws of the lioness and into her mouth.

My student's siblings shouted the appropriate, "Oh, gross!" The adults (including myself) chuckled indulgently. The wildebeest collapsed and died.

I began to turn away from the screen, but the lioness did something wholly unexpected. It licked the carcass several times before it began to feed. Like a child licking an ice cream bar.

Nobody else noticed. Of course. But the implications were at once clear and profound. Far from distasteful, the blood running into the mouth of the lioness was like nectar into the mouth of a butterfly. Moreover, the lioness hunted every day in order to feed herself and the pride. She was familiar with every aspect of killing and she found it unutterably sweet.

A few minutes later the conversation turned to the Jonestown massacre. The first live footage had appeared on the evening news. It consisted entirely of slow pans across the bodies with appropriate pauses to show dead babies cradled in their dead mothers' arms. To me, the gas-swollen bodies resembled the puffy balloons in the Macy's Thanksgiving parade.

The narrator kept up a running commentary, assuring viewers that armed men had forced the Jonestown residents to feed cyanide-laced Kool-Aid to their children. Yet these same armed guards had, with only a few exceptions, eventually put down their rifles and swallowed the lethal dose.

My student (a master of the obvious) said, "How could anyone do that? *I* would have tried to kill the guards. If I was gonna die anyway, I would have at least tried to take one of them with me."

Humans love to go on about themselves, but the truth was that my student had no idea how he'd react to the offered cup of Kool-Aid. How could he? Nevertheless, he continued to boast to his parents and they nodded wisely. For myself, I kept out of the conversation because my own thoughts were going in a different direction.

I was watching my student closely. He believed his own boast. Perhaps he *would* fight if faced with death. My own experience is that most humans go like frightened sheep. They beg and they cry, their bladders (and sometimes their bowels) emptying convulsively.

But I *have* known people who struggled right up to the end. Looking for a way to escape or kicking out in rage. I know such people exist.

I excused myself and left my student's apartment, but I didn't take the subway uptown. A series of questions, a precursor of some deep understanding, so dominated my attention that I ignored everything else. Why were there no fighters in Jonestown? Why was there no sign of struggle or rebellion? Did this collection of sheep come to the Reverend Jones with its wool sheared? Or had some arrived as lions and been gradually reduced to lambhood? Did Jones deliberately design his 'message' to attract the sort of humans who would take the cup of Kool-Aid? Or is submission an inevitable part of the religious experience? And what, precisely, *are* the conditions for 'obedience unto death'?

In the suburban neighborhood where I grew up in the 1950s, those families who owned dogs let them out to run freely. I never knew these dogs to cause any trouble to humans. They sometimes fought among themselves, but most often the stronger dog would simply growl and the weaker would slink away. My own dog, King, was the king of the neighborhood. He was a malamute and dead game with other dogs. King didn't get into many fights, but the ones he got into were usually intense.

Poochie lived at the other end of the heap. He was a small mongrel with short yellow hair and a tiny tail that curled as tightly as a pig's. Whereas most of the dogs hung out together, Poochie was always alone, even when a bitch was in heat. He never got into fights either. He sunk down on shaking legs at the mere approach of another dog, male or female.

In some ways, I was similar to Poochie. I, too, usually played by myself. But I was never bullied by the others. I never pressed my belly into the ground and begged for mercy. The neighborhood kids resented and feared me, but they didn't challenge me.

In the years before we left Valley Stream, my mother insisted I play outside, in the 'fresh air,' even when it rained. (Back then, I thought she wanted to get rid of me. Now I'm not sure that she could formulate a desire that precisely.) On this particular day, it was raining hard and I was playing in the garage as usual. This was before we lost the house. I was about ten years old. I was rearranging the small jars of hardware my father had stacked in his workshop before he took off. If the jars had only been different heights, the perfect arrangement would have been easily found. If they were the same height, I could have used the objects inside as the key to their arrangement. But they were of different widths and different heights, and every arrangement seemed haphazard.

Nevertheless, I persisted. There wasn't anything else to do. Not in the rain.

About an hour after lunch, Poochie wandered in through a small door on the side of the garage. He was soaked and shivering, but he didn't try to approach me. He pressed his belly and his muzzle onto the greasy concrete floor and hoped for the best.

I was annoyed at first. The garage was uniquely mine, because my mother never went there. She didn't know how to drive and we didn't own a car. I decided to throw Poochie into the rain.

He didn't move as I approached, although he kept his eyes on me. Even when I casually kicked him (a hint and not meant to hurt), he did no more than flatten himself into greater submission.

I kicked him harder. He moved about six inches, but didn't run.

I kept him between myself and the door, offering an escape route that he didn't take. Poochie placed his faith in submission. He trusted submission to pull him through, as it had with the other dogs.

The first thing I did, once I realized that Poochie wasn't going to run, was close the garage door. I locked it, too, though I hadn't clearly formulated my experiment. Then I sat on the floor of the garage and stared at the dog for a long time.   .

Poochie was very ugly. His fur was thin and dingy. His muzzle was short and sharp. His body was too long for his stumpy legs. Without thinking too much about it, I yanked at his corkscrew tail. I expected him to squeal like a little pig, but he kept his muzzle on the concrete.

I decided to determine the exact point at which Poochie would abandon submission and decide to fight. I put my hands around his throat and squeezed slightly. No response. I slowly (and predictably) tightened my grip.

His body contracted, once he understood where the experiment was going, and his back feet kicked out. He even groaned toward the end, a high, hopeless cry so pitiful I almost let him go. But he never tried to get away. He never growled. He never tried to bite.

Poochie made a tremendous impression on me, because I *didn't* expect him to die without a fight. The experiment was supposed to determine the point at which the animal would make a stand. Before Poochie, I believed 'submission unto death' to be impossible.

How can the same species that holds Poochie hold, for instance, the hounds that corner bear and puma until the slower humans arrive with their guns? Or the police dog willing to brave clubs and knives? Or the pit bull terrier *eager* to fight to the death?

How can the same species that holds me hold the followers of Jim Jones?

There's no limit to what I could do with a few hundred Poochies at my command. That's what I kept coming back to. Of course, I knew nothing of Jim Jones' personal beliefs. He may have been absolutely sincere. Nevertheless, there was *no* limit to what I could do with a few hundred Poochies at my command.

I dumped Poochie in a bed of blossoming peonies. His carcass was found the following day. Apparently, nobody in the neighborhood was capable of what I'd done, because nobody formulated the possibility of foul play. Some of the kids thought Poochie had eaten slug poison. Others insisted he'd suffered a heart attack or a stroke. All the kids were tremendously saddened, though none of them had given a shit about Poochie when he was alive. Not even the fat girl who owned him.

As for myself, I felt only fear and confusion. I observed the children's tears and wondered why my own eyes were dry. Whereas they demonstrated their human feelings by conducting a full-scale backyard burial, I stayed in the garage, arranging bottles of nuts and bolts. Again and again, I asked myself what was wrong with me. I never once thought to ask myself what was right with me.

At that age (how could I help it?), I was afraid of my differences. (I thought I was *supposed* to feel what the other children obviously felt. That these feelings came down through some unimpeachable source, like God.) I experienced this fear as a kind of confusion. To live one's life without clarity, pushed from one pseudo-obligation to another, is a curse. To have the potential for freedom, only to be lost in confusion, is a proper cause for mourning.

Marilyn took away the confusion, which I understood as guilt and which was never more than a mistake in judgment. She gave me clarity and purpose, but never, not even for a single instant, have I been grateful.

FOUR

There was a time in Stanley Moodrow's life, a brief moment just after he joined the detectives, when he dreamed of being the kind of suave investigator associated with stolen art or Fifth Avenue jewel thefts. Stepping out of the uniform and into a suit for the first time, he entertained a goal common to many of New York's finest—they strive with all their might to project an image of classy sophistication. Some detectives succeed at this. Some don't. Moodrow was a don't.

Thirty years later, a year after turning in his gold shield for a private investigator's license, Moodrow was still a don't, but he no longer felt the need to pass for a civilian. Being taken for a cop, he'd learned over the years, had any number of potential advantages. PIs, on the other hand, are little more than ordinary citizens with gun permits—they have sleazy reputations and, as often as not, the public meets them with scorn instead of respect. PIs *buy* information. Real cops demand it.

In the decades that followed his rise to the detectives, Stanley Moodrow worked on his cop image diligently. He wanted to project the essence of cop, to reek of it so that everyone, citizen or criminal, would make him for exactly what he was. No surprise, then, that he consciously used strangers to evaluate his success or failure. Of course, most people are oblivious on the street. The rule of thumb goes like this—don't make eye contact if you don't want trouble. There are some, on the other hand, who find no safety in hiding their heads, who watch everything and everyone, especially six-foot six-inch cops.

The mutts, of course, fit neatly into this category. Crack or heroin junkies, mostly, they prowl the streets, looking for opportunity. Korean greengrocers are just as sharp. The skells have taken the Koreans for soft, and robbery is an ever-present threat. Cab drivers also learn to evaluate their customers quickly. They have to, because more cab drivers are killed every year than cops.

Doormen are as wise to the faces on the street as any of these groups, but for an entirely different reason. Doormen are not subject to robbery, because street criminals know that doormen, like joggers, don't carry enough money to buy a cup of coffee. The problem facing doormen is who belongs and who does not.

In other cities, where millionaires look like millionaires, separating the low-lifes from the VIPs is no problem. But in New York the sleaze in the torn sweat suit is likely to be a vice president at Chase Manhattan, while the odd burglar wears an Yves St. Laurent jogging outfit and sports a fifty-dollar haircut. Evaluating street action is as much a part of a doorman's job as finding a cab in the rain.

Which is why Moodrow unbuttoned his coat, exposing the worn handle of his S&W, as he approached the entranceway to 657 Sutton Place. The ancient revolver was part of the image and while the doorman, Ladislaw Wrotek, noted its presence without changing expression, he was markedly more polite to Stanley Moodrow than he usually was to strangers in cheap suits.

"Connie Alamare," Moodrow said sharply. "Apartment 28C." The sign said VISITORS MUST BE ANNOUNCED and that applied to any cop not in "hot pursuit of a felon." Moodrow noted the modest lobby with its stucco walls and worn, marble floor. Six fifty-seven Sutton Place was a pre-war building and the architect had reserved the luxury for the apartments upstairs. Modern buildings, where the residents live in white cubicles, have outside fountains and lobbies designed by interior decorators.

"You got to arrest her maybe?" The doorman grinned, exposing two gold teeth on the right side of his mouth. He was a big man, almost as big as Moodrow.

"What?"

"You are policeman, no? I wonder if you go to arrest Ms. Alamare." He dragged the word 'ms.' out contemptuously.

"You know her?"

"She is witch. No belong here with important people."

"How so?"

Ladislaw Wrotek laughed shortly. "If you no come to arrest her, then you find out for own self. Don' be worrying too much about it. She show you right away."

"Yeah? Well, thanks for the tip."

The woman who opened the door to apartment 28C did, in fact, resemble a witch. Wizened and ancient, she looked just like one of the elderly nuns who'd plagued Moodrow's early education—Sister Paulinus, a legendary disciplinarian who'd turned fourth grade into a rite of passage.

A shiver traveled up Moodrow's back, a definite presentiment of danger. "Connie Alamare," he said in his most authoritative voice. He was hoping against hope that the apparition standing before him was the maid.

The witch stared at him for a moment. "You," she demanded. "What's your name?"

"Stanley Moodrow. For Connie Alamare."

"Hey, Connie," the old lady screamed. "C'mere."

The woman who appeared an instant later was in her mid-forties. Wiry thin, her black hair was pulled back tight against the side of her head. In thirty years, Moodrow realized, she'd be the old lady's twin. "Hey, *momma*," the woman said. "This is the private eye. Remember? I told you he was coming."

"This *strunza* is supposed to help us? This *citrullo*? He's an old man." She shook her head in disbelief. "Better I should go light a candle at St. Michael's." The old lady's accent was pure Brooklyn neighborhood. She pronounced "*strunza*" as strunzzzz, leaving off the final 'a' entirely. "*Citrullo*" became sedrools.

"*Momma*, please. The man just got here. Don't drive him away."

The old lady snorted contemptuously. "You gonna find my great-grandson?"

"Maybe," Moodrow returned evenly.

"Whatta ya mean? You gonna do it or you're too old? Which one?"

"You called me '*strunza*.' That means turd. It's just possible I don't wanna work for someone who calls me names in a language she thinks I don't understand."

"You're *Italiano*? With that name? Moodrow?" She shook her head. "If this *choch* is Italian, then I must be Grace Kelly."

"Now you call me an idiot," Moodrow replied evenly.

"Enough, momma. *State citta*. Go in the back," Connie Alamare broke in. "Remember where you are."

The old lady, much to Moodrow's surprise, did a quick about face, flashing a handful of white rosary beads. Connie watched her disappear, then turned back to Moodrow. "My mother," she explained. "Maria Corrello. The whole family hates her. On Christmas they left her sitting in a nursing home with a turkey dinner from the Salvation Army. I took her out when I hit it big. I figured with enough rooms, we could stay out of each other's way. Meanwhile, I can't keep a maid anymore. I got money I ain't counted, but I gotta go through the rooms with a vacuum cleaner and a dust cloth. Life plays funny tricks, ya know?"

"Funny ain't the word for it," Moodrow sighed.

Connie Alamare led the way into the living room. It was enormous by New York standards, twenty by thirty-five feet with fourteen-foot ceilings. The southern terrace running its length faced the heart of midtown Manhattan and would have afforded the kind of view affluent New Yorkers kill for, the ultimate status symbol, if the French doors and the floor-to-ceiling windows weren't covered by thick gray drapes.

"I got an allergy to light," Alamare announced. "Could you believe that? I pay a fortune for this place and I can't open the drapes. I don't know. Sometimes I feel like throwing in the towel."

She rolled on, but Moodrow, paying little attention, swept the living room professionally. The overstuffed furniture looked as if it had been bought by the pound. The back of the chair he sat in towered over his head. The coffee table, where Connie Alamare laid her coffee cup, was solid mahogany and heavy enough to anchor a battleship. Even the dark oil paintings, depicting various aspects of the Italian landscape, were dwarfed by their carved and gilded frames.

"You want coffee? I could have my mother bring it in."

Moodrow shuddered. "No thanks. I'm gonna take notes here. I need both hands. Why don't you run down the facts. Give me a feel for the situation."

"A 'feel'? I'll give you more than a 'feel.' I'll give you the whole damn situation."

She rose abruptly, walking through the living room to a long hall-way. Moodrow had no choice except to follow. He had a good idea of what he was going to find and the intermittent hiss of a respirator only confirmed his suspicions. The small bedroom, in direct contrast to the rest of the apartment, was bright and airy. A thin breeze curling through half-open windows flicked at sheer white curtains.

"Florence always wanted to open the windows," Connie explained. "She liked to play outside. A tomboy. All the times I told her 'be a lady, be a lady . . .' I couldn't even count the times I told her."

The young woman lying on the bed was thin, but not yet gaunt, though she would be. She lay curled into a fetal position, despite the efforts of a physical therapist who straightened and exercised her muscles on a daily basis. Her eyes, wide open, stared at Stanley Moodrow without the slightest glimmer of recognition.

"She was breathing when they found her, but then she stopped. In the hospital before they identified her. They cut a hole in her throat and hooked her up to the machine. *Mannagia l'anima di che te morte.* That bastard, Craddock. I curse the souls of his ancestors."

Moodrow watched Florence Alamare's chest expand and contract in obedience to the push of the air from the respirator. He'd seen people in similar conditions, victims of gunshot wounds or savage beatings.

"See how they feed her now? They drilled a hole, then put a tube right into her stomach. I pour the food in twice a day. It's a liquid. Thick, like syrup. They say she can keep her weight up, but look how she's growing thin."

Moodrow watched for another moment, then stepped back out of the room. There was no sense in staying there, nothing to be gained by looking at the twisted wreckage of Florence Alamare. Connie followed him, closing the door gently behind her. She didn't say anything until they were seated in the living room again. Then her face turned to stone. "I want this bastard to pay," she said. The words hissed like the respirator attached to her daughter's throat. "I want to pull his heart out of his chest."

"I'm not a mercenary," Moodrow replied evenly. As a cop, he'd received his assignments from a higher authority. Now he could pick and choose.

Connie Alamare snorted derisively. "If I was a Sicilian, I wouldn't need you. I'd make one phone call and Davis Craddock would already be dead. But I'm *Napolitano.* My grandfather was a tomato farmer. He used a hoe instead of a shotgun."

"One second," Moodrow interrupted. "I know what you want. It's called revenge. It's what all victims want. But I don't do revenge. What

I do is investigate. I find facts and if they point toward a criminal act, I call the cops. You hear what I'm sayin'?"

He was lying, of course. 'Making the motherfuckers pay' was at the core of his entire professional life. But it's one thing to be an instrument of the New York Police Department and quite another to be a gun pointed by any citizen with the money to pay his fee. He wanted to be sure that Connie Alamare, consumed by hatred, was aware of his position.

"Okay," Connie's eyes narrowed. "You gotta forgive me, because I'm used to speaking the way I grew up. In Canarsie, Brooklyn. The big shot detective, Goobe, said you were a cop for thirty-five years so I figured I could talk naturally. I figured you were used to dealing with people from the neighborhoods."

She was lying, but Moodrow didn't mind. He leaned back in his chair, crossing his legs, allowing the case to sweep over him.

"Look, when I say I want his heart, I'm not saying you should hold the knife. Don't forget, I already know that Davis Craddock did this to my girl, so if I wanted him to have an accident some day, I wouldn't be hiring you to find proof. I'll settle for taking him off his perch. I'll settle for seeing him in handcuffs. Your job is to get an indictment. Then you can step out."

"Ms. Alamare," Moodrow interrupted the speech.

"Connie, please."

"Connie, fine. Why don't we start with the last time you saw your daughter."

"That was eight years ago."

"Eight?" Moodrow allowed the surprise in his voice to encourage her to open up.

"You know what I do for a living?"

"I don't. No."

"I write books about slave girls who marry princes and live happily ever after on yachts in the Mediterranean. I started reading these kinds of books when I was twelve years old. It was my escape from Canarsie. From a papa with heavy hands. From a mama with a nasty tongue who prayed five hundred rosaries a week. From the *gumbah* who wanted to lift my skirts in the hallway of St. Agnes and who I eventually married and who had hands as heavy as my father's.

"I must've read five thousand romances, before I sat down and wrote one. Florence was eleven years old and my husband, he should rot in hell, was dead. I was back to living with my family. They were very old-fashioned, so it was expected that a daughter with no skills and no husband would move back into her parents' house. I suppose that if they died, I would've been taken in by my sister, but I didn't wait around that long.

"It was a nightmare in that house. My parents didn't talk to each other. They talked to me and to Florence. They screamed their complaints and they complained about everything and everyone in their miserable lives.

"After a couple of years, I was desperate. I would've done almost anything, but I was an ex-housewife with a high school education and no kind of skills that would bring me enough money to live on my own. For most women in my class, the answer was remarriage, but I was different. I didn't wanna lay underneath some drooling guinea just so I could call myself a wife. That's exchanging one prison for another.

"So I wrote a book describing all the things I could never be and all the things I could never have. Of course, I didn't really believe that I'd be able to write a book that anyone else would want to read, so I added something that I never found in all the romances I'd read. I added sex. My heroine was a white girl who belonged to a Saudi sheik. The man is a beast, but what can she do? She has to put up with his perversions, until the sheik offers a visiting British viscount a night with his white slave. Naturally, the viscount and the slave fall in love and live happily ever after. It became the new thing in romance novels. I mean the sex, of course. Me, I took a fancy name—Roberta Chamberlain—and hired an accountant to add up the money.

"If life was fair, me and Florence would've lived happily ever after, too. She would've used the money to get an education, married an artist, lived in France, had wonderfully talented babies. But you can't escape your fate. Not me and not her. When she was eighteen, she decided she needed a psychologist and she went to one of the Hanoverians, Samuel Brooks. Only they didn't call themselves Hanoverians. They called themselves Therapists and I didn't have no idea what my daughter was getting into. Three months later, Florence disappeared into that prison they call a commune. The one on Ludlow Street. At first I got letters describing her wonderful new life, then she cut me off altogether. They told her that her family was responsible for all her suffering and she could save herself only by putting them out of her life."

Connie Alamare began to cry. Not from sorrow, Moodrow noted, but from rage and frustration. "That was the last time you heard from her?" he asked calmly.

"Three years ago, I got a snapshot in the mail. On the back, she wrote, 'Me and my son, Michael.' That was it. No return address. I tried to reach her. I had messages delivered to Ludlow Street. I hired a private detective, a *mariulla*, a thief. He tried to muscle his way into the commune, but they kicked his ass. After that he stayed in his office and sent me bills every month. I wouldn't say that I gave up, but I didn't see what I could do. I accepted the fact that I wouldn't see my daughter (or my grandson) until my daughter wanted to see me. Then, about two months ago, the cops found her in a vacant lot in the Bronx. They identified her by fingerprints and I took her into the house after the doctors advised me to put her in a home. The nurse is out picking up medicine. Usually she stays with Florence every minute."

"What was the cause of all this? What do the doctors say?"

"The doctors say she had a stroke."

"Bullshit." Moodrow was old-fashioned. He wasn't in the habit of using street language in the presence of a strange woman, no matter how coarse, but the diagnosis of stroke shocked him. "People don't get dumped in lots in the Bronx for having strokes. What do the cops say?"

Connie grinned broadly. "At last," she crowed. "At last I got a man with guts. You find a girl like this in a lot in the Bronx, you gotta know someone did something wrong. She was wearing a three-hundred-dollar outfit, for Christ's sake."

"Please, Connie." Moodrow ignored the compliment. "What do the cops think?"

"All the cops wanted to do was dump her off on me and forget about it. The doctors said it was a stroke, right? If no crime was committed, why should the cops be involved? Well, I got a lawyer, a real *finocchio* with Italian suits and a stretch Mercedes. So much marble in his house, you think you're in a Greek museum. He took it up the line, from the detective who took her fingerprints to the lieutenant to the precinct commander to the borough commander to One Police Plaza where the hotshots work. They sent some people out, but they couldn't even give her an address. They couldn't tell us where she lived for the past years. Or who her friends were. Or how she made a living. Or where her son is. Finally I get to this guy with all the white hair, the *chief* of all the detectives. 'No crime was committed.' That's all the *strunza* can say. 'No crime was committed.' If I want to take it farther, I should hire a private investigator. Then he recommended you."

"Franklyn Goobe," Moodrow sighed.

"You and him didn't get along?" Connie asked hopefully.

"He was a bigshot in the cops and I was a precinct detective. Getting along doesn't really have anything to do with that relationship. In the army, a colonel doesn't get along with a lieutenant. Orders come down and you do what you're told, like it or not." Moodrow deliberately left out the fact that he'd manipulated the NYPD (and Franklyn Goobe) as much as possible. His new employer was trying to make the cops into adversaries and Moodrow didn't see the point of it. Not at this stage. "What about your grandson? It could be anybody's kid. Maybe your daughter was trying to get back at you by inventing a grandson you'd never see."

"Smart, Moodrow. You ask smart questions. I had the lawyer check birth records for the year he would have been born and we found him easy enough. January 15 in Beth Israel Hospital on First Avenue. A baby boy, Michael, born to Florence Alamare. She listed her address as 1117 Ludlow Street which is where the commune is."

"And the cops didn't check out the Hanoverians at all?"

"They went there and Davis Craddock told them my daughter left the commune two years earlier. He hadn't heard from her and couldn't care less. Look, Moodrow, one of the reasons I picked you is you spent your career on the Lower East Side. You know the territory."

Moodrow shook his head. "It's not gonna be that easy. The Hanoverians aren't neighborhood. They're closed off."

"I want my grandson," Connie said evenly, "and I'm willing to pay. I got a check for $10,000. Put it in the bank and mail me the bills. When that check's used up, I'll send you another one. You find my grandson, you get a $15,000 bonus. You get proof on Davis Craddock, it's fifteen more. I got so much money, I need a computer to count it. What am I gonna spend it on? I need an heir and that girl lying in the bed needs justice. Do the right thing, Moodrow. Do the right thing."

FIVE

Petey Ragsdale was in seventh heaven: he had a pocketful of PURE and pretty Polly in her 13th Street apartment, the 4th of July and Christmas wrapped up in one beautiful package. More good fortune, he had to admit, than any junkie is entitled to in the course of a mostly desperate fucking life.

But fresh is fresh, and he had no intentions of not *enjoying* his blessings, deserved or not. PURE hadn't been on the market for more than a month and it was already the rarest dope on the Lower East Side. Every day (as soon as he scrounged the bank) Petey searched for

PURE, but the one lousy dealer who controlled the PURE action, Deeny Washington, didn't seem to have more than a few hundred bags a day.

The worst bitch about it was that everybody knew about PURE. Every junkie in the city was lookin' for PURE, but takin' whatever brown shit the regular dealers were holdin'. For the last five days, Petey had gotten the same crappy story from his brothers in junk.

"Maannnn, you missed the muthafucka by a hair. I got the last bags off his ass and they was tight, man. Baddest damn dope in New Jack City."

Not this time, though. Not *this* fucking time. He'd gotten lucky, today, spied an asshole delivery man leave the roll-up door on his GMC unlocked and been rewarded for his eagle eye with two thirteen-inch Sonys. You didn't need no fence for no fuckin' Sonys in the box. Just walked into the nearest gas station on Houston Street and the boss snatched them up for a buck twenty-five apiece.

As soon as the money was in his pocket, Petey hustled his ass over to the projects on Pitt Street and waited for Deeny to show up. Course, he wasn't the only sick junkie hangin' out in the small playground. The swings and seesaws were covered with freaks, half of 'em lookin' like they were dyin' of goddamn AIDS. When Deeny dragged his black ass across the parkin' lot, they moaned in anticipation. It sounded like the noise his granny made when the nurses tied her hands to the bed rails.

After Deeny was gone, Petey's best bro', a car thief named Littlerock, asked Petey did he want to go off to a squat on Attorney Street to get off.

"Can't do it, baby. Got me some new pussy," Petey told Littlerock. "Come down to the Lower East Side from Malapan, New Jersey. Like, her father does cows for a livin'. Milkin' 'em and shit. Course, the bitch don't care for no cows. The bitch wanna be hip. She wanna learn the Bohemian way and be like one of the fuckin' people."

"And I *know* you gonna be the one to show her how to be a people."

They'd slapped themselves a pair of low fives and nearly dropped dead laughin'. Pretty Polly was like winnin' the lottery. Like a good luck lightning bolt. He'd been there before (so had Littlerock), and he knew it wouldn't last forever. Most likely she'd straighten up and dump his ass into the street. Or she'd show up stoned for a family dinner and her family would lock her up in a drug rehab center. Or she'd steal from everyone she ever loved until she became the same broke and desperate junkie he was.

But right now this very goddamn minute she was waitin' for her little Petey to bring the goodies home. He'd fixed her for the first time a week ago and it was like she was made for dope. Lying back in the bed, noddin' out while the TV flickered the only light in the room. Pretty soon, he'd start charging her to get high. Pretty soon she'd be payin' to get *him* high.

He was careful to look behind him when he turned into 13th Street. Sooner or later, the vampires would be drawn to pretty Polly. That was another way he could lose her which is why he wanted her away from other junkies for as long as possible. He'd turn her loose when she ran out of money. (After all, he wasn't a fuckin' pimp. Let somebody else turn her out.)

"Let's screw first. I wanna be close to you."

She said it before he could even close the goddamned door. "There's time and *time*," he said, figurin' to confuse the bitch. Couldn't really be showin' her how sick he was, could he? Or how sick he was gonna be if he didn't get off real soon? "Appropriateness is what I'm sayin'. What's chill later ain't necessarily chill now. Like there ain't nothin' wrong with spontaneous, but life got a progress and you gotta tune yourself to it."

She looked down at the rug and said, "You're a junkie, aren't you? You can't stop yourself."

So he didn't have no choice except fuckin' her into the ground. No choice whatsoever. Not that it was all bad. Bitches that wanted to make you better sometimes fell in love with you. If she fell in love, he'd own her ass for a long, long time. If she fell in love with him, she'd escape from the drug rehab center to get back to him. She'd steal from her parents, write bad checks, carry dope . . . anything to keep her Petey from gettin' sick.

He didn't come. She was completely open to him, but his mind was on PURE and how he was gonna feel when he had it runnin' through his veins. She didn't seem to mind, though. The bitch fucked hard when she wasn't stoned, and he was pretty sure she'd gotten off a bunch of times. He took Polly's spike out of the closet and put it next to his own. ("Never use *nobody's* toys, Polly. *Never*. I seen one after another dead from AIDS." As if he gave a shit. As if he wasn't already infected.) One of the good things about PURE was that you didn't have to cook it up. Just dump it in water and watch it vanish: no quinine, no mannitol, no cut whatsoever. But today he had a few bags of brown dope one of the dealers had laid on him. The dealers were desperate because nobody wanted their product.

"Try this brown shit, Petey. Smiley D is more worser than PURE, 'cause the man loadin' up on the quality."

He set his little tripod over the candle, dropped a bottle cap into the slot on top, added half the brown dope and a syringe full of water, lit the candle. Smooth and practiced. He was about to add the PURE, enough for his needs and not for hers, when she started bustin' his chops again.

"Do me first, Petey."

Holdin' out her arm like she was cuter than the fuckin' pig on the Muppets. It was another test, but this little test wouldn't last long. Petey had the touch. Always had it. From the first time he fondled a set of works. He could get the bitch off inside a goddamned closet. Get her off in her eye in the dark if he had to. He dropped a tiny speck of PURE into the bottle cap and waited for the mixture to come to a boil.

The hit was instantaneous. Naturally. The needle slid into a thin vein on the outside of her forearm, and he grunted his satisfaction as he loosened the tie and slid the plunger home.

"Bout time you be learnin' how to do this to yourself," he said, already turnin' toward his own rush.

The feeling was glorious. Almost as good as the hit. His body began to tingle with anticipation as he prepared the cure for all disasters. The difference between so sick you wanted to die and chief kaiser of the whole goddamned universe. He watched the brown heroin until it bubbled, blew out the candle, then emptied two red vials of PURE into the cooling liquid. He let the anticipation roll up into his throat as he dropped a small tuft of cotton into the fix and drew the liquid up into the needle.

"Sweet mama on the rock," he said, turning back to find pretty Polly lying in a heap on the bed. Lying stone fuckin' cold unconscious. Nothin' moving. Not even her tits goin' up and down. He snatched her off the sheets and started slappin' her, but she didn't move a fuckin' muscle. Her skin didn't have no color at all. Except, maybe, blue.

Panic replaced the joyous buzz of anticipation. He shook her and began draggin' her ass around the room. Screamin', "Wake up, bitch. Don't die. Don't die you fuckin' bitch." Like he was in a movie, but it wasn't no good, no how. One thing he'd seen plenty of since he brought his monkey back from Vietnam was dead ODs. Pretty Polly wasn't gonna be eatin' no crackers no more.

He dumped her body on the bed and calmed himself down. Thinkin', *did anybody see your ass come into this buildin'?* Askin' himself did he have time to fix or did he have to get his Keds in gear right now this fuckin' minute?

"Nobody know nothin' 'bout me and the bitch," he said to no one in particular. "Gotta be crazy ta walk outta here without gettin' well."

He looked back at Polly as he wrapped the tie around his left bicep, feeling all kinds of regret. Thinkin' how maybe she got some cash lyin' around the apartment. Or like a 14-carat chain or a cross or one of them Jewish good luck letters the bitches like to wear. Fifteen seconds later, he was dead.

SIX

When Betty Haluka first hatched the notion of a housewarming dinner at Stanley Moodrow's new apartment, she was well aware of the fact that Moodrow's idea of a home-cooked Italian meal was limited to a crusty loaf of bread, a box of Ronzoni and a jar of Ragu. Moodrow had never learned to cook, despite three decades of bachelorhood, because he'd never needed to learn. There were too many restaurants within walking distance of his apartment, most reasonably priced and featuring a unique cuisine. As the avowed protector of his neighborhood, Moodrow was known everywhere and the usual cop discount made eating out as cheap as cooking.

Still, he did love to eat, and he wasn't entirely unhappy when Betty announced the menu. *Pasta e fagioli*; an enormous cold antipasto; fusilli with grilled hot sausage and broccoli; chicken in garlic, wine and vinegar; homemade Italian cheese cake and espresso with anisette. What bothered Moodrow was the prospect of spending four hours shopping for the ingredients.

"We could buy everything on this list within a mile of here," he'd insisted.

"We're having a housewarming, Stanley. It's a special occasion. When was the last time you moved?"

"In 1955," he'd admitted sheepishly, "when the Dodgers won the World Series."

"Then either you have to sneak into your new home in the dead of night or you have to celebrate with something special. You can't compare supermarket cheese with what you can buy at DeLuca's. And that goes double for freshly made pasta."

Moodrow had grunted into his morning coffee. "I think I'll sneak."

"You can't sneak. We already invited Jim and Rose and the kids."

"First I move into a yuppie apartment and now I'm gonna shop like a yuppie. This is culture shock and I'm too old for it. Correction: *we're* too old for it. Plus it's bad for my image. Next thing you'll be movin' me out to Connecticut."

"If it makes you feel better, you can wear a ski mask. Besides, you don't have to shop. You have to drive and wait in the car. C'mon, I want to hear about the Alamare case, anyway. We'll talk while we go."

If there was any way that Betty could have done it by herself, Moodrow would have begged off, but there are no legal parking spaces in midtown Manhattan and the prospect of taking five subways through Queens, Manhattan and Brooklyn, even without the grocery bags, was too gruesome to be contemplated. Moodrow knew he was drafted and his complaints no more than ritual.

It was nine o'clock in the morning when they left Betty's Park Slope apartment in Brooklyn. They headed toward the Manhattan Bridge, and the traffic along Flatbush Avenue was fierce. In most cities, the rush hour ends at nine, when the workday begins; in New York there are days when it doesn't end until the workers go home. Under normal circumstances, Moodrow would sooner have rescued a cat from a tenement fire than spend his morning in Manhattan traffic, but as soon as he began to talk about Connie Alamare and her daughter, Flo, he forgot the traffic altogether, steering his newly purchased '82 Mercury Marquis with the automatic professionalism of a veteran cop.

"The thing cops hate most is when witnesses start bullshitting them," he began airily. "It happens all the time and mostly there's no reason for it. Alamare's daughter has holes up and down both arms. Clean punctures from clean needles which most likely makes her a rich junkie. That's not so uncommon as you'd think, but the funny thing is her mother didn't mention it. If you listen to her, you'd think the daughter was an angel."

"Did she know?"

"She knew. She paid a lawyer two hundred dollars an hour to make sure she'd know. When the doctors saw Flo Alamare's arms, the first thing they did was test her for drugs and she showed positive for heroin."

"Did she overdose? Is that what happened?"

"I spoke to the doctor in charge of the ward where they first brought her. Doctor Johnson in Bronx Municipal which is a hellhole. He insists that she only had traces of heroin in her system. Not near enough for an OD. Then they brought in a cardiologist to do some tests. His name is..."

Without taking his eyes from the road, Moodrow took a worn notebook from the inside pocket of his jacket and began to turn the

pages with his thumb. "Merstein. Samuel Merstein. He's the one who
thinks she had a stroke."

"How does he know?"

Moodrow's thumb curled the pages for another moment. "They
took a test—a PET test. It's an unbelievable thing really. They put
radioactive glucose into your veins, then watch your brain cells with a
Geiger counter. The idea is to find which part of your brain doesn't use
the sugar. That's the dead part. Which is what happens when you have
a stroke—some part of your brain dies. Anyway, the parts of Flo
Alamare's brain that control movement and thinking don't work. Dr.
Merstein wouldn't say that she's brain dead, but he thinks she's so close
to it that it doesn't matter. Flo Alamare's never gonna tell us what
happened to her."

"Couldn't the same condition result from an overdose of heroin? I've
seen a lot of that with Legal Aid. If you stop breathing and the brain
doesn't get oxygen, you can definitely have brain damage."

Moodrow, trying to avoid the traffic on the Bowery, took the east-
bound Canal Street exit and began to work his way through China-
town. "They only found *traces* of heroin in her body."

"You did say that she'd been using for a long time?"

"She had a lot of holes in her arm. All clean, by the way. No
infections which means she wasn't sharing needles. Contrary to popular belief, not all dope addicts are poor."

"If she was that much of a junkie and that rich, how come she only
showed *traces* of heroin? It doesn't make sense. She should have been
stoned."

Moodrow grinned. "There's a lot of things that don't make sense.
That's why they call it a mystery. That's why I was hired. If it made
sense, they wouldn't need me to straighten it out."

They ran up Allen Street to Houston, then turned west. They were
heading for the west side, to DeLuca's cheese shop and Manganero's
Grocery, both left over from the day when Italian immigrants, looking
for work on the Hudson River docks, had flooded into Hell's Kitchen.
DeLuca's would supply the creamy ricotta for Betty's cheese cake and
the sharp crumbly provolone she'd throw into the antipasto. Manganero's would supply prosciutto, cappicola, stuffed cherry peppers, a
garlicky salami and freshly made pasta.

"What if she'd taken the overdose a couple of days before she was
found?" Betty, one foot out of the car, turned back to Moodrow.
"Maybe in someone else's apartment. If they hoped she'd come around,
they might have waited, then decided to dump the body. She would

have metabolized most of the heroin by then, so she'd only show traces."

Moodrow giggled his appreciation. "I spent most of my career hating lawyers. That's because they're smarter than me, and they think like cops. I spoke to the uniforms at the Four One, in the Bronx, the ones that found her. She was tossed in the middle of a vacant lot. Just left on top of the garbage. There's two people living in cardboard shacks at the back of the lot. Two old-time juicers. They're the ones who found her, and they swear she had to have been dropped off that night. The point I'm making is that I think whoever dropped her there meant for her to die in that lot, so it doesn't seem likely they'd keep her in an apartment for two days, then bring her out alive. Also, I asked the doctor who first examined her if she had any fresh punctures. He said she did. In fact, they tested the tissue around it for traces of poison. The doctor said the puncture was still open when she came in. It had to've been made within twenty-four hours."

Moodrow waited until Betty disappeared into Manganero's before descending on the nearest hotdog wagon. Hell's Kitchen, below 42nd Street, had escaped the wave of gentrification sweeping across Manhattan's poorer neighborhoods. By day, workers streamed into the small warehouses, filling the coffee shops and delis. At night, the crack dealers huddled in doorways near the Lincoln Tunnel exit ramps, feeding the shoppers streaming in from New Jersey to get stoned. It was New York without tourists and Moodrow, smiling to himself, absorbed it the way other retirees soak up the Florida sun.

When Betty finally appeared on the opposite side of Ninth Avenue, weighed down with two huge sacks of groceries, Moodrow calmly opened the Mercury's enormous trunk and waited for her to thread her way through the traffic. Dodging traffic is a necessary survival strategy for New Yorkers, and Betty was a master, even remembering to look out for crazed bicycle messengers.

"I got it," she said, dumping the groceries into the trunk. "Flo Alamare had a stroke. Just like the doctors say. But whoever she was with couldn't know that. They just assumed she overdosed and dumped her in the lot."

"It's possible," Moodrow admitted, "but I don't like it. Only street junkies dump people in lots. And they don't do it if the person is still alive."

"I take it there's no chance she got a hotshot? That she was deliberately poisoned."

"Hotshots are mostly rat poison or bug poison. That would mean stomach cramps, diarrhea, vomiting. There was nothing like that."

Moodrow cut west to Tenth Avenue, then headed straight uptown. The next stop was a Greek delicatessen in Astoria, Queens, because Betty insisted that Greek olives were more Italian than Italian olives. She'd also decided to surround the antipasto with stuffed grape leaves, but she kept that anomaly to herself.

"What do the cops think?" Betty asked. "You said you spoke to them."

"The cops say no crime was committed. Every other question gets an 'I don't know.' How did she get to the Bronx? Where did she spend the twenty-four hours before she was found? Where did she spend the last two years before she was found? How did she support herself? Who did she associate with? Same bullshit: 'I don't know.' After the old lady started busting chops, they sent a detective over to Hanover House. He interviewed Davis Craddock who says Flo Alamare took her kid and walked out of the cult two years ago and hasn't been heard from since."

Betty shook her head in disbelief. "Didn't they check phone records? Credit cards?"

"Not until after the lawyer got involved. His name is DeVilio, by the way. When the lawyer started screaming about lawsuits, the detectives put a trace on all the paper, including motor vehicle records and tax returns. Flo Alamare had a driver's license with Hanover House as the address, but it was three years old and maybe she forgot to file a change. Other than that, *nada*."

"Then Connie Alamare was right. Flo must have been in the commune when this happened to her. If she was living on her own, she would've at least had to pay taxes."

"Unless she was living with another rich junkie. One who was rich enough to support her, too."

Moodrow inched the Mercury up to the toll booth on the Triborough Bridge. The toll was $2.50 each way, about five times as much as it took to keep the bridge in repair. The surplus, the profit, was used as a subsidy for the buses and subways. Somehow, the politicians, city and state, had decided that driving a car into Manhattan was an immoral act, like drinking alcohol, so immoral that any tax was justified. A year earlier, Moodrow would have flipped his badge and been allowed to pass without paying, one of a number of perks available to cops. Now he forked over the toll like everybody else.

"The thing about the Hanoverians," he began, once they were moving across the bridge, "is that they've always kept themselves away from what was happening on the street. That part of the Lower East Side was dope heaven when they started their commune. Heroin, cocaine, speed, acid, dust. Meanwhile, the Hanoverians went around looking like office workers. Even the kids were turned out. The antidrug thing was one of the fronts they put up to curious reporters. Here they lived in the middle of the drug war and they kept themselves straighter than straight. I'm gonna go out and talk to some of the people I used to know on the street, but I doubt very much if things have changed."

They came off the bridge at 31st Street in Queens. A quick left turn would take them directly to Mediterranean Foods, but the signs hanging from the el were clear. Moodrow would have made the turn anyway, if he was still a cop, counting on his badge to get him through, but now he feared the forty-dollar ticket like any other civilian.

"What about the kid? What's his name?"

"Michael Alamare." Moodrow pulled the car alongside a fire hydrant. The Greek store was just up the block, but Betty made no move to open the door. "Kids are another problem altogether. Kids don't leave paper trails. No driver's license, no credit cards."

"What about doctors? He must've been to see a doctor within the last couple of years. I mean that's the whole thing, isn't it? To place Flo or her son inside the commune within the last two years? That makes Davis Craddock into a liar."

"Making a false statement to a cop," Moodrow continued, "is at least a misdemeanor. It's a wedge we can use to find the kid."

"Exactly." Betty opened the door and stepped out onto the curb. "What I can't figure out," she said, closing the door, "is what the Hanoverians want with a five-year-old kid."

She was walking down the street before Moodrow could answer. The question had already occurred to him and the answer, given a little thought, was obvious. If Hanover House (or Davis Craddock) was responsible for Flo Alamare's condition, denial was the only way to save the commune from an intense police investigation. The Lower East Side, long a haven for the city's freaks, had seen its share of communes. Moodrow didn't know of one that could stand close scrutiny.

He looked around for a coffee shop. Though the books about cops are filled with alcohol, it's coffee that fuels the department. There was a small candy store up the street that looked promising, but even as he started to get out of the car, Moodrow spotted a brown Plymouth slowly cruising down 30th Avenue. He didn't have to look for the word TRAFFIC on the doors. New York City's third major source of revenue, after real estate and the income tax, is traffic. If he left the Mercury, the Brownie would wait until he was out of sight, then write him a thirty-dollar ticket. A year ago, like every other cop, he'd had a restricted parking permit . . .

Moodrow shook his head. Why was he thinking about the cops so much? He rolled the window down and watched the human parade. Astoria is primarily a Greek neighborhood and the widows, in their shapeless black dresses, were out on the street. There was a fair sprinkling of Asians, too, as there seemed to be in every New York neighborhood. Most of the Asian women pushed strollers and a few were obviously pregnant. The scene was as close to bucolic as the city ever got.

Moodrow stepped out of the car, then leaned back against the door. The Brownie was ticketing a Toyota by an expired meter, and Moodrow wondered if he'd have enough time to run over to the candy store for a container of coffee. But the Brownie was already giving him a speculative look. Tickets were expensive and if you got too many of them, the state wouldn't renew your registration. He waited until Betty came back, then left her to guard the Mercury while he fetched coffee for both of them.

"There's something I think you should do," she said when he got back. She was sipping at her coffee while Moodrow, one-handed, headed off to Court Street in downtown Brooklyn. "I think you should save the blood and urine. If it's still there."

"Say that again?"

"When Flo Alamare was in the two hospitals, they took blood and urine samples. For testing. If the samples haven't been destroyed, you should have the hospital hold onto them. I got somebody off on that, one time."

"You're still thinking it's poison." Moodrow shook his head.

"I had a client about two years ago. I don't even remember his name. That's how many there are. Anyway, his wife goes in the hospital with severe stomach cramps, diarrhea and dehydration. She starts running a fever and, for a day or two, the doctors think they're going to lose her. Then she recovers. Six months later, the husband gets drunk in a bar and brags to his pal about how he poisoned his wife with bug poison. It turns out the pal is a cop informant, and he repeats the story before the husband gets out of the bar. The cops investigate and make an arrest, but all the blood and fluid they took when the wife was in the hospital had been destroyed. Meanwhile her body metabolized whatever he gave her. I don't have to tell you the rest."

For a quick moment, Moodrow felt a rush of familiar male annoyance. Where did Betty get off—a woman and an amateur—telling him how to operate? Then he came back to the professional cop, the capital 'D' detective willing to accept any help from any source, especially when the suggestion was eminently reasonable. He recalled a time when he'd jumped at the chance to use a psychic in the search for a missing girl. The psychic turned out to be a miserable asshole who'd led him from one vacant lot to another. "This is the one I see in my vision. This is the one I see." Moodrow had dug up half of Brooklyn before he dumped the psychic. The girl was never found.

"That's a good idea. I'll get the lawyer to get the cops to call the hospital. You never know what's gonna happen down the road."

"There's one other thing I think we could do. I think we should trace the kid, Michael, through pediatricians."

"That's another good idea." Moodrow was a little surprised by the 'we' in Betty's suggestion, but he let it go. "How would you go about that?" he said, pointedly.

"I guess I'd call pediatricians in Manhattan and ask them if they've ever had a patient named Michael Alamare."

"Forget it. You're talking about a thousand doctors. At least. You'd never get to them on the first call and most of them wouldn't cooperate, even if you did. You're not even law enforcement. Just a private citizen taking up time when the doctor could be making money. Most of those offices are geared up to bring in three hundred bucks an hour and the last thing the doctor wants to do is spend twenty minutes bullshitting with a lawyer." Moodrow had spent most of his career canvassing neighborhoods. Or contacting 'every car rental agency in the city.' Sherlock Holmes would not have understood, but the main thing separating good from mediocre detectives is efficiency.

"So what are you saying? Give it up?"

"Not at all. You just have to be a little smarter. First, do it by mail. You can address, stamp and seal a thousand envelopes in one day, if you organize it right. Second, Connie Alamare has a picture of the kid when he was around two years old. Get it blown up and copied. Third, write a tear-jerker letter: 'Please help me find my grandson.' No mention of any criminality. Just a missing kid and 'can you help me.' That'll get the attention of whoever opens the envelope. The Medical Society'll be glad to supply you with a list of New York pediatricians."

"Why do I get the feeling I'm being hustled?"

"When you thought you were doing the hustling?"

"Yeah."

"I think your idea is good. I just don't have the time for it, right now. I'm gonna spend the next few days trying for a quick pay-off. I got an interview with Davis Craddock."

"I can't believe he's willing to talk to you."

"First call I made. No problem. I'm gonna see him on Monday morning, after I track down a few ex-Hanoverians. There's a special

NYPD squad that keeps track of cults. I got one of the detectives to give me a list of Hanoverians who've left within the last two years."

"You think they'll cooperate?"

"I think so. There's bound to be some who're nursing a grudge. Maybe they lost their money or something. Anyway, all I need is one to either put Flo Alamare in the cult or say that she left when Davis Craddock says she did. I don't wanna go out there with a closed mind, one way or the other. I saw Flo Alamare's picture when I was in the apartment and she looked like the Virgin in all the paintings. A small face, all dark eyes and curly dark hair down over her shoulders. There's no doubt in my mind that she could trade that beauty for a free ride, if that's the way she wanted to go."

They got as far as the Queens Boulevard exit on the Brooklyn-Queens Expressway before the traffic stopped dead. Moodrow waved his miniature retired cop badge at a cruiser, then asked for the cause of the problem. A jacknifed tractor trailer, he was told, on the far side of the Kosciusko Bridge, with a resulting fuel-oil spill. A story so commonplace that alternate routes had already been prepared. Moodrow, still thumbing his notebook, steered the Mercury onto the Queens Boulevard exit ramp. He'd weave through industrial Queens, head into Brooklyn over the Pulaski Bridge, pick up the expressway at McGuiness Boulevard.

"What do you think about a salad of escarole and arugula?" Betty asked. "With capers."

"I think it's the real me," Moodrow said, still thumbing through the small notebook.

SEVEN

The food at Moodrow's housewarming was so good that nobody noticed the house. Which was just as well, because the white cubicles with their two-inch plastic baseboards had about as much charm as the view of the tenements south of Houston Street, the view from the front window. The drinks helped, too. They made it easy for Jim Tilley to forget the mornings he'd spent in the kitchen of Moodrow's old apartment, drinking coffee and talking shop. The kitchen in Moodrow's new apartment was an elongated rectangle the size of a coffin. It would never be cozy and it was painted an even glossier white than the rest of the place.

Moodrow had lost some furniture in the fire that forced him out of his old apartment, more to smoke than to flame, but what he managed to salvage easily filled the small rooms in his new home. Moodrow had bought his furniture in the fifties when the word mahogany meant more than a nearly transparent veneer. The table and chairs which had fit comfortably into Moodrow's old kitchen, now crowded the sofa in his new living room. Moodrow, who was subletting the apartment, couldn't believe that someone had paid more than a hundred thousand dollars for its 1250 square feet.

But the food definitely made it better. Rose Tilley (formerly Greenwood, formerly Carillo) had been born into a family of Italian immigrants. Her mother had made ravioli by hand, carefully folding the homemade strips of dough over little piles of ricotta cheese. The result had been exquisite, but not better than the meal cooked by Betty and Moodrow. Rose couldn't imagine what role Moodrow had played in the preparation of the meal, but he was still wearing his apron when he met them at the door. Rose's oldest child, Lee, had been especially amused.

Rose, a cup of espresso liberally dressed with anisette in her hands, was happy to see her son laughing again. The last few weeks had been very troubling, ever since he'd come home with the question she'd been dreading for years.

"Mommy," he'd asked, "what color am I?"

Lee's father had been very dark and both Lee and his sister, Jeanette, were a definite light brown. This would not be a problem if his mother and stepfather were black. It might even have been livable if *one* of them was black, but Rose's skin was china-white and Tilley, the Irishman, was fair as well.

Rose had been expecting the question. (In African-American families the question would have been, "Mommy, what's a nigger?") But she had no ready answer, only a series of linked understandings that were far too complex for a nine-year-old child who needed a simple concept to defend. Of course, both children would have to see themselves as black, because that's the way America would see them. But to lock a child (her child) into a fixed, self-limiting category was heartbreaking for Rose. Like most parents, she instinctively wanted her children to reach a place she had never seen. A place not marked by concepts like African or Italian or any kind of hyphenated anything.

Jim Tilley had been more practical. "What you wanna be," he'd explained to Lee, "is your own color and not take a lot of shit from people who don't like it." Tilley had been a fighter. Over the course of a long amateur and a short professional career, he'd stopped caring what other people thought of him. He'd met his fear every time he went into the gym to spar and had beaten it down with courage. After a few years, he'd developed a rock-hard sense of his own personal value. Now he claimed that all fighters, from the flashiest champion to the most hapless 'opponent,' if they stick with their profession long enough, go through a similar evolution.

Tilley (along with Moodrow) still worked out in a local club, coaching the kids and staying in shape. When Lee had expressed an interest, Tilley had jumped at the chance to bring him down, and Rose, after a week of terrified refusal, had finally given her blessing. Now Tilley was bragging about Lee's skill to Moodrow and Betty.

"He's got attitude which is the first thing," Tilley explained, looking over to Rose for confirmation. "He's not afraid to throw punches and take his chances, which is what it's really all about. He's also fast as hell and get this, Stanley—he doesn't blink in the ring. I've got him sparring two-minute rounds, and he doesn't blink."

"You better watch out," Moodrow said to Rose, "or Jim'll put him in the ring with Mike Tyson."

"He's nine years old," Rose said.

Tilley, emboldened by the food and the alcohol, threw his hands in the air. "Hey, if the money's right, what's a few pounds?"

The object of their speculation, along with his sister, was in Moodrow's spare bedroom, the one that passed as his office. They were watching a cop show on a small TV set. Lee was fascinated by cop shows and though Jeanette, at seven, would have preferred a sit-com (*any* sit-com), she worshiped her older brother. After all, he was almost through fourth grade while she was still in first.

Betty looked back toward the small room where the kids were playing. For what seemed the tenth time, Rose was praising her cooking. Asking her how she learned. Who taught her.

"It was straight compensation," Betty finally announced. She was well on the way to getting plastered and she knew it. The knowledge, instead of making her cautious, only pushed her into speaking out. "I was married when I was twenty-one, right after I graduated from NYU. My husband was a high school teacher. I wanted kids, like every other woman in my generation, but I had four miscarriages in two years. The last one was really bad and the doctors predicted the next one would be worse. So I forgot about kids. I went to Brooklyn Law and I learned to cook. Both at the same time. My girlfriends showed off their babies and I showed off my coq au vin and my career. Twenty-five years later, my girlfriends' kids are grown and gone, but I still have my chicken and my law degree. None of us, by the way, have our husbands. Which is a long way of saying I wish I had your problems with Lee and Jeanette."

Nobody said a word. Moodrow took Betty's hand under the table and pulled it over against his leg, but Betty wasn't looking for comfort. "What I've been thinking about is Connie Alamare's grandson, Michael. What if he's really being held prisoner? He's got no one to protect him out there. As far as the police are concerned, he doesn't even exist. When I think about him, I think about the faces of the kids on the backs of the milk cartons."

"*If* he's alive," Tilley said quietly. "You have to figure that if Michael Alamare's existence is some kind of threat to the commune, Craddock wouldn't be likely to keep him around."

Rose threw her husband a dark look. "Aren't we making some big jumps here? We're taking a group of people who have a reputation for being straighter than straight and first making them drug addicts and then murderers. It's nothing but speculation."

Moodrow glanced at Betty before he decided to respond. She was following the conversation attentively. "It's not as far-fetched as you think," he said to Rose. "I took a walk around the neighborhood last night. By the Hanoverian commune. I found a character over there named Ephraim Borrano. The mutt's been a junkie for thirty years. A genuine homeboy—born in the building where the commune is now. He says there's no rumors that the 'blancos' (which is his name for all non-Latino white people) have started using drugs. But he did tell me one interesting story. You know how teenage kids are, right? Some of them have to show their macho every minute of the day. A few of them accomplish the transition from boy to man by attacking weaker people. I don't know how they figure that sadism is macho, but I've heard it so many times, I have to believe it. On the Lower East Side, the twelve-year-olds mostly attack Jews, especially Jews with beards and long coats, but it seems that Ephraim's cousin, Oliver, decided that the Jews were okay, but the Hanoverians had to go. He and his pal, Berto, started picking them off, pelting the men with stones, fondling the women, punching the kids. It was so much fun, that some of Oliver's other playmates began to join them. Now I gotta admit that this is a pretty common story when ethnic groups are mixed together, but there's a couple of interesting twists here. First, the Hanoverians never called the police. Second, Oliver and Berto were found in an abandoned building a month ago. Both dead. Both executed with a .22. Both shot behind the right ear."

Rose was the first to speak. "That's a good story, but it doesn't prove anything. If Oliver and his pal were street kids, they might have been killed by anyone."

"Oliver and Berto were part-time crack dealers, though Ephraim swears Oliver didn't use crack. You know the bull—his family's very poor and the kid was just trying to help out. Ephraim also swears that Oliver and Berto weren't killed over drugs or territory."

"How does he know that?" Tilley asked.

"Mostly, when street dealers are killed by their competitors, the word gets out right away. The executions are supposed to have a deterrent effect on future competitors. That's half the point."

Tilley nodded solemnly. "I remember Oliver and Berto. It was just after I got put on homicides. Me and my partner responded to the scene. We made the killing for drug related, but we couldn't trace it to a particular crew. Nobody makes a big deal about a couple of crack dealers, but I remember thinking it was strange."

"Even if the kids weren't killed by drug dealers, that doesn't mean they were killed by the Hanoverians," Rose said.

Betty and Moodrow stood up simultaneously and began to clear the dishes. Jim and Rose stayed in their seats. The couples saw each other often and had decided that visitors were not allowed to help, which meant that, at every other party, you could stuff yourself without paying the consequences when you did the dishes.

"One thing for sure, if the Hanoverians actually did kill Oliver and his pal (and Ephraim is *sure* they did), they're keeping their mouths shut. I guess that means they're not drug dealers."

Tilley said, "Which makes the Hanoverians the only people on the Lower East Side who aren't."

"Excuse me," Rose stood up. "If you're gonna talk shop, I'm gonna check on the kids." Not that she wouldn't like to talk about her own profession, but she was an accountant and there was just no way to make her job in New York City's Department of Sewers and Waters very interesting. Rose was trying to transfer to the comptroller's office, which at least promised greed and corruption.

"Wanna hear the latest?" Tilley continued, ignoring the jibe. "PURE. It's a joke right? There's a new brand of dope on the Lower East Side. Everybody wants it. Junkies and cokeheads both. PURE. Maybe they wanna be virgins again."

"So what's the big deal about a new brand name for dope?" Moodrow called. "Smiley D, Blue Thunder, Beam-Up . . . Every dealer on the street has a cute name for his drugs."

"This is a little different, Stanley. This comes in vials, like crack, but it's a powder, not rock. The vials are sealed with different colored caps according to potency. The seal proves that the dope is pure."

"Have the narcs seized any of it?"

"We got a few empty vials from a snitch, but whatever was inside them, wasn't heroin or cocaine."

"What was it?"

"When I find out, you'll be the first to know. The junkies seem to love it, but the word is there's only a little bit of it on the street."

Moodrow, a stack of plates in one hand, half a cheese cake in the other, marched into the kitchen. Betty was standing by the sink.

"I know that kid's alive," she said. "Michael Alamare." She looked sideways at Moodrow, not wanting him to be teasing or even tolerant, and found him composed and serious. "I think the cult has him and he's in trouble. I see him as a prisoner, as a caged animal."

Moodrow stood over the garbage pail, patiently scraping the dessert plates. He and Betty could barely fit into the tiny room. "I once had a supervisor who kept talking about 'trust your instincts, trust your instincts.' What I found out is that sometimes my 'instincts' were nothin' more than a bullshit ego trip. Not all the time, but enough so I made a decision to check *everything*, no matter what my instincts told me. You have to do all the little things right, because if you leave anything out some Legal Aid lawyer's gonna shove your search warrants so far up your butt, you'll be able to read them without your glasses."

EIGHT

Abou Jefferson was still in a sulk. Scrunched down behind the wheel and not saying a word even though he usually never shut his face. That was all right, though. Wendell Bogard could understand that. All those years wearing rags and eating with the roaches. Abou wanted no part of driving his old man's shitbucket when he could be toolin' down the boulevard in the red Benz or the black Samurai with the black windows and the Pyle Driver pushing out beats at 700 watts per channel. Shaking so loud even the cabbies turned to look.

"Hey, Abou, we havin' a good time," Wendell said, business being, after all, nothing but business. "This here shit is chill, man. Like these faggoty rags and takin' yo daddy's old Buick, 'stead of the Benz. We playin' like James Bond. Y'understand what ah'm sayin'?"

What Abou wanted to answer was "you ain't payin' me to drive my daddy's shitbox car. If I wanted to drive my daddy's shitbox, I wouldn't be puttin' my ass on the line every goddamn day." But nobody played that shit with Wendell Bogard, because Wendell Bogard would pull your ticket in a minute and he could *think*, too. That's why Wendell was sitting in the backseat and Abou was driving and saying, "Oh, man, ain't this some fly shit? I ain't wear these rags since I been singin' in the reverend's choir."

And that was that. Now it was official: they were having a good time. Something very important was about to happen to Wendell Bogard, something that might move him as far ahead as he'd already come. He had to keep his mind free of bullshit like Abou's sullen expression. That was how he'd busted loose of the projects. By out-thinking the b-boys who thought a nine was the answer to every problem. "Man get hissef in *mah* way, Ah jus' *serve* his cherry ass."

Only thing was, the violence kept on coming back to chill *everybody's* ass. Your nine would roll on one night. Your enemy's 47 would roll on the next. The first night you serve him. The second night he serves you. The corners were always there. The corpses were always there. The dealers milled about, looking over their shoulders for crime cops and competitors. Only things that changed were the faces.

Wendell remembered the faces who'd come up with him. Come up and gone back down. Bozo White catching a case that equaled life plus twenty years in Attica. Essy Freeman capped thirty times from a van. (The 47s had *smashed* his body; in the coffin, he looked like he'd come through the window of his Benz and the mortician couldn't put his face back together.) Little Milton Thomas paralyzed in a wheelchair and talking about the Reverend Farrakhan. Using his one good hand to pop the pain killers they laid on him.

But mostly they'd lost by being their own best customers. Living off their fucking *product* when they knew it was the fastest way to get their asses beat back down. That they'd fall right through the dope cracks and end up sleepin' in cardboard boxes. End up in a lot with the rats and the garbage. End up like they began.

If anybody was hip to that shit it was Wendell Bogard. He'd been on the street since he was five years old. Running from the beatings his mama's boyfriends put on him. (And the times when his mama was out on the street and the boyfriends touched him and made him touch them. "You say shit to yo mama, Ah kill you, boy.") Runnin' from his mama's beatings, too. She didn't say anything when he left. Just kept on collecting the welfare until the case worker made a visit and she couldn't produce her little boy.

The welfare ran him down on the street. They put him with his auntie which was the luckiest thing that ever happened to him. His auntie didn't care what little Wendell did. Didn't hardly ever beat his butt. Didn't cook for him neither. Or buy him clothes. Or send him to school. Just produced him every month for the welfare, so that it got to be like making beats—them steady sending her the money every month and the bitch steady buying that wine and steady drinking it down with her girlfriends. Drank it on the same bench every afternoon, then staggered back into the projects to check out *Wheel of Fortune* on the television. Look at Vanna White's dress and never, never get the phrase.

"Man," Abou said, jarring Wendell, "these here maggot neighborhoods get me crazy. People lookin' at me like I'm comin' out they nightmares."

Wendell chuckled appreciatively. Even though he'd given up that bullshit about dope dealers being some kind of heroes. Wasn't no hero to it, as far as he was concerned. There was just blood and money and living large. The trick was keeping heart, mind and body alive.

Which is why he'd found his place. His place among the dealers. His place on the corner, though he never went near the corner these days. The dealers had taken him in when he first come out on the street. Like he was a pet. Feeding him when they ate, which wasn't too often. Letting him hang loose in the shooting galleries and the crack houses where a kid could see everything there was to see about the life.

Wendell was eight years old the first time he helped the brothers drag an overdose out of a busted-up house. By the time he was ten, it didn't bother him anymore. It was just something that could happen to people. Like the coke freaks fucking themselves into oblivion. No shame—just drop them pants and get down to it. Like dogs in a vacant lot.

Crack was sexual money. Twenty dollars or a hit on the pipe. Fuck as long as the hits keep coming. Fuck until the AIDS is ripping your body to pieces. Draggin' crack babies. Draggin' AIDS babies. Beamin' up till it don't matter. Until you get to some place where nothing matters, but staying stoned.

The kiss-ass years as a little kid on the corner allowed Wendell to see the traps before he stepped into them. Never touched drugs in his life. Instead, he found a dynamite dope connection and got himself nodded onto a crack corner where his product only improved business. Worked himself backward, into a better and better connection, then moved his own people in whenever a 'face on the corner' went down.

Now he was 'livin' large' and the pigs were after his ass. Every time they busted a junkie from the neighborhood, they were askin' after Wendell Bogard.

"Do you know Wendell Bogard? Can you get close to him? Will you sell the nigger out for another chance at life?"

The brothers who refused the deal came back and told him all about it. The brothers who took the deal (or pretended to take the deal) didn't know him well enough to take him out. So far, anyway.

"Turn left here, Abou," Wendell said. "We almost there."

"Man, we goin' from bad to worse. These motherfuckers so white, they invisible."

"Abou, you're a damn fool. Why don't you get smart and think about what your mouth is runnin'?"

"You hard, Wendell."

Now the boy was sulking again. Playing that pussy shit like his feelings were hurt. Wendell wanted to remind Abou that it was the *white* man who first brought dope to the brothers. The *white* man who first brought the cocaine. Now the white man was making them a new offer. A free sample and a deal to follow. Wendell had never seen dope with the power of PURE. The junkies had gone crazy. Of course, there was only that little bit, just enough to tease. Just enough to get Wendell into old clothes and an old car, to get him out to maggot heaven. Look to see if the pennies from heaven were gonna fill his tin cup.

The motel was down at the end of College Point Boulevard, where the white man had said it would be. Abou parked the car as far from the office as he could and Wendell stepped out onto the asphalt. Under other circumstances, he wouldn't walk into a situation like this without a dozen brothers to cover his play. But there was something about these little white boys in their gray pants and blue jackets, their ties and white shirts . . . you just couldn't take it seriously.

But it didn't turn out that way at all and Wendell was caught by surprise when he walked into room 35 to find the walls lined with little white faggots in stupid blue blazers carrying very large, very black AK47s. Calculating real quick, Wendell figured they could put about eight hundred rounds in his black ass before those banana clips were empty. Still, he wasn't afraid, just surprised enough to laugh out loud when Abou started shaking.

"Be cool, brother," Wendell whispered into his chauffeur's ear. "These white boys just for show. They got no reason to dog us."

Because that was the way it *had* to be. The white man had control of some very valuable property. No way he could do business with the brothers, unless he showed he had full intentions of protecting his property. Dress them maggots all alike and put them along the walls with their blank white faces and they looked bad enough to stand up to the street. Put them in that house on Ludlow Street and it'd be like going up against an army.

And the army wasn't the only surprise in the room, anyway. Maybe not even the biggest surprise. The man, himself, Davis Craddock, was sittin' on a couch with his bitch. Short and muscular, he wore a white suit and a white hat pulled down so far it nearly hid his small black eyes. The bitch was stuffed into the tightest green leotard Wendell had ever seen. No panties under or over. The leotard jamming into the crack of her ass.

"Mr. Bogard. Welcome. Davis Craddock, here." Craddock stood up and stretched out a small hand. His nose was sharp and prominent, dominating his face. "This is Marcy Evans."

Wendell, much to Abou's surprise, grinned broadly and gave Davis Craddock a full-out Iowa pump handshake. It was a marriage made in heaven, as far as Wendell was concerned, because if there was anything he loved, it was a crazy white man. Mostly, the white people in his life had been welfare workers who talked shit like, "Did anybody touch you in a bad place?" Instead of, "Did the nigger make you suck his dick?"

Wendell had known some crazy white people on the street. Bad motherfuckers ready for the first asshole to get up in their faces. Didn't care about shit like jail or pigs or even about keeping their asses alive. 'Death Before Dishonor' tattooed on the arm and the motherfuckers steady believin' it.

"How are you, Mr. Craddock?" Wendell, catching the look on Abou's face, dropped the smile and thanked the good Lord that Abou wasn't strapping tonight. "I'm Wendell (he pronounced it wen-*dell*) Bogard and this here is Abou Jefferson."

"Mr. Jefferson?"

Craddock extended his hand, but Abou wouldn't even look at it. Wendell wasn't sure whether Abou was scared or mad. Didn't care much, either. He could feel opportunity reach out to him like all the dope-high promises that kept his customers coming. Wendell didn't shoot dope or smoke crack. Wendell was high on success.

"Abou's hostile," Wendell explained, breaking the tension. " 'Course, that's the way the jam's supposed to go, right?"

Craddock looked at him for a moment, then laughed. No satire in it, though. A pleasant 'we're all good fellows here' chuckle. "You're a wonder, Wendell," he said, glancing toward the woman. "Isn't he a wonder, Marcy?"

"Sure, Davis."

Her eyes rose to meet Wendell's. They promised anything but the truth. It was a game, pure and simple. Which didn't bother Wendell. Not as long as it was crazy.

"Let's go into the other room," Craddock said, indicating a door connecting to the next suite. "Where we can have some privacy." When Abou started to move with Wendell, Craddock put out his arm. "I don't wanna be pushy, but we're gonna talk about matters that cops call 'incriminating.' If we make a deal, the secret's gonna come out. I accept that. But if you refuse, it'd be better if the rumors are unsubstantiated."

"I think the man is sayin' that you gotta chill out in here," Wendell said to Abou.

"If the bitch go in, I go in," Abou said.

"You go where I motherfuckin' say, punk." Wendell gave Abou his hardest cold killer smile. Cold enough to freeze Abou's black balls. Abou was *permanently* pissed, pissed from the day he was born. Which was cool, as long as he was pointed in the other direction. Wendell Bogard didn't have no partners. "Anythin' else you say be dissin' me. You dis me, I don't forget."

Abou read the message and let his eyes drop down. There wasn't no shame, because Wendell might as well have been speaking Urdu for all the white man, crazy or not, understood.

Marcy Evans led the way, with Wendell following and Davis Craddock bringing up the rear. Abou, left standing among the enemy, looked around the room, then snorted decisively. "White motherfuckers," he muttered, before going off to the kitchenette in search of a beer.

Davis Craddock locked the door as soon as they were inside. "You want a hit?" He held up a small vial of white powder.

"Sorry, but I don't use no dope. Man who *sells* death, got no business eatin' it."

"I'm disappointed. I was hoping you'd personally try the sample I sent you."

"Why's that?"

"I think the reasons are obvious."

"Shi-i-it. I *do* love a crazy white man. 'Course, that don't mean I wouldn't spray the motherfucker who tried to make me look like a chump. Crazy or not."

Craddock only smiled and spread his hands apologetically. "You're an amazing man, Wendell. Wonderful, really. But I understand you better than you think I do. You pretend that you don't care what happens here, but I know you didn't drag your butt out to Whitestone just to put me down. I think you're full of shit."

Wendell looked into Craddock's eyes. Threw him the baddest badass stare in his arsenal, but there was no fear. The man looked happy. Like he was playing and winning. "Must be the army," Wendell said, relaxing into acceptance. He'd caught himself a crazy white man with a bottomless bucket of gold.

"Army?"

"The army in the other room. A man with a army don't have to fear too much. I'm sayin' this like from one general to another."

Davis Craddock accepted the compliment, then gestured to a club chair drawn up in front of an easel. "Fair enough," he said, all business now. "Let's get down to it." He uncovered a bright green chart drawn by hand on oak tag paper. "I'm going to make a bunch of assumptions here. Don't bother confirming. I'm going to assume that you received the product I sent over to you, that you've given it a fair trial and that you like the results. I further assume that you see a chance to advance your own economic interests by purchasing this product from me. You're here tonight to find out exactly what PURE is and what it will cost you to obtain it in large quantities."

"That sounds good," Wendell said evenly. "Sounds like you makin' me a proposition. Only thing about it is I know you already set up somebody else. Nigger called Deeny Washington. If you lookin' to have a man of my size for a partner, you got no bidness settin' up a junkie asshole like Deeny Washington."

Craddock smiled. "Can we get to that later? I promise I'll make it clear."

"As long as we get to it."

Craddock took the pointer and tapped the chart on the easel. "The first thing I did was make the decision to create PURE. The second thing I did was define the drug I wanted before I went into the laboratory. I was determined not to settle for the first compound that made a mouse tipsy. This chart lists the qualities I decided on. First, the consumer should be able to use the drug in a variety of ways: injection; inhalation; smoking; eating. Second, the purity of the compound should be carefully controlled so that accidental poisonings and overdoses are eliminated. Third, the drug should be physiologically addicting. Just as morphine is ten times as addicting as opium and heroin ten times as addicting as morphine, the new compound should be ten times as addicting as heroin. In fact, carefully controlled studies with laboratory animals have shown PURE to be thirty times as addicting as heroin. Fourth, the drug should produce the exhilaration of cocaine, along with the compulsion to repeat the experience as often as possible. Fifth, the duration of the cocaine-like high should be increased to match that of the heroin-like high. Sixth, the compound should be packaged in tamper-proof containers so that the consumer, no matter where he or she purchases the compound, will receive exactly the same product. Seventh, the drug should be marketable at competitive prices. A single dose for a casual abuser should not exceed ten dollars. Eighth, the drug should be as profitable as heroin or cocaine in order to attract retailers.

"The final compound, which has all of the above qualities and which I intend to market under the name PURE, is similar to heroin in that it reduces anxiety and eliminates the sickness associated with heroin withdrawal, but it is *not* heroin or any other known opiate. PURE is also similar to methamphetamine in that it fills the consumer with energy and confidence, but it is *not* methamphetamine. These *nots* are very important in terms of my goals."

Craddock turned back to the charts. He nodded to Marcy, who made a little curtsy before removing the top chart to reveal another. "This chart describes the process by which the government could make PURE illegal. I should say the process by which PURE *will* be made illegal. Sooner or later, the cops will call PURE to the attention of the legislature and the legislature will add PURE to its schedule of forbidden drugs. Until that moment comes, no one can be prosecuted for selling or possessing PURE. The one-hundred-million-dollar question, of course, is how long entrepreneurs, like ourselves, can expect this situation to last."

"That *is* the question," Wendell interrupted. "If there's enough time and enough PURE, the dope could be all across the country before the pigs figure it out."

"My sentiments, exactly. Now here's how it works. The basic federal narcotic law was written in 1970. It's called the Federal Comprehensive Drug Abuse Prevention and Control Act. The law has a number of schedules. Drugs are put into one schedule or another according to how dangerous they are. New compounds can only be added to the schedules after a series of steps are taken. First, the Attorney General of the United States must determine that the compound has a high potential for abuse. Second, the Attorney General must go to the

Secretary of Health, Education and Welfare, present his evidence and gain approval."

Craddock nodded to Marcy who removed the chart to reveal still another piece of carefully lettered oak tag. "Assuming agreement between the AG and the Secretary, a committee would be created and asked to make the following determinations." He banged the pointer against the oak tag, smiling like a stand-up comic anticipating a good punch line. "First, establish the new compound's actual or relative potential for abuse. Second, collect all scientific data regarding the molecular structure of PURE. If this structure is not known or is still being studied, the proceedings must stop until the psychoactive molecule or compound is identified. Third, determine the history and current pattern of abuse involving the new compound. Fourth, determine the risk to public health, if there is a risk. Fifth, establish the potential for physiological and/or psychological dependence.

"I don't think they can do this in less than two years. A year to figure it out and a year to do the research. That's federal. The states are less predictable, because each state has its own laws, but I'd be shocked if the states, with the possible exception of New York and California, move more quickly than the federal government. Most likely, the states will let the feds do the work, then follow behind. The trick is to set up national distribution before introducing PURE to the general public. By the time the legislatures act, PURE will be the hottest drug in the marketplace. Hotter than crack ever was."

Wendell allowed himself to relax into the chair. Crazy white men. They were the wonder of the world. Stand out there in a suit the color of vanilla ice cream and point at motherfucking *charts*. Like they were two executives in an office. Funny how when white men wanted to do business with a brother, they learned to talk without saying the "n" word. "What's this shit gonna cost me?" he asked.

"Thirty-five hundred an ounce. It'll be the cheapest drug ever seen."

"Shi-i-i-it. That's more than what coke's goin' for right this minute. How you gonna sell it to dudes buyin' ten keys at a time?"

"PURE is much more powerful than cocaine. I'm talkin' about twenty-eight hundred doses in an ounce. Twenty-eight thousand dollars on the street. There's room for two or three mark-ups between my price and retail. And there's a bonus, too. Once PURE is established as a force in the marketplace, the formula can be sold to the highest bidder. As I see it, Americans are being forced out of the drug business. South Americans and Asians are taking their place, because most drugs, at present, originate in foreign countries. PURE will not have to be smuggled across international borders. It will be a hundred-percent American. Red, white and blue. Tried and fucking true."

"How'd you get hold of my name?" Wendell abruptly changed the subject.

"I got it from the aforementioned Deeny Washington. Marcy's recruited him for our test marketing project. At first, he was afraid. Afraid of *you*. He said you were the big dope man for the Lower East Side."

"I don't see why you set up that loser with this good dope. Man don't know shit about dope."

"Deeny Washington wasn't chosen for his knowledge of the drug business. I want to test PURE on the open market before I begin to manufacture in large quantities, but it's very important that any undue attention generated by this test marketing come to a dead end. And I do mean a *dead* end. Deeny Washington is the ultimate expendable. A terminal junkie with every disease known to man. Once our project is completed, Deeny Washington is gone."

"And you want me to do it?"

Craddock laughed shortly. "I can see how you'd arrive at that conclusion, but appearances are deceiving. I presume you'd have no trouble dealing with this kind of problem—you *are* a businessman, after all— but I'm looking forward to eliminating Mr. Washington myself. Mr. Washington has become Marcy's slave. He'll do whatever she tells him to do. In fact, he's come to trust her so much, he lets her prepare his injections."

"I get the picture." Crazy white motherfuckers. The wonder of the world. The wonder of *his* world. Old Davis wasn't gonna do it to show Wendell how bad he was. Davis was gonna do it because he liked to do it.

"Then I invite you to watch closely while PURE enters the marketplace. There's plenty of competition in our test marketing area and PURE is priced competitively. In effect, the heroin and crack addicts are deciding just how desirable our product is. But let's assume that all goes well. Let's assume that our consumers love PURE. In that case, I'll put the manufacturing end into high gear while you set up local, regional and, eventually, national distribution. My goal is to market two hundred pounds of product, then sell the formula and get my white ass out of the business. I intend to accomplish that before PURE becomes illegal. And, of course, I guarantee you exclusive right to market PURE. Assuming you can handle the weight."

"Man, you must be jokin'. Two hundred pounds? That ain't more than ninety kilos. Shouldn't be no problem whatsoever. Long as I get first bid on the formula when we're done."

"I believe we understand each other."

Wendell took out a handkerchief and blew his nose. Crazy was what the man was. Crazy and beautiful. In the meantime, Wendell Bogard's future was looking like more than a jail cell and a series of high-priced lawyers. Imagine, a get-rich dope and the pigs can't bust your ass. Goddamn miracle is what it was. "We got to find some way to seal this shit," he declared.

"A handshake isn't enough?" Craddock asked.

"African-Americans don't do no handshakes. We do that slappin' and bumpin' shit."

"Perhaps we could put Marcy into some really humiliating sexual position. She'd love that."

"No, man, pussy ain't strong enough for what we gonna do. Y'understand what I'm sayin'? We ain't got no contract, so we got to find another way of statin' our intentions."

"And what would that be?"

"A song, my man. We gonna seal the deal with a song."

"A song?" Davis Craddock couldn't repress a wide grin. "What are we gonna sing, Wendell?"

" 'Pusher Man.' It's the national anthem of dope. 'Oh, say can you see' and that shit."

When Abou heard the words coming from the next room, he damn near shit his pants. The blonde bitch was snapping her fingers and screeching: "Yeah, yeah. Yeah, yeah. Yeah, yeah. Yeah, yeah." The other one, the maggot, was doing the lyrics in a deep baritone while Wendell stayed a little behind, working the beats. Singin' about niggers in alleys, about the pusher man being the only daddy and momma a dope addict would ever have. It was a song for the brothers and sisters, not the maggots.

Abou sucked hard on his beer. All kinds of crazy thoughts ran through his head, confusing him until they resolved themselves into a single idea: *what the fuck am I doin' in a room with thirty armed maggots when all I got is my motherfuckin' dick to shoot with?*

Because if there was one thing Abou hated more than anything else in the world, it was a crazy white man. Never knew *what* the fucker might do.

NINE

from *The Autobiography of Davis Craddock*

Heeeeeere, Poochie, Poochie, Poochie. Here, Poochie. Here, Pooooooochie. Hop! Skip! Jump! Fly! That's a good Poochie dog. That's a good doggie.

Dear Marilyn provided the answer for my Poochie obsession. As she has for so many other obsessions.

I couldn't get the cult thing out of my head. It seemed such a simple thing. There had to be tens of thousands of poochies out there and I only required a couple of hundred. Unfortunately, poochies are solitary creatures.

Imagine a lake filled with ravenous piranha. A few tiny goldfish cower in holes at the very bottom of the water. You are the fisherman. Your task is to catch the goldfish, but you keep hooking piranha. They swarm over your bait while the goldfish live on whatever crumbs fall to the lake bed.

The challenge? To manufacture a bait that attracts the goldfish without interesting the piranha. Ordinary human beings (as voracious as piranha—just ask any dolphin) would be a constant source of friction and dissent. My vision was of obedience unto death.

The classic answer, of course, has always been 'esoteric' religion and the search for 'enlightenment,' but can you see me as Guru Davis?

Perhaps I should change my name. Swami Rumphump. That has an esoteric Indian ring to it. What Poochie could resist Swami Rumphump?

Simple truth, boys and girls: I don't know a chakra from a mantra. Worse still, it has long been my opinion that religion is the most pitiful of all human endeavors.

Nevertheless, I spent the month following the Jonestown massacre in the library, researching cults. All were based on religion. Even the ones that encouraged the use of drugs had some spiritual message at the heart of their bait. "Trust in me and I'll set you free."

I imagined myself in white robes. My followers sat before me (in full lotus position, of course), begging for spiritual enlightenment.

"Enlightenment? That will come in time, my little butterfly. First you must cast off your ego. You must remove your inhibitions. Along with your panties."

I might be a Christian or a Hindu or a Buddhist or . . .

After a month of intense fantasy, I was forced to admit that I could not be a priest. Even if I learned to bring off the role, it would take me years to gather my disciples. The admission depressed me and, as compensation, I seduced Marilyn.

It came as a surprise, even to me. Such a mousey little woman. She moaned slightly when I cupped her tiny breasts, but she didn't resist. For all her talk about sexual repression, she was near to being a virgin. When I laid her out on the bed, she (just as she advised her clients) lost all inhibition.

Marilyn was the first poochie. Perhaps I should have had her stuffed and mounted. With her short, straight butchy hair and her uncorrected rabbity overbite, she would have done well in a display case.

No bait was used, of course. We were thrown together by circumstance and once Marilyn set me free, I simply lacked the inhibition to keep my hands to myself. I wanted her and I reached out. Later, I discovered that Marilyn, from the psychological security afforded by her profession to the greedy wet nature of her sexuality, was a very typical Poochie.

Instead of a post-coital cigarette, Marilyn began to talk. Lying back on the pillow and seemingly oblivious to the wet sheets beneath her butt, she outlined her 'dream.' She had developed a unique therapeutic method and was in the midst of writing a book outlining her theories. Her method involved intense interaction between therapist and patient. Patients, she insisted, would become therapists themselves, creating a mutual interdependence that would eventually counter the damage done by the nuclear family.

That was her bug—the nuclear family. She blamed all the ills of the world on this 'unnatural relationship.' It was certainly unnatural in her case. She'd been molested by *both* her parents. (A fact which intensified the sexual fantasies that allowed me to match her sexual ardor. I imagined her, five years old, naked in front of her naked mother. She lies back on the bed and . . .)

What did I know about psychological theory? Not a damned thing. I'd been training to be a chemist when my crime occurred. Therapy was a condition of my probation. Far from choosing Marilyn, I had been assigned to her by a computer that keeps track of analysts who accept Corrections patients with no resources beyond medicaid.

Of course, I made the cult connection immediately.

Here's my crime. See if you think it reprehensible.

I killed thirty-six rabbits in an unauthorized experiment at CCNY's College of Engineering.

Rabbits! For this slight indiscretion, I was expelled. (I love that word: expellllllled. As if academia decided to shit me out.) I was also charged with breaking and entering, destruction of school property, cruelty to animals and assault.

(Here's an interesting notion: human concern for the welfare of other species can be seen as a measure of human evolution. By this standard, I am a throwback to *australopithecus*. I have no concern for *any* species. Especially my own.)

The university's chemistry department had received a shipment of neurotoxic venoms for an experiment on the use of poison in the treatment of various diseases. *My* experiment, which I intended to write up for my biology class, concerned the speed with which these venoms dispatched rabbits.

I think I had the faculty convinced that my experiment was sincere. Until my roommate, Bernard Epstein, brought in the video tapes.

I ask you: was it wrong of me to record the demise of my rabbits? Aren't the convulsions of rabbits as relevant as heartbeat and respiration? I caught up with Bernard Epstein a couple of hours after my expulsion and beat the living shit out of him. That's when the university decided to press criminal charges.

My attorney, court appointed, pleaded me guilty after working out a deal with the prosecutor. Naturally, my background was taken into account: my disturbed mother, my violent, long-gone father, my social isolation. The judge delivered a lengthy lecture, the gist of which was, "If I find your ass in my courtroom again, I'll put you in jail for a long, long time. You need restraint, boy, and if psychology can't provide it, the penal system will."

Marilyn was delighted to have a collaborator who fucked her three times a day. And I was able to shape my bait with malice aforethought.

Marilyn thought of me as cured. I was the living embodiment of the efficacy of her theories. All that and an active penis too? Here, Pooooochie.

Those were wonderful times for me. Marilyn was very generous. She'd inherited money from her parents and could afford to keep me in style.

I lived without economic anxiety for the first time in my life. I moved into Marilyn's apartment. I ate her food, used her credit cards for clothing, drove her car. After a few months, she listed me as a therapist and paid me a salary. My own therapy stopped and I began to see patients.

Meanwhile, she continued to write her book and I was able to manipulate her theories so that (coincidentally, of course) the dynamics of her therapy paralleled those of every cult I'd studied.

I cut the patients off from their families, drawing them into the bosom of the cult. I discouraged single partner sexual relationships. I separated children from their parents. I established a commune for advanced therapy. I found repressed, frightened little poochies and made them feel powerful. I took compulsive masturbators and let them fuck like bunnies and told them indiscriminate sexuality would cure them of their psychological ills.

Along the way, I invented a little method for separating the piranhas from the poochies. I called it confrontational therapy. The name describes the experience exactly. Therapists were trained to humiliate the patient from the *opening* session. Names were used: coward, wimp, faggot, pussy, bitch, cunt. The method was supposed to shock patients into receptivity. Here, Poochie, Poochie, Poochie.

The piranhas never made it past the first session. In fact, most of the piranhas didn't make it *through* the first session. But all the poochies came back and as one session followed another, the poochies became poochier and poochier.

Here's how it worked: we did a certain amount of advertising, but we didn't accept referrals, either from other psychologists or from the various social agencies that plague New York City. Our patients had to seek us out at our Union Square offices. After a few sessions, assuming the Poochie returned for subsequent appointments, he or she was invited to join a group therapy circle. These circles consisted of six or more new patients led by an experienced therapist. Eventually, poochier patients were invited to become 'part of' Hanover House, the cult commune. Results: uncontrollable piranhas were eliminated before they got close enough to cause any damage, while the poochies were properly prepared for life on Ludlow Street before they came through the doors.

Here's how it worked: Early on, when I was still a Therapist, a young woman named Marcy became my patient. In the course of our first sessions, she related the recurring dream which had moved her to seek therapy. The dream took place in a courtroom. She was on trial for something—she wasn't sure exactly what—unrelated to sex. One of the lawyers called her to the witness stand and she was about to begin her testimony when the judge suddenly interrupted. He ordered her to remove her clothing, explaining that her testimony could only be delivered in the nude. The agony engendered by this experience was so intense that she inevitably woke up before her bra hit the floor.

I didn't use the standard confrontational techniques on Marcy. Her poochiness was more than obvious. I was kind to her, instead, and she was properly grateful. She was a chubby girl (as are so many poochies), but she thought of herself as grotesquely fat. She hadn't worn a swimsuit in years, hadn't worn shorts or a sleeveless T-shirt.

When she admitted her virginity (in a halting, pitiful, poochie voice), I nodded my head thoughtfully. But I *knew* that if I managed to penetrate that puss, she'd be my slave for years to come.

After a few months, I invited her to join a circle I was forming and she readily agreed. The first sessions passed uneventfully. The poochies were sizing each other up. They were afraid of rejection, but, later, when they were more secure, the stronger members would rip the weaker ones apart. Leaving *me* to pick up the pieces.

We were in the middle of our fifth circle, when I ordered Marcy to stand up. She complied, but she was obviously frightened.

"I want you to expose your breasts," I said solemnly.

"Please . . ." she whispered.

I ignored her, turning back to the others as if my request were commonplace. She looked around the room wildly, but there was no way to get out of it. It was either bare tit or out the door. I didn't particularly care which.

She finally did it. Her skin reddened from her waist to her ears, but she unbuttoned her blouse, removed it. Then her bra.

She had large firm breasts. I was glad to see that, because I knew I'd have my head between them before too long. She stood there for the remainder of the session. Her shoulders were slumped, but she didn't try to cover herself with her arms. Nobody spoke to her. They thought I was punishing her, and they didn't want to share her fate. Several potential piranhas kept looking at her. They wouldn't be back, which was, after all, the point of the exercise.

I left as soon as the meeting was over. Marcy was buttoning her blouse as I opened the door. She was crying softly. An hour and a half later (after a decent supper in a small Italian restaurant), I knocked on her door.

There was no hesitation on her part. She bled so much I wanted to announce my triumph by hanging the sheets out the window. I told her that she'd come over an enormous therapeutic hurdle. She was light years ahead of the others, and Hanover House was open to her whenever she wanted to come.

She bought every word. Toward sunrise, I had her walk around the room, then pose. The poses became more and more provocative as she overcame her inhibitions. In the years that followed, she proved herself the most promiscuous of all my little horny poochies.

Here's how it worked: Marilyn wrote a veritable tome. *The Human Reality: A Manual for Growth*. Five hundred pages of unproven speculation (supposedly based on the work of mainstream psychologist Martin Hanover) describing every aspect of human development within the nuclear family. And how to fix it.

Integrated Affect. Interpersonal Pathology Systems. Repressive Dynamics. Confrontational Therapeutics.

It was all bullshit and the academic world threw up a shit storm of scorn. That was our second success. Religious cults are inevitably cast out by the mainstream. That's why they can claim to offer the one true real knowledge that ordinary humans fail to perceive. That's how they convince society's rejects that they (the rejects) are the elect, the worthy, the saved.

How does it go? Blessed are the meek, for they shall have sex? No, that's not right . . .

Our patients studied Marilyn's book. They were invited to participate in their own therapy. Within a few months, the more talented were cursing back at their Therapists. Then they became Therapists themselves.

Two years after Marilyn completed *Human Reality*, I had a hundred poochies dangling from my belt.

Five years later, I convinced my poochies (Marilyn included) to buy three joined tenements on Ludlow Street, near Delancey.

Two hundred poochies—that was my vision and I had them.

I fantasized an apartment-cleaning business and my poochies put it together. They worked it, ran it, advertised it and gave me the profits.

I fucked all the women. The chubby ones, the ugly ones, the hairy ones, the dirty ones. I didn't have to search them out. Contact with my penis became a ritual test of worthiness for admission to Hanover House. They came to us. They lived with us. They worked with us. But they were not *us* until I fucked them.

The men had to fuck Marcy, my first and my best.

I exercised enormous power in the lives of all Hanoverians, and I was arbitrary in my exercise of that power. I humiliated some and exalted others. My rejection was tremendously painful, but the most common reaction was a desperate attempt to understand the rejection in terms of *Human Reality: A Potential for Growth*.

Some days I humiliated every blonde I met. On other days I chose left-handed women. Or balding men. Or Jews. I was unveiling the putrid core of their psychological disease and they often came to thank me for bothering to show it to them.

The women had permanent beds. The men rotated on a weekly basis. *Everybody* got laid.

I encouraged them to have children, but kids were separated from their mothers shortly after birth and raised communally. Hanover House would command their deepest loyalties.

Money was communally held. Workers signed their checks over to Hanover House, then filed weekly requests for an allowance.

Decisions concerning Hanover House were decided by democratic vote and subject to my approval.

I siphoned off nearly fifteen percent of Hanoverian revenues. Less in the beginning, when we were struggling to pay the mortgage. Then more and more as my 'project' developed.

The young girls were the absolute best. As I said, we pulled them away from their parents in infancy. Their only loyalty was to Hanover House, and *I* was Hanover House. My rule of thumb was 'old enough to bleed, old enough to butcher.'

Droit de seigneur, señor?

Here, Poochie.

TEN

In some ways, Stanley Moodrow's afternoon was going splendidly. Traffic in Manhattan, for instance, was almost nonexistent. The warm Sunday afternoon, the first of the new year, had lured many New Yorkers away from their island, to the country or the beach. Still, luckily enough, Moodrow was having no trouble finding people at home. He was interviewing former Hanoverians, trying to place Florence Alamare and her son, Michael, within Hanover House in the recent past. The list of ex-cultists had been compiled by an unofficial

NYPD squad that dealt with subversive organizations, political or spiritual, passing (also quite unofficially) pertinent information to other individuals or organizations with a 'need to know.'

Private Investigator Stanley Moodrow certainly had a need to know, but as he was a nothing PI instead of, for instance, chairman of a congressional subcommittee, his need would have gotten him exactly nothing, if he hadn't been a friend of Detective Lieutenant John Flaherty, who ran the squad. Flaherty was on a list of acquaintances Moodrow had begun several years before. The list included every precinct and every special squad and who, in the course of a thirty-five-year career, Moodrow knew well enough to ask for a favor.

Moodrow had begun his interviews at ten in the morning, working patiently through the afternoon and early evening. Now it was nearly eight o'clock and he was headed out to Brooklyn and the last of the ex-Hanoverians living in New York City. All told, he'd seen seven people. Or yelled at them through closed doors. Or cursed them quietly as he walked away from total silence. That was the one fly in the day's ointment. The witnesses were easy to find, but they wouldn't talk to him about Hanover House and its master, Davis Craddock.

They were afraid, of course, obviously afraid. The few who'd spoken to Moodrow civilly had given the same message: upon leaving the cult, they'd signed a 'contract' in which they'd 'agreed to keep silent' about 'day-to-day life' in Hanover House. The words and phrases were repeated exactly. As if they were created for district attorneys or reporters or nosy rent-a-cops like Stanley Moodrow.

Moodrow knew that only fear could evoke such precise responses. The one woman who'd opened up a little (strictly 'off the record'), Felicia MacDowell, had admitted as much. "Look," she'd said, "the way I feel is that I was lucky to get out at all. It's like applying for an emigration visa in Moscow. 'Many are called, but few are chosen,' if you take my meaning. Everybody I know who left Hanover House (I'm talking about the ones who were there for more than a few months) made the same deal. We don't talk about it. Not even to each other. Not ever."

"What are you so afraid of?"

The question had been purely rhetorical, but MacDowell had answered anyway. "Maybe some of us left people behind, boyfriends or even children. Maybe some of us were born scared."

"Scared of *what*? Violence? How tough could they be? They're psychologists, for Christ's sake. I know cops who'd love nothing better than..."

Felicia MacDowell had smiled, then started to close the door. Moodrow, in good cop fashion (once you get 'em talkin', don't stop for nothin'), had sputtered one more question.

"Off the record. Okay? We're trying to get a slant on a Hanoverian. Florence Alamare. Did you know her?"

He went on to describe Florence's present physical state, hoping to elicit a sympathetic response, but MacDowell had only hesitated for a second before closing the door.

"Florence Alamare," she said softly, "is—or was—one of the reasons we're scared."

The one thing Moodrow had never done was work for the money. Not that he hadn't cashed his paycheck readily, but the amount had never been large enough to influence his decisions. A cop who's in it for the money, he'd concluded early in his career, is bound to put his hand out, sooner or later. Now the money had become important (especially because, at Betty's insistence, he'd spent a good piece of it on a paint job and a rug for his new apartment) and, whenever he thought about it, he was convinced that Connie Alamare would use the fact to bludgeon him if he didn't get quick results.

Of course, he could always walk away. From the daughter *and* the money, but the problem was that he liked the problem. It had all kinds of interesting complications. In the past, he'd most often beaten his way to the solution of the crimes he'd investigated. Pick up the neighborhood and keep on shaking until the guilty party falls out—that was one of the pieces (and there were many) of advice he'd given Jim Tilley when they'd partnered together. Who would he shake now? He'd have to unravel the whole mystery before he could start with the heavy hands.

Connie Alamare, Moodrow finally decided, was like the traffic in Manhattan or the assistant district attorneys who sneered at you when you came to them for warrants. Or NYPD sergeants who chewed you out in the locker room while the whole precinct watched. She was going to be a pain in the ass, no question about it, but New York was filled with pains in the ass. As for her daughter, Florence . . . A detective's cases are assigned. (The detective who receives a case is usually said to be 'catching.') In reality, the victim, as often as not, is as low a low-life as the perp. If it wasn't for the money, the Alamare case would be like hundreds of cases he'd handled in the course of his thirty-five years in the job. Maybe he should phone Connie Alamare and reduce his fee . . .

"Stanley, you must be getting senile," he said aloud. He was driving along Ocean Parkway, in Brooklyn, enjoying the warm evening and the large, stolid homes that marked the overwhelmingly Jewish neighborhood. "A house on Ocean Parkway" had summed up the dreams of two generations of Jewish immigrants. It was where you went when you worked your way out of the Lower East Side. Ocean Parkway, Grand Concourse, Queens Boulevard, Eastern Parkway. Broad, solid roads lined with the kind of austere brick housing that excites middle-class New Yorkers. Two of them had lost all pretense of gentility. The Grand Concourse, in the South Bronx, had become a desperate slum and was now making a comeback, while Eastern Parkway, in Brooklyn, was surrounded on both sides by some of the most devastated black neighborhoods in the country.

But that was New York. That's the way Moodrow had always known it. Immigrants arrived, first from Europe and China, but, then, from every part of the globe. They clustered together for obvious reasons, not the least of which was the suspicions and prejudices of the immigrant populations that preceded them. Moodrow's destination—Brighton Beach Avenue, near the southern end of Ocean Parkway—was in the center of a neighborhood undergoing just such an ethnic change. Brighton Beach, like neighboring Coney Island, had been Jewish, originally. Then Coney Island became Latino, mainly Puerto Rican, and slid from working middle class into stunning poverty. Brighton Beach, the locals predicted, would be next. It was already happening . . .

Urban blight was the phrase used by the media to describe the phenomena. People in the threatened neighborhoods characterized it somewhat differently. *They* were coming. With their dark skins, their drugs, their poverty and their crime. The inevitable result (given the understanding of the players) was white flight and what had happened in Coney Island was, according to the cynics, certain to happen in Brighton Beach.

There was no way, of course, for the locals to anticipate the actual course of events, that *they*, though undoubtedly foreign, would turn out to be Jewish. How, when you get right down to it, could the citizens who packed their worldly goods and took off for Long Island or New Jersey, know that the Soviet Union, pressed by every Western government, would allow its virtually imprisoned Jews to emigrate in larger and larger numbers? Who could predict that these Jews, who were not particularly religious, would reject Israel and choose America as their homeland? What crystal ball, in 1975, would have foretold that Brighton Beach would be their eventual destination?

They came all through the 1980s, just another wave of immigrants looking for a place to live. Until the media was as likely to call the neighborhood Little Odessa as Brighton Beach. For Moodrow, stepping out onto a street where the only language to be heard was Russian, it was like coming home. The Lower East Side of Manhattan, where he'd grown up, had been harboring immigrants for a hundred and twenty-five years. He was looking for a Russian nightclub called HEAVEN (perhaps in reaction to religious suppression back home) and Alyosha Budnov, father of ex-cultist Natasha Budnov.

Natasha had been the only former Hanoverian that Moodrow had bothered to phone. According to the NYPD, she'd lived in the commune for less than three months and he didn't want to come all the way to Brighton Beach if she wasn't about to cooperate. To his surprise, he'd gotten the father, Alyosha ("you will call me please Al, yes?"), on the phone. Alyosha had begged Moodrow to come out for an interview.

"Excuse me, please. Let me to explain. My daughter is from old schools. She will obey her father. I am promising this. And may that bastard, Davis Craddock, go forever to hell."

The only problem was that HEAVEN wasn't on Brighton Beach Avenue, where it was supposed to be. And the people Moodrow asked only shrugged their shoulders and muttered something in Russian. Even the counterman at the pizzeria and the proprietor of O'Roark's Fine Men's Furnishings. It is at such moments that the exotic is transformed into the annoying and Moodrow found himself wondering if the good citizens of Little Odessa were making him for a cop. Perhaps from the KGB?

It was a question that never got an answer. Moodrow finally found a Korean greengrocer who willingly (perhaps because Moodrow was looking for a Russian and not a Korean) pointed out HEAVEN's true location on Brighton 6th Street, a few yards from the main boulevard. Moodrow had never been inside a Russian nightclub, but he'd imagined the scene on the drive over. He'd pictured a small grimy room with an enormous bearded folk singer engulfing a battered guitar. The patrons would be huddled over glasses of vodka and rickety chess boards. A great, Russian soulfulness would permeate the room—the ancient wail of the oppressed made into flesh and blood.

From the street, HEAVEN met all of Moodrow's expectations. The capital letters were a faded green against a faded gray background. A peeling steel door, painted the same color as the peeling brick wall, might have led into the basement of KGB headquarters. Moodrow, smiling to himself, pulled the door open and stepped into a Russian birthday party.

The tables were covered with small plates of food, the plates stacked on top of each other with the smallest empty spaces occupied by bottles of vodka. The walls were lined with strips of aluminum that moved with the air currents, reflecting the light from a dozen chandeliers. On the bandstand, a sextet in designer clothes sang, "She loves you, yeah, yeah, yeah."

Moodrow recognized the old Beatles' tune immediately. In a way, he also recognized the men and women on the dance floor. They spanned every age, from eight-year-old girls unable to get a boy interested, to aged grande dames squired by adolescent grandsons. The men wore suits and smelled of after-shave. The women wore sequined evening gowns and sported diamonds and gold.

"It's the fuckin' Elks Club," Moodrow muttered in disbelief. "They're more American than I am." His eyes swept the room, looking for some sign that the patrons of HEAVEN were Russian. There was the food, of course. He didn't recognize anything on the plates. Then he saw a bone-thin, middle-aged woman in a low-cut satin gown fill a tumbler with vodka. Neither orange nor tomato juice was added, but the woman pulled on the drink as if it was a glass of lemonade. The gesture seemed purely Russian to Moodrow, even if the bottle of Absolut jarred somewhat.

A waitress in a gray T-shirt and plain black polyester skirt came up to him and shouted over the noise of the band. Unfortunately, she shouted in Russian.

"Alyosha Budnov." Moodrow pronounced 'Budnov' like he was ordering a beer.

"Sorry," the waitress said, throwing up her hands.

"The manager," Moodrow persisted. "Al."

"Al," the waitress repeated, smiling this time. "Budnov." She pronounced it 'Boodnuv.'

"Yeah," Moodrow said, handing the waitress a business card. "He's expecting me."

The music from the bandstand built up to a terrific crescendo, then stopped abruptly. The following silence was quickly filled with excited conversation. The only language was Russian. Then the bandleader, a platinum blond kid with hair down to his shoulders, announced, in English, that he was about to play, " 'The Russian Dinosaur,' but first . . ."

The band launched into a slow, dirge-like rendition of "Happy Birthday" while the bandleader sang, in English. Moodrow smiled at the homey touch. Then the band repeated "Happy Birthday" eight times, the only variation being the name of the celebrant and Moodrow realized that the entire crowd consisted of birthday parties. Looking more closely at the tables stacked with food, he estimated the bill couldn't be less than fifty dollars a person, even though the party closest to the bandstand consisted of more than a dozen people.

Russians must love birthdays, Moodrow thought. Followed by, *Stanley, you shoulda been a detective*.

"Mister Moodrow, hello to you." The man rushing up to pump Moodrow's hand was as tall and broad as Moodrow. He sported a thick, black beard that seemed to reach up into his eyebrows. Its color matched his double-breasted silk suit and tie. Moodrow, reading automatically, made the suit for a thousand dollars. The ruby tie-tack and the star sapphire pinky ring . . . probably another two. Of course, it didn't matter to Moodrow, but curiosity is a given with good cops and Moodrow's first glimpse of the new immigrants was having the same effect on him as Toys "Я" Us would have on a two-year-old.

"Mr. Budnov . . ."

"Please, I have ask you before. Al is my name. And I will call you Stanley."

"Moodrow," Moodrow said.

"Pardon me?"

"Call me, Moodrow."

"Ah. I have known such people who wish to be called as such."

The band began to play again. Moodrow didn't recognize the tune although it must have been "The Russian Dinosaur," as promised by the bandleader. In any event, the music was too loud for conversation and Moodrow, watching Budnov's lips move without understanding a word, shrugged his shoulders helplessly.

"We go to outside," Budnov shouted, leading Moodrow through the crowd. It was cooling off rapidly, but neither man noticed the temperature.

"You want to know about Mister Davis Craddock. Here I will tell you the story and you will understand completely. One year ago my daughter calls me on telephone to say she has found true meaning to life and she don't want to see her family no more. She is going into place called Hanover House where she will find inner self. Me, I am nearly falling down in faint. My heart is stopping in my chest. All time I was thinking she goes to the New York University where she will become doctor. Doctor is what I was to be until I ask for exit visa."

Moodrow leaned back against the fender of his Mercury. He wasn't going to have to push for this story, which probably meant that Al Budnov was proud of whatever he'd done.

"I understand that your daughter, Natasha, was in the commune for less than three months?"

"Three months?" Budnov snorted into his beard. "Is maybe more like three weeks. And even that because I have become soft American liberal. After I receive phone call, I am talking to everyone. Even great Russian Rabbi. 'Relax Al,' they tell me. 'Don't be doing foolishness. Daughter is twenty years old. She is free woman. Wait for her to come around.' I hear this for two weeks, then I go to see Davis Craddock. You want to know what I say to him?"

"As a matter of fact, I do."

Budnov smiled, rubbing his hands together. "Is no big mystery. Davis Craddock meet me with big grin on face. I say, 'Let me tell you simple life story. You don't have to make comment. Just please to listen.' He say nothing, so I go right away into life story. I say, 'When I was student in Moscow, my professors tell me to join Communist Party. This way I am certain to become doctor which is what I am wanting. Instead, I become refusenik. You know this word? I apply to state for exit visa and state respond by sending KGB. They come in black car and take me right off street. Down to Lubyanka Prison for beating. Not bad beating, just warning for foolish student.

" 'Next day, I demonstrate in front of American Embassy with fellow refuseniks. This time KGB only watch. Beating comes from Moscow police. Soon, I am expelled from university. I cannot get decent job. My wife and baby daughter suffer. I think this is worst thing that can happen to me. Then KGB searches my apartment. They find leaflets which the day before I was handing out in the street and they say I have done treason. I go to jail and wait ten months for trial without seeing lawyer or judge. Trial takes fifteen minutes. Five years in labor camp for being social parasite.

" 'Mister Craddock, are you knowing how cold it is in labor camp when you go out on January morning wearing only rags? You know how body feels when you live on soup which is water and half-rotting vegetables? Many people give up and die and sometimes I think they are smartest. Better to die than to live among people who kill each other for crusts of bread. But these things are not always according to will. I survive anyway. I return to Moscow and find my family living like worst families in South Bronx. My wife is washing laundry. Daughter is sick.

" 'I go to uncle who is in Party, borrow five thousand rubles. Then I find Americans with dollars and offer them two times regular currency exchange rate. At first, other money dealers are angry, but in Gulag I learn how to make my will felt and I am very large man, so I am accepted. I think all will be well, until I am given by informer to Moscow police and Lieutenant arrests me. He says, "Alyosha, why are you so foolish? Police know everything that happens in Moscow. You must learn to get along."

" 'He takes my day's supply of rubles and shoves it in pocket. Tells me please to call him if other police ask me for money. Otherwise he will see me each month. Soon, I branch out. I buy American products, blue jeans and radios and tapes of forbidden Beatles music. Möscovites are going crazy for such things. They buy and buy and police come only once each month to give me beating for show. My family now lives well. We have large apartment, like party apparatchik, and it is no trouble to get exit visa if dollars are passed on to proper commissar.

" 'Now, Mister Craddock, I am in America. I am part owner of nightclub. I also have taxi fleet and operate limo service. Last week, Mayor of New York comes to my nightclub looking for votes. He shakes my hand and tells me I am wonderful man. Inspiration for whole generation of Russian Jews. Only one dream left for me, Mister Craddock. That daughter become American doctor. You will help me to get this dream. In three days you will bring daughter back to me. You will not tell her that I come here. I have made so much friends in America. Believe me, friends are very, very necessary in nightclub business, because of so many commissars who must be made happy. I have discussed this with them and they are agreeing when I say I have not come all this way, from gulag to America, only to lose dream.'

"Three days later Stasha come home. Craddock has told her she is unacceptable candidate for new world he is building. I am not fool. I find proper therapist for Stasha and now she is back in school. See how dream can come true, if human being does not give up?"

Moodrow, his arms folded across his chest, smiled patiently. Budnov's tale came as no surprise. Any South American illegal could tell stories of fierce determination in the wake of enormous obstacles. Budnov, who thought he was fleeing to a new world, had brought the old one with him.

"Craddock did nothing? No threats? No explanations?"

"He look me straight in the eye whole time. He is smart, Moodrow, not afraid. I think he is thinking why he wants so much trouble for one Russian girl. When I finish story, I leave without one word passing between us."

The door opened and a young woman stepped out of the club. Short and slender, with thick black eyebrows over deeply set black eyes, she approached tentatively, like a child expecting a punishment. "You called for me, Daddy?"

"Yes, Stasha. This is private investigator I am telling you about. He wishes to be asking you about someone you knew in Craddock House."

"It's Hanover House, Daddy."

She spoke with so little accent, that for a moment Moodrow thought her father had been putting him on. "Ms. Budnov," he began. "I hope we're not disturbing you." He kept his voice very soft, his tone sincerely questioning. "I know you're busy."

"No," she said, glancing at her father, "I will help you. My father told me you were asking after someone at the commune."

"Right, Florence Alamare. They may have called her Flo."

"She was a Therapist."

"You mean a psychologist?"

"The Therapists were the ones closest to Davis Craddock. They took their therapy directly from him. There were lots of regular members giving therapy. We all did that. The Therapists kept the commune running."

"Does that include internal discipline?"

Stasha looked up quickly. "Yes," she said. "I didn't understand it at the time. I thought they were there to protect us, but now I know they were there to control us."

"Florence Alamare was one of these Therapists?"

"She was very close to Craddock. She'd been with him a long time."

"Did she have a kid, by any chance?" Moodrow deliberately failed to mention the child's sex.

"Yes, a son, Michael."

"Do you know his age?"

"Four or five. I'm not sure. I left Hanover House nine months ago."

"And that was the last time you saw Florence Alamare."

"That's the last time I saw any of them."

"One more question, all right?" Moodrow smiled and got a smile in return. "I really appreciate what you're doing. Answering questions like this. I'm a complete stranger to you. You could tell me to take a flying leap and I'd have to walk away with nothing . . ."

Natasha Budnov blushed. Moodrow was making a point of suggesting that her presence was not commanded by her father and she was grateful. "Please go on."

"Did you ever observe anyone using drugs in the commune?"

"Never. Drugs were forbidden."

"And there were no rumors?" Moodrow noted Natasha's surprise. The question had been totally unexpected.

"None."

Moodrow nodded his acceptance, then abruptly changed the subject. He described Florence Alamare's present situation, as he had earlier in the day, then asked if she would sign an affidavit that she had seen both Florence Alamare and her son at Hanover House within the last nine months. Moodrow wasn't surprised when she quickly agreed. Not with her father towering above her, as fierce as old Stalin himself.

ELEVEN

from *The Autobiography of Davis Craddock*

Riddle: When is a poochie not a poochie?

Answer: When he lives entirely in the company of other poochies.

When a poochie lives entirely in the company of other poochies, he becomes a *relative* poochie. And a royal pain in the ass.

Another, equally exciting point of view?

Most of my poochies "studied" with someone else before they came to me. They'd been Zen Buddhists or Born-Again Christians or Hindu Hare Krishnas or Sufi Muslims or all of the above.

How they loved to go on about the esoteric teachings imparted to them in the course of their studies. "Well, Muhammad says . . ."

I usually put these rantings down. It was part of the confrontational technique: "Religion is bullshit. If it weren't bullshit, you wouldn't have had to drag your sad ass into therapy."

By carefully differentiating between Hanoverian science and every other form of salvation, I made my poochies feel special.

We weren't a cult. *We* didn't refer to heaven and hell or God and Satan. *We* were a scientific investment in the future. *We* were the shining path to Utopia. *We* were the . . .

(What a bore. The only things more pitiful than Hanoverian theories are the assholes who swallow them up.)

One day a patient of mine was rattling on about his experiences with some guru or other. We'd been in Hanover House for a couple of years and by that time I rarely paid attention to what they said. I let this one go on until his bullshit passed the point of no return. Then I exploded on him in typically aggressive Hanoverian fashion.

"What's the point?" I demanded. "What's the goddamned point?"

He took it the wrong way. Naturally. He said, "The point was about the development of our efforts. Nothing proceeds in a straight line. We make real progress in the beginning, but sooner or later we come up against a stone wall. Usually, we just stop what we're doing, but if we force ourselves to continue, the line bends and the qualitative nature of the project shifts slightly. No matter how hard we try to pursue our original goal, these shifts continue periodically. If we persist over a long period of time, it's quite possible to have a project become its opposite."

He gave Christianity as an example. Christianity begins with simple, communal spirituality, then gradually becomes the Inquisition (a far more amusing enterprise, by the way).

Another example: the guru named Rajneesh. What began as a spiritual quest by sincere and motivated seekers became an armed camp wherein spirituality was maintained by assault rifles.

As it turned out, the name of the guru putting forth this idea was George Gurdjieff. The changes he described were in accordance with a (what else?) cosmic law. All human beings are bound by this law. Unless they (like Gurdjieff) have developed a soul. Once a human has a soul . . .

When is an obsession not an obsession? When it leads to a decision. When it *resolves* itself in action.

I couldn't get the Gurdjieff garbage out of my mind. Like the Jonestown massacre, it became part of every waking moment.

There were other problems, too. We were being investigated (to no avail) by the New York State Attorney General. (Doesn't that look imposing: *New York State Attorney General*. How 'bout, *The United States of America vs. Davis Craddock?*)

While the investigation proceeded, I discovered a completely unexpected by-product of my efforts. Some of our poochies had shed their poochiness altogether. Isolated from the pit bulls of this world, they'd developed the confidence to assert their pitiful individuality.

Most of them were content to split into factions. (Marilyn, of course, was leading the faction that repudiated . . . Guess who?) Others announced their intention to reenter the real world. After a year of vicious attacks (by themselves) on the weaker poochies, they felt completely confident.

This sudden resurrection should have been useful as part of the winnowing-out process described earlier, but a few of the poochies (for reasons *I* can't imagine) retained a certain amount of resentment over the methods used to effect their cure. The hope of revenge, of course, made them even stronger and there was talk of lawsuits and tabloid investigations.

To further understand my state of mind, add this: The Reverend Sun M. Moon was in jail. Rajneesh had been kicked out of the country. The Hare Krishna cult was under an all-out attack for alleged murders committed at their West Virginia commune.

Every mass media periodical was running stories about evil cults and how they enslaved their followers. As if my Hanoverians were common citizens and not a bunch of desperate poochies seeking any refuge from the big, bad world.

Now I ask you: how did I proceed? Make your best guess. The grand prize will be an expense-paid trip to freedom. How did I deal with the treachery from within? Or the threat of continuing investigations? Did I manage to keep the evolution of Hanover House on a straight line? Did I dig in my heels and fight for the purity of my experiment? Did I ride off into the sunset?

Let's back up a little. Let's back up all the way to my innocent youth. I'm twenty-two years old and a college student. Even though I'm attending City University and the tuition is negligible, my mother has been institutionalized for several years and I have to support myself. With no skills and no ability to work for someone else, I begin doing burglaries on Long Island.

Late at night (I don't sleep much, don't feel the need for it) I get into my little black Comet and drive out through the Midtown Tunnel and onto the Long Island Expressway. I watch the names of the towns. Roslyn. Glen Cove. Smithtown. I find one that appeals to me and glide off the highway.

The middle-class neighborhoods I haunt are incredibly quiet in the early morning. Thirty miles east of Manhattan, nothing moves after midnight. Apparently, the good burghers need to rest their shoulders before reapplying them to the wheel.

I search for empty houses. Look for the signs. In certain neighborhoods, the garbage men come in the early morning. I cruise at night. Which house doesn't have trash cans in front? Has the lawn been cut recently? Are there newspapers piled up on the porch? Excess mail?

I find several potential targets and note which windows are lit. Several days later, I return. Each target is carefully reviewed. Are the same windows lit? Vacationing families always leave a few lights on. The lights are supposed to frighten the burglars, but at three o'clock in the morning, a well-lit house might as well have an EMPTY sign tacked to the aluminum siding.

For six months, it all works according to plan. Breaking into empty homes thrills me in unexpected ways. I feel as if I control the lives of the families I hit. Of course, I take only cash, jewelry and the odd mink. No television or stereos; I'm a student, not a junkie. In fact, I sometimes leave with nothing.

One cold February night, the inevitable happens. I'm in the dining room and I've found a treasure. An old collection of sterling silverware. Solid, not plated, and worth at least a grand, even to a fence.

I make a noise, a thin cry of pleasure.

"Is anybody there?" A woman's voice. Unsure. Hoping against hope for a bad dream.

I conceal myself alongside the doorway and she pads into the room. For a moment, the light from a full winter moon streams through her nightgown. Then she flips the lightswitch and I take her down from behind. My arm goes around her throat, choking off her scream.

My own fear is indescribable. I tighten my hold reflexively as I listen for the sounds of a husband or children. By the time I realize no one else is in the house, the woman is nearly unconscious. Still without a coherent plan, I release her.

"Please don't hurt me," she sobs. "I'll do what you want."

Pardon me? Have I uncovered the archetypal rape fantasy? Pick a hole, any hole?

I look into her dark blue eyes and see no emotion beyond terror. My choke hold, inadvertently extended, has convinced her that her life is in danger. She hopes only for survival.

I force her into the bedroom. By now I know what I'm going to do. She has a large bed with brass foot and headboards. I tie her with strips of sheet.

As I stroke her body, I watch fear, hatred and loathing flick across her eyes. She has not been gagged, but makes no effort to scream. I take her breasts in my hand. Squeeze them hard. Tears begin to flow from the corners of her eyes.

"Please don't hurt me. Please don't hurt me."

Here, Poochie. Heeeeere, Poochie.

The sex, when I finally get around to it, seems an afterthought. As if sex was never the point. I have not hurt her (not physically), but I have been thrilled beyond my understanding. The affair, which began as an accident, seems part of my destiny. I have recognized a reality that was always present: the boogeyman in the closet come out to play.

Obsession follows. I go into homes looking for women. I begin to carry weapons: a knife, chemical mace, a blackjack. I create a disguise, a black silk hood with eyeholes, and cinch it around my neck with a red bandana. The disguise becomes my trademark and the cops dub me 'The Executioner Rapist.'

After a dozen adventures, outwitting the police becomes as important as subduing the husband and humping the wife. Though I know nothing about the men who hunt me, I give them comic book names: Dick Tracy, Dirty Harry, Charlie Chan. What will they do next? Where will they concentrate their undercover operations? Beef up ordinary patrols?

I've always worn surgical gloves, but now I use stolen license plates. I take a different route each time I visit a given community. I extend my field of activities to include Westchester County and northern New Jersey.

Though driven by desire (how I love to see their faces, the husband angry *and* aroused, the woman's flesh jerking in spasms at the touch of my fingers), I practice the art of patience. I reject one target after another. This one is too close to a neighbor's house. That one has older children. Or a large dog or an alarm system or . . .

By my twenty-third birthday, I've claimed more than thirty victims. I'm still at City College and doing quite well, financially as well as academically. For some utterly mysterious reason, in addition to the required science courses surrounding my chemistry major, I elect to take abnormal psychology. It's in this class that I come face to face with myself.

The instructor, a young woman named Roberts, is taking her Ph.D. The topic of her thesis is serial criminals, their motivations and potential treatment. "Although we ordinarily talk about serial *killers*," she carefully explains, "there are other criminal activities (especially *rape*) that also fit this category." Then she enumerates the characteristics of serial crimes:

The same crime (except for location) is committed in the same way, again and again.

The crime is committed more and more frequently as time goes on.

The crime becomes more and more violent as time goes on.

The crime does not, primarily, involve economic gain.

The criminal personifies the men who pursue him.

The criminal takes trophies.

The criminal tortures (not always physically) the victim.

The criminal feels increased by the crime, perhaps even to the point of grandeur.

The criminal believes he can never be caught.

The criminal cannot stop committing the crime.

Taken all together, Ms. Roberts calls these characteristics, "The Presence of Ritual." It is the name she will give to her doctoral thesis. And the book that follows.

In any event, the topic fascinates the entire class and we carefully dissect the psyches of various serial luminaries.

One point Ms. Roberts makes (and which, of course, fascinates yours truly) concerns the apprehension of the serial criminal. She begins by denying the old cliche: serial criminals do *not* want to be caught. In fact, the most notorious serial criminals (the ones who've been studied) took great pains to conceal their crimes. Even those who send letters to the police or to reporters.

Serial killers are caught because they commit the same crime in the same way over and over again. Eventually, the possibility of apprehension becomes statistically probable. Then inevitable. Incarceration can only be prevented by death or disabling injury or complete psychological breakdown.

I raise my hand innocently. "Are there no cases in which a serial criminal simply stopped through an act of will?" I was carefully imagining what she'd look like as I lifted her skirt with the point of my knife.

"Serial criminals are entirely compulsive, though rarely delusional. The inability to stop is what separates the serial criminal from the garden-variety psychopath."

Thus ended the career of 'The Executioner Rapist.' I never went back out. I needed to prove something to myself. Was I, in fact, a serial criminal? Or was I a mere garden-variety psychopath?

Call me Cabbage.

Nothing proceeds in a straight line. The certainty of change applies to quality as well as quantity. I had vainly boasted that, given two hundred poochies, I would rule the world. But, in fact, the poochie business is self-limiting. The bigger it grows, the more attention it draws. First the media, then the cops, then the politicians. A parade of pigs worthy of a midwestern county fair.

I needed (I concluded) *a new line of work*.

I decided to abandon the poochie business within five years. Without knowing where I would go, I decided to exploit Hanoverian therapy for all it was (economically) worth and to use the capital thus accrued for some new endeavor.

But first, of course, I had to straighten out the Grand Poochie Rebellion.

In accordance with my short-term ambitions vis-à-vis Hanover House, I devised a decidedly short-term solution. I took the *least* aggressive poochies and created a special cadre. I called them Therapists. The rest, the rebellious ones, became Counselors.

I then armed the Therapists. I also gave them better food, better housing and their choice of sexual partners. Most of all, I fed their poochie fears by insisting that they *deserved* their status. As the living embodiment of Hanoverian therapy, they were the hope of the world. The aggressive poochies were (what else?) trying to destroy everything we had built. We were, therefore, justified in doing *anything* to them.

Poochies who wished to leave were encouraged to get out. Without their children and with a deep appreciation of the three taboos: lawyers, reporters and cops. Many of them, to my relief, did so.

There remained one further impediment to the successful resolution of the Great Poochie Rebellion and that, of course, was dear Marilyn.

Instead of becoming the Queen of Hanover House, she fought me every step of the way. I tried to reason with her, but the stupid bitch really believed in Hanoverian therapy. She thought she was forging links to a better, brighter future for all human beings.

Finally, she became repulsive to me. I loathed her for her stupidity. Her ultimate essential poochiality. And I decided to make her pay.

I took out the black silk hood (holding onto potentially incriminating evidence was another characteristic of serial criminals) and the red bandana.

Marilyn had never lived at Hanover House. She had a cheap, rent-stabilized apartment on West End Avenue and she was too greedy to give it up. I had a key to this apartment. One night, when I knew her to be occupied, I secreted myself in one of dear Marilyn's spare bedrooms. When I heard her key in the door, I slid the hood over my face and tied it down.

I soon discovered that I'd lost none of my technique. I hit Marilyn extremely hard, disabling her completely for a moment. By the time she reoriented herself, she was gagged and cuffed. Staring into her eyes, wondering if she'd know me, I found only the requisite fear. Fear which increased to terror when I opened the knife.

I began to cut Marilyn out of her clothes. It was old hat to me (especially as I had no sexual interest in Marilyn), but it held her attention nicely. Of course, she begged for mercy. With my ear close to her mouth, I understood every word.

(I'd been hoping, by the way, that being a renowned psychologist, she'd come up with something unique, but it was the usual blabber: "Please don't hurt me. Please don't hurt me. No, no, no, no.")

When I cut through the center of her bra, she grunted as if I'd turned the blade inward. When I did her panties (when she felt the cool steel against the lips of her sex), she passed out.

I tied her down, then patiently waited for her to revive. When she was fully awake, I removed the hood.

Her eyes bugged out of her head. It was funny enough to laugh at, but I kept a straight face. I flicked the tip of the knife across her belly. Just deep enough to draw a single drop of blood. She began to beg again, but I continued on. A dozen flicks that would be no more than scratches within a few minutes. Then I laid the knife blade against her breast and left it there until I saw death in her eyes. Not physical death, but a bitter and absolute and irrevocable loss of will.

I untied and uncuffed her. She removed the gag from her mouth, but said nothing. While she watched, I burned the hood in a metal wastebasket.

If she chose to make a complaint, the ashes would, of course, be evidence. But she wouldn't. She would (and did) separate herself from Hanover House. She would (and did) stop seeing her old patients. She would (and did) accept a job in a public hospital. She would (and did) keep her little poochie nose out of my fucking business.

(Incidentally, I never intended to kill Marilyn. Her body would have drawn the messiest of messy investigations. From the beginning, I merely intended to exploit those qualities which made dear Marilyn so endearing.)

Heeeeeeere, Poochie.

TWELVE

Stanley Moodrow had a number of excellent reasons for being on foot. In the first place, his newly purchased, barely used, eighty-thousand-mile Mercury wouldn't start. Not even with the help of jumper cables, a

five-dollar bill and a passing cabbie. In the second place, it was a
beautiful day. A night of rain and a brisk northerly wind had rid the
Manhattan air of its customary soot and small sunny clouds were
dodging behind the sharp peaks of the skyscrapers like street criminals
avoiding a patrol car. In New York, never noted for its climate, days
like these are rare enough to draw attention and Moodrow, if he'd
bothered to lift his head, might have taken a deep breath and enjoyed
his stroll.

But Moodrow, stepping out of his new digs, kept his eyes on the
pavement. He was on his way to interview Davis Craddock at Craddock's Hanover House office. Under normal conditions, Moodrow
would have been looking forward to this initial contact with his 'prime
suspect,' but an eight o'clock phone conversation with Connie Alamare
had soured his morning considerably.

Her attitude was not entirely unexpected, of course, but it had come
so early as to be disconcerting. Sure, later on, if the investigation stalled
. . . Crime victims and/or the families of crime victims, as Moodrow
knew from his years as a precinct detective, sometimes become frustrated and take it out on the investigators. But this was only the first
week, *and* he was making progress. He had found someone to stand up
and say she'd seen Florence and Michael Alamare inside Hanover
House within the last nine months.

Not that that particular piece of information would produce any
immediate results. Moodrow and Betty had taken the promise of a
sworn affidavit to an old friend, Leonora Higgins, an assistant district
attorney with the Manhattan office. Betty had been convinced that
Leonora could get a judge to sign a search warrant. Moodrow had
disagreed and been right.

"*If*," Leonora had carefully replied, "your informant had seen Michael Alamare within the last nine *days*, instead of the last nine months
and *if* there was an intense police investigation already under way, you
might get a warrant."

"But if we can get in there," Betty had pleaded, "we can almost
certainly find some trace of the child. Davis Craddock is a proven liar."

"Listen, Betty, I know that Legal Aid people think we can put a
judge's signature on a recipe for buttermilk pancakes. That's the general myth—judges are rubber stamps for gung-ho cops and assistant
DAs—but it's simply not true. Just because the child was at a certain
location nine months ago, doesn't mean he's there now. Hanoverians,
like all other Americans, have a constitutional right to privacy and no
judge will violate that right on the basis of information that's nine
months old. Especially, when there's no real evidence of a crime."

"What about kidnapping?"

"Do you *know* that the grandmother has legal custody of the child? I'd say she's going to have to prove the child *exists* before she gets custody. And even if the Hanoverians are holding the child, it can't be kidnapping. At best, they could be fined for not notifying Special Services for Children. And that's if the father, or someone claiming to be the father, isn't lurking in the background. You want a warrant? Have the grandmother get legal custody, then prove that the cult is *currently* holding the child and that you know *where* the cult is currently holding the child. You're as familiar with the routine as I am."

"Look, Leonora," Betty had said, "the Hanoverians aren't a group of benign eccentrics. I'm convinced that Michael Alamare's at serious risk."

"All of the Hanoverian children are at risk. As are half the children in this city, for one reason or another."

"Maybe we could do something *here*," Betty had insisted. "Maybe in this one small instance, we could eliminate the risk."

"Now you know how the DA feels when a defense lawyer gets the bad guy off the hook."

Leonora's voice, in deference to their friendship, had been gentle, but the message had been clear enough. Or, if it hadn't been, NYPD Chief of Detectives Franklyn Goobe had made it clear enough. Moodrow had wanted Goobe to reassign the Flo Alamare investigation to the Seventh Precinct, where Moodrow had considerable influence. It had taken three separate calls to get past Sergeant Ryan Reilly, Goobe's fifty-year-old answering machine.

"How's it hangin', Moodrow? You solve the case yet?" Goobe's voice, when he came on, oozed jocular authority. It was his favorite posture when dealing with subordinates.

"Not yet, Franklyn."

"Whatta ya waitin' for, guy. Sam Spade'd be lining up his next caper by now."

Moodrow hastily outlined his progress and got the response he'd expected. At best, Michael Alamare's situation was a problem to be resolved in family court. How could Moodrow expect the Seventh, set in the heart of a drug-infested neighborhood, to accept another burden?

"Prove," Goobe unknowingly echoed Leonora Higgins' advice, "that Flo Alamare was the victim of a crime and we'll investigate. Get custody of the kid and prove the Hanoverians are holding him, and we'll put Davis Craddock away for twenty years. Remember, the reason why I recommended you to the old lady is because I don't think it's a problem for the cops. You hear me?"

"I hear you, Franklyn."

"Good. And one more thing, Moodrow: don't call me anymore. You're getting paid, so accept the responsibility."

Connie Alamare's call had come the next morning. *Before* Moodrow's first cup of coffee. Her voice was amazingly sharp over the phone and Moodrow, sitting at the edge of the bed, bleary-eyed, had had trouble formulating coherent responses.

"Hey, Nero Wolfe," she'd said, referring to Rex Stout's fictional detective, "today's the big day, right?"

"Huh?" The alarms going off inside Moodrow's skull sounded as if they were underwater. He shook his head, turning to read six-thirty on his clock.

"C'mon, Stanley . . ."

"Don't call me Stanley."

"What are you gonna turn out to be, sensitive? I hope I didn't buy sensitive, because what I need is tough. We're raiding Hanover House, in case you don't remember. This is the day I get my grandson back."

Moodrow hesitated, imagining himself and Connie Alamare charging into the commune. It was funny, but it didn't give him a clue as to what she really meant.

"I don't know what you're talking about," he finally admitted.

"You don't recall what you told me yesterday? Wake up, Nero, it's daytime."

"Just barely."

"You're a comedian, now?"

"What I am is a hired professional. Not your dog."

"You don't recall telling me that you were going to try for a warrant. I seem to remember that phone call took place less than twenty-four hours ago."

Moodrow hesitated for a moment. Part of the deposit she'd given him had already been spent on a car. A car which wouldn't start. "What I remember about last night is trying to find out why you lied to me about your daughter. Why you didn't tell me she'd been a junkie? You painted your daughter to be Mother Teresa, but the evidence says she was a doped-out enforcer for Davis Craddock."

"I didn't know, all right? Whatta you makin' such a big fuss about?"

"You keep saying that, but you had to know she was using drugs because the doctors told you she was."

"Does it matter that I wanted to keep her pure for a few more days? You were gonna talk to the doctors anyway."

"What matters is that I might not have taken the case at all. I don't like cases where the victim's a perp."

Connie burst into rapid-fire Italian, speaking far too fast for Moodrow to understand. Which was just as well, because he probably wouldn't have cared for the plans she had for him and the donkey. When she was finished, she took a deep breath before switching back to English. "Hey, Nero," she said. "Let's not make a fight about it. You want out of the case, send me a check and we'll forget we ever met."

Moodrow felt Betty's fingers on his neck. He'd been trying to keep his voice down, but, of course . . . Her arms slid around his chest, fingers barely reaching his nipples, as she molded her body to his back.

"What about the work I already did? The way I figure it, my hours, plus my associate, Betty Haluka's hours, plus my expenses, which have been considerable, add up to more than the deposit. I think you owe me money." Betty, having slipped her nightgown over her head, was gently rubbing her large, dark nipples against his back. A circumstance which considerably strengthened his determination not to be bullied.

"What'd I just say? Let's not make a fight. You told me last night that you were trying to get a search warrant for the commune. Why don't we start from there?"

"I made the phone calls and nobody wants to know about it. Which, if you recall, is what I told you would happen. There's progress, because we now *know* that Davis Craddock lied about when Florence left the cult. Assuming he's not psychotic, his only conceivable reason for lying is that he has something to protect."

"Get to the point, Moodrow."

"I'm tryin', okay?" Betty had his left nipple between two long red nails. She was pinching it right to the threshold of pain. "This is not gonna get done in a few days. Ouch!"

"What?"

"Nothin'. Listen. I can't get the cops to act. As far as law enforcement is concerned, the case is dead. I have a completely different angle in mind. Damn!" He snatched Betty's hand away, pulling it, quite accidentally, down into his lap. "I don't buy that Flo had a stroke and neither do you. Maybe we can find other doctors to take a look. I'll go back to the former Hanoverians, too. Be a little harsher, this time out. If nothing pops loose, I'll set up surveillance."

"That'll take a year."

"Did I promise quick results?" He groaned, a morning man to his bones. "If you wanna take me off the case, send me a release and I'll send you a statement."

With the sound of Connie Alamare's machine-gun Italian still echoing in his ear, Moodrow wrestled Betty down to the bed. He knelt above her for a moment, looking down at her body. She was heavy, maybe fifteen pounds over her best weight, but the underlying muscle was heavy enough to keep the smooth curves of her body well defined.

"You know what the old lady calls me?" he asked.

Betty ran her hand over the hair on his chest. "No, what?"

"She calls me 'Nero.' "

"After the Emperor? I don't get it."

"She calls me 'Nero' after the detective in the Rex Stout books."

"Nero Wolfe?"

"Yeah, that's him."

"Why would she do that?"

"It's a fat joke."

He waited a few seconds, hoping her laughter would subside. It didn't.

"I don't like this," he said. "I don't like it at all. Don't you remember what Dear Abby said about laughing at the male partner before intercourse? It don't promote enthusiasm."

Despite the morning sex (he was still without his first cup of coffee) and his successful squelching of the widow Alamare, Moodrow was lost in gloom as he ducked the traffic on Houston Street. He was thinking, naturally enough, about the Alamare case, but he couldn't keep his thoughts focused. He did have an immediate course of action in mind, but little expectation of results. He would interview Craddock, but the interview, though it might be amusing, would almost certainly come to nothing. He would go back to the former Hanoverians as well, looking for the names of cult members who'd been close to Flo Alamare. If he could, for instance, find an ex-lover and separate him (or her) from the cult for a few hours . . .

But the problem was that, despite his best intentions, he continued to jump from 'what' to 'why.' Why, for instance, should he give a damn about Flo Alamare, a junkie enforcer for an asshole like Davis Craddock? He wasn't a cop anymore. He had no obligation to investigate just because a crime might have been committed.

When he thought about Michael Alamare, it got even worse. Betty kept trying to make the child into the victim, but Moodrow couldn't imagine himself handing the little boy over to Connie Alamare. "Here's ya granny, kid. Have a nice life." Who was to say the child wasn't better off with the Hanoverians?

And the widow was going to become more abusive as time went on. More abusive and maybe she'd hold back on the money, too. Try to beat him over the head with the checkbook. And that was the answer to the 'why' of it. No sense pretending. Whenever Moodrow thought 'why,' he thought 'money.' He needed it and she had it. He felt like a junkie watching a busy cash register.

It was just a little past eight-thirty as Moodrow made his way down Clinton Street, but some of the shopkeepers were raising the steel gates protecting their merchandise and a few of the stores were already open for customers. Delancey Street, west of the Williamsburg Bridge, had been a haven for 'smart' clothing shoppers since the early part of the century, when Jewish immigrants had flooded the Lower East Side. The small shops, cluttered together and serving a clientele that expected rock-bottom prices, had no hope of maintaining themselves on shopping mall hours. They wouldn't close until late evening.

Moodrow knew many of the owners from his years with the Seventh Precinct. They'd been mostly Jewish, at one time, but now they came from a dozen countries spread over three continents. Moodrow nodded to the ones he recognized. A few years before, when he was still Detective Sergeant Moodrow, they would have come over to discuss their problems. These days, they waved and went back to their work.

Moodrow glanced at his watch and frowned. Once again, the sins of the flesh had come between him and the performance of his duty. If he was to keep his nine o'clock appointment with Davis Craddock, he was going to have to hustle. Nevertheless, believing, as he did, that there was, in fact, *no* life before caffeine, he turned into a small restaurant at the corner of Delancey and Clinton. The Latino behind the counter, recognizing him, grinned broadly.

"Hey, you, Moodrow, who you bustin' now?"

"Balls, José. The only thing I'm busting these days is balls. Gimme a coffee, light and sweet. Wait a second. Pour me a cup. I'll take the container when I go." Late or not, Moodrow wanted to be awake for Davis Craddock. It was the least he could do.

"Maybe you could bust the guy who fucked up Armando." José nodded to an older man, the owner, who had his back turned to them. The man was slicing onions, already preparing for the hamburger crowd. The Crown Coffee Shop was famous for its hamburgers. "Armando, come and say hello to the old man."

Moodrow was fishing for a proper retort (and hoping that José was trying to be funny), when Armando turned around. Both sides of his face were grotesquely swollen and the skin over his brow had been split. It was being held together by stitches and small pieces of tape.

"What happened to you?" Moodrow asked, the question no more than ritual.

"It was the crack, man," Armando answered. "They didn't even have enough money to buy a gun. They used pipes."

"You should've given 'em what they wanted." Moodrow felt the emptiness of the cliche, even as he spoke it.

"They didn't ask for nothin', Moodrow. They just hit me in the face and kept on hittin' me until I went down. Crazy men. If I didn't block most of the shots with my arms, I woulda been dead. And I wasn't comin' home with the receipts, either. I was on my way *to* the job. One dude was wearing a purple sweatshirt with Minnie Mouse on the front. He didn't even bother takin' it off. Alls he could think about was crack. The cops grabbed him an hour later in front of a drug house on Forsythe Street. He was still wearin' the Minnie Mouse, but he was stoned out of his mind."

"Did he snitch on his friend?" Moodrow asked, mildly curious.

"Of course," José interrupted. "They all snitch. What does it matter? The cops say these particular ones got long records, so they'll do a few years. I told the cops, 'Big deal, there's always ten more takin' their place.' I don't understand why the cops don't stop the dope and the crack."

"Just wave their arms and make it all disappear?" Moodrow snorted. "Like when your mama kissed the booboo and made it better?"

"Okay, wise guy," José said seriously, "but I remember twenty years ago, when the heroin was coming into the *barrio*. My cousins turned into *maricón* fucking junkies. So bad they beat up my grandmother for money to buy dope. I thought I was in hell, then, but if you're in hell, that's supposed to be the end of it. So tell me how it could be that hell got worse? And what kind of hell is comin' next? I got a fourteen-year-old boy and I'm afraid to send him to the corner for a loaf of bread. How's he gonna become a man when he's fourteen and too scared to go into the street?"

"Look here, José." Moodrow, unruffled, stirred his coffee. He'd been living with the failure of law enforcement for a long time. "What'd you call me a minute ago? 'The old man'? I'm retired, remember? The only thing I'm responsible for is my rocking chair. Make me a container. Light and sweet."

"Hey, Moodrow," Armando called, walking over close to the register, "wanna go double or nothin' for the coffee?" He turned his face from side to side. "How long since the *maricóns* beat me down?"

Moodrow gently pressed the swelling on Armando's face, examining the bruises carefully. "Four days. Maybe four and a half the most," he said without hesitation. "Not less than four."

Armando began to laugh. "You're still *muy hombre*, Moodrow. You're still the big fat king cop of Loisaida. Today, I buy the coffee. Tomorrow, we clean up the drugs."

THIRTEEN

Deeny Washington had never been happier in his life. He was even happier than before that fateful day, twelve years ago, when the pigs stuffed his butt into an impossibly crowded Riker's Island bull pen and he got so sick he *had* to admit that he was a miserable piece of shit of a black dope addict and would never be anything else.

Of course, the fact of it was that dope *made* you happy, even *if* a junkie's life was hell on earth. Even if a heroin addict with infected arms (like *his* infected arms) could expect nothing more than a short life and a common grave dug by prisoners from Riker's Island. Prisoners who were, most likely, junkies themselves.

Unless, maybe, some piece of heaven reached itself down to lift you up. Unless you somehow teamed up with a bitch like Marcy Evans and she fucked your wasted black ass into oblivion. Unless she gave you a place to stay and turned you on to the *baddest motherfuckin' shit ever to find a home on the Lower East Side*. Unless she made *you* the *only sole source* for the baddest shit ever to find a home on the Lower East Side.

PURE, baby! The one, the only, the greatest dope in the whole of New Jack City. The Big Rock Candy Mountain come to feed Deeny Washington's *personal* monkey.

When he thought about it (and he seemed to think about it every moment of his waking life), he kept concluding that it couldn't be happening to him. There he was, prowling the streets, an inch from being too sick to function, when she'd stepped in front of him with her palm outstretched. He'd expected to find a quarter (or, better yet, a motherfuckin' *dime*), which would be the ultimate confirmation of his slide into subhumanity, but her fingers held several small vials of white powder and when he looked back up at her, she said, "Your fucking dreams, nigger. That's what's in here. Your fucking dreams."

Of course, he was *supposed* to beat her down because she called him a nigger, but he was so sick that he let her drag him, like a dog on a leash, to a small apartment on Broome Street. The dope was like nothing he'd ever used. It took away the sickness, but it didn't leave him nodding out on the floor. There was something else in it, like cocaine, but it didn't make him want to use more ten minutes after he got off, either. It made him want to get in the bed with the little white bitch. It made him want to hump the living shit out of her, which is exactly what he did.

Or exactly what *she* did to *him*. He was never really sure, because she was as eager as any woman he'd had in his life. Even if she *did* make him take a shower before they got started. Even if she *did* wash him down with a soft, soapy washcloth. Even if she *did* clean him up like a housewife preparing a chicken for dinner and make him wear a condom *every* time they did it. (Which he couldn't really bitch about since the last time he tried to give blood, they told him he had the virus and it was only a matter of time.)

Deeny Washington giggled as he strutted along Delancey Street. The white bitch had set him up as the *sole* source for the heaven called PURE and now he had some decent bank in his pocket, as well as dope in his veins. He also hadn't been sick in weeks and his weight was back up to a hundred and sixty pounds. No more rags from the back of the soup kitchen either. Deeny's big black ass was squeezed into designer jeans, his broad back caressed by a safari jacket from Banana Republic.

But none of those particular accomplishments protected him from the sickness that hovered above him like some black vulture in a cowboy movie and he began to pick up the pace a little. He hadn't gotten off for more than six hours and he could feel the vulture dropping down from the sky, smelling the sickness as it itched and scratched beneath his skin.

Not that he couldn't put up with it. Deeny remembered days when the vulture was *this* close and he didn't have an unlimited supply of shit waiting for him a few blocks away. Days when he *prayed* for death. But that was all in the long ago, gone away past and *no* junkie ever lives in the past. If a junkie lived in the past, he'd remember the sickness and he wouldn't go back to junk after weeks of getting clean in a jail cell. After weeks of *absolute, motherfuckin' hell*. Deeny had picked up his monkey in Vietnam after he'd been wounded. The scars on his belly ran in every direction and the pain had been incredible, but, of course, he would go through *that* bullshit again and again before he'd face the sickness of being without dope.

Marcy was calling to him before he got the door open. "That you, Deeny?"

"Who were you expectin'?" He might as well play it a little bit bad, because he was sure as shit gonna melt when she held out the PURE.

"How'd it go, today?" She was standing next to the bed, wearing a Mickey Mouse T-shirt without a bra and red gym shorts over black panties that were no more than wishful thinking.

"Sold out, like every day." Deeny's cock began to rise, despite the impending sickness. "They beggin' for PURE. They cryin' for it. We got as many crack addicts as dope junkies now. I swear for a fact, Marcy, if you give me enough PURE, we are definitely gonna *own* the Lower East Side."

She only grinned at him, tossing her blonde hair back over her head, pulling her small perfect features into a baby-pout. "Didn't I ever tell you 'Pleasure before business'?"

Then she was handing him a brand-new spike and he was sitting on the edge of the bed, wrapping a piece of rubber tubing around his bicep, slapping at a vein on the outside of his arm. There were no abscesses, now that he was using a new .22 gauge needle each time he got off, and he found a vein without any trouble at all.

The vulture drifted off even before he pushed down on the plunger, even while the blood boiled up into the transparent syringe. It wasn't much of a hit, just enough to push the sickness a few hundred feet into the air. But there was plenty of PURE for later on and Marcy was already pulling the T-shirt over her head. Her shorts were already sliding down over her thighs. Her panties . . .

She took her time with him, keeping him on the edge, but not letting him get off. She did things to him that she hadn't done before, not even bothering with a rubber, and Deeny thought her abandon was due to the way his tongue moved over her swollen flesh. Not that he really cared. His body was on fire and when he finally exploded, he screamed a scream loud enough to scare away the most determined vulture in the desert sky.

"One more time, Deeny. Then a big reward." She turned completely around, putting herself astride his hips, then pushing him up into her. They were both pouring sweat when she leaned forward, laying her small dark nipples against his lips. He could feel her reaching up for her orgasm. Her whole body shook violently, then seemed to melt. He was coming, too, screaming again, though he was too lost even to hear his own voice.

She got off the bed as soon as she caught her breath, going into the bathroom, as usual, while Deeny lay back against the pillow. She would come out with a spike in her hand, a spike filled with enough PURE to keep him happy until the morning. Maybe he'd watch the Mets game if it was on TV. Order in some Chinese food . . .

"Here you go, baby." She was standing by the bed, a loaded spike in her hand. Two months ago, he'd been a terminal heroin addict waiting for the first infections that signal the onset of full-blown AIDS. Now he had dollars in his pocket and the taste of a sweet, clean woman on his lips. It was a miracle. The kind Jesus gave to His believers. Not to some miserable junkie who hadn't done a good deed since the day his grandmother kicked him out of the house.

"Thanks, Marcy." Once again, he found a vein without having to probe. Then he closed his eyes, pushed the plunger home and was dead before he could take the needle out of his arm.

Marcy sighed and began to pack her few things. She was going to miss Deeny even though she had to admit that he couldn't be left alive when they ended their test marketing. Deeny was so eager, so grateful for the changes in his life. But, then, she concluded, Deeny didn't get such a bad deal, after all. A quick, unexpected death was an improvement on the future that awaited him before he was selected to implement the program.

Fully dressed, now, she zipped the small suitcase closed, then fished the house keys out of her pocket. "Bye-bye, Deeny," she said, gathering the small cardboard box that held the still-running video camera, flicking off the lights, locking the door behind her. "Bye-bye."

Wendell Bogard watched the video tape four times. He watched in wonder, all the while thinking how the tape was evidence (but not against *him*, of course) and how only a crazy white man would be crazy enough to keep it. Two crazy white people really. The bitch was crazier than Craddock. The both of 'em cold enough to keep souvenirs. Like cowboys notching their six-shooters after the big gunfight.

At first, Wendell had supposed that his new partner was dangerous crazy. Burning with the kind of fire that sizzled until the pigs dipped it in the sewer of American justice. Only the truth was the pigs were miles from Davis Craddock's door. But not from his own. The pigs were steady scratchin' at Wendell Bogard's door.

Davis Craddock rose abruptly and stopped the VCR. "I guess that's the final proof, right?" he said, turning from blood to business with a suddenness that made Wendell want to applaud. "You heat PURE to the boiling point, it's gonna kill you. That's what happened to Flo."

"Flo's not dead," Marcy said. "Flo's still alive."

It was a game they played. Him sayin' his old girlfriend was dead and the new girlfriend sayin' she was alive. Thing about it was that the old girlfriend and the new girlfriend used to do each other. Lovers, more or less. Marcy Evans also loved to put PURE in her veins. Maybe she was wondering when she'd be dead, too. And if ol' Davis C. would give a shit.

Craddock pressed the rewind button and the machine began to hum. "I have to admit it was a mystery, at first. I'm talking about when Flo died."

"Flo isn't dead."

But Craddock was ignoring her, speaking directly to Wendell. Knowing Wendell would eat it up.

"Seems like the mystery got solved when you injected the mice," Wendell observed mildly.

Craddock shook his head. "C'mon, Wendell. Where's your scientific spirit? It's up to men like us to keep the spirit of honest inquiry alive. Sure, we did boil up a batch of PURE and inject fifty times the normal dose for a human into fifty little white mice. Sure, all fifty twisted themselves into pretzels before their tiny brains exploded. But to the scientific fucking mind, that is not proof that PURE, when heated, kills humans. It doesn't, for instance, prove that PURE killed Flo."

"Flo isn't dead." Marcy Evans was lying back against the sheets, her small hard breasts pointing straight up. To Wendell, her nipples looked like an extra set of pale, pale eyes. One time, Wendell, dreaming of chocolate brown skin against blue-white flesh, had tried to bring his own woman, Jo-Dee, into their little circle, but Jo-Dee had freaked. Jo-Dee didn't like white people very much.

Of course, Wendell didn't like white people, either, but the craziness changed it for him. Jo-Dee couldn't see that. "The white man likes to use us for sex," she'd said. "Nigger might sometime get so close to the white man, he think the white man finally love him. But in the end, the white man gonna take his white pussy and his white money and leave a nigger to face the mob. Check it out."

"So, what I had was a mystery," Craddock continued. "And a number of questions. Like, why hadn't PURE killed Marcy? She'd been using it for months without any ill effects. Why didn't PURE kill *all* of Deeny Washington's customers? Was the process of decay continuous or was it due to some external factor? If the process was continuous, all the PURE would eventually become a neurological poison and the formula would have to be discarded. But, if the process was due to external factors, maybe the factors could be avoided. And maybe PURE had nothing to do with Flo's death. The fact that Marcy found Flo with the needle still in her arm is only circumstantial. It does not represent proof to the scientific mind."

Marcy went into the bathroom. She sat on the toilet with the door open and peed loudly. Craddock took the video tape out of the VCR and walked over to the closet. He knelt down and pulled up a section of the floorboards. The space was crowded with papers, but he forced the tape inside.

"Seems to me," Wendell said, "that there's only one question here. Can we sell this shit the way it is?"

But Craddock ignored him, too. "Somehow I got stuck on the idea that our customers mixed PURE with something else. There was a chemical reaction and the new compound became poisonous. The literature is full of cases in which two ordinarily harmless compounds become deadly when mixed. I experimented with every substance a junkie might combine with PURE. Including all the adulterants commonly added to street heroin and street cocaine. Nothing."

Marcy Evans came out of the bathroom and took the syringe Davis Craddock held out to her. Wendell watched her tie up her right forearm, then slide the needle into a vein on her wrist. Finished, she lay back against the pillow, her eyes closed, her legs open. "Wasn't it amazing how fast he went?" she said. "I mean Deeny. He was alive and then he was dead. It was like there was no transition."

"Man, that was bitchin'," Wendell admitted. "Which is why I'm wonderin' if we can jus' lay this shit on the masses. Might also be the pigs'll dig like rats to find out who's sellin' dope that kills."

But the man wasn't in no mood to listen. Standin' there in the middle of the room with his little white dick hangin' down.

"My problem is that my inner cadre is *too* goddamned obedient. When I first began to test the effect of PURE on humans, I told Marcy and Flo and the others not to heat the drug because it would dissolve without heating. Naturally, they obeyed and PURE's dirty little secret remained hidden. The junkies and the crack heads, on the other hand, have no discipline whatsoever. They undoubtedly combined PURE with heroin, which has to be heated to a boil. Of course, that doesn't explain what killed Flo. She wouldn't have knowingly heated PURE. But Flo's death, I suspect, will remain a mystery. An unexplained accident."

"Flo's still alive," Marcy insisted.

"Really?" Craddock acknowledged his woman for the first time. "If you call that living, Marcy, you and I have different definitions of the word 'life.' "

"Hey, man, I don't wanna sound radical." Wendell's voice dropped down a notch. He was starting to get mad now, and he reminded himself about the money and how much he liked crazy white men and crazy women like Marcy who fucked without shame. Like whores, but for the pleasure, too. "But it's past time we killed the hype. This is s'posed to be a business meetin' and the only business we got is if we can sell this shit or do you gotta go back and make somethin' else. Ah'm talkin' about PURE. The question is can we sell it the way it is? I mean, how many junkies will it kill?"

"That's two questions, Wendell. Two."

FOURTEEN

The sixteen-family tenement on Ludlow Street bearing the small plaque reading HANOVER HOUSE was as nondescript as any of its neighbors. South of Delancey, the Lower East Side loses much of its artistic pretensions. There are no punks or dancing Hare Krishnas to lend atmosphere. When the Hanoverians had moved in, the area had been populated by Latinos. Now the Chinese had come, pushing up from the Brooklyn Bridge, paying exorbitant prices for the red brick tenements. Ironically, Hanover House and its 'weirdo' inhabitants had become the fixed point in a changing cosmos.

The man who opened the door to Moodrow wore the prescribed uniform for Hanoverian male Therapists—dark trousers, white shirt, gray sleeveless sweater, navy blazer. He consulted a clipboard, then nodded shortly.

"You're expected," he said. "My name is Peter Johnson. I'm Davis Craddock's personal secretary. I'll take you up."

Though Hanover House consisted of three tenements joined to each other by the removal of several walls, the fact could only be seen from inside. The central building, including the first floor, where Moodrow now stood, housed the cult's general offices as well as the offices and warehouse of Hanover Housecleaning. The building to the south was divided between therapy rooms and Davis Craddock's private quarters. The building to the north was a general dormitory. The rank and file lived in tiny rooms on the first three floors. The Therapists, though much fewer in numbers, lived on top.

Moodrow looked wistfully at the passageway leading to the north building. He could hear the laughter and shouts of small children at play. If he could get to those kids, even if Michael Alamare wasn't present, he could find answers to the basic questions.

"Please stay close to me."

The secretary, tall and spectral thin, turned toward the stairway and Moodrow saw the bulge of a small revolver beneath the dark jacket. It was a bit much, here in nerd heaven, but in keeping with the level of fear expressed by the ex-Hanoverians Moodrow had visited. Not that Moodrow could do anything about it. If he was still a cop, he might have demanded a permit, hoping the jerk didn't have one. If he didn't, he could be removed to an interrogation room at the Seventh Precinct. Would Johnson-the-Jerk trade his freedom for a small piece of information concerning a kid named Michael Alamare? Does a bear . . .

"This way."

Johnson's curt instructions jolted Moodrow out of his fantasy, and he followed the secretary to the fourth floor. The layout was typical of New York tenements. A narrow stairway led to a narrow landing punctuated by narrow wooden doors. You could paint the landing and the doors with subtle shades of beige and gray, but the economics of the design still prevailed. There was no ornamentation, no wasted space. The landing floors were concrete, the walls were stucco, the railings and stairs were steel.

Johnson stopped in front of a doorway. He knocked rapidly before pushing the door open.

"This is Mr. Moodrow," the secretary announced. "To see Davis. Mr. Moodrow, this is Kenneth Scott." Then he closed the door without bothering to say good-bye.

Moodrow was left standing in a small front office. A young blond man, seated behind a metal desk in the center of the room, gave Moodrow the obligatory hard stare of the trained sentry.

"You have a weapon?" he asked.

"I'm a licensed private investigator and a retired NYPD detective. I have a gun and a permit to carry it. How about you?"

"You can't bring a weapon into the presence of Davis Craddock."

The injunction *never* to surrender your weapon is drilled into every cop from the day he steps into the Police Academy. The only acceptable defense for the loss of a weapon is unconsciousness. "Why's that? Someone out to kill him?"

"No one is allowed to bring a weapon into the presence of Davis Craddock."

Kenneth Scott was much bigger than Craddock's secretary, though still inches short of Moodrow's six-foot six. His weapon was bigger, too, and more obvious beneath his coat. The temptation was to view the Hanoverians as harmless societal rejects. That, Moodrow realized, would be a mistake. Like being surrounded by a pack of twelve-year-olds on a subway train and seeing them as cute.

"If I was a cop, I'd be allowed to take a weapon into the presence of Davis Craddock, wouldn't I?"

"You're not a cop. You're a private investigator."

"Yeah, but you said *no one* is allowed to see Davis Craddock if they have a gun. What I'm saying is this: if you could be wrong once, why not twice? Maybe it's okay for a private investigator to carry a gun if he has a permit. Maybe the rule only applies to illegal guns like the one you got in the shoulder holster."

Nothing. No reaction whatsoever. Moodrow looked closely, searching the man's eyes for signs of drug abuse, but could find neither the torpor of heroin nor the exhilaration of cocaine. Kenneth Scott seemed in perfect control, almost indifferent to any potential threat from Stanley Moodrow. Which would, of course, give Moodrow a big advantage in a confrontation.

"The rule is that nobody, except a policeman, can bring a weapon into the presence of Davis Craddock."

Moodrow pulled a battered leather wallet from his back pocket and waved it in the man's face. "What about *ex*-cops. See that miniature badge? See the ID card? I'm a retired NYPD detective sergeant and that's what makes it okay for me to carry a weapon into the exalted presence of Davis Craddock."

"I keep repeating myself." The sentry finally showed his annoyance. "That's a waste of time and time is all we have. Let's make it absolutely clear: either you leave the gun with me or you turn around and go home. Do you understand?"

"What about the New York State rules for people with gun permits? What about the law that says I can't voluntarily surrender my weapon to anyone except an agent of law enforcement? I mean, if I give you my gun and you go out and kill someone, I'm up shit's creek. I don't like shit's creek. Up *or* down."

"Look here, Mister. . . ."

In the sequence of movements that followed, Moodrow was proudest of the way he dipped his hip. True, his move was very fast. It would have been quick, even for a much younger, much lighter man. For a fifty-five-year-old retired cop with a build like a coffin, it was impossibly fast. Much too fast, for instance, for the confident sentry who stood in front of him. The only part of Kenneth Scott that moved was his jaw. It dropped open in shock.

Of course, Moodrow was also proud of his preparation. As he'd stuffed the wallet into his back pocket, he'd slipped his left foot forward and rotated the right side of his body backward. He'd done this *before* he'd really begun to move and he'd done it without alarming Davis Craddock's sentry. That had gotten his back into it and when he finally committed himself, the punch hadn't come from his arm or even from his shoulder. He'd felt the tension begin where the broad muscles of his back joined his spine, then flow through his shoulder and into his arm. It was the fist, the knuckles, that finally absorbed it, but the power came from the very first part of the movement.

Taken all together, those efforts alone would have been worthy of a pro, but there was still one more element to be tied into the move that Moodrow (already thinking of how he'd describe it to Jim Tilley) had decided to call Operation Coldcock. It came from the legs and was known to fighters like Mike Tyson and Joe Frazier, who'd perfected it. The right knee bends, the hip drops and rotates backward, the body comes *up* as well as forward. The result, as Moodrow had often observed, on a well-muscled individual like the guard who lay in front of him, was a solid chunk, like a tree hit with a sledgehammer, and an unconscious state that cannot be readily distinguished from a coma.

Moodrow disarmed the man, then took a few seconds to enjoy the fruits of his labor, staring down at the unmoving Hanoverian, before pushing open the door to Davis Craddock's office. A huge wooden desk with ornately carved legs rested on a deep gray carpet in the center of the room. Behind it, Davis Craddock, wearing a blue cashmere sweater over a white silk shirt, reclined in an upholstered chair with a carved wooden edge. A blonde woman perched on his knee. Her mouth opened in surprise at the sight of Kenneth Scott stretched out on the floor behind Moodrow. Craddock, however, remained impassive, his hand resting lightly on the desk.

"Davis Craddock, I presume," Moodrow said affably. "I'm Stanley Moodrow. We had an appointment."

"You didn't knock."

"You don't miss a thing, do ya?"

"Marcy, leave us alone, will you."

The blonde left without protesting, without looking back. Craddock, his eyes riveted on Moodrow, waited until the door closed before speaking.

"What happened to Mister Scott?"

"He fell asleep." Moodrow slowly crossed the room. He kept coming until he was leaning over the desk. Craddock had sent the woman away because he was afraid that Moodrow would humiliate him and he didn't want any witnesses. Finding personal weaknesses and playing them out is standard procedure for cop interrogations. A newspaper lay on the desk, the bulge beneath it was obvious enough. "What's under the paper? You got a surprise for me?"

"Mister Moodrow, I want you to leave. Right now." Craddock's eyes were filled with hate, but there was something else behind his rage. There was just a hint of the frustrated child about to burst into tears.

"Let's take a look." Moodrow lifted the newspaper and tossed it onto the carpet. The vintage World War II .45 automatic looked like it weighed a hundred pounds. "That's a lot of gun you got there, Davis. Shoots every way, but straight. You gotta be a real good shot to hit anything with it. That what you are? A good shot? Tell you what—I'm gonna give you a chance to show off." He stepped back a few paces, then drew the left side of his jacket aside to reveal his own .38. He noted that his heart was beating normally. He'd been in violent situations many times in the course of his career and his heart had always pounded like it was about to come through his chest. But there was no threat of violence here. Davis Craddock would shoot you in the back. Or stab you while you slept. Anything, except risk his own life. Moodrow waited, letting the seconds tick away until Craddock's fear registered in his eyes, then stepped forward and picked up the .45. "You got an awful lot of guns here. I mean, for a psychologist. What do you need with all these guns? They part of the cure?"

Moodrow was about to put the automatic back on the desk, when a door at the back of the room opened and several male Therapists burst into the room. Their ragged breath and red faces indicated they'd come in haste. And that they'd been summoned. They stopped dead, of course, when they saw the .45 in Moodrow's hand. There's something about a very large gun in the hand of a very large man that scares the shit out of amateurs.

And the Hanoverian Therapists, Moodrow realized, were nothing, if not amateurs. He held the gun up for their inspection. The room was under his control, but there was no telling who'd come in next. Or which door they'd come through. Or exactly what he stood to gain from his present advantage, since he had no good idea what, except for Michael Alamare, he was looking for.

Moodrow began to back across the room. Better to get out without doing any more damage. The Hanoverians were already beginning to relax. Sooner or later, one of them would decide to impress the boss.

"Wait a second. You came here to ask about Flo Alamare, right?"

"Keep going." Moodrow stopped in the doorway to the outer office. The sentry he'd disarmed was moaning softly.

"A miserable bitch. Just like the mother. We threw her out two years ago."

"Is that right?"

"That's the reality of it."

"Bullshit."

Craddock folded his hands and began to speak rapidly. His breathing was shallow, his anger and fear barely under control. "Flo Alamare was always a problem. She liked to act out, to test us with displays of her anger. I can't count the number of times she told me that one day we'd throw her out. 'Dump me' was the expression she used. I didn't say it to her, but I did believe that she'd eventually go too far and I was right. First she began to use drugs, then to bring them into Hanover House, then to offer them to other Hanoverians. What could I do except ask her to leave? Which I did more than two years ago."

Moodrow waited a moment before responding. "You're not bad, Craddock. Your face doesn't show any of the lie you're putting out to me. That's very good for an amateur. Take it from someone who's done thousands of interrogations. But the thing of it is that I've got witnesses who say Flo Alamare was living here after you say she left. These witnesses will sign affidavits, give depositions, testify in court. That's bad for you, Craddock. Bad for your bullshit commune, too. Of course, if you wanna give me the kid . . . If you wanna hand over Michael Alamare and answer a few questions about what happened to his mother . . . Plea-bargaining *is* the name of the game in law enforcement these days. Who am I to buck the tide?"

Craddock managed a smile. He was good at legalities. "What sort of 'witnesses' are we talking about? Are they, perhaps, former Hanoverians with a grudge against Hanover House? I know you don't care for me or for the philosophy I espouse, but believe me when I tell you that hell hath no fury like a human being after a failed therapy. Patients, in the course of therapy, often reveal the most personal aspects of their pitiful lives. Later on, if things go bad, they resent having exposed themselves. It's all so common really."

He would have gone on, but Moodrow interrupted with a wave of the .45. "If that was true, I wouldn't have to beg people to talk to me. You think you're in control of your situation, because you've been getting away with your bullshit for all these years. You stood up to investigations, lawyers . . . everything they could throw at you. But as far as I'm concerned, all those little victories did was set you up. What is it that Rambo says in that movie? 'I'm comin' fa *you!*'" Moodrow paused long enough to smile. It was the first time, in the course of a long career, he'd dealt with a criminal who was both crazy and controlled. It was going to be better than he'd expected. "You got any idea how much money the widow's offering for your ass? This is a bounty hunt for me. Like goin' after a lion that kills sheep. If I bring back the hide, I collect the reward. Of course, like I said, you could always hand the kid over. I don't *have* to skin the lion to get paid."

FIFTEEN

from *The Autobiography of Davis Craddock*

I'm going to give this chapter a title. I'm going to call it:
  "Munching the Meeses" or "Life's Little Consolations."

Of course, there's a moral here. Something about snatching victory from the jaws of defeat. Or finding the silver lining supposed to inhabit every cloud. Or strolling on the sunny side of the street. Or, simply and wonderfully put, how to take advantage of life's little consolations.

I had nearly two hundred poochies by this time. They were more quarrelsome than ever. My Therapists needed weapons to keep the peace.
    Whereas in the past I'd made sure that all my little poochies got laid, now I used sex as a reward. Indiscriminate fucking was restricted to the Therapists. Ordinary poochies were assigned wives.
    (A perfect example of accepting those little consolations, by the way. I was besieged on all sides by relatives and lawyers and agencies. In some ways, my life was a living hell. [Do I sense a lack of sympathy for my plight? Remember, in the final analysis, there are only two categories: poochies and me.] But I made the best of it by enjoying the little things. Especially the assigning of sexual partners. By examining the files, I determined the most painful combinations. I put grossly obese men with women who worshiped athletes. I put obnoxious, angry women with men who feared their mothers. I put perfectly matched couples together, then ripped them apart a month later. It wasn't much, let me hasten to admit the obvious, but the follow-ups offered just enough amusement to make life bearable.)

The worst part was the money. There was too much of it. Why do revenues running into the millions inevitably draw the eye of the greatest of cult killers: the Internal Revenue Service? Nine hundred and ninety-nine thousand dollars and they ignore you. Another grand and you're public enemy number one.

We'd been a nonprofit organization for many years, but that only made it more interesting for the gray suits who came to examine the books.

Guess what condition the books were in?

"We are scientists, sir, not *bookkeepers*." (Imagine James Mason addressing W.C. Fields.)

Nevertheless, poor record keeping or not, they continued to harass me.

"Mister Craddock, was the five-thousand-dollar pool table in your private quarters purchased with corporate funds?"

"Yeah, I guess it was. Where do I pay the 'tax plus penalties'?"

"Mister Craddock, did you funnel fifteen percent of all incoming revenues into many, extra-large, safety deposit boxes?"

"I'm being persecuted for my beliefs. Call the ACLU."

Enough with the whining? Appetizers are fine, but let's admit the truth: it's the meat course that counts.

I had come to the point where I believed that my best move was to ride off into the sunset. *With* the contents of my safety deposit boxes tucked neatly into the saddlebags.

But running away doesn't suit my style. Not that I couldn't run, if I had to, but somehow my personal danger never became so imminent that instinct took over. No, what I did was vacillate until inspiration came. Curiously, it came through a combination of personal observations and a television show. Just as it had when I decided to build Hanover House.

My personal observations?

The neighborhood surrounding Hanover House is as drug ridden as any in New York. When we first established Hanover House, the drug of choice was heroin, with an occasional sprinkling of Angel Dust or methamphetamine. (Marijuana was taken for granted.)

Then cocaine and crack made their appearances and within a few months it seemed like there was nothing else. Whereas heroin junkies, undeniably dangerous when sick, kept their action off the streets, crack dealers chased people down the sidewalk.

"Jum's, baby. The fines', the bes'."

The television show:

One boring evening, a Therapist named Flo Alamare and I (yes, I'd taken an intimate; which only goes to show that even psychopaths have feelings) were watching a PBS analysis of the drug trade on our 60-inch, rear-projection, Sony TV (purchased, by the way, with foundation funds). Though rather stylish, in its own way, the documentary lacked the glitter of network efforts. There were, for instance, no pictures of children selling crack to undercover cops. Only a sober professor, wispy white hair drifting away from his enormous skull, with a pointer and a series of slides.

The modern drug trade, he explained, began after World War II, when organized crime families began to smuggle heroin. The typical operation involved purchasing opium in southwestern Asia, transporting it to Marseilles or Palermo; processing it into morphine, then heroin; smuggling it into the United States.

Curiously, all of the above steps were accomplished within a few years. The problem was distribution. Customers. It took the mafia thirty-five years to establish the marketplace that existed when large quantities of cocaine first became available. It took ten years for cocaine to penetrate every aspect of American life.

The cocaine originated in South America and South Americans controlled the entire industry, which made prosecution extremely difficult. Ironically, the coke smugglers had established their routes in the late 1970s.

When the United States government began spraying the Mexican marijuana crop with the herbicide Paraquat, it created an enormous vacuum in the marketplace. The entrepreneurial attitude, as we all know, abhors a vacuum, and so, enormous quantities of marijuana began coming up from South America. Specifically, Colombia.

The switch to cocaine was simply a matter of dollars and cents (dollars and sense?). Cocaine, on an ounce-for-ounce basis, wholesale or retail, sells for nearly ten times as much as marijuana.

At this point, the old man on the screen made an abrupt switch to the problems associated with drug rehabilitation and my thoughts drifted away.

I had never, I reflected, seen a more simple example of laissez-faire capitalism. (Talk about caveat emptor!) A previously unknown human need asserts itself. Entrepreneurs spring forth to fill the need. A marketplace is established, growing slowly and organically until it can support the ultimate capitalist tool: the fad.

Which is what cocaine was, at first. A fad. Then the peculiar addictive properties of the cocaine fad drove the marketplace into a frenzy. There was money for everyone. It spilled over into ghetto homes that had never known a positive bank balance. It resulted in an orgy of expansion.

Enough with the lecture. On to 'munching the meeses.'

After all, while interesting enough in their own right, drugs had nothing to do with me or with Hanover House. I had kept drugs out of Hanover House (more than one poochie was shown the door because of an inability to control his habits) for purely practical reasons.

I tried to switch my thoughts to an upcoming IRS interview. They were going to question me about a property on Long Island, a summer retreat that I called the Cycle Research Center. Ostensibly, the 'cycle' was the endless infection and reinfection of humans caught in the neurotic swamp of the nuclear family. In fact, it was used for no other purpose than to observe my poochies in their bikinis.

If rented, the property, just blocks from a white sand beach on Shelter Island, would have brought Hanover House a tidy sum. On the other hand, if I was using the house for my own purposes, the rent would be a perk and very, very taxable.

I was going to claim (at my attorney's suggestion) that the house was a retreat for *all* Hanoverians, but the truth was that only a few Therapists knew about it. It wouldn't take a hell of an investigation to prove me a liar.

The going rent for large summer homes on Shelter Island is about two thousand dollars a week in season. Add up the weeks and months and, even if I paid the 'tax plus penalties,' IRS auditors would have every right to ask where I'd gotten the money. Ugh!

Once again, the idea of a graceful retreat entered my consciousness. The powers that be had made it clear to my attorney: if I quit the guru business, I'd be allowed an unexamined exile.

Then Flo interrupted me. "Do you believe this?" she asked, pointing to the screen. "I mean, what's next? First marijuana, then heroin, then cocaine. What's coming next?"

What I wondered, later on, was how, with my background in chemistry, I hadn't asked the very same question myself?

Here's how it worked: I had extensive files on every one of my poochies and I went through them until I found John Blumberg. His father owned a chemical supply house in Queens. Even though John had broken off all relations with his parents, they continued to write him every week. He was an only child and had apprenticed in the family business.

I made John a Therapist, introducing him to Flo's sexual prowess along the way. Within a month, when he was thoroughly addicted to the sex and the power, I approached him with my 'Plan for America.'

"John," I told him, "although I haven't spoken of these matters before, I've been studying Eastern philosophy for some time. Especially the pharmacology of enlightenment. As a result, I've decided to set up a small lab and do experiments. Unfortunately, given current levels of drug-related paranoia, chemical purchases, especially by newly established labs, are often subject to special scrutiny. Let's face it, John, the *last* thing Hanover House needs is another investigation."

By this time his head was bobbing up and down and I had little trouble convincing him to reconcile with his family. A simple promise that Flo would continue to fuck the living shit out of him sealed the contract. He left Hanover House and, within a few weeks, resumed his place in the family business. Within two months, his firm was supplying us with chemicals.

Here's how it worked: chemistry terrifies the average man. Directions like 'stir and reflux for 27 hours.' Or, 'dissolve oily residue in 160 parts di-isopropyl ether.' Or, 'collect crystalline plates by filtration.' Or (my personal favorite) 'add 250 mg of compound C in 5.0 ml of tetrahydrofuran to a stirred suspension of 200 mg of lithium aluminum hydroxide in 5.0 ml of tetrahydrofuran.' All guaranteed to keep the potty flushing.

But the truth is that chemists are no more than cooks. True, the chemist's pots and pans are more elaborate than the tools of the housewife, but the principle remains the same: ingredients are combined, then processed by various means. If the same ingredients are combined in the same proportion and under the same conditions, the results are *always* the same.

Here's how it worked: my goal (after considerable research) was to marry an analogue of a medically useful synthetic opiate called fentanyl (which is ten times as powerful as heroin) to an analogue of synthetic cocaine. The resulting compound would combine the tranquility of heroin with the energetic euphoria of cocaine. It would also combine the eventual physiological addiction of an opiate with the compulsion to immediately repeat the experience which typifies cocaine.

My compound would have other advantages as well. I decided to name it PURE because of its most basic attribute. Heroin might be ten- or twenty- or even thirty-percent pure and is cut with any number of substances. Cocaine is often cut with compounds like lidocaine or novocaine to increase the skin-numbing effect. PURE would be pure.

PURE would be marketed in vials with heat-sealed plastic caps. The caps would be red, white or blue (catchy combination, eh?), depending on the size of the dose. PURE would be so pure, it could be smoked, shot or snorted. Unlike heroin, it would dissolve in water without heating. Unlike cocaine, the effects would last for hours instead of minutes.

Are we talking user-friendly, or what?

Here's how it worked: an analogue is a compound which is identical to another compound except for one or two atoms. To one extent or another, morphine, heroin and all the synthetics, like Demerol, are analogues of opium. Which is why they're called opiates.

My goal was to create a new analogue with all of the previously mentioned attributes. The advantage of a new analogue is that it would not appear on any drug schedule and, therefore, *not* be illegal.

Here's how it worked: I obtained the formulas (or recipes, for you cooks out there) for the production of fentanyl and synthetic cocaine from the U.S. Patent Office. (We *are*, after all, talking capitalist here.) Then I examined their molecular structures carefully.

Oh, look, I said to myself, *here's a hydrogen atom off by itself. It's 'vulnerable' out there and you know how I hate vulnerability.*

'Vulnerable' hydrogen atoms can be knocked off and replaced with other atoms or groups of atoms by combining certain chemicals under certain conditions. For instance, if I partition a mixture of ordinary fentanyl and methyl sulfate in a Kugelrohr apparatus at 40–60 degrees for six hours, my 'vulnerable' hydrogen will fly the coop. An atom of carbon with three attached hydrogen atoms (all 'vulnerable,' by the way) will take its place.

Other chemicals attack other points and the possibilities are nearly infinite. Hydrogen, nitrogen, oxygen . . . atoms can be made to tap dance around a central core. The effect (to a chemist, anyway) is kaleidoscopic.

Here's how it worked: there's a level on which the analogy (please note the relationship: analogue/analogy) between chemistry and cooking is false, and that is the predictability of results. The housewife, adding cinnamon to an old recipe for the first time, pretty much knows how the cake will taste before it comes out of the oven. The results of chemical reactions *cannot* be predicted in advance.

For instance an analogue of cocaine may not have any narcotic effect whatsoever. Or it may have undesirable side effects. Or it may be far weaker than the original. Or it may be a deadly poison.

Imagine the drudgery implied by this particular piece of information? Yes, I could make the atoms dance a thousand dances, but each dance had to be set up, thoroughly tested and carefully recorded. The chances of finding a dance that would produce the results I envisioned were very small. Perseverance is a given for experimental chemists.

The really amazing part was that once I decided to pursue the creation of PURE, my other problems began to drop away. The IRS concluded its investigation with a bill for $5,000 in back taxes and a $2,000 fine. The district attorney's office decided (according to my lawyer) that Hanover House was no worse than most of the other cults on the Lower East Side and definitely not involved in drug use or crime.

The angry families, of course, never go away, but the difference was amazing. Despite the drudgery of the lab (until my specially chosen poochies were trained, I had to do most of the work myself), I woke up each day with a smile on my lips.

True, my good fortune could evaporate overnight. The IRS could descend with renewed fury or the DA find some new avenue of investigation. But a man who fails to enjoy good fortune for fear of the future is a slave and I was not born to be a slave.

Besides, there was always munching the meeses.

Here's how it worked: the only test for the potency of an opiate involves the opiate's effect on pain. For instance, I could have taken ten or twenty milligrams of one or another analogue, injected it into a vein, then smashed my finger with a hammer. Gee, did that hurt or didn't it? Am I stoned, or what?

Though not a coward, I rejected this method as too subjective. No, I said to myself, you're a scientist and you'll proceed in a scientific manner. Besides, that's why God made meese.

Ten animals were used to test each compound: little white mice with little pink eyes. The kind pet owners feed to their snakes. All aggression had been bred out of them and they wouldn't bite no matter how much pain I inflicted. (Here, Poochie?)

The mice were anesthetized and catheters inserted into the tail artery and the external jugular. A thermometer probe was pushed up the poop.

In this way, blood pressure, anaerobic blood gases, respiration, body temperature and the speed with which the compound left the blood-stream could be measured from moment to moment.

Then the noses and tails of the mice were inserted into clamps.

Anesthesia was discontinued and thirty minutes later a tiny, tiny amount of the new compound was administered.

Then the clamps were tightened.

The dosage was increased every five minutes for thirty minutes and the results carefully recorded.

The screams of the mice were ignored. (Except by those who like music.)

Each time the dosage was increased, the clamps were tightened. I didn't want the mice to become jaded.

After the experiment, each mouse was taken gently into the hand and carried to a far corner of the lab where it was held over a large gray cylinder bearing a sign that read GARBAGE. The scientist in question placed the ball of his/her thumb on the animal's skull and snaked his/her forefinger around the animal's throat.

Proper technique? Squeeze and drop.

Munching the meeses.

Life's little consolations.

Here's how it worked: the cocaine analogue was never found. The duration of injected cocaine, fifteen minutes, could not be stretched to four hours. After a year, I switched my focus to another stimulant, methamphetamine, and managed to find a compound which, though far less potent, had none of the jangling paranoia that characterizes the end of an amphetamine high.

My neo-speed was a perfect complement to an astonishingly addicting compound I obtained by rearranging the atoms attached to an asymmetric carbon on a molecule of fentanyl.

The marriage of neo-speed and neo-dope produced PURE. There was no need to clamp the mice. (But, of course, I did, anyway. Plastered on PURE, they didn't mind all that much.) Their little mouse euphoria was palpable from the moment of injection.

As was the euphoria of Flo Alamare, chosen to be the first human to know PURE. She was thrilled by the honor and accepted the needle like Joan of Arc accepted the pyre. But when I shot the plunger home and PURE flooded her blood for the first time, she moaned in ecstasy.

Flo was psychologically addicted within days. Severe physiological addiction took less than one month.

*   *   *

Here's how it worked: due to market conditions, a single dose of PURE (enough to make a nonaddict high for about six hours) had to sell for $10. The amount of PURE needed to make a nonaddict high was 10 mg. It cost me fifteen cents to produce.

One gram of PURE would produce 100 doses. Street value: $1,000. One ounce of PURE would produce 2800 doses. Street value: $28,000. One pound of PURE would produce 44,800 doses. Street value: $448,000. One ton of PURE would produce 89,600,000 doses. Street value: $8,960,000,000.

Let's say that I, as the wholesaler and after manufacturing costs were deducted, could only realize ten percent of the retail price. That would be . . . $896,000,000.

Bye-bye, Poochie.

Late at night. Insomnia is the great curse and the great blessing. It is the place of decision.

I admit that I have no desire to occupy the crime stratosphere currently inhabited by the Colombians. (Do you think mafioso sigh and count their blessings each time a newsman mentions the awful, evil cartels?) The high-profile drug life is a direct road to long-term incarceration.

From my point of view, beating the odds can be defined as living a long criminal life without attracting the attention of the 'po-lease.'

A ton of PURE? A motherfucking *TON*?

Why not ten tons? Four hundred billion dollars worth of PURE. It would only be a drop in the country's collective drug bucket.

But my plan calls for a maximum of the old 'in and out.' In fact, although I've kept it quiet so far, my role model is David Rockefeller, not Scarface.

As of this writing, I've just finished setting up a laundering operation to handle the revenues from two hundred pounds of PURE. A series of corporations, each in a different state and ostensibly engaged in professional housecleaning, will funnel revenues into a number of offshore banks. A clumsy operation, but adequate for its decidedly short-term purpose.

Two hundred pounds of PURE equals ninety million dollars on the street. My end: no less than nine million. Plus the auction, of course.

The auction is a matter of conscience. How could I deprive America of the fruits of my labor? No, I say, PURE, the finest expression of the American entrepreneurial spirit (the spirit that made this country great and don't *you* forget it), should not and shall not pass from the Earth.

Once I've established PURE as the product of the future, I intend to auction the recipe. I predict that the highest bidder will be every bit as sweet as I am. In fact, we will differ in only one respect: the purchaser will have no fear of incarceration.

SIXTEEN

Jim Tilley was fighting exhaustion when he walked into the Roberto Clemente Gym on Houston Street. He was coming off a fifteen-hour drug surveillance and wanted nothing more than to pass Moodrow a small piece of information and get home to Rose and his bed. Nevertheless, the sight of Stanley Moodrow working on the 'problem' of a tall, bony middleweight named Harold 'Boomer' Blevins lifted Tilley's spirits immediately. Moodrow had been coaching young fighters for years, but it'd been a long time since Tilley had seen him in the ring. Not that Tilley was really surprised. Moodrow had called him with the details of his Hanover House adventure (including 'Operation Cold-cock') the night before.

Tilley also knew 'Boomer' Blevins and was thoroughly familiar with his problem. A talented prospect at sixteen, Harold Blevins was quick and smart but had the unfortunate habit of dropping his left hand after throwing a punch. He'd been doing it since he'd started boxing and his success in YMCA tournaments had only reinforced the habit. Now he was entered in the Golden Gloves and the competition would have no trouble either finding or taking advantage of such a fundamental error.

Moodrow kept his massive arms down over his ribs and chest as they moved across the ring. His hands were uncovered, though he held a loose glove in his right hand. Blevins wasn't throwing punches to the head, which made it that much easier for Moodrow to block most of the body shots with his arms. But 'most' isn't 'all,' and Blevins, at 158 pounds, was very quick. He was also pissed off, even though he understood that it was 'for his own good.' Moodrow was slapping the side of 'Boomer' Blevins' face with the loose glove each time Blevins dropped his left hand.

It was the 'by the book' way to deal with a bad habit—punish it in the gym, before an opponent punishes it in competition—but that didn't prevent the side of 'Boomer' Blevins' face from turning bright red. Blevins had been nourishing his untested amateur ego for a long time and Moodrow was supposed to be an old man. In some ways, the humiliation was as important to his budding career as the education of his lazy left.

"Hey, Stanley," Tilley finally called.

Moodrow looked over and nodded. "Jim. What's up?"

'Boomer' Blevins, noting his trainer's distraction, took the opportunity to load up on a straight right hand. The sound it made echoed through the little gym, but Moodrow didn't seem to notice. "Awright, Harold," he said. "Let's call it a lesson for today. Get some ice on your face before it swells up."

Tilley shook his head. He recalled being up in the Bronx with Moodrow when they'd gotten a flat tire. Moodrow had insisted on changing it instead of calling for a tow from the police garage. He'd managed to get the spare and the jack out of the trunk, but had somehow pulled the wrong way on the lug wrench. First the wrench had bent in half, then the lug had sheared off the axle.

"I think I've maybe got something that ties in with Alamare," Tilley said. "It's worth a look."

"Yeah?" Moodrow stopped running the towel over his face and chest. "Tell me the widow was found in the river. Make my day."

"No such luck. Just a couple of ODs that turned out to be poisonings."

Moodrow's ears went up and he smiled. "Poisonings?"

"Ten days ago, the uniforms get a call about an apartment with a bad smell. They break down the door and find two stiffs, one male and one female. They *both* have spikes in their arms. The suits come an hour later and make the stiffs for ODs. They take evidence, seal the apartment and send the stiffs over to the medical examiner for autopsies. The ME also suspects an overdose, but then he cuts open the male's brain and finds part of it turned to charcoal. Then he cuts the female's brain and finds an identical condition. Naturally, the ME tests for every kind of poison, but he can't make a match. Result: suspicious death resulting from unknown compound."

"When was this?"

"Ten days ago. But, wait, it gets even better. Three days ago, two uniforms check out another DOA. One of the uniforms was present at the first apartment and remembers finding these unusual little vials of white powder on the male DOA. Now, here they are again. Being an ambitious sort, the uniform tells the detectives and they get a rush autopsy on the third stiff. Same poison killed all three."

Moodrow leaned back on the edge of the ring and ran the towel over his short gray hair. "What about the evidence? Were the stiffs identified?"

"The vials were sent out to a DEA lab in Maryland. The report came back positive for opiates, but not for any particular opiate. The drug isn't heroin or Demerol or morphine or any drug we know about. The three stiffs consist of two HIV-positive junkies and one pretty young runaway from New Jersey."

Moodrow tossed the towel into a corner and began to walk toward the lockers at the far end of the room. "Unless I'm missing something, whatever it was in the vials didn't kill the junkies."

Tilley grinned. "Well, I didn't actually inject myself with it, but according to the lab, it doesn't kill mice. It gets mice stoned out of their minds. You remember that new drug I told you about, PURE? Well the rumor was that PURE was being sold in vials, not bags."

"Didn't you say PURE was a brand of heroin?"

"My own snitches told me that junkies were using it, so I naturally assumed it was dope. Which it is. It just isn't heroin."

"You think it's a designer drug, like Ekstacy?"

Ekstacy, created in a clandestine California lab, had swept into New York's discos in the mid 1980s. For the first year, until the legislature added it to the drug law, it had been sold quite openly.

"Or LSD," Tilley said. "That was made in a lab, too. It was legal for years. By the way, the only reason I know about this is because Izzie Malkin asked me if any of my snitches were talking about the stiffs. One of them, Deeny Washington, was the main source for PURE."

"I know Izzie. I know him pretty good."

"He says you should come down and talk to him, if you want more information."

Moodrow began to work the combination lock on his locker. "I don't wanna seem like a party pooper, but how does this new drug relate to Flo Alamare? The doctors said she was positive for heroin."

"Only that it was a case that looked like an overdose and turned out to be something else. Of course, Flo Alamare's alive, so the docs can't slice her brain open to look for poison. Anyway, I just mention it as a possibility."

"All right, Jim. I know you're tired." Moodrow pulled on his shirt, working the buttons with massive fingers. "Wanna hear something funny? All day I been thinking about how I fucked it up yesterday. I should've checked the arms of that bodyguard. What's his name? Kenneth Scott? When I had him alone, I should've rolled up his sleeves and checked his arms for needle tracks. What happened was I got caught up with the bullshit, with playing the big, bad cop. The Hanoverians didn't look like junkies to me, not even middle-class junkies, but there's no question I should've rolled up the bodyguard's sleeves and checked it out once and for all."

SEVENTEEN

It was nearly eight o'clock when Betty Haluka bustled into her lover's apartment. Her arms were full of groceries and she was bursting with news, but the sight of Stanley Moodrow bent over the kitchen table, a slender pencil clutched in his right hand, brought her up short. There were times when Moodrow seemed to live in the small notebook he kept with him twenty-four hours a day, but this time he was working with a sheet of writing paper. Betty had never seen him write a letter before.

"What're you doing?" she asked, dumping the packages on the table.

"I'm writing a letter." He held his cheeks up for a kiss, then began to inspect the goodies in the bag, his face impassive, as always.

"I can see that," Betty said. "I'm not blind. What kind of a letter?"

"A friendly letter."

"You mean, as opposed to a business letter?"

"Something like that."

"Stanley, why are you busting my balls?"

"I don't wanna be the one to tell you this, but . . ."

"Who's the fucking letter to, Stanley?"

Moodrow giggled. "Davis Craddock." He started to return to his work.

"Stanley, if you don't stop it, I'll throw out the ice cream."

"What kind of ice cream?"

"Dark chocolate peanut butter swirl."

"That's extortion."

"Right now. Right in the garbage. Read the letter."

"All right. You want me to read the letter, I'll read it. But I'll never forget this. You shouldn't even *buy* chocolate peanut butter if you're gonna play that kind of a game with it."

"Right now, Stanley."

Dear Davis,

Please excuse my addressing you as 'Davis.' I know it is presumptuous of me, but all of us at the Royal Society for the Promotion of Creative Hand Humping (you may remember that we created the now commonly used slogan, *Do it Quick or Do it Slow—Your Hankie Never Says No*), feel we have recognized a kindred spirit in you. In fact, in appreciation of your efforts to destroy the nuclear family, you have been nominated for our Jerk-Off of the Year award. This prestigious award, last given to Mike Dukakis for his promotion of defensive tank driving, is symbolized by a bronze miniature of our famous Betty Boop Blowup Doll (created by yours truly) and a lifetime supply of fuzzy tube socks. We'll be having our annual dinner in two weeks, so please RSVP if you can make it.

Sincerely and with warmest regards,

Vinnie Vaseline

When Moodrow looked up, Betty was standing in the middle of the kitchen, a quart of ice cream in her hand. She stared at him for a moment, then down at her wet hand. "I want a divorce," she announced calmly.

"You can't have a divorce," Moodrow reminded her, "because we're not married. In fact, we're not even cohabiting together."

"In that case, I want a psychiatrist."

"You could try Davis Craddock. I hear he's getting an award."

Betty smiled in triumph. "That's just what I did. This afternoon I went to my first Hanoverian conference." She noted Moodrow's astonished look, then continued. "I begin therapy two days from now."

Moodrow took a deep breath. "Listen, Betty, Davis Craddock is no joke. This guy would kill you in a minute if he thought you were a threat to him."

"I suppose your letter isn't a threat. I suppose your letter is an example of classical drama."

"The letter's going out to him *because* he's crazy. I'm trying to reach a crazy man, to make him paranoid enough to take me personally."

"How will he know who it's from?"

"He'll know. And he'll know that I'm coming for him. I wish I could show you the expression on his face when I called his bluff with the .45. Craddock is nuts, but he's in control. I want him to lose control, to panic. Fear isn't going to make him less dangerous, just stupid and careless."

Betty began to sort the groceries, taking them from the bag and arranging them on the table. She was trying to phrase her answer in a way that truly represented her feelings. The problem was that she didn't even like to *think* about the story she would have to tell. She shuffled cans of peas and corn and tomatoes for a minute, then took a deep breath. "This happened to me a long time ago, sixteen, seventeen years. I can't remember anymore. I never told you about it, because I could never make it good in my own mind. I tried for years, then I stopped thinking about it.

"One day, I picked up a client named David Teitelbaum. He was charged with abusing his two daughters, Anna and Toby. Anna was the oldest. She was eight. Toby was six. The evidence against Teitelbaum was persuasive, but not conclusive. That's usually the way it is in sexual abuse cases. There were the children's statements, of course, but the mother hadn't actually witnessed the abuse and would not be a witness. A medical examination showed some evidence of vaginal and anal scarring, but the doctor who conducted the examination wasn't willing to swear that it was *absolutely* due to sexual abuse. The trial, if there was to be trial, would hinge on the testimony of the children.

"Teitelbaum swore he didn't do it. He told me he was a nice Jewish boy with a wife who happened to hate him. Why did she hate him? He didn't know. Their marriage had been arranged, and he hadn't gotten to know her before the wedding. True, marriages weren't really *arranged* anymore, but in the tight, Orthodox community where he grew up, boys and girls were kept apart. One day you came home to find a girl sitting at the dinner table and all the relatives, yours and hers, grinning like idiots.

" 'Mona hates everybody. Ask her what she thinks of her parents. Ask her what she thinks of the rabbi. Ask her anything. You'll see she's crazy. *Goyim* get a divorce from women like this. Jews shoulder the burden. I tried to be a good husband and this is my reward.'

"I didn't believe him. I believed the children. But that didn't mean I couldn't get him off. The children's statements were full of hesitations and contradictions. That's normal. Kids can't appreciate the importance of clean, emphatic testimony. If you want to get them to talk about something they don't want to talk about, you have to coax it out of them. But juries don't necessarily understand children and the hesitations bring doubt. If I put Teitelbaum on the stand and he repeated his accusations against his wife, the doubt could easily blossom into reasonable doubt. I wasn't afraid of the prosecutor's cross-examination because there were no witnesses to the abuse and Teitelbaum didn't have a criminal record.

"The ADA who handled the prosecution, a veteran named Max Bauer, had no illusions about the case. He offered me a plea bargain three days after Teitelbaum was arrested. One count of abuse and five years Upstate. I took it back to Teitelbaum, but I advised him to turn it down. If we waited, we'd do better.

"Teitelbaum was a tailor, a working man struggling to move up into the middle class. The community had already convicted him, and his wife had control of his meager assets. Bail had been set at $50,000 and he had no hope of making it, so if he wanted to sit it out, he would have to survive in the Brooklyn House of Detention. I don't have to tell you what the other prisoners think of child abusers. In order to make his wait a little easier, I notified the court that my client's life had been threatened and that the Department of Corrections wasn't taking adequate measures to protect him. If he'd been black or Latino, I doubt if I would have gotten a response. But David Teitelbaum was a skinny Jewish man who walked with a stoop. His glasses were so thick that looking into his eyes was like peering into the wrong end of a pair of binoculars. If he was assaulted in prison, no matter what he did, the Jewish community would have been up in arms, so Corrections moved him into protective custody and set up a twenty-four-hour guard in front of his cell. It was like a suicide watch, but it went on for three months.

"I ran into Max Bauer in one of the courtrooms the day before Teitelbaum's trial was supposed to start. He asked me to meet him in his office after court recessed for the day. I wasn't surprised when he upped the ante. The kids, he told me, were reluctant to testify with their father present. Not reluctant, I take that back. They were *afraid* to testify. He'd filled their heads with tales of dybbuks and imps and devils, all the horrible creatures who'd attack them if they told their mother what he was doing. (I already knew this from their statements; that was one of the advantages of waiting it out.) In order to avoid a trial, Max would allow Teitelbaum to plead to a single count of neglect. He'd get six months and do three. On the other hand, if we insisted on a trial and Teitelbaum was found guilty on all counts, the DA's office would push for the max on every count, sentences to run consecutively.

"The trial judge was a tough old bird named O'Brien. He was usually fair to both sides during a trial, but, upon conviction, he gave away time like Santa Claus gives away Christmas candy. I took the plea and the threat back to my client. Teitelbaum accepted the deal without hesitation and did the time, as they say, standing on his head. Three months in the same secure cell and he was back out on the street. A year later, he was arrested for the rape-murder of an eight-year-old Dominican girl.

"I know it was just my job, Stanley. I know all the bullshit rationalizations. The truth is that Teitelbaum was evil in just the way Davis Craddock is evil. He had no conscience, no sense of what he did to those girls. They were objects to be used for his pleasure, like an air conditioner or a toilet bowl. And I helped him get off. Instead of doing five years, he did three months . . ."

Moodrow got up and took two bowls off the shelf. "I don't see where this is getting us. Does Teitelbaum make Craddock less dangerous?"

"After Teitelbaum committed the murder, I refused to handle any more child-abuse cases. Technically, Legal Aid lawyers are supposed to take whatever comes along, but the turnover at Legal Aid is so great, the administration tends to compromise, especially with experienced trial attorneys. But that didn't make it right for me. I carried it around for years. Until I realized that *nothing* could make it right. The system would go on and on and on. Teitelbaums would continue to get off with light sentences, then go out and commit murder. I happen to think, on balance, our system is the best. It's not perfect, mind you, just better than anything else I know about. But that belief doesn't make it better. Teitelbaum was a tailor. He didn't know a damn thing about trials or rules of evidence. If I'd told him there was no chance that a jury would find him innocent, he would have accepted the five years like any good psychopath. There are a number of prisons with specialized programs for sexual offenders. *Maybe* he would have gotten into a program. *Maybe* some psychiatrist would have reached him. One thing's for sure, that particular little girl, Inez Escobedo, would be alive today. She'd be twenty-two years old."

"I still don't see how that makes it safe for you to go into Hanover House," Moodrow insisted.

"Look, I don't see how there could be any danger to me. I'm not going to walk up to the nearest Hanoverian and ask if I can speak to Michael Alamare. Davis Craddock doesn't know anything about me. And I've also got the perfect background: a burnt-out Legal Aid lawyer searching for 'something to believe in.' "

Moodrow pulled up short. "That's pretty good. 'A burnt-out Legal Aid lawyer . . .' What happened at the conference?"

"It took place in the third building. The one farthest away from Houston Street. There were about a dozen Hanoverians in the room. One of them was wearing a jacket and a tie. He told us about the family and how destructive it was. He said that Hanover House is a greater threat to the culture than Communism, because it offers an alternative to the nuclear family. That's why the media and the government constantly attack Hanoverian ideas. Then he went into the therapy itself. He said it was confrontational, designed to produce quick results for people who were strong enough to take it. There are rules that we're supposed to follow from the first day. Like no drugs, ever. And no fighting with the other Hanoverians. 'Minimum responsibility for our manifestations' was the way he put it."

"How many other candidates were there?"

"Four."

"Did you see how many others signed up for therapy?"

"I was the only one who signed on the spot. The others said they wanted to think it over."

"That's because the cult's reputation is so bad." Moodrow began to spoon ice cream into two bowls. "That'll also make Craddock suspicious about strangers coming in." He shook his head firmly. "It's not worth it, Betty. Not for the slight chance of coming upon Michael Alamare."

"You know what's bothering me, Stanley? It looks to me like everyone's in it for the wrong reasons. Connie Alamare's obsessed with her anger. You're playing games with a maniac and cashing a paycheck. What about the child? How do you know the child hasn't been killed? Or isn't about to be killed? If you were responsible for the mother's death, would you keep the child around?"

Moodrow, to Betty's surprise, replied evenly. "Craddock's gotta keep the child handy in case one of Flo Alamare's pals decides to drop a dime about the kid. That's assuming Flo was living in the commune before they found her in the Bronx. Which is not entirely clear." Quickly, he outlined the information given to him by Tilley a few hours before. "I'm beginning to think Flo Alamare was part of whatever crew was handling this new drug, PURE. I remember a case in California about five or six years ago. Someone was making a drug in a lab and calling it China White. It killed a number of people before it disappeared. That was a lab mistake that caused that. Maybe it's coming up the same way here. In fact, I wouldn't be surprised if every half-assed chemist in the country was dreaming of some new drug to replace crack cocaine in the hearts of America's drug consumers. Why not? Every time you turn the TV on, they show an eight-foot pile of money the cops took off some dealer. You know how that affects the creative criminal mind? They don't see the bust or the skells in their handcuffs. All they see is the money."

Betty poured herself a mug of coffee from the pot on the burner. She'd been after Moodrow to get himself a Mr. Coffee, but he preferred to make a pot in his old percolator, then reheat it on the stove. Betty poured milk into the mug, but it seemed to have no effect on the inky liquid.

"I screwed it up yesterday," Moodrow said. "When I had the body-guard alone in the office, I should have rolled up his sleeves. I should have checked his arms for tracks. But after I left Jim, I was walking toward Broadway, when I saw one of the Hanover Housecleaning trucks parked outside an office building. I went into the lobby and the Hanoverians were waxing the floors. Except for one guy in a blazer, they were wearing identical white short-sleeved shirts. I didn't see any sign of tracks."

Betty drank from the cup, then shivered. It was as bad as she'd expected. "I think you're telling me that you don't think Davis Crad-dock is holding Michael Alamare."

"Yesterday, I was sure the kid was there. Now, I don't know. I gotta go back up to the Bronx and talk to the doctors who treated Flo Alamare. Maybe she really did have a stroke. I mean Jim says PURE was being sold by a terminal street junkie named Deeny Washington. How could Deeny Washington get near Hanover House?" He stopped, then put his hand on Betty's shoulder. "The thing of it is that Craddock's dangerous. I know I can't stop you from going in there. Maybe I don't want to stop you. It's what I'd do, if I were in your place. But if you're gonna do it, I want you to take it seriously."

Moodrow went to a closet in the hallway outside the kitchen and unlocked a small toolbox. The object he took out of it looked like a thick fountain pen.

"This is a one-shot, .38 caliber gun. We'll go down to the range tomorrow and I'll show you how to cock it and fire. I want you to carry it into Hanover House whenever you go there."

"Stanley," Betty said softly, "I really don't think I could kill anyone."

Moodrow's face turned to stone. He smacked his palm down on the kitchen table. "In that case," he said, his voice dripping sarcasm, "you oughta think about dropping the Mata Hari impression and just accept the guilt for Teitelbaum. Because, sure as shit, Davis Craddock wouldn't have any trouble killing *you*."

The call came in at ten-thirty and Moodrow, despite not having thought of Connie Alamare all evening, knew who it was before he picked up the phone.

"Hey, *paisan*, I just phoned to let you know that somebody's doing something."

Moodrow was tempted to hang up without replying, but that would only bring another, probably longer, call. "Like what?" he asked.

"My attorney dropped a subpoena on the big *gumbah*, himself. Davis Craddock has gotta come into court and testify about exactly when Flo and Michael left Hanover House."

"When is this supposed to happen?"

Connie Alamare's voice was more subdued when she replied. "Next month. It was the earliest date on the judge's calendar."

"What do you wanna bet Davis Craddock is gonna be out of town on the particular day? I got a fifty says he gets two postponements and then he lies. You want the bet?"

"So what are *you* doing? Eh, *capotesta*? Such a tough guy, but all you do is cash the checks. Maybe you were in it with that detective, Goobe. You and him—*imbroglioni. Maledizione* . . ."

"Stop working yourself up, Connie. What I'm doing is what I'm doing. You want a report, you'll get one in writing. At the end of the month."

"I don't wanna wait to the end of the month to get my grandson." She was shouting into the phone.

"For what?" Moodrow asked quietly.

"What is that supposed to mean?"

"Why do you want the kid, Connie? You bored? You need a toy to play with? A little kid, maybe? So you can make him into another Florence?"

"You bastard," the old lady yelled. "You dirty bastard. You're gonna hear from my lawyer."

The phone went dead in Moodrow's ear and he managed to find the receiver without turning his head. He wondered, for a moment, just what he'd do if he was taken off the case. Would he simply walk away, a mercenary without a paycheck? Or would he settle down and enjoy the game he was playing with Davis Craddock?"

"Was that Connie Alamare?" Betty's voice drifted in from the bedroom.

"Yeah, that was the good widow herself."

"She still crazy?"

"Actually, she's gettin' better. She's cursing me in English, now."

EIGHTEEN

Kickin' on the boulevard is how the brothers put it. Drivin' a big, black van with big, black windows. Scratchin' out beats with the point of a knife against the dashboard. Rip this one up today, buy another one tomorrow. Singin' about the heavy bread and all the sweet, sweet bitches that came with it. Singin' about the "Pusher Man."

"Song gotta be at least fifteen years old," Wendell explained to his companion, Davis Craddock. "Back before nobody never heard about crack. Same shit, though, between them old days and right now. Nigger ain't seven feet tall and can't jump over the roof got only one way to get out. And it ain't by steady beggin' the white man for no bullshit job."

They were driving north on FDR Drive, heading for the Bronx and a short conversation with a pure fool by the name of Billy Williams. Gonna pull the motherfucker's card was what they was gonna do, but the crazy white man was actin' like it wasn't no more than a walk in the park.

"See here, Davis. Nothin' make a brother feel better than pushin' it back in the white man's face. When a white man see me cruisin' through his neighborhood, he thinkin' one word: 'nigger.' When he see that my wheels costin' twice more than his, he say that word out loud. When he see the gold hangin' down my chest, he scream it: 'Nigger, nigger, nigger, nigger' till his tongue fall out his head."

Craddock turned off the radio (he was taking it serious and Wendell appreciated that) and began tellin' about how crazy his momma was and how his daddy hit the road and how he lived his life without no family and without no street either. How there was nothin' in his life at all and how he made his life inside himself.

"That's the only place to live it," Craddock finished. "Inside yourself, so you know just who you are. I'm a nigger, too, but I'm invisible. Citizens who see me on the street don't know what's inside. I can't change that . . ."

"Yeah, baby," Wendell said playfully, "you can show the world your true intentions. Be like them jailhouse white boys. Get yo' face tattooed. Little spider webs comin' out from the corner of yo eyes. The pig see you cruisin' down his street, he right away throw yo ass up against the car. Jus' like they do for a brother."

"I got a question," Craddock said. "If our enterprise makes you rich and you move to a Caribbean island where everybody has black skin, are you gonna paint yourself white so you'll be called a honkey?"

"We don't call 'em no honkeys no more. We call 'em maggots now."

"C'mon, Wendell, answer the question."

"Shi-i-it. Be real int'restin'. Jus' another black face in a black country? Maybe I try it on. See how it fits me."

"Not 'just another black face,' baby. You'll be the richest black face on whatever island you go to. But that's not what we're talking about. See, the thing of it is that I can walk around thinking thoughts from Adolf Hitler's autobiography and nobody reads my mind. You can walk around thinking thoughts from the goddamned Gospels and the whole white world thinks you're plannin' to smash its collective head. It's really fucking stupid, but it's there, too. Like mountains or sewers. The only thing you get to control is what's inside. Inside, you can be whatever you want to be and the best thing, the funniest thing, is that if you look inside, you and me decided to be the same person."

Wendell cranked up the amps and they listened to Curtis Mayfield tell his stories: "Freddie's Dead," "SuperFly," "Pusher Man," "No Thing On Me." The jam was definitely goin' down. In the dash and in the world. Wendell had lined up wholesalers in Philly, Boston, New Haven and D.C. The man in D.C.—a white Italian man by the name of Rafe Antillo—was very large in the life. A *player*. Wendell would have to be careful or Rafe Antillo would take his shit off, but Wendell just loved bein' a brother who sold shit to a white Italian man. Motherfuckin' Italians were the ones who brought dope to the ghetto in the first place.

But white or black, everybody loved PURE and when he explained what would happen if the junkies cooked it up, nobody seemed to be too upset. A few dead junkies, more or less, until they learned, wouldn't bother the man. Look at what AIDS was doin'. Junkies dyin' everywhere and nobody didn't give a shit. Meanwhile, PURE was the baddest dope ever to come down the line. Have to be altogether crazy to fuck with it. Davis Craddock wasn't crazy. Wendell Bogard wasn't crazy either.

They got to Billy Williams' apartment at four o'clock in the morning. Billy was at his night job, as expected. Wendell and Davis carried small, hooked pry bars, but they didn't need them to get in. Davis had taken the set of keys Terry Williams kept in the property room at Hanover House and copied them without anyone knowing. Now he used them on Billy Williams' lock, and in the quiet of a weekday morning in a middle-class working neighborhood the two men slipped into the empty apartment.

Billy came home at six-thirty. When he turned on the light and recognized Davis Craddock sitting on his living room couch, his face seemed to collapse. He was pale and blond, and the blood draining from his face gave his skin a transparent quality. He didn't notice Wendell, who was sitting in the kitchen, until Wendell walked back into the living room. There was no pity in Wendell's eyes, no humanity, either, but somehow Billy rallied. Billy, in his days as an acolyte, had been one of the most vocal of a small group of Therapists who fought against the admission of blacks to Hanover House.

"I knew you'd come," Billy said directly to his former mentor. "But why this?" He gestured toward Wendell.

"Oh, man," Wendell moaned, "the maggot done dis me. I mus' be gettin' to be a old motherfucker or somethin'."

"What is he talking about?" Billy continued to speak to Davis Craddock.

"See," Wendell said, "if I was a maggot, the bitch'd introduce hisself. Soft as he is, he oughta be takin' care he don't disrespect a man like me. 'Stead, he talkin' like I'm his punk. No way I can eat that. I eat that, all the niggers be steady sayin' *ah'm* soft. That shit is bad for bidness."

Wendell took a long, slender folding knife from his jacket pocket and flicked the blade open. Billy was sure the knife was meant for him, but Wendell went to the sofa and quickly slit the cushions and the backrest. He pulled out a small amount of crumbly yellow foam and threw it into the center of the room before repeating the action on the single club chair next to the couch. For a moment, Billy thought Wendell was searching for something, but Wendell wasn't even looking at the cushions when he cut them open.

"What . . ." Billy began. "I don't understand." Then he noticed that both his visitors wore gloves and his heart sank.

"Who'd you talk to, Billy?"

Craddock's voice was devoid of amusement. Billy Williams had never heard it this way. Neither had Wendell Bogard, who grinned in appreciation before turning his attention to a sideboard in the dining room. Very quietly, he began to pull out the drawers and empty them onto the dining room table.

"I haven't spoken to anyone since Flo came to see me."

"Flo Alamare came out to see you?"

"Some time ago. That's why I sent my daughter back to Hanover House. Flo must have told you."

Craddock shook his head. "Flo's dead. She never came back to Hanover House after she saw you, Billy. I hope you didn't kill her."

"Are you crazy?" Billy spoke without thinking, but Craddock didn't react to it. "I've never been violent. You used to tell me that I needed to be violent, but I could never even manage to get angry. How would I kill Flo?"

"Maybe you didn't kill her out of anger. Maybe you killed her out of fear. She was found a few miles from this apartment. In a vacant lot."

Wendell was in the kitchen, quietly emptying the cupboards and the drawers onto the floor. "He killed the bitch," Wendell said. "I know he done it. He got guilty all over his face."

"Look," Billy said, "Flo came here and told me that I couldn't keep my daughter." His voice broke for the first time. He didn't know what they wanted, but he knew they were going to hurt him. It was all so unjust. He'd worked as hard as anybody to establish Hanover House. Now he was being rewarded. "If I wanted to be defiant, I wouldn't have sent Terry back to Hanover House. I mean Terry was with Flo when Flo came here. If I killed Flo, I would have had to do it in front of my daughter."

"So, who'd you talk to?" Craddock seemed more relaxed. He was beginning to smile.

"Nobody."

"Bullshit, I *know* you were talking to a lawyer and a writer."

"I mean after Flo came to see me. I haven't spoken to anyone since then."

Craddock sighed. "I realize that you didn't kill Flo. How could an asshole like you kill Flo Alamare? You gave up your own daughter because you were afraid. Because you were the same chicken-shit pussy who first walked into my office. Because you were, in fact, my greatest fucking failure." He paused, waiting for a response, but Williams refused to look up. "So who'd you speak to, Billy?"

"Please..."

"You didn't by any chance speak to a fat detective named Stanley Moodrow?"

"Oh, God . . . Yeah, a detective came out here asking about Flo, but I didn't speak to him. As soon as he told me what he wanted, I sent him away. I swear it, Davis. I sent him away without another word."

"This fat detective says he can prove that Flo Alamare was living at Hanover House right up until her death. Now you tell me how a fat detective could prove a thing like that if you didn't speak to him?"

Davis was lying. Moodrow had only said he could put Flo inside Hanover House within two years, but the good fisherman feels no conscience when he disguises the bait. Craddock wanted to get a feel for how much Moodrow knew.

Wendell broke in before Billy could reply. "What we oughta do is fuck this little bitch in his ass, *then* ask the questions." He came back into the living room, pulling at his crotch while he stroked Billy Williams' hair. "Lil bitch fall in love when he feel mah dick in his butt. Ain' that right, lil bitch?"

Billy shuddered, but made no effort to pull away from the much larger Wendell Bogard. "I don't know who told him," Billy said to Craddock. "Anybody at Hanover House could have told him. There's probably another ten people who've left within the last year. Suppose he visited all of them?"

"But they didn't see her on the day of her death."

Bogard playfully tugged Williams' head into his lap. "C'mon, Billy, tell the man what he want to hear. He's yo goddamn psychiatrist. He doin' this shit for your own fuckin' good. Ain' that right, Davis?"

"Maybe we're being too hard on Billy," Craddock said.

"Did y'all say 'hard-on'?"

Davis ignored his partner's humor. "I mean we have to do what we have to do. Even if Billy didn't snitch us out to the fat detective, he knows all about PURE. He's the only one outside Hanover House who does."

"Maybe I could go back into therapy," Billy whispered. The black man holding him was incredibly strong. As strong as all the people he'd feared in his life. He felt like a child lying in the dark. Watching the closet door for the slightest movement.

"I don't think so, Billy. I think we should take a little walk."

Billy Williams didn't resist Craddock's gentle tug. He allowed himself to be led across the room to the front door of the apartment.

"All right, Billy," Craddock said. "Far enough. Now turn around. That's good. Just a little to the left and it'll be perfect."

Davis Craddock, anxious to impress his companion, put all his strength into the first blow, swinging the pry bar in a long arc from his knees to the top of Billy Williams' head. Craddock had expected Billy to fall unconscious, but the slender, balding man only dropped to his knees. There was plenty of blood, though, which was encouraging, and Davis Craddock was too professional to let disappointment interfere with the pursuit of his declared intentions. He raised the hooked bar above his head and again brought it down on a whimpering Billy Williams. Still, the job wasn't done.

"Lemme hit the bitch one time," Bogard whined. "I can't watch this 'thout gettin' in mah shots."

"No way," Craddock said firmly. "You're left-handed and I'm right-handed. All these wounds have to come from the same hand. Besides, you lost the coin toss."

"Shi-i-i-it."

Craddock decided to get it over with quickly. He began to work the top of Billy Williams' now-unmoving head with short, chopping strokes. Davis was not a doctor and he'd been a little worried about whether he would know the moment when Billy Williams died. He'd feared he might continue pounding until he made himself a fool in Wendell's eyes, but Billy Williams' bladder and bowel untied at the moment of death and the stench left no doubt in either of the partners' minds.

The man was motherfuckin' amazin'. Goin' through the door alone. Just the way they planned it. It was closin' in on seven AM and there'd likely be people on the street. Black and white together looked wrong. White neighbors see that, they gon' remember.

A few minutes later, Wendell followed Davis through the front door, closing it softly behind him. Then he slid the hooked end of the pry bar between the jamb and the lock and popped the door back open. Nobody around. Nobody to see that he was bustin' out the lock *after* he was finished in the house.

The porter was in front, messin' with the garbage cans, when Wendell pushed the door open and walked down the stoop. A nigger from the old school, shufflin' his appreciation of the white man's shitty job. Wendell gave the nigger his hardest badass look and the man turned away. But he'd remember. Which was the whole point.

A moment later and Wendell was around the corner where Craddock was waiting in the van with the engine running. Smilin' his happy maggot smile. Crazy as crazy could be.

"What'd I tell you?" he asked. "Did I tell you he wouldn't scream? Did I tell you he'd take it like a bitch takes cock?"

"Got to say for a fact that yo peoples go easy. He knew what we was gonna do to his ass, but he didn't even *think* about fightin' back. You white boys got some strange ways. Nigger don't go out like that."

"Yeah?" Craddock quickly outlined the realities of the Jonestown massacre, emphasizing the large number of blacks who drank the Kool-Aid. Then he told his partner about Poochie and his own theories. "The poochie," he concluded, "stretches across all barriers. Race, religion, nationality. It may be that conditions for blacks are so harsh that most of the weak are eliminated, but there are always a few. In fact, if it wasn't for the poochies, men like us would be in deep trouble."

Kickin' down the boulevard. There was about ten million cars all goin' to work. Suckers for that nine-to-five bullshit. Wendell knew he could never have that. Couldn't even goddamn read was the truth of it. But his partner coulda done it. Could still do it. Still turn back to the world. If he wasn't so crazy.

"What do you say we celebrate?" Craddock said. "Seeing as we're going to be a long time getting back downtown." He waved his hand at the sea of cars, trucks and buses.

"What you wanna do? *Pusher Man*?"

"Let's have a little *white* celebration for a change. Reach around in the back and get that box behind the seat. Got a little surprise in there."

Surprise? Man had a whole ice chest in there. Had two glasses so thin they'd break if you spit on them. Wendell fumbled with the cork until it blew, bouncing off the windshield, then whistling past his ear. He peered at the label, puzzling out the letters, but unable to make sense of the words. *L. Roederer Cristal*.

"Don't usually drink this shit," he announced. "Too faggoty. Too maggoty. If you catch my meanin'."

"Make an exception, Wendell. It's been a good night."

Drivin' in silence. Crazy maggot and his crazy nigger partner sippin' on French champagne. Wendell hadn't ever had no best bro'. DTA was the motto on the street—Don't Trust Anyone. But there was definitely times when he wanted to. When he sometimes *did* feel like he was in the presence of the twin brother he used to imagine when he was a kid.

NINETEEN

Betty Haluka pushed open the door to her lover's apartment, stepped inside, then deliberately slammed the door shut. The crash echoed through the tiny apartment, freezing Moodrow in his chair. Leaving him to wonder exactly what he might have done or said to merit such a greeting.

"You wanna write a letter?" Betty shouted. "You like letters? Well, take down this and address it to Davis Craddock: 'Dear Motherfucking Piece-of-Dog-Shit Cocksucker . . .' "

Moodrow let the breath he'd been holding ease out of his lungs. Betty had just finished her first therapy session.

"Didn't you get along with your shrink?" he asked, trying both to keep his voice innocent and to control the giggle that pushed against his lips.

Betty looked at him for a minute, daring him to make a smart remark. "Stanley, you have no idea what that bastard said to me."

"You want a drink?"

"Yeah. And I'll take that slop *you* drink. No water."

Moodrow got up and Betty sat down. Neither spoke as Moodrow retrieved the bottle of Wild Turkey from a cabinet over the sink and poured two inches of bourbon into two glasses. He put Betty's on the table in front of her and she drank it in a single gulp. The coughing fit that followed (not to mention the flame in her throat) did nothing to improve her mood. She continued to stare at Moodrow, fire in her eyes, until the firewater in her stomach began to have its pacifying effect.

"You won't believe what that son of a bitch of a Therapist called me," she said, her voice considerably softer.

"After seeing the way you came through that door, I'm ready to believe anything."

Betty ignored him. "The first thing he does—his name is Jack Burke, by the way—is sit me down on a wooden chair in a small, dirty room. Then he lowers himself into a leather chair that's almost a damn throne and we start talking. I tell him about my career and how, after all my years of work, the criminal justice system is more perverse than ever. I tell him that I have no relationships. No children or family. I feel like my whole life is over. I'm just a fat, middle-aged woman with no prospects. I realize I should be looking for a second career, but I can hardly get myself to leave my apartment.

"He lets me go on for about half the session, then breaks out laughing. Which is something *you* better not do."

"The furthest thing from my mind," Moodrow protested.

"Don't interrupt." She tossed Moodrow another hard look, then continued. "So we get halfway through the session—a session that *I'm* paying for—when he waves his hands and shakes his head. 'Jesus,' he says, 'you *are* a wimpy cunt. I see it all the time and I guess I should be used to it, but when it comes to me like this, it makes me feel like I have to puke.'

"Jack Burke is a little man. Like five-foot four and maybe a hundred twenty pounds. I wanted to jump off the chair and smack him in his smirking face, but . . ."

Moodrow poured another inch of bourbon into Betty's glass, then refilled his own. "Ah, the woes of the undercover cop. You're gonna have to get into the role. You've gotta *become* the wimpy . . ." He noted the look on Betty's face and didn't add the epithet. "You have to become the person your target expects you to be."

"I managed not to bash the bastard," Betty said. "I tried to tell him that if I was able to control my feelings, I wouldn't be there.

" 'You want mood elevators?' he says. 'Placodil, Elevil, Melloril? Valiums, perhaps? You're not gonna get that here, lady. All you're gonna get from us is the opportunity *not* to be the whiney bitch sitting in that chair. When we finish with you, you'll be a prosecutor instead of a public defender.'

" 'But I spent my whole life defending people.'

" 'And look where it's gotten you.'

"At that point I decided to keep my mouth shut. Which only encouraged the prick. 'There's all kinds of sick people out there. Schizos, psychopaths, deluded people of every shape and variety. But they never come to us. We get sad little misfits like you. *Oh, can you help me? I feel so sad and I'm such a good little bitch. I spent my whole life trying to help people and now everybody mistreats me. Boo-hoo-hoo-hoo* . . . Isn't it about time you stopped being a baby and helped yourself up?' "

Moodrow sipped at his drink. Despite his best efforts, a grin began to pull at the corners of his mouth. "Did he expect an answer?"

"That's just it, Stanley. He leaned back in his chair like he was goddamned Sigmund Freud directing a movie. Folded his arms across his chest and fixed me with a hard stare. I said, 'That's why I came to therapy. Because I want to help myself.'

"He goes, 'You came here because your friends won't put up with your crybaby act anymore. In fact, I'll bet your friends don't even come around to visit.'

"By that time I'd gotten a little control back, although I was still steaming. 'Nobody comes around,' I admitted. 'I feel so alone. Sometimes I start crying and I can't stop. Sometimes I can't get out of bed in the morning.'

"The prick only laughed. 'I think I'll give you a name. I'll call you the Boo-hoo Girl. You get your real name back when you earn it. That's assuming you show up for the next session. Personally, I don't give a shit. In fact, nobody at Hanover House gives a shit.'

"I said, 'What kind of therapy is this? I come here in pain and you attack me.'

" 'It's called therapy that works. As opposed to therapy that encourages Boo-hoo Bitches to become drug dependent. You wanna know if we care? Look back at your parents. One or both of them was just as depressed as you are. They *gave* you depression as surely as they gave you the color of your eyes. And you can *never* change that simple fact until you stop being a pussy and start acting like a *man*.'

"He waited again, smirking at me. Pushing my buttons. I couldn't think of anything, so I repeated myself. I said, 'Do you think I want to be this way? If I didn't want to change it, I wouldn't be here.'

"He said, 'Wanting isn't enough. Look, I'll be frank. In my opinion, you're too old. You should have started twenty years ago. I think what you'll do is give up on Hanover House and dig up a mainstream shrink with a prescription pad. What *we* do is strip away all your illusions about your wonderful family and how much you love your mommy and daddy. All Hanoverians are family. We don't support you with drugs. We give you the chance to help yourself through hard work and group effort. That's assuming you come back, which, as I said, is very unlikely.'

"Stanley, I got myself through it by remembering the child. I kept thinking about Michael Alamare trapped in that hell. We know that Davis Craddock is a killer. We know that he uses violence to control his people. What's going to happen to the child? Assuming he's still alive. And what about all the other children? It's just not right. It's not right at all. He has to be stopped."

Moodrow grunted his agreement, then got up, walked to his desk and picked up a legal pad and two pens.

"What's that for?"

"We're gonna write a letter."

Dear Mr. Craddock,

It's a sad fact of human life that few of us prepare for future events, even when those events are inevitable. For instance, only ten percent of all Americans buy a funeral plot before they pass away. Pity the poor relatives who, lost in grief, have to deal with the financial realities of a proper funeral and a decent burial. We at the Royal Society for the Eradication of the Terminally Undesirable are determined to educate the public about this sad failing. Because, Mr. Craddock, death is inevitable. It comes to all of us and often when we least expect it. We may wake up each morning with a smile on our lips and a song in our hearts. We may spend happy hours in the gymnasium, lowering our weight and our resting pulse rates. Then, despite our best efforts, we drop dead for no good reason at all.

Our American Boy Scouts have a motto: Be Prepared. If little children can understand the necessity to 'be prepared' for an unknowable future, how can we, as adults, allow ourselves to live in ignorance?

We at the Royal Society for the Eradication of the Terminally Undesirable, in an attempt to end human delusion, are prepared to make a guaranteed offer. If you mail us a check for $1,000, we will arrange for your burial in a pit on scenic Hart's Island. Uniformed, respectful prisoners will dig your grave and drop you into it. For a small extra fee (one pack of cigarettes per man), they will each shed a tear and refrain from pissing on your coffin.

Please don't delay. Mail your check immediately. After all, you may be dead before you have a chance to take advantage of our generous offer. And won't you feel stupid if that should happen?

They wrote it over three or four times before Betty announced her satisfaction by tossing the pen onto the table. She got up and circled the table to sit in Moodrow's lap. Without preamble, she began to unbutton his shirt.

"Now, listen up, Stanley. This is what you're gonna do. And I don't want any lip. After you get your clothes off, you're going to undress me. Slowly and carefully. Then you're going to put your head between my thighs and manipulate my clitoris until I have an orgasm. Then you're going to take your penis, place it inside my vagina and move it in and out until I have another orgasm. You got that?"

"Yeah, I got it. I got it. But there's something I feel I should tell you."

"Like?"

"Like kissing on the lips costs extra."

"I don't want you to go back in there."

They were lying in bed, almost ready to drop off into sleep. Moodrow had long ago accepted the fact that Betty was tough, that she made her own decisions. It was one of the things he liked best about her. Now, however, he was really afraid. Afraid that she had no idea what she was getting into and no idea what to do if her 'plan' fell apart.

"I have to go, Stanley." It was the reply he expected.

"Are you scared?"

"I'm not scared. What I am is pissed off."

"That's what bothers me." He turned onto his side, propping himself up on one elbow. "A question: if you're so sure that Craddock is a killer and that Michael Alamare is in grave danger, why aren't you afraid for yourself? You *should* be afraid."

"How's he going to know? I'm just another wimpy cunt to them. Another potential slave. They're trying to drive me away, not lure me in."

"Craddock's paranoid. And there's very few applicants these days. I know he's got some way of checking on the ones who stick around."

"Stanley, I *have* to go."

"You're not qualified." Moodrow knew he was taking the wrong tack, but he couldn't keep the anger out of his voice. "What is it they say? Anyone who tries to be their own lawyer has a fool for a client? You're trying to be your own cop and you don't know the first thing about it."

"I'm going back, Stanley. I have to."

TWENTY

from *The Autobiography of Davis Craddock*

GRACE under pressure. PERSEVERANCE in the face of adversity. Eventual TRIUMPH despite all the unexpected obstacles this bastard of a universe can throw at me. That's the ticket, right? That's the proper attitude for get-going tough guys. Right?

And then there's Wendell the Wonderful.

When Flo Alamare went down, I hoped I'd fall apart. I freely confess to this last desperate grab at normalcy. Flo had been my consort for years. My chosen favorite. If, on learning of her demise, I had descended into grief it would have proven what Marilyn had always insisted. It would have proven that a feeling human being still lived at the core of my utterly perverse psyche.

I accept this 'hope' as a lesson. Because what I felt was, first of all, nothing. Then minor annoyance. Then anger as the ramifications of whatever shithead thing she did to poison herself began to manifest themselves.

I suppose I should be grateful that Marcy found Flo and the van before the police did, but Marcy, instead of bringing Flo back to Hanover House, dumped the paralyzed bitch in a vacant lot.

Once the body was found, the arch-cunt of Manhattan, Mama Alamare, got into the act. She brought in the police and when they gave up, hired the fat detective to bust my chops.

The fat detective won't play by the rules. Not that I have any rules. And not that I won't enjoy playing with the fat detective. But the truth is that I only need a month. At most.

Flo's body should never have been found. Who would have noticed her disappearance? My poochies? I would have had no trouble convincing my poochies that Flo simply took off. Most poochies, when the time comes, sever their relationship with Hanover House by flight.

Flo's disappearance would have been yesterday's news within a few weeks. Marcy would have stepped into Flo's role and life would have gone on.

Marcy was Flo's lover. That's the *real* reason why she didn't bring Flo back to me. After all, Flo was still alive and Marcy knew what would happen to Flo if I got my hands on her. I *have* my hands on Marcy and Marcy will pay.

Because the reality is that I only need one month to complete my project.

The fat detective writes me funny letters. He makes his intentions clear. He's going to get me. How? By sending his bitch into Hanover House.

I underestimated him. I admit it. *Everything* I did was wrong. I should have, with all due courtesy, passed him to one of my asshole administrators. Poochies unto death, one and all, they would have told him exactly what we told the cops.

Or better, yet, I might have played the outraged victim. First the DA's office. Then the IRA. Then Connie Alamare's obnoxious lawyers. Then the fat detective.

How much could I be expected to bear? Especially since my only concern has been to forge a path to the future. To ease the suffering of a psychologically burdened humanity.

I should have given the fat detective to my attorney. I should have begun an action against Connie Alamare, accusing her of harassment. I should have . . .

Two can play the game of underestimation. I've been screening all new clients for months. What I feared most was some undercover narc sniffing out the connection between Deeny Washington and Hanover House. All it would take is a street snitch running into Marcy and Deeny Washington and recognizing Marcy as a Hanoverian. Or a loving relative come to rescue an enslaved sibling. Or a big fat detective sending his fat girlfriend to find a little bastard who isn't a little bastard, but my own rather repulsive flesh and blood. Which is why he's alive. Even Marcy would turn against me if I dropped my first born (an obnoxious little rat, by the way) into the East River.

*   *   *

The one thing I cannot risk is a recent association of that petrified corpse, Flo Alamare, with Hanover House. All those little holes in her arm would undeniably tie Hanover House (and, of course, yours truly) to the world of drugs.

Because I only need one month. One month to manufacture two hundred pounds of PURE, dismantle the lab and hide the drug in a dozen locations in as many states.

Another month to sell it off? Two months? As of this writing, Wendell the Wonderful has orders for sixty-five pounds of PURE. He also tells me that his clients are very, very curious about PURE's origins.

As a matter of routine, I've been having new clients followed to their homes (or to the local precinct, in the case of a narc; or to a hotel, in the case of a relative; or to a fat detective's apartment, in the case of Betty Haluka) for the last six months.

We have few applicants these days. Over the last year or so, our publicity has gone from bad to worse. Unlike the Moonies, we have never recruited street people. My poochies are educated and our techniques deliberately confrontational.

In prior years, our initial free seminar brought out dozens of applicants. These days we rarely get more than four or five and very few of those return for therapy. Fewer still come back for the second therapy session.

The fat detective pays. The fat detective finds me amusing. As of this writing, I have no way to put my hands on the fat detective's flesh. But I *will* put my hands on the flesh of his bitch. I will *own* the flesh of his fat bitch and the vehicle of her enslavement will be PURE.

TWENTY-ONE

The uniformed doorman standing guard at the entrance to Connie Alamare's Sutton Place apartment building snorted derisively when Moodrow stepped into the lobby on his second visit.

"You are no cop," he said decisively. "You have not arrested bitch. Bitch is still residing here. What you are wanting?"

"Don't bust my balls."

Moodrow was in no mood to be reasonable. If talking to his client on the phone was thoroughly unpleasant, a face-to-face visit was like preparing yourself for a raid on a well-defended crack house. Not that he could have avoided it. He needed a signature and signatures cannot be gotten over the phone. Even though homicide-by-poisoning is extremely rare in New York, suicide-by-poisoning is common and the medical examiner gets the job of determining exactly which poison was used. Whenever the medical examiner's own lab tests come up negative, he farms the work out to Toxilab, Inc., an independent specialty house in Queens. Moodrow planned to pick up the blood and urine stored at the Bronx hospital that had first treated Flo Alamare and deliver it to Toxilab. He was certain both that Flo had been poisoned and that the Bronx doctors who'd declared her a stroke victim were not going to help him prove it.

Not surprisingly, the doctors at Bronx Municipal had refused to release the fluids without a notarized request from the next of kin. Moodrow had gotten Connie Alamare to call the toxicology department at the hospital, but procedure being procedure, especially in city-run institutions, the department head, Dr. Federico Benari, had refused to budge.

"You have not to arrested her," the doorman insisted.

"Sorry to disappoint you. Wanna get on the intercom and 'announce my presence'? I'm in a hurry."

"Why such hurry just for getting ass kicked?"

"It's like going to the dentist, pal. Dragging it out only makes it hurt more."

The doorman burst out laughing. "You are with me okay. She is definitely great bitch of New York. On other day it is pouring rain and she calls down for cab. How can I get cab in rain? For fifteen minutes she scream in face. In my country such woman is beaten unmercifully."

"You don't have cops in your country?"

"Is no crime to beat great bitch of New York."

Moodrow, bored, nodded at the phone. "Just announce me. I'm going up."

"Okay, but I can already hear drill going bzzzzzzzzzzzzz."

Despite his bravado, Moodrow felt his heart quicken as he stepped out of the elevator. Dealing with Connie Alamare's mouth, he quickly decided, was worse than preparing yourself to raid a well-defended crack house. It was like being taken prisoner by the Inquisition.

When the door was opened by Connie's mother, Moodrow let out a tiny groan of anticipation which the woman, quite correctly, took for abject terror.

"Eh," Maria Corrello almost shouted. "It's the *strunza*. Whatta you come for, *strunza*, another check? My daughter hasn't thrown away enough money?"

"Why do you care? You afraid she'll run out and you'll have to go back to the old ladies' home? Excuse me, I forgot. They're not called that anymore. Now they're retirement communities."

"Retire? While there's *citrullos* like you in the world, I'll never retire."

"Ummmm." Moodrow couldn't get past the fact that grandma thought ball busting was a legitimate occupation. He'd known any number of silks in the job who'd put this idea into practice, but they'd always justified their sadism with sanctimonious pronouncements about protecting the job from cops like him. This woman was blatantly throwing it out there.

"I came here to see your daughter," Moodrow finally muttered. "If I remember correctly, she doesn't *allow* you to write checks."

The woman ignored his comment. "What's with you, anyway?" She gestured at his best brown suit. "*Sciofoso*. You can't afford clothes? You spend our money on dope?"

Moodrow leaned in close. "You know what you are? *Una chiachierona*." He was calling her an old windbag. The carefully researched epithet had been intended for the old woman's daughter.

"*Va fancula*," she replied evenly. "*Va fa en Napoli*."

Va fancula, Moodrow knew, meant 'up your ass.' The rest of it was beyond him. In desperation, he turned and began to walk back to the elevator.

"Hey, *paisan*," the woman shouted. "Where you goin'?"

"I had enough bullshit," Moodrow called over his shoulder. "If your daughter wants to speak to me, let her come to my office."

"You don't have an office."

"Now you're gettin' the picture." He pressed the elevator button, then folded his arms across his chest.

"C'mon, *gumbah*, what's the matter with you? I'm just an old lady. I thought you were a tough guy. My daughter's alone in there with Florence. You come on."

"Are you sorry?" Moodrow asked without turning.

"*Ammaza tutta la familia*," she muttered.

"Uh-uh. None of that. I asked if you were sorry."

"I'm sorry, all right. Go talk to Connie." The old woman turned and began to walk away, leaving the door open. She took five or six steps before she lost control and spit on the floor.

"Your daughter's gonna have your head for that, Maria," Moodrow called after her. "Because I'm gonna tell on you."

The woman continued to mutter softly as she walked back into the depths of the mammoth apartment and Moodrow almost laughed. Then he remembered that he still had Connie in his immediate future and sobered up. He hunched his shoulders and made his way back through the living room and into the hallway leading to the bedroom. To his surprise he heard the sounds of conversation along with the hiss of the respirator coming from Flo Alamare's room.

"I got a letter this morning from Aunt Bella in Columbus." Connie Alamare's strident voice was instantly recognizable. "The fat one who threw up at your cousin's wedding. You remember? The *chooch*. She's as stupid as ever. Her youngest boy was arrested for dealing cocaine and she moans and groans. 'I didn't know. I didn't know.' Meanwhile, he's got a hole where his nose should be. It's disgusting. Her husband only cares about his silk suits and his guido shoes and the *grappa* he drinks with his friends at the social club. He won't even talk about getting a lawyer for the kid or posting bail. That's why she writes me after five years. All the money is in Frank's name. She can't even find the check-book. I told her years ago to put the horns on him. 'Why do you let this *citrullo* step on you? Your children are all grown. Get yourself a young boy to make you happy and a lawyer to make you rich. Your husband has money. You don't have to live like a servant.'

"Not Bella, Flo. Bella's a guinea from the old country. Her husband is God. 'What would I do without Frank? Divorce is forbidden by my religion.' I tried to explain that divorce isn't forbidden. Only remarriage. 'I don't know how to live by myself. I only know how to take care of the house. Cooking, washing, cleaning. This is my life.' I told her, 'If that's your life, you'd be better off dead.'

"Flo, it's sickening. Believe me, I know because I once had to live that way. If it wasn't for your father's passing, I'd have ten kids and a forty-inch waist. The world is set up to make men happy. Why shouldn't it be? It's men that set it up in the first place. Women are just whores. A man can go on the street and buy a woman for twenty dollars or go in a church and get a lifetime contract for nothing. For room and board. That's what they give the slaves. Clothes for their backs and a place to sleep.

"I didn't want that to happen to you. That's why I was so hard on you when you were growing up. I wanted you to be strong enough to resist the crap. I wanted you to be a woman who stood up for herself."

In the silence that followed, Moodrow, curious, stepped into the doorway. Connie Alamare was sitting next to Flo's bed, holding her daughter's hand, a hand that was little more than twisted bones, and crying softly. "I don't know. I don't know." She murmured the phrase again and again.

Flo had gotten noticeably thinner. Her dark, empty eyes stared, unblinking, at the ceiling. Saliva dripped from the corners of her mouth to form a dark stain on the sheets. A tube ran from beneath the sheets to a half-filled bag of urine while the IV bottle slowly emptied into a vein on her throat. The respirator continued to push air into her lungs, then pull it out again. Over and over.

It didn't seem possible that she could still be alive. Her body was little more than a shadow beneath the bedclothes. Moodrow, taken by surprise, felt himself drifting back to those first years in the job. There were times, before he'd hardened himself, when the unrelenting misery had threatened to overwhelm him. When he'd seriously considered leaving the job. The victims, the families, even the criminals—it was ugly beyond description and the realization that he would have to deal with it for the length of his career made him want to run as far away as he could get. Eventually, he'd learned to ignore it. You took the man's pay and did the man's job and sending the mutts Upstate was all the consolation you were going to get.

But there were times when the old feelings returned. You walked, unsuspecting, into a crime scene and found all the misery summed up in a single image. He recalled an incident that had taken place in his last year in the job. He was summoned to the scene of a homicide involving an eighty-one-year-old woman. She'd been raped first, then beaten to death with a tire iron. Moodrow, preoccupied, had stepped into the apartment to find the woman's husband, in violation of all crime scene procedure, cradling his wife's bloody head in his lap. He'd looked up at Moodrow and his eyes held every inch of the suffering that would dominate the rest of his life.

"Hey, Flo, look who's here. It's Nero the detective." Connie Alamare, her dark eyes glittering through her tears, had turned toward him. She continued to stroke her daughter's hand as she spoke. Her voice was defiant.

"Your mother told me you were in here." If there was anything else to say, Moodrow couldn't think of it.

"Did he come for another check, Flo? What do you think?"

"You know why I came here, Connie. I spoke to you about it yesterday."

"He wants to send your blood to a laboratory, Flo. After three weeks of work, he gets a brilliant idea. Check the blood."

"I want to find out exactly what happened to her."

"If you want to find out what happened to Flo, all you have to do is open your eyes."

"Look, Connie, your daughter was using drugs when this happened." Moodrow's voice was calm and steady, his anger entirely gone. "I've talked to the narcs in the Seventh Precinct. I've talked to the mutts on the street. Everyone tells me there are no drugs in Hanover House. We may have to look elsewhere."

"You're sniffing up the wrong tree, Nero." She finally dropped her daughter's hand. "Flo was crazy about Davis Craddock. She thought he was some kind of a god. She *worshiped* him. If she left him, she would have come home. And what happened to my grandson? You want me to believe that little Michael is a prisoner of some drug addicts? I don't believe it. What would they do with him?"

"I don't know."

"Nero doesn't know. Ten thousand dollars and he doesn't know."

"For Christ's sake, Connie . . ." The woman's ability to get under his skin was maddening. He'd come prepared to challenge her acid tongue, epithet for epithet, but the scene had disarmed him. He found himself wanting to ease her suffering. Ease it or kill her. "This isn't getting us anywhere."

"It's getting *you* somewhere. It's getting *you* rich."

Moodrow looked back at Flo Alamare's twisted body. Her narrow chest, pumped by the respirator, was moving up and down. "I haven't given up on Davis Craddock. I'm doing what I can to draw him out. I promise you, if Craddock did this to your daughter, I'm going to know how and why. If your grandson is still in Hanover House, I'll eventually be able to prove that, too. But I also think you should prepare yourself for the possibility that she left Hanover House and got into trouble later on."

"You should send someone inside. Pretend to go for therapy. My grandson isn't invisible. You get inside, you're going to find him."

"I'm already doing that, but maybe there's something else you better consider. Michael has a father, biological if not legal. The father could have a claim on . . ."

"Leave that for the lawyers, Nero. You just find him. That paper you wanted is on the table in the living room. Pick it up on your way out." She turned her back on Moodrow and began to caress her daughter's face. "You see, Flo," she said, "pretty soon you'll have Michael back with you. We'll be a family again."

TWENTY-TWO

It was only ten o'clock when Moodrow left the Alamare apartment on the Upper East Side of Manhattan. He would have liked to go directly to the hospital, but the chairman of the toxicology department, Dr. Federico Benari, would be unable to see him until four in the afternoon. Benari had insisted on the hour, just as Connie Alamare had insisted Moodrow pick up her notarized request in the morning. It was frustrating, at the least, but Moodrow had already decided to make the gap productive by trying to answer one of the questions that had been jumping out at him since he'd begun the investigation. What was Flo Alamare, a middle-class white girl, doing in a part of the Bronx dominated by unrelenting poverty? Of course, without any recent history, the question had remained unanswered and it was tempting to think of her as just another junkie looking to get stoned, but the emerging picture of Flo as one of Davis Craddock's enforcers suggested that she may have been on official business.

Moodrow had a list (by no means complete) of former Hanoverians. Reviewing them, he found only one with a Bronx address: William Brandeis Williams. Flo Alamare's body had been discovered a few blocks north of the Bruckner Expressway, the logical route for anyone traveling between Williams' east Bronx apartment and Hanover House. Moodrow had already been to see Williams. He'd gotten nothing from the man besides a muttered "I don't know anything" and a hastily closed door. As this same response had come from virtually every other ex-Hanoverian, Moodrow had drawn no conclusion, but with time to spare, he decided to pay Mr. Williams a second, unannounced visit.

The late morning traffic was extremely light and Moodrow made the run to Williams' Throgs Neck apartment in under an hour. He was looking forward to a quick, productive conversation and a long, cholesterol-filled lunch before he went to the hospital. Williams, according to Moodrow's notes, worked nights and Moodrow hoped to find Williams sleepy and vulnerable. What he found was a spider's web of yellow crime scene tape covering Williams' door. Apartments are only sealed in suspected homicides. Williams lived alone.

Moodrow, his instincts quickening, drove to the nearest precinct, the Four Five. The duty sergeant informed him that Williams was indeed a homicide victim, but the case wasn't being handled by the precinct detectives. It had been turned over to a borough-wide homicide task force.

"They don't trust the precincts no more," he announced. "We're not professional enough."

"Where's the task force operating from?"

"They're housed in the Four Six."

"That's on the other side of the Bronx."

"Very good. I see you know your geography."

Moodrow ignored the sarcasm. "What about the uniforms who responded to the scene. Maybe I could speak to one of them?"

"We had a suit who heard the squeal and made an initial response. Calaverri. He closed off the scene until the task force dicks showed up. I think he's at his desk. Straight through to the back."

Moodrow made his way to a large room filled with back-to-back desks. Calaverri was a short, thick man with a scruffy salt-and-pepper beard. He was sitting behind a mountain of paperwork and was none too pleased by the unexpected visit.

"Williams? Yeah, I responded to the scene. Unfortunately, I'm not competent to handle a simple homicide. It don't mean shit that I spent the last nine years building up a list of snitches in the precinct. Now we got scientific detectives with computers sitting on the other side of the goddamn borough. They don't clear half the files, but they fit the latest professional fucking model. Me, I'm just a clerk."

"That's how come I retired." Moodrow shook his head. "It doesn't make sense, Calaverri. Thirty years in the Seven and they tell me I don't know the territory. I said, 'Here's my papers. I'm outta here.' "

It was bullshit, of course, but it was the kind of bullshit Calaverri wanted to hear. They gossiped about mutual friends in the job for a few moments, then got down to business.

"Williams got his head busted with the traditional blunt object," Calaverri announced. "Probably a tire iron or a pipe. I only got a look at the guy's brains. The autopsy report went to the task force. The apartment lock was busted out and about three quarters of the apartment was trashed. Williams most likely surprised the burglar who then went crazy. The victim looked like a dog run over by a truck."

"That seem right to you?"

"Whatta ya mean?"

"Most burglars only do what's necessary to get away from the scene. Why'd the perp hang around long enough to kill him?"

"It's the crack. It makes 'em crazy."

"Yeah, sure, maybe it was crack, but there's another possibility. Maybe Williams knew the intruder. Maybe the perp *had* to kill him."

Calaverri shrugged. "It ain't my business, really, but I'll tell you something weird. This guy must've lived like a goddamn monk. You know how when you lift prints you always come up with a dozen that turn out to be friends and acquaintances? The only prints we picked up in Williams' apartment were his. The scene wasn't wiped clean, either. This guy was a hermit."

"Did you canvass the neighborhood? Before you got pulled off?"

"Are you kidding? Solving crimes ain't my job. *This* is my job." He held up a handful of files. "The only people I spoke to were the nosy neighbors hanging around the scene. The porter says he saw a colored guy come outta the building an hour before the body was discovered, but he didn't see the guy's face well enough to make an ID. I think the porter's name is Jackson, but don't quote me."

Twenty minutes later, Moodrow was sitting in Calvin Jackson's basement apartment, pulling on a cup of coffee. Jackson was a slow-moving, elderly man who'd been working in the building for ten years.

"Wasn't anyone I ever seen in this neighborhood. My eyes ain't much good no more, but I could see the boy was an African-American. Big bastard. Ain't no African-Americans livin' round here. 'Cept for me."

"Did the man look like a drug addict?"

"Shi-i-i-it. Every time you white folks see black skin you start thinkin' crack and dope. This boy was dressed too good. Had on a leather sport jacket must've cost near five hundred dollars. Shined up shoes and a big diamond on his left hand. Crack addict? The man looked more like a pimp. I been tryin' my whole life to get along with you people, but it ain't no use. I still get watched every time I walk into the five and dime. We all thieves and dope addicts to you."

Jackson's tone was matter-of-fact and Moodrow, knowing he was right, took his time asking the next question. "You say there are no black people living in this neighborhood. Weren't you suspicious when you saw a black man come out of the building at that hour of the morning?"

"That's just it. The boy didn't *act* suspicious. He come down the stoop like he was the damn landlord. Didn't try to hide his face or nothin'. There's a couple of airline stewardesses livin' on the top floor. I figured maybe they was havin' a party. Them airline women do like to party. Maybe they was changin' their luck."

"Did you speak to them after the body was discovered?"

"Naw. Turns out they was in Seattle that night. Most likely partyin' with them pilots. Say, I gotta get back to work. Don't mind chattin', but if them garbage cans ain't by the curb, they ain't gonna get picked up and the tenants'll be all over my black ass."

"Just a couple more questions. Please?"

Jackson shrugged and looked at his watch. "Got five minutes, maybe."

"What's your impression of Williams? You know him?"

"The man was only here a couple months and he mostly kept to himself. Nod at me when he seen me, but nothin' more. Funny thing about it is he had a kid with him when he come here. Little girl name of Terry. She was the friendly one, but she up and disappeared one day. Never did find out where she went."

"You never asked him?"

"Damn, man, don't you know nothin'? Calvin Jackson is the god-damn colored *porter*. I ain't no tenant to be socializin' with the white folks. When I'm lookin' for company, I go back where I come from. Back to Harlem where I still got some family."

Moodrow nodded thoughtfully, but he felt his pulse quickening as pieces of the puzzle began to come together. This was the way all his investigations worked. You pushed and pushed until the parts made a whole. He took out a copy of the photo Flo Alamare had sent to her mother. He'd been carrying it in his inside jacket pocket since the case began and this was the first time he'd found anyone to show it to.

"You ever see this woman around here?" he asked, passing the photo to Calvin Jackson.

"Shit, 'thout my glasses, that just look like someone done spit on the paper." He fumbled through a kitchen drawer for a moment, then came out with an ancient pair of glasses. Both eyepieces had been taped and he had to hold the glasses to his face while he peered at the photo. "Yeah, I seen the woman. But not with that kid."

"You sure."

"I said I seen the woman. Nasty bitch walked right past me with her nose in the air. She was with Williams' little girl. That's Terry. Terry's face was all painted up. That's how come I remember. That little Terry was the *nicest* child, but when she stopped to talk to me that day, the bitch kept on pullin' her along."

"When was this?"

"Can't really say. Maybe three weeks ago. Maybe a month. Fact, now that I think on it, Terry disappeared right after. You ain't hintin' this bitch had nothin' to do with that?"

"If her father didn't complain to the cops, I doubt there was force involved."

" 'Less she done scared the shit out that white faggot. Boy always looked scared to me."

"Yeah, well I'm a detective, Calvin, and right now I'm still detecting. I don't wanna make any judgments until I'm sure. Do me a big favor and take another look. Make sure this woman is the woman you saw that afternoon."

"Don't gotta look. What I seen, I seen. Damn but that child was nice. Used to talk to me every afternoon on her way home from school. When she didn't get off the bus that afternoon, I was surprised. Then she come walkin' up with the woman in that picture."

Moodrow nodded thoughtfully. "Can you describe Terry Williams to me? Anything I can use to identify her."

"Williams didn't have no picture of his own daughter?"

"It's a crime scene, Calvin. I don't wanna bust through the tape and I don't have time to get permission." Moodrow was thinking of the task force on the other side of the Bronx. Did he know anyone in the Four Six? Would they be willing to let him in without some clear connection between Terry Williams' disappearance and the murder?

Calvin Jackson looked at Moodrow in disbelief. "Never met no cop with scruples before. Guess it's true when they say you ain't never too old to learn. Lemme see. She was a pretty little white girl. Blonde hair and blue eyes. Them kind all look alike to me, but there's one thing you might use. Her right eye was kind of out to the side a little bit. Not real bad, now, but if you looked close you could see it."

Moodrow managed to contain his excitement long enough to put away a meatball parmigiana hero and a bottle of beer. Then he surprised himself by calling Betty Haluka instead of Jim Tilley. The phone rang a dozen times before he gave up and dialed his ex-partner's number. Tilley's phone only rang twice.

"Hi, we're not home now, but . . ."

Moodrow hung up in disgust. Betty was after him to get an answering machine *and* a beeper, but he hated the idea of being available every minute of the day. His uncle had expressed a similar emotion when he spoke of the transition to radio that had made every cop a slave to the precinct dispatcher.

Still, Moodrow was definitely disappointed. He needed to go over it with someone, but it was clear that he was going to have to settle for his own counsel. He consoled himself with two slices of pizza and a large Coke, then pushed his thoughts back into the investigation. He had absolutely no doubt that Hanover House and Davis Craddock were at the center of the puzzle. Williams had been silenced because he had seen Flo Alamare on the day she had her . . . Accident? Attempted murder? Illness?

The heroin in her body had come to her through Craddock. Despite all the evidence, Hanover House was somehow involved with drugs. Of course, that didn't explain the black male Calvin Jackson had seen on the morning of Williams' murder. As far as Moodrow knew, the commune had no black or Latino members. Maybe they'd brought in a professional to handle Williams, although it didn't seem likely that Craddock had those kinds of connections.

Bits and pieces. It still came down to that. Bits and pieces and how to prove the final piece at the very center of the puzzle was Davis Craddock. For the first time Moodrow entertained serious doubts that Michael Alamare was alive.

Restless, he went back to the phone and dialed Betty's Brooklyn number. He expected her answering machine, but she picked up on the third ring. He quickly outlined his conversation with Calvin Jackson, then begged her not to go back into Hanover House.

"Williams was viciously beaten," he explained. "Way beyond what was necessary. Craddock is a psycho. He'd kill you without thinking twice. We're not talking about a stroke victim and a missing child anymore. We're looking at drugs and murder."

"But if I could find Terry Williams, wouldn't that prove Flo Alamare had been inside Hanover House recently?"

"And what are you gonna do with that information? Start a lawsuit? I gotta tell you the truth, Betty, I don't think Michael Alamare is alive. And if he's not, why are you risking your neck? What have you got to gain?"

"Suppose he is alive, Stanley. Then he'd be in grave danger, wouldn't he? My therapist told me if I came back for a few more sessions he'd introduce me to the other Hanoverians. And I don't think there's much risk, either. You've got a lot of possibilities, but no proof of anything. Maybe they'll offer me drugs."

"You're a goddamned amateur. You're gonna get yourself killed."

"Don't yell at me, Stanley."

TWENTY-THREE

Abou just *wouldn't* understand. Wendell Bogard was trying his best to kick it out there, but Abou kept shakin' his head. Wouldn't even *hear* about it.

"White man *cannot* be no brother," Abou said for the tenth time. "When the shit come down, the white man will leave you to eat it. Nothin' wrong 'bout usin' a white man to get some bank. Can't get *around* the white man when it come to money. They owns every goddamn thing. But when you talkin' 'brother,' you talkin' crazy."

"Now look here, Abou." Wendell's voice began to rise. "You workin' for *me*. Ain't no reason I got to explain nothin'. I'm tryin', cause *y'all* my brother, too."

"That's what I'm *talkin'* 'bout." Abou kept calm. No sense in messin' with the man. "Ain't too many brothers on the Lower East Side and them Puerto Ricans wouldn't never give me no chance to show my bidness side. You picked me up when I didn't have nothin' and I'd damn near die for you. Ain't no white man gon' do that. Specially no *crazy* white man. You call a crazy white man yo brother, sooner or later, you gon' get fucked up."

That was the *hardest* part for Wendell to explain. About the craziness. About singin' songs in the van and sharin' the white man's personal bitch. About how he was *sure* the white man loved him.

"Check it out, Abou. Like I *seen* Davis Craddock do murder. Like he didn't ask *me* to pull nobody's ticket. Most white men expect the nigger gon' do the dirty work. Craddock be fightin' *me* 'cause he wanna do the killin' for *hisself*. And he done it cold, Abou. The man is *altogether* cold."

"Okay. I ain't disputin' that Craddock ain't no punk. He's hard, Wendell, but that don't make him no brother. The way I know is do bidness with the white man, then come home to yo *real* brothers. That's the way I know. Mus' be ah'm too old to change." Abou was twenty-three.

Abou was drinking Glenfiddich, a single malt scotch. Wendell had picked that up from Craddock and Abou didn't have a problem with the juice. Abou liked livin' large and Wendell didn't allow him to do drugs.

Wendell filled their glasses and decided to give up on the convincing business. "Lemme tell y'all what the white man done last night," he said.

Abou drained his glass, then leaned back to hear the story. The white man *was* crazy and the stories were bad. Be even badder if they was in a movie instead of fuckin' up Wendell Bogard's life. "I spose ya'll be singin' or some shit."

Wendell's face turned to stone. "You dissin' me, now."

"I ain't poppin' junk, Wendell." Abou beat a hasty retreat. Wendell's temper was legendary. "Jus' playin'."

"Best chill, Abou." Wendell refilled his lieutenant's glass, then waited. He wanted Abou's cooperation, if not his approval. The money here was large and he didn't need to be watching his back.

"I'm chill, bro." Abou drained his glass for the fourth time that night and found that he was, indeed, 'chill.'

"What it's about is *time*. You seen the merchandise and you know its power. Ain't no question about the power of PURE." Wendell paused, got a nod of agreement, then continued. "The man is busy makin' this shit happen. Only need a month or so and he ain't lettin' *nothin'* get in his way. You know that white man got his ticket pulled in the Bronx? Name of Williams?"

"You done told me all about it."

"Yeah, well I didn't tell y'all 'bout Williams havin' no kid. Check it out. Other day this kid name of Terry start axin' 'Where's my daddy. How come my daddy don't come see me no more. I wanna go to the Bronx. See my daddy.' Ain't no way the bitch gon' see her daddy 'cause her daddy done got his ticket pulled."

"That *do* make it hard," Abou observed. He was feeling no pain whatsoever.

"Yeah, that make it *impossible*. Meanwhile, the little bitch be stirrin' up trouble with them faggots live in the commune. Like you can *see* the shit gon' come down if the man don't do nothin'. We up in Davis' room one night. Me, him and his bitch, Marcy. Davis say, 'We have a serious problem here. We have to deal with it before it gets out of hand.'

"Marcy say, 'I know what you're thinking, Davis. You can't hurt that child.'

"Davis say, 'You know how much money we're talkin' about here?'

"Marcy say, 'Money isn't everything, Davis. She's just a little girl.'

"Davis say, 'We're talking about murder, Marcy. So far, the cops haven't connected us to Mr. Williams' demise, but if they stumble onto Mr. Williams' daughter and she starts talking about the time her Auntie

Flo picked her up at the circus, *you'll* be eatin' pussy for the next fifty years.'

"Now check this out, Abou. We all sittin' butt naked in the bedroom. Marcy's in a chair with one leg thrown over the arm. Little blond pussy jus' winkin' at us. Invitin' us. Me and Davis be on the bed with our dicks hangin' down. Talkin' 'bout killin' some little kid."

Abou let his head wobble a bit. It was as close as he could get to a nod of agreement. "That's hard, man. I said that before. The man is sure as shit hard."

"Marcy say, 'I don't care about that. Ever since Flo got hurt, I've been Terry's bonding mother. I can't *kill* her. For cryin' out loud.'

"Davis Craddock get this big smile on. Say, 'You're not afraid to go to jail, Marcy?'

"Marcy say, 'You've got to draw the line somewhere, Davis. You just have to.'

"Davis say, 'Okay, that's good. But we can't let the child stay here crying for her daddy, can we? That would be suicidal.'

"Marcy say, 'You're right, Davis. What should we do?'

"Davis make a face like he thinkin' deep on the subject. Then he look straight across at his bitch, lookin' at her eyes. He say, 'Let's take the kid out to the lab and stash her with Michael till we finish the manufacturing phase. Once we have our product secured, we can let her go.' Michael is Davis' kid. He keepin' his kid away from the commune for some reason I ain't heard about.

"Marcy run across the room and give Davis a kiss. A real wet motherfucker. She mostly a kid, her own self.

"Davis push her away. Say, 'But we can't tell her she's going to meet Michael, because she thinks Michael's living with Flo. We have to tell her she's going home to be with her daddy. You tell her we'll be starting out for her daddy's tomorrow night at seven-thirty. Tell her to pack some clothes. Enough for maybe three days. If she asks why her daddy isn't coming to pick her up, say that her daddy's angry with the people in the commune. He won't come to us, so we'll take her to him.'

"Marcy get dressed and go out to find the little bitch. Davis take off, too. Say he got bidness. Next night at seven-thirty we bring the little bitch out to the van. Davis axe me to drive and we start workin' our way out to Long Island somewheres. Davis and the two bitches is sittin' in the back, singin' songs."

"*Singin'*," Abou interrupted. He was drunk, now, and suddenly happy. "Motherfucker *always* be singin' somethin'. *Crazy* white man." He was lost in admiration for a moment. Then he remembered that he *hated* crazy white men.

"I got to take the heat for that shit," Wendell observed. "I done started the man up on makin' beats."

"Look like he caught on fast."

Wendell shook his head, laughing. "Well, this time it ain't *my* music. They goin' on 'bout some small world. Same words over and over. The little bitch don't even notice that we ain't goin' to the Bronx. Probly don't know nothin' 'bout geography. Course, I don't know shit about no Long Island either, but he get me on a parkway and say just keep drivin'. Then they goes on talkin' and singin'. Me, my mind ain't tight to they bullshit. Ah'm mostly thinkin' 'bout how ah'm gon' see the lab. Ain't seen it up till that point. Then I hear a loud crack like a stone done hit the back window. I turn around and Davis be holdin' the little bitch and her head be layin' down on her chest. When I was a kid, I remember pickin' up a dead mouse and its head done flopped over jus' like that little bitch's head.

"Marcy done went crazy. Screamin', 'How could you do it? How could you do it?' Ah'm thinkin the white man ain't gon' take this shit off his bitch and sure nuff I hear the bitch start chokin' and Davis got his hands round her throat. The bitch is kickin' out and scratchin' at his arms, but he hold on tight. Davis ain't big, but he *strong* and he got no mercy in him. Meanwhile the bitch eyes buggin' out her head and she slowin' fast. Stop kickin', stop scratchin'. She starin' in Davis' eyes and he steady laughin'. Then the bitch's eyes freeze up and she shit her pants.

"Davis drop her down and climb up next to me in the front. He say, 'Wendell, in life you got to have a goal. You got to put that goal in front of you and not let petty concerns prevent you from reaching it. I *had* to eliminate Terry, because she stood between me and my goal. But I knew that if I eliminated Terry, I could never trust Marcy again. In a month, I'll be far away from Hanover House. There will be no way for the cops to put it together, even if they find the bodies.'

"I say, 'That's chill, baby, but for now, I settle for rollin' down the window. What the bitch eat for dinner?'"

"Now *you* start singin', right?"

Wendell worked up a wide grin. There was no disrespect in Abou's voice. "Ah'm teachin' the boy 'bout how to make beats."

"Now I *know* you done gone crazy. The white man got to be near forty years old. How you gon' teach a old white man to rap?"

"Yeah, well I ain't expectin' the man to make no *dope* beats. But he tryin'. When you cruisin' down the parkway with two dead bitches in the back and shit stink in your nose, y'all don't have to be good. Fact that you singin' at all be enough."

"Can't argue with the straight truth. The white man is *crazy*. What you do with the bitches?"

"Oh, man, Davis got that shit *down*. We drive out to some kinda woods, find this little dirt road goin' in. He got the graves already *dug*. We drop the bitches in, push down the dirt and spread leaves and rocks. Time we done it, look like we never been there, and ah'm wondrin' what we gonna do for pussy."

Wendell looked down at his drunken lieutenant. The man he called his 'Crew Chief.' "I got big plans for us, Abou. Davis say he gon' sell off his formula once I distribute this first bit. Bro, I got that shit three quarters sold already. Gon' spread it out 'cross the whole motherfuckin' *country*. Then, when PURE be more famous than Batman, ah'm gon' take mah bank, *buy* that formula and take it to *Africa*. We be kings, Abou. Shippin' PURE all over the *gottdamn* world. Fuck them Colombians and their cocaine. Africa, baby. We goin' home."

Abou opened one eye. Tryin' to keep his voice cool. "You ever get to see that lab, Wendell?"

"I can hear your brain grindin', Abou. No, we come right back after we buried the bitches."

"The white man know the people you sellin' to?"

"No, he don't know nothin' 'bout it."

Abou finally smiled, turnin' his face into the couch cushions. His head was spinning, but he held onto one idea until he lost consciousness. He *hated* crazy white men.

TWENTY-FOUR

The most vicious four-letter word in New York these days, *the* four-letter word for the 1990s, has nothing to do with excrement or the various forms of human sexual expression, though it's definitely a curse and rarely uttered in polite company. The word is AIDS and the damage it has done to certain segments of New York's population would, if those segments were white, middle-class and heterosexual, have drawn a massive response from the politicians who control the American tax dollar. If the victims lived in Bayside instead of Harlem (or if they had insurance and the costs of their medical care would have to be paid), the medical community would have long ago mobilized all its resources in pursuit of a cure and the Nobel Prize sure to follow. But, of course, the victims of AIDS have not, by and large, been middle class and the words used by impolite society to describe the victims include epithets like fag, nigger, spic and junkie. In the minds of most voters (especially in the era of 'read my lips: no new taxes'), fags, niggers, spics and junkies are the ultimate expendables and New York politicians have responded to the will of the electorate by refusing to provide money to expand the public health-care system.

The footage, on the other hand, has been great. Skeletal victims dying in the subways, in shelters, in abandoned tenements, in packed emergency rooms—it all makes for powerful theater. Just as in the 1960s and 70s, families could gather round the roast beef and watch the carnage in Vietnam, New Yorkers can view elderly black women caring for terminally ill two-year-olds without the slightest sense of personal danger. Statistics like the projection that 30,000 to 40,000 black and Latino children will lose both parents to AIDS before the decade draws to a close can be dissected with the detachment of agricultural bureaucrats discussing a plague on Australian chickens.

Meanwhile, the victims keep dying. The junkies continue to use infected needles and the crack addicts continue to engage in mindless promiscuous sex. Stanley Moodrow, as cynical as any cop who ever carried an NYPD shield, had understood the situation on the day the politicians decided not to give clean needles to the junkies. As a cop, he'd been forced to view the carnage directly, but his post-retirement clients had usually been a step above the denizens of the Lower East Side, so except for the odd junkie with the *chutzpah* to die on the sidewalk, he'd been able to avoid the physical reality of AIDS. This critical distance forms part of the explanation for his shock upon entering Bronx Municipal's emergency room. The rest of it stems from his preoccupation with Davis Craddock and what Craddock would almost certainly do if he uncovered Betty's true intentions. Moodrow felt there must be some way to communicate his fears to Betty without seeming like a typical male trying to bully his girlfriend, but he hadn't been able to find one.

The noise hit him first. The emergency room was packed with poor, sick people. A half dozen babies were crying loudly. Families gathered around improvised meals, chatting in English and Spanish. Moaning junkies, too sick to go out in search of a fix, sat as close to the bathrooms as they could get. One man, his shirt pressed to a bleeding head wound, was having an active conversation with the empty air.

A tall, thin woman with a child in her arms stood at the information desk, screaming at the nurse-receptionist. "I don't care about how many doctors you *don't* have," she shouted. "My baby is sick and I want one of the doctors you *do* have to examine her."

"You'll have to go to the clinic and make an appointment with the pediatrician," the nurse said patiently.

A security guard stood behind the woman, one hand on her shoulder, making it clear that it was all right for her to voice her complaint. As long as it didn't find physical expression. He, too, seemed bored.

"I been here for ten hours," the woman continued.

"Hell, you just arrived," the guard explained. "We got folks in this room been here two days. There ain't no beds. Ain't no gurneys. Ain't even no room in the hallways. The evening clinic opens at seven o'clock. They'll most likely see you tonight."

"How come nobody said anything about the clinic when I came in this morning? I been sittin' here all day with a sick child. Why didn't somebody say something?"

Moodrow stood in the doorway, staring at the scene as if trying to retrieve a lost memory. He flashed back to Connie Alamare holding her daughter's hand, then walked quickly to the receptionist's desk and tapped the guard on the shoulder. The guard turned angrily, only to receive the full force of Moodrow's best blank cop stare.

"I'm lookin' for the toxicology lab," Moodrow explained.

"You go through that door over there," the guard replied impatiently, "and all the way down the corridor to the exit door. That'll put you in the main entrance where you should have gone in the first place."

Moodrow was sorely tempted to go back outside and walk around the building, but it was almost four o'clock and he suspected that Dr. Benari would seize on any excuse not to see him. Steeling himself, he pushed through the door into the treatment area. Despite the fact that virtually every square foot seemed to be occupied by a gurney with a patient on it, his first impression was of motion. The staff, aides, nurses, doctors, all seemed to be running. Patients, reaching out with a hand or a complaint, were ignored. The only exception was a knot of white uniforms gathered around a bleeding man who'd just come in a side entrance used by ambulances. Even here, instruments and commands flew through the air with equal speed as the doctors and nurses struggled to keep the man alive while surgeons were located and the operating room prepared.

You're gettin' to be an old man, Moodrow told himself. You used to be able to walk past this without thinking twice.

He gathered himself once again and threaded his bulk between the gurneys and down the corridor. The reception area was much quieter, with only the occasional visitor stopping to make an inquiry. Moodrow waited his turn, then asked for toxicology, adding that he had an appointment with Dr. Federico Benari. The receptionist patiently wrote out a pass, then directed Moodrow to the fourth floor.

"Try the elevators," the receptionist advised, "if they're working today."

The elevators were, in fact, working, but they kept arriving full of doctors, aides and patients. If Moodrow had been a little smaller, he might have pushed his way between the odd gurney and wheelchair, but his six-foot six-inch frame would have brushed the elevator ceilings, and the aides and doctors glared instead of making an effort to find room for him.

"Why don't you try the stairs?"

Moodrow turned to find a security guard standing by his elbow.

"This time of afternoon, all the basement services are trying to clear enough time for dinner. Radiology and physical therapy and like that. You could stand here for an hour."

"What about them?" Moodrow gestured toward a knot of visitors.

"They gotta take the elevators. You're here on business. I heard you tell the lady you were going up to see Benari and he's never in his office after four. I'm the guy who checks the doors to make sure they're locked, so I know."

Moodrow took the stairs two at a time. For the length of one flight, he congratulated himself on his youth and agility. By the time he reached the third floor, however, the sweat was running freely and his heart was pounding in his chest like a speed bag in the hands of a prize fighter. He took the last flight one stair at a time, forming, as he went, an enormous respect for the athletes who participate in a yearly run up the one hundred flights of the Empire State Building.

There were no patients in the toxicology lab, a fact for which Moodrow was infinitely grateful. On the other hand, there were no doctors, either. Just an open area lined with chairs, a locked door and a Plexiglas window which revealed the desk ordinarily occupied by the receptionist. Moodrow tried the door, but he knew it would be locked before he touched the brass knob. He felt the anger rising, as real as the .38 pressed against his waist, but he fought it down, lifting his fist to knock. The door opened before he could finish and a small, fat man carrying an attache case rushed through. Unfortunately, with Moodrow's bulk directly in front of him, there was nowhere to go and the resulting collision, though mild enough by Moodrow's standards, rippled through the man's body as he bounced several steps backward.

"Who . . ." the man began.

"Doctor Benari?" Moodrow grinned.

"Yeah?"

"I'm Stanley Moodrow. You were expecting me." The statement left no room for argument.

"You're late."

Moodrow glanced at his watch. "Five minutes."

"Five minutes is exactly as much time as I *was* prepared to give you."

"You're in a hurry?"

"Very observant."

"Then this is your lucky day, because if you don't back up and do your fucking job, I'm gonna toss your fat ass through the window and you'll be in the parking lot before you know it."

Moodrow folded his arms across his chest, giving the good doctor a moment to think it over. Of course, Benari *knew* that Moodrow was bluffing, but the fact that he, Benari, was five-foot six while Moodrow was six-foot six and both weighed 250 pounds mitigated any desire to call that bluff.

"Make it quick," he said, backing into the small office behind him and setting down his briefcase.

Moodrow took the notarized request from his back pocket and handed it to Benari. "I just have a few questions. Then I'll let you go. According to the doctor who treated Connie Alamare, she had a stroke. I guess that's what the tests revealed. But everything I know about her recent history suggests that she was poisoned. That's why I'm taking the blood to . . ."

"You're wasting your time. We ran a standard tox screen while she was in here."

"I didn't know that." Moodrow felt his heart sink. Another dead end. If he'd known about this earlier . . .

"Let me make this quick. We tested for all the obvious poisons. Arsenic, curare. Every insecticide, rat poison or herbicide on the market. We tested for a number of industrial poisons as well as drugs that become toxic when combined. We're satisfied that she was *not* poisoned, either deliberately or accidentally. Now, if you're asking if we tested for every toxic substance known or unknown to man, I'll admit we didn't. There are literally thousands of poisonous industrial chemicals. We didn't test for all of them. We didn't test for South Australian seasnake venom, either. Nor the toxin of the African green mamba. Without a recent history to point in some direction, it would take a year to do what you want done. On top of which the cardiologists are sure she had a stroke."

Moodrow stepped into the room and sat on the edge of the receptionist's desk. The cops hadn't mentioned the tests. Maybe they hadn't known about them. On the other hand, the cardiologist in charge of Flo Alamare's case must have known all about it, but hadn't seen fit to communicate the information.

Dr. Benari, encouraged by Moodrow's apparent confusion, picked up his briefcase and prepared to exit. "Go back into the lab. Tell Mr. Goss who you are and he'll give you fluids." He stepped through the door, punched the elevator button, then couldn't resist a final shot. "What you want to do, Mister Moodrow, is hope she dies. Then you can physically examine her organs and prove your theory, one way or the other."

Moodrow didn't bother to respond. He was sorely tempted to leave Flo Alamare's bodily fluids where they were and go about his business, but he'd pushed hard for this and the lab in Queens had agreed to stay open late so Moodrow could deliver the frozen blood and urine before it spoiled. Sighing, he walked into the back and entered the laboratory.

"Mister Goss?"

The man sitting in a chair behind the counter was no taller than Federico Benari, but he was thin and wiry with a full beard and a halo of thick black hair surrounding a small face. "Misha, please. Call me Misha." He put down the book he was reading and got to his feet.

"Okay, Misha. My name is Moodrow and Doctor Benari told me to see you about picking up Flo Alamare's blood samples."

"They're in the freezer. I'll get them." A moment later, he was back with a half dozen vials of blood and urine which he put in an insulated bag and handed to Moodrow. "You should refrigerate these as soon as possible."

Moodrow took the small package and prepared to leave. It was well into the evening rush and he was anxious to get to the labs of Toxilab, Inc.

"By the way, Moodrow, how'd you like Bo-bo?"

"Bo-bo?"

"Bo-bo Benari. The fattest fuck at Bronx Municipal."

"He's not the sweetest guy in the world," Moodrow answered evenly, "but he seems to know what he's doing."

"He doesn't know shit." The technician's face was impassive, but his voice dripped with contempt.

"You talking about this particular case?" Moodrow held up the package.

"Yeah. See, Alamare was a problem and the one thing we don't like at

Bronx Municipal is a problem. These are the plague years in New York. Nobody's got time for mysteries."

"You got my attention, Misha. Don't stop now."

"Alamare was a puzzle right from the beginning. Pretty white girl in a vacant lot. Needle marks on her arm, but no sign of the infections every junkie gets. Doesn't add up, right? On the other hand, Bronx Municipal is operating at a hundred and forty percent of capacity with a third less staff than our budget calls for. People don't want to come here. Doctors, nurses, aides, techs. Most of the AIDS patients in New York are bottled up in municipal hospitals because private hospitals don't want to treat them. More than half the blood we draw in this hospital is saturated with the virus. You stick yourself with a needle, which happens fairly often, you could get the disease. It's not very likely, but we're talking about a condition that's a hundred-percent fatal. Figure it out for yourself."

"What you're saying is that patients at Bronx Municipal don't get proper medical care."

"It's not as bad as it sounds, because the staff is very dedicated. That's why they come here. But what they don't need is a mystery. Mysteries take all kinds of extra time and time is the scarcest resource in this hospital. So when they got Flo Alamare, they took the easiest way out and called it a stroke."

"You're saying it wasn't a stroke? Are you a doctor?"

Misha Goss blushed and started to protest, but Moodrow interrupted him. "Don't take it the wrong way, Misha. I just need to know why you're so sure."

"I'm not positive that she didn't have a stroke. What I'm saying is her condition is more consistent with some kind of poisoning. Especially the muscle rigidity. When she came into the hospital, she was stiff as a board and that's *very* unusual. I'm telling you, Moodrow, if she'd been taken to a private hospital, this would have been handled differently."

"Benari told me he tested for poison." Moodrow felt his interest rising again. He wanted to reach out and hug the little technician.

"I ran the tests myself. A standard tox screen. We tested for thirty-five toxic substances. Out of maybe a thousand possibilities. What does it prove?"

"Benari says it would take a year to test for all of them."

"Benari's an asshole. I have a test we could do in ten minutes. If it works, we'll be ninety-five percent sure she was poisoned. I tried to get Benari to okay it, but it's a little unconventional and he hates my guts."

"What do you want to do?"

"I'll take a small amount of Alamare's blood, spin it down in a centrifuge until the serum separates out, then inject the serum into a mouse and see what happens."

"Why does Benari object to that?"

"Well, for one thing, even if the mouse dies, it's possible that whatever killed the mouse didn't hurt Flo Alamare. Very unlikely, but still possible. Also, if the mouse lives, it doesn't mean that Alamare wasn't poisoned. Maybe she metabolized the poison before we drew the blood. Maybe the concentration in her blood isn't great enough to kill the mouse. Maybe the poison never entered her bloodstream. Maybe. . ."

"All right, I get the picture. Let's just go ahead and do it. We'll figure out what happened after we're finished."

Fifteen minutes later, they stood in a small room at the rear of the lab. Goss held a tiny, white mouse in his hand and when he injected ten cc's of clear serum directly into its abdomen, it began to struggle madly, though it made no attempt to bite. Ten seconds later, it was dead, its small body as stiff as if it had been taken from a freezer instead of a cage.

"Jesus," Moodrow whispered, "that was fast."

Misha Goss smiled, nodding his agreement. "Right. Now give me your arm and we'll try it on a human."

Moodrow jumped away and Goss began to laugh. "Just kidding, bro," he announced.

"Your wife must get a big kick out of you." Moodrow, despite his embarrassment, was laughing, too.

"She always enjoyed my sense of humor. Right up until she left for Australia." He looked down at the mouse for a moment, then back at Moodrow. "There's one favor you can do for me, Moodrow. When you get to Tox, Inc., don't mention what happened here. Just give them the fluids. I have a friend over there and I'll talk to him privately."

"What's the problem?"

"The problem is what we did here is unauthorized *and* unscientific, *and* I'm hanging onto my job by my fingernails."

"Yeah?"

"Yeah. I played a little joke about a month ago and it didn't go over too good."

Moodrow leaned back against the wall. "You gonna tell me what you did?"

"It happened one day when Benari was taking a delegation of Japanese doctors through the lab. This was during the day, when we have eight techs working. I was racking urines when they came over to me. You know . . ."

"What the hell is 'racking urines'?"

Goss grinned. "When a patient is passing urine that's cloudy, we sometimes take samples every four hours or so, put them in test tubes in a rack, then watch to see how fast the solids settle to the bottom of the tube. It gives us an idea of whether or not the patient is improving and it doesn't cost anything. Anyway, I was by the racks when Benari came in with four Japanese doctors. You know how the Japanese are? They bow like penguins. 'Hai, hai, hai.' No expression whatsoever. Dead blank. Benari goes through this explanation of how we rack the urines, then finishes by saying, 'And how's the patient doing, Mister Goss?' I take the urine at the end of the rack, uncap it and drink it down. 'This one looks pretty clear to me,' I say. Of course, it wasn't urine in that test tube. It was apple juice and I was making a little joke. Meanwhile, the Japanese don't even blink. They watch me drink the juice down, then start bowing like crazy. 'Hai, hai, hai.' Benari was so pissed off, he transferred me. I'm the only one here at night. They even lock the doors, because some of our patients have been known to roam the corridors looking for controlled substances. Me, I'm a sociable guy. I don't like being alone."

"Okay, I don't have a problem keeping my mouth shut. Meanwhile, let me get this stuff to Queens before it goes bad." Moodrow gathered up the insulated bag and began to walk toward the door. "There's one other thing I wanted to ask you about, Misha. I wanna know if you think it's possible that Flo Alamare overdosed on heroin? I know the tests only showed *traces* of heroin, but . . ."

"Wait, wait. Back up. The test we did on Alamare isn't specific. All it can do is show the presence of an opiate. It can't tell us *which* opiate. In a criminal case, you have to determine the exact nature of the substance, but from a medical point of view, the treatment for an overdose of heroin is the same as the treatment for an overdose of any other opiate. Flo Alamare could have been using anything from morphine to Dilaudid."

"Then why did the doctor say she showed positive for heroin?"

Goss shrugged. "Maybe he didn't. Sometimes, people hear what they want to hear. Remember, this wasn't a criminal case. There was no need to be that accurate. They do gas liquid chromatography at Toxilab, Inc. That should pin it down."

"You wanna hear something funny? All of a sudden I don't have any doubt about what it was. Now I'm sure. And I'd thank you from the bottom of my heart. If I had a heart."

TWENTY-FIVE

Four days later, Stanley Moodrow made a decision that surprised everyone who knew him. He decided to call for help. Perhaps it was the weather, a series of perfect spring days that stretched out for more than a week. The sun-drenched afternoons had lured normally jaded New Yorkers out of doors and the streets were crowded with joggers and bicycles. The parks had exploded with blossoms. Azaleas, tulips, daffo- dils, cherry and apple trees, elegant dogwood and opulent magnolias. The new leaves on the trees in Central Park glowed with energy, matching the intensity of grassy lawns that leaped from dingy yellow to bright green overnight.

Moodrow had found it impossible to stay inside his small apartment, but there was nothing for him to do outside except rework opinions he'd already formed. Even though all the evidence led to the conclusion that Flo Alamare had been poisoned, accidentally or deliberately, and that Billy Williams had been killed as part of a cover-up and that the deaths of three drug users on the Lower East Side were somehow related, there was little he could do about it. He could not, for instance, enter Hanover House and demand to interview Terry Williams. Or obtain a warrant to search the commune for drugs. He was tempted to set up surveillance, but without adequate manpower or the vans, high- power directional microphones, telephone taps and video cameras available to the police, the most likely outcome would be discovery and the removal of evidence.

So he filled his afternoons with long walks through the neighbor- hood. Through *his* neighborhood. He'd been born on the Lower East Side in 1935, in the middle of the depression. He'd known a time when drugs were nonexistent. When the loser in a fight would be allowed to rise and shake his opponent's hand instead of being stomped into the concrete. In the 1950s, when he'd joined the cops, an adolescent with a knife was condemned as an incorrigible juvenile delinquent. Now the kids packed 9mm machine pistols with thirty-round clips. They feared nothing. Incarceration was a rite of passage and an early death part of the territory.

The prevailing mood was helplessness. The Lower East Side of Manhattan had always been poor and the currently predominant Latino population struggled to move up, just as the Italians, Jews and Poles had struggled in past decades. Only now there was the sense of events out of control. The reality of drugs, especially the lure of big money, had transformed an already violent neighborhood into a war zone. Divisions of heroin and crack junkies, faced with habits that cost hundreds of dollars a day to support, prowled the streets in search of money and dope. Undercover cops, looking exactly like the mutts they planned to arrest, pursued buy-and-bust operations that often resulted in shootouts as likely to injure the citizen as the criminal.

Moodrow walked past Hanover House a dozen times. He found it hard to imagine the life of the average Hanoverian. Despite the fact that his sense of Betty's fate, if she was found out, was sharply defined. As was his sense of what he would do to Davis Craddock if Betty got hurt.

His own assessment of Betty's danger was one of two factors that pushed him into contacting the NYPD. Maybe if the cops began an intensive investigation, she'd back off. Maybe. The second factor was the preliminary report from Toxilab, Inc. The poison in Flo Alamare's body fluids had not been identified, but the techs were certain that the opiate detected at Bronx Municipal was not heroin. Or any other known drug. The hospital had concluded that Flo Alamare had been positive only for *traces* of heroin, but Toxilab's preliminary opinion was that the unidentified opiate in Flo's body was so powerful that the small amount detected at Bronx Municipal was more than enough to make her very, very stoned. In addition, the lab had discovered a compound that resembled the crystalline structure of methamphetamine.

"What you've got," Doctor Murillo, the president of Toxilab, Inc., had explained, "is a pair of analogues. Think of it this way. Opium, morphine and heroin each have an identical central core that produces narcosis. This central core is surrounded by atoms that have no real part in the effect. It's like a planet with a dozen moons. A chemist can take these moons and rearrange them. Or eliminate one. Or even add a moon. The planet isn't changed very much. Which is why the non-specific testing they did in the hospital came up positive."

"Is it possible that this . . . What'd you call it? Analogue? Is it possible this analogue also poisoned Flo Alamare?"

Murillo had grinned. "Would you believe that I *love* mysteries. I read at least two a week. I even have a couple of writers who use me for research."

"That's funny," Moodrow had responded. "Because, as a cop, I *hate* mysteries."

"I can understand that. It's not a hobby for you. But to answer your question, I'm a Ph.D., not an M.D., and I'm not terribly familiar with the testing that led the cardiologist to diagnose stroke. Nevertheless, proceeding as a detective and not as a scientist, I'd say that the number of puncture wounds in the patient's arms precludes the possibility that the narcotic also poisoned her. *Unless* that narcotic was somehow altered. I'm sure you've noticed that all medications, even over-the-counter remedies, are stamped with an expiration date. The consumer thinks that an aspirin is an aspirin, but most compounds remain chemically active and lose their effectiveness over time. Fortunately, aspirins don't become toxic. They simply stop relieving headaches."

"I'm not following you. Are you saying that she *couldn't* have been poisoned by the analogue?"

"Not really. All medications are subject to elaborate testing designed to eliminate the possibility that chemical changes will produce toxicity. If we assume that some amateur chemist with a lab in the woods has created a new drug, we must also assume that the new drug was not subjected to exhaustive testing. The drug Alamare used to get high may have been altered in a number of ways. Even something as innocuous as sunlight can change the atomic structure of a compound. Which is why so many medications come with a warning to keep them away from light. Heat can also cause sudden shifts in atomic structure. We haven't been able to isolate any toxin in Alamare's fluids, and we've tested for more than fifty poisons. My opinion, again as a detective, is that whatever poisoned Alamare, if she *was* poisoned, is as new as the compound that got her stoned. I also believe that the poison was created both accidentally and environmentally. In other words, it occurred in the natural course of day-to-day life. If I had a sample of the drug she used to get high, I could probably run down the poison in a few days."

Moodrow had taken this conversation with him as he walked the streets of the Lower East Side. If he was still a cop, he would have gotten his sample, one way or the other, but the new drug Tilley had spoken to him about, the drug called PURE, was no longer on the street. The only potential samples were in the hands of the police.

In the end, he'd called Jim Tilley and Leonora Higgins, detailing the results of his investigation and asking for help. They'd gone back, Jim to the precinct and Leonora to the DA's office, and presented the evidence to their superiors. Now they were meeting in Tilley's apartment and the news was all bad.

"I spoke to Captain Ruiz," Tilley began, "and I guess it's to his credit that he listened to me all the way through. He wasn't very enthusiastic, Stanley. As far as he's concerned, the only pieces of your case that mean anything to the Seven are the dead junkies and dead junkies just don't have priority. In the Seven or anywhere else. Even if they were poisoned, which hasn't been proven, that doesn't mean a homicide occurred. I . . ."

"Actually, it's manslaughter," Leonora Higgins interrupted. She was as carefully dressed as always, but the severity of her navy blue suit was softened by the two children perched on her knees. "Technically, a dealer who sells a controlled substance that results in a death can be prosecuted for manslaughter. Unfortunately, as far as I know, it's never happened."

"We're not talking about a controlled substance," Moodrow reminded her. "This drug, PURE, is completely new."

"That doesn't matter. It was sold or given to the victims with the full knowledge that it would be consumed. The result is a homicide. By the way, your dealer can't be prosecuted for possession or sale of narcotics. Until PURE is chemically identified and added to the schedule of controlled substances, it can be sold quite openly."

"When will that happen?" Rose Tilley's question surprised everyone. She usually avoided discussions of police matters, but now she sat on the edge of her chair and her voice was insistent. "My children are prisoners in their own home. I take them to school in the morning and arrange to have them picked up in the afternoon. They never go out to play by themselves. That's no way for kids to live, but there's too much violence out there and the violence comes from drugs. Now you're telling me there's something worse than cocaine and it's not even illegal."

Moodrow laughed out loud. "They used to talk about heroin like it was the plague. Like it was the devil's final assault on the human race. Then the cocaine began to flow and cocaine became the end of the world. Then some smart businessman figured out a way to make coke smokable and crack magnified everything a hundred times. Why should we kid ourselves? If those radar ships around Colombia manage to stop the cocaine, somebody's gonna figure out a new way to feed the junkies. If you remember, about fifteen years ago we got the farmers in the golden triangle to switch over to alternative crops. Put a real dent in the amount of heroin on the streets. Then the Mexicans started growing poppies and heroin became more plentiful than ever. If you don't want your kids to use drugs, then you're gonna have to make them strong enough to resist, because the drugs aren't going away. And if you want your kids to be safe on the street, you're gonna have to let the junkies have their dope cheap. You're gonna have to legalize it or give it away in clinics."

"Then why are you so upset by Davis Craddock and PURE?" Betty couldn't resist asking the obvious question.

"I don't know if I do care about some new drug. Except that people are out there getting poisoned. That puts a whole new light on it."

"Wait a minute, Stanley," Tilley corrected. "PURE is killing junkies, not people."

Moodrow glared at his former partner. "It could be your kids, too. Nobody's immune. Junkies turn into animals because that's what it takes to maintain the habit. I don't think addiction warrants the death penalty."

Tilley started to answer, but Moodrow waved him off. "We're not gonna solve the drug problem this afternoon, Jim. Let's get back to business."

"Fine," Tilley said. "The Captain sent your information on Williams' death up to Bronx Homicide. They seemed interested, but who knows what they'll do. The samples of PURE we picked up at the two homicides were sent to the DEA for analysis. There's *zero* chance of getting any back."

"Why didn't you hold onto a piece of it?" Moodrow asked.

"I can answer that," Leonora said. "PURE isn't illegal. It would be like holding onto a comb."

"That's right," Tilley said. "There wasn't any point in keeping it. By the way, I've been working my snitches hard for the last few days. Trying to get you a sample from the street. The junkies went crazy for PURE. That was all they wanted. Then it disappeared as if it was never there. What I think is that the chemist who made it, Davis Craddock or whoever, took it off the market when he found out it was poisonous."

"You think so, huh?" Moodrow straightened in his seat. "I've been walking through the neighborhood for the last few days, just looking around, and I saw an old friend of ours go into Hanover House. Wendell Bogard. He was still coming up when I left the job, but I hear he's a high roller these days. It looks like Craddock's getting ready to make some kind of a move and if we can get Captain Ruiz to set up twenty-four-hour surveillance, we'll probably find Craddock's lab in a week."

"You may be right," Tilley said, "but it's not happening. The Captain thinks it's a problem for the DEA, not us. You gotta remember that if PURE isn't illegal, then the lab isn't illegal."

"He's right," Leonora said. "He might be in violation of some federal statutes if he's using certain chemicals called precursors, but it's not a problem for local law enforcement."

Suddenly, Lee, Rose's oldest, slid off Leonora Higgins' lap and stalked off to his room. "Drugs, drugs, drugs," he complained. "That's all I hear about at school. It's boring."

"That's right. It's boring." Lee's sibling and shadow, Jeanette, followed him dutifully.

Tilley watched them go for a moment, then turned back to Moodrow. "The thing about PURE that makes it really different is that the coke freaks want it as much as the heroin junkies."

"I'm not surprised. The lab says there's some kind of speed in it. The lab also claims the opiate in PURE is twenty or thirty times as powerful as heroin. Plus it sometimes kills people. And nobody wants to do anything about it."

"That's not completely true, Stanley," Leonora said. "I've also spoken to the DEA and they say that if PURE comes back on the market, they'll begin the process of adding it to the list of controlled substances."

"And how long will that take?"

"Two years."

The afternoon ended on the worst possible note. Moodrow, in a last, desperate attempt to keep Betty away from Davis Craddock, told Rose, Leonora and Jim about her visits to Hanover House and all three fell on her. What she was doing, they declared, was crazy. No good result could come of it. Hanoverians were *leaving* the commune. If they wanted her to keep coming for therapy, it was probably because they already knew who she was. Craddock was both murderous and unpredictable. Wendell Bogard, if he was now associated with Craddock, was suspected of a dozen homicides. Betty simply *had* to stay away.

Betty's face reddened as the assault grew in intensity, but she waited until they were finished before she got up and put on her jacket. Moodrow's desperate 'please, Betty,' went entirely ignored. Betty didn't say a word until the front door was open. Then she turned back and stared directly into Moodrow's eyes. "You don't own me, Stanley. Men have been trying to own me since I reached puberty, but I've somehow managed to live my life without chains. Do you really think that I'm about to let some *cop* put me in handcuffs?"

TWENTY-SIX

from *The Autobiography of Davis Craddock*

Four days ago, I reread the last segment of my autobiography and discovered, much to my chagrin, that I sounded like a petulant child. A *whiner*.

God doesn't like a whiner. He maketh calamities to rain upon a whiner's head.

Besides, I do not wish to project self-pity. Self-pity is, in fact, the antithesis of the image I see in the mirror every morning.

I now view my previous writing as a moment of weakness. A moment of self-indulgence. The story of my life.

But I've taken the pledge. I've turned the leaf. No more self-indulgence. I'm a new man, now. Or an old man, resurrected. When I look in the mirror, I see cold calculation. I see determination.

Praise the Lord, and pass the chicken.

Marcy has gone to her reward in the sandy soil of a Long Island pine barren. She first hurt me when she allowed Flo to live. She hurt me a second time when she balked at the elimination of a 'little' problem.

It would have been sheer self-indulgence to keep her on simply because she was the best pussy I've ever had. On the other hand, squeezing her neck until her tongue popped like a New Year's Eve noisemaker was mere problem-solving.

Cold calculation.

Just the image I wish to project.

A sudden thought. My autobiography has become a journal. I've caught up with myself. Which makes it quite interesting. I now record decisions before the results of those decisions become manifest. The creature to emerge, should I screw it up, would be little more than a buffoon. Of course, I could always do a quick rewrite (or a leisurely rewrite, since my autobiography will not be published in my lifetime), but I'm much too *honest* for that. Of course.

*   *   *

Inspired by my resolution vis-à-vis Marcy Evans, I set out to deal with three problems: the pussy problem, the poochie problem and the fat detective (plus fat bitch) problem.

Curiously, my primary project, the manufacture and distribution of two hundred pounds of PURE, is ahead of schedule. The manufacturing phase will be completed within two weeks. (My safety deposit boxes, on the other hand, will be as empty as the space between the fat detective's ears.) The finished product will then be removed to secure locations in a dozen cities. Finally, piece by piece, PURE will be turned over to Wendell in exchange for cold cash.

Wendell the Wonderful claims to have pre-sold three quarters of the product. His phone, he says, is ringing off the proverbial hook.

Most of his clients are black. This pleases him immensely. The Italians, he says, had their turn. The Colombians came next. Now it's the time of the brothers. Which, since blacks consume most of the drugs, is only fair.

I asked him what fair has to do with it. I lectured him on the beauty of individuality. "Don't limit yourself with unnecessary labels," I advised. "Don't put yourself in a box."

Nevertheless, he retains a blind loyalty to his race. In fact, he declared his intention to buy the PURE formula. How much did I want for it?

Naturally, I refused to forego the obvious benefits of a competitive auction. I made only one concession. I agreed to sell the formula to Wendell for fifteen percent less than the highest bid. Is this love? Or what?

I expect—I *will*—come out of this with twenty million dollars. I shall take the cash and flee to Brazil until the fallout (should there be fallout) settles. I shall wait until PURE rules the American drug scene, then journey to Colombia. Faced with a shrinking market, the cocaine cartels will be eager to acquire the PURE formula. Their access to chemicals (a problem which Wendell has yet to recognize) will make the switch from cocaine to PURE a simple matter. Whereas Wendell might be able to produce a hundred pounds per month, the cartels will produce tons of PURE.

But on to the pussy problem.

With Marcy gone (the only thing she'll be sucking is Long Island sand), I suddenly became the most eligible celibate in Hanover House. When I told my poochies that Marcy had elected to pursue her own ends, the response was overwhelming. Instead of asking questions, the females projected lust.

The Queen is dead. Let's fuck the King.

Ordinarily, I admire ambition, but I was busy formulating a plan to shed my poochies and I was sorely tempted to limit my sexual expression to a handkerchief. (Could the fat detective be right, after all?)

On the other hand, I recognized that sex with Marcy had been an important part of the bonding process Wendell and I had gone through. I *need* Wendell.

After long and deep consideration, I developed a set of criteria that allowed me to leave the frying pan without jumping into the fire. The new bitch would be hot enough.

I wanted a female who would be utterly obedient. When Marcy first came to Hanover House, she was a shy and frightened little girl. So drab as to be almost devoid of personality. She huddled in corners, avoiding even the pretense of friendship. I took her under my wing and personally created the flamboyant, uninhibited woman she became. Under my tutelage, Marcy's life was enormously enriched. And far preferable, despite its brief duration, to the life she would have lived without me.

If the first criterion was obedience, the second was a female without close ties to the other poochies. Wendell is a bit of a mystery to the Hanoverian community. Whereas the average poochie rarely has access to my genius, Wendell comes and goes at all hours. The last thing I need is a bitch jumping off his cock to "share" with her sisters.

Finally, my new consort had to be sexually interesting. Both Wendell and I were accustomed to unfettered sexual expression. A frigid bitch who laid beneath us, unmoving, simply wouldn't do.

Or would it?

If I wanted a shy, obedient female, how could I expect sexual experience?

The solution was to go the other way. To find a bitch whose *lack* of experience, in combination with obedience unto death, would hold our interest. For a month or two.

Once the criteria were established, the solution was simple enough. For some time, I'd been cultivating an eighteen-year-old Cambodian girl. Blossom Nol. My initial interest was purely selfish. I thought it might be amusing to put her with Marcy for an evening's entertainment. My and Wendell's entertainment. Of course.

Blossom Nol is an amazing creature. She has the body of a twelve-year-old and the face of an angel. Large dark eyes. Button nose. Soft, heavy lips. Tiny chin. All framed by thick black hair.

Her breasts are so small they make almost no impression on her white blouse. Her arms and legs are pitifully thin. Her hips are nearly invisible and her black skirt falls in a straight line from her waist to her knees.

I'd become her personal Therapist a month before my pussy problem existed and discovered a bizarre life history. Like many Cambodians, her family had fled the murderous politics of the Khmer Rouge. Fortunately, they'd left *before* the fall of South Vietnam, when the competition for U.S. visas was less keen. When it was still possible to bribe Cambodian officials to advance families to the top of the emigration list.

Luckily, Blossom had never experienced the horrors of the new Kampuchea. Unluckily, her father made Pol Pot seem like Santa Claus.

Blossom was unable to recall a time in her life when she hadn't been routinely beaten.

Her father used a four-foot length of quarter-inch wooden doweling to drive home his personal idea of proper human behavior. He called these lessons "stripes."

Spill your milk: one stripe. Cry over spilled milk: two stripes. Pee your pants: one stripe. Poop your pants: two stripes. Disobedience meant blood.

The discipline continued as she got older. Despite manifest obedience that, she claims, was immediate and complete. Her only solace was a loving grandmother who died when she was seven years old.

Boo-hoo-hoo.

The grandmother's death left Daddy Nol with a big problem. He and Mommy Nol (whose only attempt to interfere with Daddy's discipline earned her a personal set of stripes) owned a small restaurant in the West Village. The economics of immigrant life were such that both were forced to work.

With granny gone to the big rice paddy in the sky, who would supervise young Blossom? Professional child care was never considered. In the first place, the Nols worked at night. In the second and most important place, outsiders would infect young Blossom with, curse of curses, "American nonsense."

Daddy had even resisted sending Blossom to school. Until Immigration threatened to reject his application for citizenship.

The solution was simple enough. Each afternoon, Daddy Nol left his restaurant to meet Blossom as she came out of school. Ever the concerned parent, he escorted her home, waited while she used the toilet and undressed, then tied her to her bed and went back to work.

Leaving her with a single injunction: "No pee sheet. You pee sheet, you get stripes."

Blossom spent the *next ten years* tied to her bed. (On weekends she was allowed to scrub the apartment before her parents went to the restaurant.)

She ran away from home when she was seventeen and was raped four times in the first month.

Naturally enough, given her circumstances, Blossom considered suicide, but was afraid to go through with it. Somehow, she wandered into Hanover House. She told me that she knew she'd found a home when her Therapist began to curse her. She didn't mind the shouting as long as it wasn't followed with stripes, ropes and rapes.

Blossom spent her first year at Hanover House in routine therapy. The therapy had been worthless, but she'd proven herself a willing worker and our cleaning business always needed bodies.

"You're a very brave girl, Blossom," I told her after three or four therapy sessions. "But bravery isn't enough. You must heal yourself."

"How can I do this?" She kept her bony hands on her bony knees and her eyes on her hands. She *never* looked up.

"Do you trust me, Blossom?"

"Yes."

I heard adoration in her voice. I swear it.

"You've been running away from your past. You'll never heal your wounds by running away. Do you understand?"

"Yes. No. I'm not sure."

"Until you confront the damage done by your family, the wounds will remain open. No matter what happens to you, even if it's all good, the wounds will continue to fester. By running away from the demon of your father, you keep him alive. You must descend into the abyss and you must do it *voluntarily*. Do you know the story of St. George and the dragon?" My tone, in direct contrast to that of her regular therapist, was kind, almost paternal.

"Yes."

"If St. George had surrendered to his fear, he would have been haunted for the rest of his life. No matter how fast or far he ran, he would never escape the dragon. The dragon would own his soul. Of course, if he fights the dragon, it *might* kill him. But if there's no risk, there's no possibility of gain. Are you following me?"

"I. What? I."

She shook her head, sending her long, glossy hair swirling about her face. In some ways, she was quite attractive. Suddenly, I found myself looking forward to the night when she would step into my bedroom. Suddenly, I was no longer bored.

"You must live the wounds. You must allow yourself to experience the totality of your pain. Knowing full well that you can walk away any time you wish. Make no mistake, Blossom, it won't be easy. Your past is a powerful dragon. You must anticipate a long and bitter fight." A fight, I didn't add, which would end on the day I became bored with her.

"What do I have to do?" Her voice was high and tiny with just a hint of the sing-song of her native language.

"You must re-create the entire experience. The ropes, the stripes, the obedience. Even the rapes. If you win, if you see the fight through to the end, you will *have* the inner strength you desperately desire. Look at me, Blossom." I lifted her chin until our eyes met. "Make no mistake, here. This is not a quest to be undertaken lightly. If you make the attempt and fail, the dragon will grow stronger. Don't try it unless you mean to see it through."

Just a thought: although I characterized Blossom's history as bizarre, very few of my poochies enjoyed mainstream childhoods. Blossom was an exaggerated version of the average poochie. She was the archetypal poochie.

When Blossom came to me, she was wearing the white, cotton night-gown common to all Hanoverian females. It covered her body completely, from her shoulders to her ankles. Blossom's eyes were riveted to the floor and if she noticed Wendell the Wonderful perched on the edge of the bed, she gave no sign.

"Blossom?" I asked.

"I've come to fight the dragon." Her thin voice held all the conviction of a chicken announcing its intention to eat the hawk. Yet I must admit that I took a moment to admire her courage. She had no real weapons and the dragon (meaning me) would surely devour her.

"Come here, Blossom."

Wendell's eyes were on fire. I hadn't told him about Blossom. She was to be a gift and the best gifts come as a surprise. Blossom was my 'bizarre pussy surprise.'

I was sitting in a leather club chair and I took Blossom on my lap and began to stroke her hair.

"Are you sure you want to do this, Blossom?"

"Yes. I know I must."

"Are you afraid, Blossom?"

"Yes. I'm afraid that I'll fail."

Her body was feather light, yet the sharp bones of her left shoulder and hip pushed against me as I cradled her in my arms.

"Have you ever had sex with a man, Blossom?"

She hesitated and I knew that she was aware of Wendell. "I've been raped."

"Have you ever been with a man for pleasure?"

"No."

"Were any of the men who raped you black men?"

"Two were black."

"How did the rapes happen?"

"I didn't have a place to live and the men told me I could stay with them. I didn't know I was supposed . . . That I had to do it with them. When I refused, they made me do it."

"Are you afraid, Blossom?"

"Yes."

"Are you going to see it through to the end?"

"Yes."

I trussed her up like a chicken. I tied her elbows to her ribcage and her wrists to her thighs. She could not lie flat on her stomach. Nor could she lower her legs. Wendell, in the process of shedding his clothes, took a moment to admire her body. Blossom's tiny breasts were little more than dark circles against pale ivory skin. Her sex was prominent and virtually hairless. With her legs drawn up, her narrow buttocks disappeared altogether.

After we finished (there was more, of course, much, much more, and for only $79.95 and the genitalia of your first born child, I'll be glad to send you the unedited video), I untied her without comment, then took several blankets from the linen closet and tossed them on the floor at the foot of my bed.

"You will sleep here," I announced. Having secured her obedience by feigning paternal concern, I switched over to the 'master mode.' With all my obligations, I didn't have time to coax her. She'd already taken enough of my energies.

She started to put on her nightgown, but I took it away from her. "You are not to cover yourself unless I tell you to cover yourself. You're in a different phase, now, and I must be a proper dragon." I held up my final surprise, a four-foot length of wooden doweling. "Obedience, Blossom. Obedience or stripes."

Hello, Poochie.

Bye-bye, Poochies.

Hanover House was a convenience I could no longer afford. The constant quarreling. The bullshit politics. Enough was enough.

Time is the limiting factor in all great efforts. I was needed at the lab, but I was forced to spend long hours baby-sitting two hundred neurotic poochies. (*Neurotic poochies*? An example of redundancy fit for the dictionary.) Originally, I'd planned to simply disappear, but that course of action had obvious flaws. My deserted poochies would first grow resentful, then seek out lawyers, investigative journalists, fat detectives, *Geraldo Rivera!*

I decided to end the Hanoverian experiment by uniting my poochies. By keeping them distracted while I made my getaway.

My performance was masterful. I had them gather in the meeting room, then wait a half hour before I made my appearance. When I entered by the rear doors, all eyes turned to me.

I literally dragged myself to the front of the room. "The time has come to end the great experiment," I announced.

The melodrama of the moment was so overwhelming I allowed a tear to form in the corner of my right eye.

"No. No. No." They stood in their seats, shouting.

"As most of you know, we've been investigated by several agencies over the last two years. In each and every case we've been cleared of any wrongdoing. Yet each investigation has taken its toll. Our legal costs have been enormous and contributions have virtually stopped because of the bad publicity."

This last was a complete lie. There had never been any 'contributions.' My only source of income was the slave labor I exacted from my poochies.

"The wolf is at the door," I continued. "The buildings are about to be repossessed." (Of course they were. The properties were heavily mortgaged and I hadn't made a payment in eight months.) "We can't even afford to buy food and clothing. It's . . ." I began to sob and moan. "Hanover House is gone, but you must not let the Hanoverian system die. You have the *knowledge*. You have the *strength*. Stay close to each other. Meet in small groups. You must live as the early Christians lived. You must be aware of your enemies at all times. As for me, I must go into a brief exile, but I *will* return to you if you keep hope alive. If you do not forget that the Hanoverian system is the *last great hope* for mankind."

At this point I broke down completely. Most of my poochies broke down as well. They forgot about the quarreling, the complaints and the bullshit poochie politics.

When I recovered somewhat, I tossed them a bone. Our cleaning business was still viable. I'd gotten offers from prospective buyers, but I would not sell. Instead, I would turn the business over to the Therapists who'd been running it all along.

Most of my poochies hadn't had to look for a job in years. Few of them were psychologically prepared for the rigors of mainstream employment. Their jobs would keep them together. That and the hope (should I say the *threat*?) of my return. By the time they sorted it out, I'd be gone.

"It's possible to view these events as a stroke of good fortune. As an opportunity. Some of you have become more dependent on Hanover House than Hanoverian psychology. Some of you have become dependent on *me*. What you must remember is that your therapy was designed to give you the strength to meet crises. I've always counseled you on the dangers of drug addiction. Well, you can also become addicted to situations and individuals. Withdrawal from addiction, from *any* addiction, is inevitably painful. Withdrawal is also *necessary*."

I ran the St. George and the dragon bit up the flagpole, then paused, giving them a chance to swallow the bait. What choice did they have? My bait was the only food in the sea. Not that I harbored any romantic delusions. Without me, their *real* addiction, to their neurotic poochie egos, would blow them apart within six months. The ones who didn't leave immediately, would separate into pockets of orthodoxy, neo-orthodoxy and outright heresy.

But, of course, I only needed a month to become yesterday's news. If not to my poochies, some of whom would surely keep the myth alive, then to any official agency with the ability to make my life miserable.

I sent the few Therapists addicted to PURE out to the lab where they would function as security. I gave the rest of the poochies five days to get out.

I endured their good-bye hugs until I could stand it no more. Pleading an imminent breakdown, I retired to my quarters. Blossom was sitting in a chair instead of on the floor, and I was forced to give her stripes. She received them with resolute determination.

I enjoyed the stripes, though I lacked the energy for sex. My performance had taken its toll, but its success filled me with a sense of accomplishment. I slept the sleep of the truly innocent.

I woke at four and began to write. It's now seven-fifteen. The writing was so effortless that I begin to believe that I missed my true calling. I should have been a writer instead of a psychopath.

The fat detective *must* pay. The fat detective's payment begins this afternoon with the arrival of the fat detective's fat bitch. I have judged her to be seriously disturbed and the only remedy to be chemotherapy. How does the saying go? The dope shall make you PURE?

Here, Poochie.

TWENTY-SEVEN

Betty Haluka, despite a perfunctory description provided by Stanley Moodrow, had entertained many images of the cult leader, Davis Craddock. She'd imagined him to be anything from a white-robed guru to a tweedy academic, eventually settling on a tall, slender figure, an urbane maniac whose glittering eyes revealed his underlying insanity. She'd been expecting to meet Craddock all along; her Therapist had assured her that Craddock personally interviewed all patients before they became part of the Hanoverian community. Still, the summons came as a shock. Betty was marched up to Craddock's suite before she could shed her coat.

"The thing is to just be yourself," her Therapist, Jack Burke, advised. "No pretensions. He'll see through you in a minute." He smiled as he advised her, thinking of Craddock's penchant for seduction as a test of worthiness. For most of Hanover House's existence, a night with Davis Craddock had been an absolute precondition to the admission of females. But over the last year, what with all the problems, Craddock had become less concerned with day-to-day Hanoverian life. Now the experiment was entering a new, unpredictable phase. Yet the great man could still take the time to counsel a patient. That's what made him a great man.

Betty, following her Therapist up the stairs, was aware of the general agitation within the community. Knots of Hanoverians, their bags already packed, talked excitedly. Many were crying. If Betty had had the instincts of an ex-cop, the alarm bells would have been ringing loud enough to wake the dead, but Betty deliberately refused to speculate, focusing her attention on what she would say to Davis Craddock.

"This is it. Good luck." Burke held the door to Craddock's suite open.

"You're not coming in?"

"It's a personal interview." He grinned lewdly. "I'm sure you'll find it enlightening."

Betty stepped into what real estate agents like to call an eat-in kitchen. The counters, sinks and stove gleamed with the efforts of Hanoverians to please their master. The floors and walls were spotless.

"Are you Betty?" A small, Asian girl sat by a white Formica table. Her hands were folded on her lap, her eyes downcast.

"I am."

"You can go inside. Davis is waiting for you."

Betty expected to enter an office or, at the least, a cozy living room. Instead, she found an enormous bedroom, big enough for a pool table and a bank of electronic gear against the far wall. She let her eyes wander for a moment, trying to take it in, then noticed the black man sitting calmly in an overstuffed chair. He was enormous, almost as big as Moodrow, and he regarded her with curious, amused eyes.

"Wendell Bogard," he announced. "At your service."

Without answering, Betty turned her attention to the man sitting at the foot of the bed. Far from her expectations, Davis Craddock was short and wiry, with a thick head of stiff, black hair that hung over his brow, dominating his small dark eyes. Looking into those eyes, Betty found no trace of the glittering insanity she'd anticipated. The man's eyes were dead black circles, as blank and empty as the eyes of a cooked fish on a plate.

"Please," Craddock said, "sit down." He indicated a straight-backed chair a few feet from his knees. "You're Betty Haluka?"

"Yes. You'll have to excuse me. I'm a little nervous."

"I can see that." He waited a moment, as if expecting a response, then continued. "You know I've been very lax these past few months or we'd have met before this. Things haven't been going too well for Hanover House. I'm sure you noticed that everybody's getting ready to leave. Have you noticed that?"

"There does seem to be a lot of activity, but I don't know what it's about."

"It's about the end of Hanover House. The end of the *great* experiment. I'm sending my children out into the cold, cruel world. Now, they'll have to maintain their various neuroses without my tender ministrations. Do you have any idea how many have come to me, begging to remain by my side? I'm not an emotional man—I admit it—but I was deeply touched by the response. I thought they'd hate me. After all, I lured them into Hanover House, made them my slaves, destroyed *any* chance of a normal life . . . Wouldn't you hate someone who did that to *you*?"

This time the pause went on so long, Betty felt obliged to make some sort of a response. "I don't understand." She'd been nervous before coming into the room. Now she was afraid. It was one thing to be face to face with a criminal psychopath in a courthouse interview room and quite another to be a potential victim.

"Well, that's neither here nor there. The important thing is that I'm making a few exceptions. I'm looking for Hanoverians with very, very special qualities to accompany me into exile. Tell me, do you fuck?"

"Mr. Craddock . . ."

Without a hint of warning, Davis Craddock drove his right fist into the side of Betty's face. "Call me Davis."

Betty scrambled to her feet. Her mind formed a dozen responses, all equally meaningless. She looked toward the door, but Wendell was already there. He was laughing.

"Please," Craddock said, "sit down. Right here. Next to me. Trust is very important to a successful therapeutic relationship. Don't you think?"

Betty touched her fingertips to the side of her face. The swelling beneath her eye was noticeable. There was anger, now, to go along with the fear, and the notion that perhaps this was still a test. It was an idea that could only have been formed in desperation. She set the chair upright and sat close to Craddock, trying to feign a sincerity that went against everything she was feeling.

"What was I saying?" There was life in Craddock's eyes now. A glow of anticipation. "Oh, yes. I was talking about special qualities. I'm looking for middle-aged women with fat detective boyfriends who manage to insinuate themselves into my life. I'm looking for creative letter writers who amuse themselves by pretending I'm an asshole. But most of all, I'm looking for insurance. Do you know anybody with all those qualities?"

"Fuck you."

Craddock's fist shot out again. "I think I like you better on the floor." He regarded her for a moment. "Yes, I definitely like you better on the floor. I only wish your skirt had ridden up over your thighs." He sighed loudly. "But in the course of a long and troubled life I've learned that you can't have everything. Wendell, will you ask Kenneth and Blossom to come inside?"

The Asian girl appeared a moment later. A blond man wearing the blue blazer of a Hanoverian Therapist stood behind her. He glared at Betty through unblinking eyes.

"I believe you've already met Blossom," Craddock said. "You should take a lesson from her. In my opinion, obedience is natural to the human female. Doesn't she look happy? And this is Kenneth Scott. Kenneth has a personal interest in the fat detective. Show her, Kenneth."

Kenneth Scott took off his blazer, then opened his white shirt and pulled it to one side. The round bruise on the upper right side of his chest was a few days old. The reddish purple had faded to a dull greenish yellow, but it was clearly visible. "The detective is Satan," he whispered. "And the woman is Eve."

"Please, Kenneth," Craddock laughed. "Enough of the Bible bullshit." He turned to Betty. "Poor Kenneth. He was raised in a good Christian home and he can't shake it off. I think you should know that Kenneth and Blossom are personally responsible for your well-being. If you want anything, just ask one of them. I promise they'll be attentive to your needs.

"Stanley's going to kill you for this," Betty answered.

"Kenneth, would you go down to the van and get it running?" Craddock waited until the door closed before continuing. "Stanley Moodrow is *my* problem. And we're not here to talk about *my* problems. We're here to talk about *your* problems. Blossom, get some ice and wrap it in a towel. By the way, Betty, would you like to see Blossom naked? No? Gee, and you look so butch. I thought for sure . . . All right, Blossom, go fetch the ice." He waited patiently until Blossom returned. "Give the ice to Betty." The Asian girl, without a trace of emotion, crossed the room and offered the towel.

"Blossom is learning obedience," Craddock continued, pulling the girl onto his lap. "She's proven herself an excellent pupil." He slid his hand into her blouse. "Notice that her expression doesn't change. Hopefully, you'll reach this level before our relationship comes to an end. But all in good time."

Betty got to her feet and moved to a chair several yards away from Craddock's fists. Her mind was in turmoil, anger and fear mingling with self-recrimination. How could she have been so stupid? Moodrow had warned her. Jim and Rose had warned her, too. What would Moodrow do when he found out? If he exploded, Craddock could easily kill the both of them. She needed to get herself under control, but her thoughts were tumbling through her mind like handkerchiefs in a clothes dryer.

"Now, let's talk about your problems," Craddock said mildly.

"Fuck you."

"Shi-i-i-it," Wendell interrupted. "Lemme teach this white bitch some lessons about disrespectin' her superiors. Bitch got herself a attitude that don't fit her position. I fix it so's when you say 'hop,' she say, 'on yo dick or on yo face.'"

"I don't think so, Wendell. Remember, Betty's an insurance policy, not an experiment. Eventually, she'll come to us, but we don't want her so shaken that she panics the fat detective when we put her on the phone. Now, Betty, let's talk about your problems. Your biggest problem, as I see it, is that I could kill you without thinking twice. I could shoot you. Or stab you. Or crush your fucking skull with a brick, then wash my hands and go to dinner. I *enjoy* killing, but, let me hasten to assure you, I *don't* kill without a reason. I've been thinking about the fat detective. *Why* does he persist? The police investigated my activities, then gave up. The IRS gave up, too. Even the Attorney General gave up. Why, I keep asking myself, does the fat detective persist? The fat detective persists because he's paid to persist. Connie Alamare's money motivates him and he'll keep coming as long as she keeps paying. Unless, of course, I supply him with a reason to stop. *You* are the reason. Any questions?"

"If you hold me forever, he'll haunt you into the grave."

"Good point. It shows that you're thinking and that's all to my benefit. I need three weeks to complete my project. A month at the outside. Then I'll let you go. As I told you, I don't kill without a reason. I'm a businessman."

"And your business is dope."

Craddock laughed out loud. "Very good, but not entirely accurate. My business is PURE, not ordinary dope. PURE is to dope as Botticelli is to Norman Rockwell. But why should I convince you with words, when I can demonstrate the genuine article? In fact, I've already prepared a sample just for you." He removed a small syringe from his shirt pocket and held it up for her inspection. "You can fight, of course, but what good would it do you? What's the old saying about rape? 'When rape is inevitable, just relax and enjoy it.'"

Betty expected to die. PURE had killed two junkies and reduced Flo Alamare to an existence far closer to death than to life. What better way for Craddock to eliminate her? She would die silently, without a scream or the sound of a gunshot.

Fear overwhelmed her. She had never experienced terror like this before, not even in her worst nightmares. The room jumped into focus. She felt herself to be aware of every single atom, of whirling electrons, of worlds that stretched to infinity. Yet she couldn't move, couldn't even beg.

Tears began to flow from her eyes, but she didn't sob. She didn't seem to be breathing at all. She could sense the molecules of blood rushing through her veins, the molecules that would carry the toxins to her pounding heart. Craddock lifted her arm and nonchalantly strapped a rubber tourniquet to her bicep.

"Good veins," he said to Wendell.

"Won't stay that way long."

Craddock waved the syringe in the air. "Not so, Wendell. The use of sterile needles and a little alcohol can keep the veins alive for years. You know, when I first decided to create a new drug, I toyed with the idea of packaging it in a syringe. But, of course, needles are illegal in New York and PURE is not." He broke into a laugh. "Wendell, look at Blossom." The girl was staring at the syringe in Craddock's hand. "Don't worry, little one, your turn will come."

The tip of the needle slipped easily into the large vein just in front of Betty's elbow. A single drop of blood pushed back into the clear liquid, then Craddock snapped the tourniquet off and slowly depressed the plunger.

Within seconds, Betty's fear vanished. Despite the danger, despite the manifest insanity of Davis Craddock, she felt perfectly at ease. The sensation was almost entirely physical, but she didn't feel slow or sleepy. In fact, her consciousness was dominated by a single, simple realization, a truth she could have gotten from any junkie on the street. The lure of dope stems directly from the quality of the high. It feels good. At least in the beginning. That's why people do it.

She recalled an anti-drug ad she'd seen on TV. Fat hissed and crackled in a hot frying pan while an off-screen voice intoned, "This is drugs." Then an egg dropped into the pan and the same voice announced, "This is your brain on drugs. Any questions?"

Betty smiled. She had a question. Why did the creators of the ad feel it necessary to lie to kids who already knew the truth? Maybe the ad wasn't meant for people at risk. Maybe it was meant for middle-aged women, like herself, who rarely had more than a glass of wine at dinner. Anyone seriously interested in helping kids would tell them the truth. That it feels so good, you want to do it again and again. You want to do it until it owns you.

"A week, Wendell. Four injections a day for one week and I'll own her. She'll beg for it. Beg. She'll willingly perform any act I demand. She'll set up the fat detective for a single dose of PURE." He walked back to the bed and took a syringe out of the nightstand drawer. "Here you go, Blossom."

Blossom needed no help. Within a minute, she was pushing the plunger home, her eyes half closed in anticipation of the rush.

"Get dressed, Blossom. We're going for a ride."

With all the nonchalance of a veteran prostitute, Blossom shed her robe and walked naked to a chest of drawers. She slid into panties and a bra, blue jeans and a red Donald Duck sweatshirt.

"I'm gon' miss that little yellow bitch," Wendell said. "Gon' miss this whole scene."

Craddock raised his eyebrows in surprise. "Marcy was much better. She was inventive. But if you want Blossom, you can take her with you. It doesn't matter to me and it won't matter to her. As long as you keep her supplied with PURE."

"You temptin' me, Davis, but ain't no way I can bring the bitch back to my crew. Raise too many jealousies."

"Then say good-bye, Wendell. You won't be seeing her again until we're ready to deal."

Craddock showed Betty a small revolver and made the predictable threats before hustling Betty down a back stairway and into an alley that ran out to Orchard Street where the van was parked. He needn't have bothered. Still overwhelmed by the effects of the drug, Betty followed obediently. Even when he ordered her to sit on the floor of the van, even when he blindfolded her with a strip of soft cotton, she made no protest. But as they moved through Manhattan, the first effects of the drug began to recede.

It wasn't much, just a slow lessening of the physical sensations, but it enabled Betty, locked in darkness, to come to grips with her situation. Craddock was insane. His surface control had to mask an underlying desperation. How could he get away with this? Where could he go? Her fate didn't really matter. Moodrow would never stop looking for Craddock, even if Craddock released her unharmed. And Stanley Moodrow had less than no interest in the niceties of the law. Betty's value to Craddock was decidedly short term. If he held her too long, Moodrow's patience, assuming he decided to be patient, would dissolve and he would act. If Moodrow thought Betty was dead, he would call in the FBI and a hundred agents would scour the country. Kidnapping is a federal crime and carries a life sentence.

The truth was obvious enough to Betty, though she experienced it without a trace of emotion. There was no 'joy of enlightenment,' just a quick, calm understanding. Davis Craddock wasn't stupid, despite his theatrics. He needed a month to complete his 'project,' a project that could only involve the manufacture and the initial distribution of the drug called PURE. After that, he would be *forced* to disappear which meant that he had no intention of remaining active in the drug world. A quick hit. Over and out.

She recalled her only prior experience with narcotics. Following an emergency appendectomy fifteen years ago, she'd been given a prescription for thirty tablets of a painkiller called Demerol. The pain had disappeared after a few days and she'd flushed the mostly unused prescription down the toilet, despite (or, rather, because of) its narcotic effect. The painkillers had cost her fifteen dollars and seemed, to her, to be very powerful. Curious, she'd asked one of her junkie clients what Demerol sold for on the street and been told that, depending on how much heroin was available, black market Demerol sold for eight, ten or twelve dollars per tablet. Her prescription had a street value of three hundred dollars. If the cost of manufacturing PURE was in any way similar to the cost of Demerol, Craddock stood to make an enormous profit from a very small amount of the drug.

A month to complete his project? He would have to keep her alive and able to communicate until he was ready to run. The physical danger was not immediate. She would have time to think, to prepare. On the other hand, the psychological danger was much more imminent. She was already anticipating the next injection. And the one after that and the one after that. Craddock was determined to humiliate her, to enslave her until she no longer wanted to be released. It would be so easy for her to acquiesce, to slide into acceptance. She was in the back of a locked van, headed for an unknown destination, imprisoned by a madman, yet she felt no anxiety whatsoever. If PURE was powerful enough to overcome fear, it would certainly overcome shame or pride. Her survival—physical, emotional and psychological—depended on her ability to resist the drug. The simple fact that the clarity of her understanding was also an effect of PURE was an irony that escaped her altogether.

TWENTY-EIGHT

For the first ten or fifteen miles, Betty tried to keep track of the van's progress. It bumped over New York's potholed streets for a few minutes, then took a left and accelerated onto FDR Drive, the only highway within miles. That much was easy. The left turn meant they were running north, toward upper Manhattan and the Bronx. A short time later they stopped to pay a toll and Betty assumed that Craddock had taken the exit for the Triborough Bridge, which connects Manhattan to the Bronx and Queens. She tried to concentrate. Which way had they gone? North to Upstate New York and New England or east to Long Island? Then she realized that Craddock could easily have passed the exit to the Triborough Bridge and taken the George Washington Bridge which ran west through New Jersey. But, no, that was impossible, because there was no outbound toll on the George Washington Bridge. The Port Authority, which controls the bridges and tunnels leading to New Jersey, had doubled the inbound toll and fired the toll takers who worked the outbound booths. They were driving north or east.

Craddock didn't help matters. He not only chattered continually, but he expected her to respond and, Betty, sitting in darkness, realized there was nothing to be gained by provoking him. Craddock was unpredictable at best. The better she understood him, the better her chance of survival.

"You know something?" he asked. "This is really a treat for me. It's been years since I've had an opportunity to chat with someone of your intelligence and independence. That's the problem with being the chief deity to a congregation of assholes. You can never let them see who you really are. You, on the other hand, already know who I am, right?"

"Yes, I know," Betty replied. She wasn't surprised to find her voice steady and strong. PURE had erased her fear altogether. For a brief moment, she entertained the idea that she could manipulate Craddock into actually liking her. If she could forge that link, perhaps he'd be reluctant to hurt her. Or to kill her. But in the course of a long career, she'd defended too many psychopaths to grasp at that straw. The emotional ties that bind human beings—friendship, loyalty, love—are no more than abstractions to a psychopath like Davis Craddock. In the end, his decision, to kill her or release her, would be based on utterly selfish considerations.

"I wouldn't admit it to his face, but the fat detective is pretty good at his job. He found out about Billy in the Bronx, didn't he?"

"Yes."

"And I'll bet he figured out what happened to Flo Alamare?"

"Something with the drug. Some problem."

"Yes, the problem. The problem is that sooner or later the fat detective's going to get his hands on a sample of PURE and run it down to a lab. Then his speculations will become what you lawyers call evidence. Of course, it doesn't matter, now that I have you." He sighed deeply. "The serpent in paradise. The worm in the apple. PURE is everything I hoped it would be. I'm sure you can attest to that. It dissolves instantly.

Why would anyone heat it? But they did. A few of them cooked it up the way you cook up ordinary heroin. It's an easy death, really. Quick and unexpected, which is about the best you can hope for in this life. But I still don't understand what happened to Flo. I suppose she must have heated it accidentally."

"Then Flo's poisoning wasn't deliberate."

"Oh no, I liked Flo. I really did. She was smart and energetic. I liked her even before I began my project, before she began to use PURE. I haven't liked too many people in my life. That's because very few people have managed to like *me*. I can play the cold, distant therapist and win the trust of fools, but I'm terrible at personal relationships. Even my mother didn't like me. She tried, though. I was her only child and she tried very hard to like me, especially after my father took off. I can remember the day she gave up clearly. Are you interested in all this, Betty? Am I boring you?"

"Go ahead. I don't have all that much to do, back here."

"Very good. A little humor. You're spunky, Betty, and I appreciate that. Not like old Blossom over here. I want you to know that I don't have anything against you. I hate your boyfriend, though. *Stanley*. What kind of faggoty name is that for a detective? It's not interesting like Hercule Poirot. Or tough like Mike Hammer. *Stanley*, take out the garbage. Did you walk the dog yet, *Stanley*? Of course, I wouldn't expect you to see it that way, but you can understand my position. I can accept adversity, but I don't care for humiliation. He shouldn't have sent me those letters."

"He wanted to draw you out into the open. He was deliberately trying to make you angry."

"Well, he succeeded, didn't he? I hope he's happy."

The van rolled on. They were obviously on a highway, but Betty couldn't determine which one or where they were headed. The hum of the tires on the road, of the transmission and differential, numbed Betty despite the drug, but she forced herself to consider her situation. They'd left the black man, Wendell Bogard, behind, but Kenneth Scott was sitting next to Craddock in the front of the van. Blossom was in back, next to Betty, a hand resting on Betty's knee. At first, Betty thought the touch was sexual, but the hand merely rested. Was it meant as a consolation? Reassurance? Betty didn't know, but it was more than obvious that the weak link in the chain (if there was to be a weak link in the chain) had to be Blossom. Kenneth Scott was lost in a mix of implacable hate, blind belief and physiological addiction. There was no way to reach Kenneth Scott, and any attempt was likely to result in a bullet or a beating. Blossom's submission came from another place altogether. Her posture, from her downcast eyes to her slumped shoulders and the way her arms hung limply at her sides, revealed depression and resignation, not anger and hatred. There was at least a chance that, being a victim herself, she would identify with Betty, not Davis Craddock.

It was more than two hours later, after they bumped onto a ferry and the van began to rock gently, that Betty got a hint of what direction they'd probably taken. The eastern end of Long Island splits into two long peninsulas. There are several islands between these forks, and some of them, Betty knew, were connected to the mainland by ferries. She had to be out on the eastern end of Long Island, which at least indicated a fairly dense population. There'd be some place to go, if she managed to get away from Davis Craddock. If they'd been traveling north to some remote farmhouse, any escape would be into dense forest. Betty was city-born and city-raised, and the deep, dark woods frightened her.

The ferry ride was brief, less than ten minutes. The ferryboat continued to sway as the cars ahead of them pulled off, then they were moving again. Craddock chattered away, bragging about his evil deeds the way an adolescent brags of a sexual conquest. Ten minutes later, the van stopped and Craddock shut the engine off. Betty, still blindfolded, was led inside.

"Welcome to Frankenstein's castle," Craddock said, removing the blindfold. "The House of PURE."

The young man standing by the rear door cradled an M16 in his arms. His face was turned to the darkness outside. Another sentry stood guard at the front of the house. He turned briefly and Betty knew immediately that he, like Kenneth Scott, was an addict and that his addiction guaranteed obedience. He would discharge his duty faithfully and without emotion.

"Come see the lab," Craddock commanded. He led her down a short flight into a windowless basement. The single room was enormous. They'd dug out to the foundations of the house, removing walls as they went, adding narrow housejacks for support. Six workers, all women, scuttled from one apparatus to another. To Betty, totally unfamiliar with chemical laboratories, the scene was as exotic as any mad scientist movie set. Which made sense, because Craddock was obviously crazy.

"There's enough PURE down here to keep Blossom high for ten thousand years," Craddock bragged. "Not that I plan to keep Blossom high for ten thousand years. All my workers know that our stay here will be temporary, but I've promised to send each of them off with a year's supply of PURE and enough money to get started in the real world. The last thing I need is an open rebellion. The product itself is stored in a temperature-controlled safe. Needless to say, I'm the only one with the combination."

"How much PURE will you have when you're done?" Betty couldn't resist the obvious question.

"Nine million doses, more or less. PURE is much more powerful than cocaine or heroin which makes packaging the trickiest part of the operation. You can't just spoon it into little envelopes. Weighing out millions of 10-mg doses by hand would have taken forever. I'm proud to say that I found the solution myself. That's why I'm so far ahead of schedule. I bought a machine to package PURE at the liquidation sale of a small pharmaceutical house that'd falsified information on an FDA form and had its license yanked. You know, I originally planned to package PURE in heat-sealed vials which is how crack is sold. But the machine I bought was designed to fill capsules. When in Rome, eh? PURE will be sold in gold or silver capsules, depending on the quantity. The capsules can be swallowed or broken open and the powder injected or inhaled. The machine can package one dose per second. In case you don't have a calculator implanted in your brain, that comes out to 3600 doses per hour, 86,400 per day. Faster than I can produce it."

"Why did you decide to package it at all? Why not just sell it in volume?"

"Good question. I wanted PURE to be pure. I didn't want the consumer to have to worry about overdoses or adulterants. Remember, PURE can't be heated. There are going to be some dead junkies no matter what I do. If I just sold the powder, how could I be sure the wholesaler wouldn't cut it with something that doesn't dissolve unless heated? I'm a businessman, Betty, and I know how important first impressions are when you introduce a new product into the marketplace. Our test marketing clearly indicates that PURE is the drug of choice, for heroin and crack junkies alike. But PURE must reach the national marketplace in a clearly recognizable, unadulterated form."

Betty felt a quick surge of anticipation. If PURE became readily available, she wouldn't be cut off when Craddock released her. Then she realized that she was already looking forward to her next dose. And that she had no reason to believe that Craddock would ever let her go. "If you're only in it for the short term," she said, "why do you care what happens after you sell it?"

"Because I intend to auction off the formula." He looked around the lab, checking each facet of the operation. "I've got a lot of work to do here. I think it's time you saw your new home. Plus, I have a big surprise for you. Then we'll call the fat detective."

He led her back up the stairs, then up a second flight to a locked door at the end of a long hallway. "You'll notice," he said, "that this door is made of steel. The frame extends six inches into the wall. The door opens outward and is secured with a steel crossbar." He removed the crossbar, unlocked the door and pulled it open. "*Voila.*"

The room was small: a bed pushed against the wall, two wooden chairs, a table, a threadbare woven rug over rough planks, a tiny bathroom with a toilet and a sink. A young boy sat on one of the chairs. He was shivering and his knees were drawn up to his chest. A long stream of mucus ran from both nostrils.

"Please, Daddy," he said, holding out one thin arm.

"Ugh," Craddock muttered. "Disgusting." He took a syringe from his pocket, crossed to the child, and pushed it into the child's shoulder. "Kids have terrible veins," he announced to Betty. "The addicts call this skin popping. It's not as fast as mainlining, but it works. It also makes the high last longer. Not long enough, though. By the way, this is Michael Alamare. My son. The object of your investigation. Blossom, get me the cellular phone from downstairs."

A minute later, Michael Alamare stopped shivering. His nose dried up and his eyes were clear. He watched Betty carefully, though he said nothing. He was waiting. As he'd been waiting.

"Michael," Craddock said, breaking the silence, "has been using PURE for about a month. My motive in giving it to him was purely charitable. He was *so* bored. I mean I *had* to take him out of Hanover House. Even before she hired Stanley, Connie Alamare had her lawyers busy looking for Michael. My story was that Flo and Michael had left the commune two years earlier. Suppose the cops got some judge to sign a search warrant?"

Blossom returned with the phone, offering it to Craddock. "What's the number?" Craddock asked. "It's time to call Stanley."

Moodrow picked up on the first ring. He wasn't surprised to hear Craddock's voice. He wasn't even angry.

"Stanley, guess who?"

"I know who it is."

"My, aren't we calm tonight? I'm not shocked, though. I've stopped underestimating you."

He paused for a reply, but Moodrow kept his mouth shut. Like Betty, he knew there was nothing to be gained by provoking Craddock.

"Nothing to say?" Craddock continued. "Well, let me fill you in on the details. I have your girlfriend. Right here with Michael. She's not in Hanover House. I need three weeks, a month at most, then I'll release her. I have no particular reason to hurt her, but if you make any attempt to find me, I'll kill her. I have no illusions. I know what will happen to me if I'm apprehended. Do you believe me, Stanley?"

"Absolutely. What do you want from me?"

"Nothing, Stanley. I want you to stay put and do nothing. I'm going to let you talk to her now. In fact, I'm going to have her call you every evening at nine o'clock."

"How did you find out what she was doing? Did you hurt her?"

"I've been having all prospective clients followed to their homes for months. I guess the attention I've received over the last year made me a little paranoid. In this case, though, you'll have to admit that paranoia paid off. Here, talk to Betty."

"Stanley," Betty said, "I was stupid. I was completely . . ."

"I don't wanna hear that crap. Tell me if he hurt you."

"No, he hasn't. He . . ."

Something in her voice triggered Moodrow's instincts. The lack of fear, the strength. Even her apology was matter-of-fact. "He gave you the drug, didn't he?"

"Yes."

"And you like it."

It was a statement, not a question, but Betty replied anyway. "Yes."

"Don't worry about it. You're not an addict and . . ."

" 'Don't *worry* about it'? That's real easy for you to say. You're safe in your fucking apartment. What am I supposed to be? Miss Liberty?"

A second later, Craddock was back on the phone. "Bitch, bitch, bitch. That's all they do, if you let them. I could give you some lessons in bitch training, if you like."

"Cut the crap."

"That's not very nice, but I'll let it go. I'll chalk it up to the heat of battle. Now, it seems to me that you have three options. You can do nothing. (By far the wisest course.) Or you can continue to work by yourself. Or you can call in the FBI and the cops. If you decide to exercise the last option, I'm certain that you'll find me. The FBI would have no trouble getting warrants to examine bank records or phone records or land titles. You'd also be able to mount an overwhelming attack on my little fortress and I'd be cooked meat. But if you do that, I'm going to take my .357, shove it in your girlfriend's cunt and blow the top of her head off. You understand me, Stanley?"

"Yeah, I understand. Just like you understand that if you hurt her, I'll find you and kill you. No cops. No FBI. Just me."

"Ah, the obligatory threat from the cornered rat. How macho. Bye-bye, Stanley. Have a nice night."

Betty lay on the bed, staring at the ceiling. The drug was powerful and sleep would be long in coming, if it came at all. Not that she was bored or anxious. Craddock had injected her before leaving to work in the lab. She had made no resistance. She would make no resistance in the morning, when he returned. At first, Michael Alamare had remained in the chair, staring at her, but after an hour or so, he climbed onto the bed and pressed himself into her arms.

"Why did my daddy put you here?" he asked. "Were you bad, too?"

TWENTY-NINE

It was just after eleven o'clock, and Jim Tilley was watching the late news and thinking about Rose and bed when Moodrow called. Moodrow's message was very simple: "Jim, he's got Betty." Tilley's obligatory response was equally simple: "I'm on my way over." He tossed a quick explanation to Rose and was out the door before she could answer.

He ran the few blocks to Moodrow's apartment, expecting to find his old friend in a towering rage, but the unpredictable Moodrow surprised him. As usual.

"There's coffee on the stove, Jim. Help yourself."

"Stanley, you okay?"

"Why would anything be wrong with me? I'm not the one who got kidnapped."

"I thought you might blame yourself."

"Bullshit. I begged her not to go in there. You and Rose begged her not to go in there. She wanted to play a dangerous game and she has to deal with the consequences. And I'm not gonna grieve while she's still alive. There's no point to it. She's my woman, not my kid."

He related his conversation with Betty and Davis Craddock calmly, going over each detail. He'd written it all down. When he was finished, Tilley articulated the most important piece of information.

"Then she's not in immediate danger," he said.

"I agree. Not that I'm buying that 'three weeks to a month' bullshit, but I think we've got at least a week. If Craddock needed less than that, he'd stonewall it. He's gonna make a move with the dope and he wants me out of the way until he's finished."

"Why is Craddock so afraid?" Tilley walked slowly to the kitchen, then poured himself a cup of coffee. "The drug is legal."

"Tell me something, Jim. What's Craddock's biggest problem?"

"You."

Moodrow shook his head. "Craddock's biggest problem is Flo Alamare. The drug isn't illegal. He's not gonna get prosecuted for possession, manufacturing or sale. But if he gave the drug to Flo and it poisoned her, he's up for reckless endangerment. If we can link the drug to the dead junkies who supposedly overdosed, it's manslaughter. And the motherfucker doesn't know that we don't have a sample of the drug. He doesn't know the DEA has the samples and we can't get to them."

"We could've had them if we'd turned the whole thing over to the department."

"You sure about that, Jim? The cops made the junkies for ODs and Flo Alamare for a stroke victim. If the DEA decides to act, it'll issue a report to the Attorney General's office and maybe, a year or two down the road, PURE will be added to the schedule of controlled substances. *Controlled substances*. Talk about bullshit. Even the word is bullshit. *Dope* is what it should be. They should call it 'the dope list' and leave it at that. If the cops had gotten into it, Craddock would have all the time he needs."

Moodrow began to unfold a Hagstrom street map of eastern Long Island. "You remember what Betty said about 'Miss Liberty'?"

"Yeah, I was kind of surprised that she'd snap at you like that."

"About a year ago, Betty and I took the ferry out to Liberty Island. Neither of us had ever been to the Statue of Liberty before, even though both of us have lived here all our lives, and we figured it was about time. Maybe I'm too much of a cynic, but I wasn't very moved by the 'Give me your poor and huddled masses' bit. I've seen too many 'poor and huddled masses' on the streets of New York to buy the dream. But Betty was really excited by the statue. Her family had come here to escape old Adolf and it'd worked out for them. We walked around for a couple of hours, then headed back for the ferry, which happened to be broken down. It was tied up to the dock, but they wouldn't let us on. We argued about it with the crew until it started raining. It had been hot as hell all day and the thunderstorms rolled in around five o'clock. There was lightning and thunder, and we were on an island in the middle of New York Harbor. I think that's what Betty was referring to when she mentioned 'Miss Liberty.' "

"You think she was talking about the ferry?"

"Betty went into Hanover House about eight o'clock. It's eleven-thirty, now. Betty called at eleven. Figure two hours, maybe two and a half hours driving. That would put them on the eastern end of Long Island, if they went that way. There's a bunch of smaller islands out there and they connect to the mainland with ferries."

Moodrow finished spreading the map out and both men leaned over it, searching. Long Island, which includes the New York City boroughs of Queens and Brooklyn on its western end, extends one hundred miles due east into the Atlantic Ocean. Forty miles from its eastern tip, it splits into two branches, the North and South Forks. Orient Point marks the end of the North Fork while Montauk Point, with its famous lighthouse, marks the end of the South Fork. Three islands lie between the Forks while a fourth, Plum Island, sits out in the Atlantic just off the tip of the North Fork. Of these, two, Shelter Island and Plum Island, are served by public ferries, while the other two, Gardiners Island and Robins Island, are privately owned. There are several other Long Island ferries, but the ferries from the north connect Long Island to Connecticut and take more than a hour to complete their runs, while the ferries from the south, connecting mainland Long Island to Fire Island, carry passengers only. Cars are banned on Fire Island.

Jim Tilley found the third possibility. "How do you know they didn't go up through Connecticut? There's an island right off New London. Fishers Island. How far is it from New York to New London?" He studied the map intently, trying to decipher the mileage chart. "A hundred and twenty-six road miles. Almost exactly the same as the length of Long Island. They could've gone to Fishers Island."

"All right, three possibilities. It doesn't matter much anyway, because we're not gonna find him by driving around. What we need is access to the paper. Bank records and like that. Maybe he made phone calls from the commune to the lab. Or maybe he's paying a mortgage."

Tilley leaned forward. "I guess that brings us to the big question."

"Which is?"

"Which is what you're gonna do. You need warrants to get that information. Warrants signed by a judge. Kidnapping is a federal crime, and I don't see how you're gonna get your warrants without calling in the FBI."

Moodrow turned back to the map without answering. What Tilley had taken for calm was actually a kind of numbness. Moodrow was well aware of the paralysis that often accompanies intense worry. Worry leads to indecision, to second-guessing. The individual knows that the wrong decision will result in the death of the victim. Better to make no decision at all than to accept that grim responsibility.

Not that Moodrow had chosen his present state. He felt like he was in a dream, like he was about to open that dark closet and confront something completely unknown. He controlled his fear by backing off, by planning, by analyzing.

Craddock, Moodrow knew, had been right. There were only three possibilities: do nothing, give it to the FBI, go it alone. He could follow the chain of events flowing from each possibility. Right up to the last link. Betty's life was suspended at the end of the chain.

"What do you think Craddock will do if I sit back and wait?" he asked finally. "You think he'll let her go?"

Tilley didn't answer immediately. He tried to imagine Craddock opening a door somewhere and Betty walking through it, unharmed. It was the least likely of all the possibilities. "We've got to assume that Craddock has some escape plan. Even if you decide to wait it out, you won't wait forever. The only real escape for him is to get out of the country. Maybe South America. Someplace without an extradition treaty. Which means that he *could* release her."

"That doesn't answer the question."

"C'mon, Stanley. I don't have a crystal ball."

"Then guess, Jim. Guess."

Tilley sighed. "The guy's ego is more important to him than the money. Success isn't enough. He wants to humiliate you. I think the least he'll do is hurt her. It could be worse."

"What happens if I turn it over to the FBI?"

"Then you'd be out of it. You're just an ordinary citizen to them. They'd have you sitting by the phone in case he calls. But the FBI would find him, Stanley. They'd get all the warrants they need. There's no way he could've set up that lab without leaving a paper trail."

"Yeah, they'd find him. But could they take him before he got to Betty? Like you said, Craddock's whole game is his ego. If the FBI surrounded the house or tried to smash through the door, would Craddock surrender? He had armed guards at Hanover House, and we'd be very stupid to assume he didn't have his lab protected. I think I should find him before I do anything. I already called Leonora. She'll be here soon."

They went back to the map and the three islands. Two, Fishers and Plum were quite small, but Shelter Island, served by ferries from the

North and South Forks, was large enough to be a popular summer resort area as well as support a year-round population of several thousand. Tilley had been on Shelter Island and he remembered it as a place of wealth, of enormous mansions looking out over Gardiners Bay. Assuming Betty had been right about the ferry ride, Shelter Island was the obvious place to look. Not that it meant very much—without enlisting the aid of the local police, they'd be as helpless on Shelter Island as they were on the Lower East Side.

Leonora Higgins arrived half an hour later. It was almost midnight and she wore no makeup. In sharp contrast to her usual business attire, she was dressed in jeans, a simple white blouse and a dark blue sweater. She, like Tilley, expected to find an enraged, unpredictable Moodrow. And, like Tilley, she was relieved by his outward calm. She accepted a mug of coffee, then listened carefully to the details of Craddock's phone call.

"Poor Betty," she said. Then, after a pause: "I hope you kill this bastard, Stanley. This bastard should not be walking around, even in a prison."

"Killing him is the easy part, Leonora. The problem is what he'll do before I get to him."

Higgins banged her fist on the table. "The one thing you can't do is wait around. Because if you wait, he'll . . ." She didn't finish the sentence. "Why did you let her go in there? What were you thinking?"

Moodrow almost smiled. *He* was the one who was supposed to be furious. "I begged her not to go, but I couldn't get through to her. She accused me of pushing her around. 'Typical male arrogance' was the way she put it."

"She should've known," Leonora admitted. "Twenty years in law enforcement. She should've known."

Moodrow surprised himself by defending Betty. "She was worried about the kid, Michael Alamare. Which was reasonable under the circumstances."

"Well, she's really helping the kid now."

"Leonora," Tilley broke in, "this isn't doing us any good. Why don't we save the guilt trip for later."

Higgins looked around the room, then sighed. "You're right," she admitted. "Let's get to work. Stanley, how many people do you think Craddock has in that lab?"

"Four or five sentries. A dozen workers in the lab. Two dozen. There's no way to know."

"How do you know he doesn't have an armed man in the room with Betty all the time?"

"I don't know, Leonora. There's no way I could know."

"Well, I don't see how you can get in there."

Moodrow spun his mug slowly on the table. He was manipulating a friend and he knew it. "What do you think would happen if the FBI showed up with an army of agents and local police?"

"There'd be no chance," Higgins admitted. "They'd never get inside before Craddock got to Betty."

"How could I do any better alone?"

"Stanley," Tilley said quietly, "are you saying it's impossible, that you can't do anything?"

"What I'm saying is that unless something unexpected happens, a direct frontal assault is not gonna get her out. But I got something else in mind. What if I set up surveillance on the lab? What if I wait for Craddock to come out, then take him? With a little encouragement, I think he'll let Betty go. Like if I offer to trade his cock for Betty's freedom. He lets her go, he keeps it. He doesn't let her go, I feed it into a meat grinder. A millimeter at a time."

"That would probably work," Higgins admitted. "But how do you intend to locate the lab?"

"The paper, Leonora. Phone records, bank records. Figure it like this. There are no apartments out there. Homes on the eastern tip of Long Island are more expensive than in the city. He didn't get that kind of money out of his own pocket. He took it from the commune and he left a trail."

"You need warrants to get that information," Tilley insisted. "And a judge has to sign the warrants. It's not like filling out a form."

Despite the gravity of the situation, Higgins couldn't hold back a smile. "I suppose that's *my* job. Getting the warrants."

"I can't ask you to do that," Moodrow said quietly.

"Don't bullshit me, Stanley. I'm a prosecutor, remember? I can smell bullshit at fifty paces."

"Look, Leonora . . ."

"Let me see if I've got it right. You need search warrants to get at Craddock's paper, but you don't want to report the crime. In order to get the warrant, I have to go before a judge with an affidavit signed by a detective. How does it begin? 'In the interests of justice'? The officer has to swear that his sources are known to him and reliable. He has to establish probable cause. Usually, the detective goes into court with the assistant DA in case the judge has questions. Is that where you come in, Jim?"

"Whatever it takes," Tilley answered evenly.

"Then you know the consequences if we're caught?"

"Whatever it takes," he repeated.

"First, we'd both be fired. Then I'd be disbarred. Then we'd be charged with filing false documents, which is a felony. To put it bluntly, our professional lives would be over."

"The idea is not to get caught," Moodrow said. For the first time, he was afraid and the fear showed in his eyes. "There's no reason why you *should* be caught. Some of those judges will sign a recipe for chicken soup. As long as we don't try to use the warrants in a courtroom, nobody will know."

"Unless there's a spectacular bust later on. You can take Craddock's body and dump it in the ocean, but you can't get rid of the lab and all the dope he's manufacturing. The papers will eat it up. GURU TURNS MAD SCIENTIST. The judge might remember. Even the easy ones read what they sign, because they don't want their warrants knocked down at trial. It makes them look stupid in the eyes of their colleagues."

"Are you saying you won't do it?"

"Fortunately, I don't have to make a decision, because there's a better way. A safer way. I can go into court and open a Grand Jury investigation into Craddock's activities. There's no paperwork involved. All I do is add it to the calendar where it'll sit for weeks before any action is taken. I don't need written approval from my superiors or sworn affidavits. Once the Grand Jury begins an investigation, I have the right to subpoena Craddock's phone and bank records. The subpoena forms are in my desk drawer. New York Telephone and most of the larger banks have departments to expedite subpoenas. After I get and copy the records, I can go back into court and withdraw the investigation. There's almost no chance of getting caught, but even if the subpoenas were uncovered, my actions would be unethical, but not illegal. As an assistant district attorney, I have the right to open an investigation and, of course, a crime *has* been committed."

"How long will it take you to do all this?" Moodrow felt no guilt, only relief.

"Half an hour. Grand Jury investigations are routinely opened and routinely withdrawn. Getting the Grand Jury to *act* is a much more difficult proposition, but, of course, we're not looking for action. There are some problems, though."

"Like?"

"Like what do I subpoena? How many foundations did Craddock set up to feed Hanover House? Didn't he have some kind of business? Before I go to the bank and the phone company, I have to know what records I want to see. I don't even know what bank, or banks, he used."

"I already thought of that," Moodrow grunted. "The state investigated Craddock last year. The attorney general's office. If you could get a look at the paperwork, it'd most likely all be there."

"You're always thinking, Stanley."

"Please, Leonora. You know what's at stake here."

"All right, Stanley." She reached out and took his hand. "Betty is my friend, too. We'll get the information you want. It's Friday night." She looked at her watch. "No, make that Saturday morning. I'll go over to the attorney general's office as soon as it opens on Monday. If the information you want is there, I'll open up a Grand Jury investigation Monday afternoon. By Tuesday afternoon, I'll have the records you want."

It was almost two AM by the time they finished hammering it out. The delay, from Saturday to Tuesday, would work in their favor. Hopefully, with Moodrow sitting on his hands, Craddock would relax. The less pressure, the better. If Craddock felt safe, he might gather up the courage to leave his fortress.

A few minutes after Higgins and Tilley left, the phone rang in Moodrow's apartment. Moodrow, thinking it was Betty, grabbed it on the first ring. Connie Alamare's voice came as a complete surprise.

"Hey, Nero," she said, "how come I haven't heard from you? You forget about me? You don't like me anymore?"

"You know what time it is?" Moodrow grunted.

"I wanted to make sure my little *strunza* would be home to take my call. I figure the rest of the time you're busy looking for my grandson."

"What if I already know where he is?"

"I want my grandson, Moodrow."

"You know something, Connie, I'm beginning to care about you and your money less and less. Handing the kid over to you is gonna be like handing a mouse to a snake."

Moodrow expected a burst of high-power Italian, but Connie Alamare's voice, after a sharp hiss, was soft, almost yielding. "Maybe I'm looking for a way to make it up. To make it right."

"Then why don't you start with me?" He waited for a response, but Connie Alamare kept her thoughts to herself. "I'll be in touch."

THIRTY

Sleep would be long in coming. It was as obvious to Betty as the fact that insomnia meant less than nothing to her. She could lie on the bed as long as necessary. She could stare at the ceiling, her body bathed in physical comfort, while a string of images slid past her unfocused attention like luminous tropical fish in an aquarium. Even the bloody nature of her thoughts (*her* blood, *her* nature) provoked no anxiety. She compared herself to an Aztec led willingly, joyously to the sacrifice. To a soldier of Allah coveting a glorious, violent death.

She would have stayed like that, like a caterpillar waiting to become a butterfly, except that Michael Alamare, though he lay unmoving, wanted to talk.

"Why did my daddy bring you here?" he asked. "If you weren't bad, why did he bring you here?"

With no ready answer, Betty replied with a question. "Why did he bring *you* here, Michael?"

"I was bad. I didn't make my bed for three whole days. That's against the rules."

"How long have you been here?"

The boy hesitated for a moment, trying to count the days. "I don't know," he said. "I've been here for a *very* long time."

"Do you miss your friends?"

"Yes. I miss Bobbie. He was my *best* friend."

"Why doesn't your daddy let you go back to Hanover House?" She sat up and looked closely at him. He was pitifully thin and pale. An image jumped into her mind. She saw golden television children playing in the sun, cheeks radiant, and for the first time began to understand the meaning of the word psychopath.

"Because I'm sick. I have to have medicine," Michael said. "If he doesn't give it to me, the sickness comes back. My daddy says my sickness is catching."

"Do you know where your mother is?"

A hint of the misery hiding behind the dope glitter rose in his eyes. "No."

"Do you know that you have a grandmother?"

The boy rolled away from her. "I don't want to talk about it."

An emotion finally rose to the surface of Betty's consciousness. Even as she acknowledged it, she found it curious that hatred could motivate her, whereas fear left her unmoved. As a defense attorney, she'd been able to find some trace of humanity in the worst criminals, some hint of the pain that had brought them to a state of permanent violence. She could find nothing in Craddock, and she decided finally that evil, stripped to its essentials, carried no emotional baggage whatsoever.

She sat up on the bed and began to take a systematic inventory of the room and its furnishings. Her mind was clear and sharp, and once she'd gotten started, she found herself completely absorbed in her efforts.

She paced the room out, placing the heel of one foot to the toe of the other. Sixteen paces by twenty with windows on two walls. Obviously a corner room. She went to the windows, one by one, and tried to peer out. They were made of thick Plexiglas and carefully painted on the outside. She could make out a piece of the world surrounding her prison through a tiny chip in the paint on the outside of the window closest to the bed, a well-lit strip of lawn with trees and bushes at the edge, then darkness. There was no road, no driveway and no other houses.

She turned her attention back to the room, noting each of its sparse furnishings. A large bureau lay between the windows of the long wall. An ancient upholstered club chair sat atop a threadbare oval rug in the middle of the floor. Two plain wooden chairs had been pushed against a kitchen table near the door. A coloring book, a box of crayons and several children's books rested on the table. A closed door between the bed and windowless wall hid a tiny room with a sink and toilet.

Betty walked over to the rug and examined it closely. It consisted of a single, thick cord spiraling out from the center and held together with thread. Unwound, it would become a rope. There was no explosion of joy at the realization, just a nod of recognition. She crossed to the windows along the short wall and examined them closely. The Plexiglas was at least an inch thick, perhaps more, and clearly unbreakable. Could it be melted? Did she have matches? The frames were made of metal and set into the wall. How far? Could she dig it out? Push the window, frame and all, into the yard? She remembered Moodrow asking her to put a screwdriver in her purse, to carry it down to the car. The panel on the front door of his Mercury was coming loose and he'd wanted to tighten it. Unfortunately, he'd taken the wrong screwdriver. He'd needed the kind with a cross, but the one he'd given her had a single blade.

Her purse was on the floor by the bed. She picked it up and began to rummage through what she liked to call 'my junk.' The screwdriver was missing, which meant that Craddock had searched her bag, probably looking for a gun. He'd left her new toothbrush, though, along with a metal nail file which she slipped into her pocket. She looked at the toothbrush for a moment, tempted to go into the bathroom and brush. She'd never had a cavity in her life, a source of secret pride, and she cared for her teeth meticulously. Then she remembered a convict she'd defended several years before. He'd killed another convict with a knife made from a toothbrush. Curious, she'd asked him how he'd done it.

"Attica is a MAX A institution," he'd explained matter-of-factly. "Everybody has a weapon, even if they don't carry it all the time. I was a new fish and I hadn't run into anyone I knew yet, so I didn't have a way to get my hands on any metal. The toothbrush was all I had and I made do with it."

"What I'm asking is how you made the toothbrush into a weapon?"

The convict, a middle-aged man with a long history of incarceration, merely shrugged. "The floor of the cell was stone. I just sharpened one end to a point. Like an ice pick. It didn't have an edge, so I couldn't cut with it. Which is why I had to kill the dude. You hold it between your fingers and punch straight in."

Betty didn't stop to consider the strong probability that she wouldn't be able to kill in cold blood. The fact that she could make a weapon was enough for the moment. She looked back at the rug. A rope could be a means of escape, but it could also be a weapon.

Michael got off the bed and walked over to Betty, pulling at her hand. "What are you doing?"

"I'm looking at the room, Michael. Is that what they call you? Michael?"

"My daddy calls me that, but Bobbie calls me Mikey. Bobbie's my best friend."

"Can I call you Mikey?"

The boy hesitated for a moment, then said, "Okay."

"And you can call me Betty."

"Betty, why are you walking around the room? You can see it from the bed."

Instead of answering, Betty led the boy to the table and began to leaf through the coloring book. The pages had been meticulously colored, though the colors chosen by the boy were a long way from the blacks and grays that dominated Hanover House. Turquoise faces, violet trousers, lime-green ties, purple trees. Only the golden sun retained its identity from one page to the next.

"Did you do the coloring yourself, Mikey?"

"Yeah. It's pretty boring here. That's why I added things. Clouds and birds."

"It's wonderful. You must have been very careful." Though Betty felt an intense desire to protect the boy, she knew that he presented a problem. An escape attempt would take a good deal of preparation. It couldn't be done without Michael's knowledge.

"Mikey, when do you think your daddy's going to let you go?"

"I don't know." The boy looked away.

"Have you asked him?"

"He usually doesn't come here. He sends someone else with the food and my medicine."

"But have you ever asked when you can go home?"

"He says I can't leave until I get better. I have something that's catching."

"Did he say what kind of sickness you have?"

"I don't want to talk about it." He flipped the pages briefly. "Have you seen my mommy?"

"Yes, I have."

"Why doesn't she come to see me?"

"She's very sick and she can't get out of bed. She's living with her own mommy, your grandmother."

Michael looked up at her, trying to read her eyes. "When I get better, I'm gonna visit my grandmother."

"Mikey, were you sick before you came here?"

"No, my daddy brought me here because I was bad. I used to be good. I was the best boy in Hanover House, but after my mommy left, I started being bad. Flo was my birth-mommy, but I didn't have a bonding-mommy like most of the other kids. That's what my counselor said. That's why I started acting out."

Betty smiled at the psychological jargon. The propaganda started early at Hanover House. "But you weren't sick before you came here?"

"No."

"Were you ever sick before your daddy started giving you the medicine?"

The boy took his time, thinking it over. PURE brought its users into an eternal present that blurred the past and eliminated concern for the future. "I don't remember. I don't think so."

"Does the medicine make you feel good?"

"It takes away my sickness."

"I know, Mikey, but does it make you feel good, too?"

"You mean like drugs?"

The idea was obviously new to him and Betty gave him time to think it over. The boy's eyes were deep brown and his gaze, driven by PURE, was intense. "Why would my daddy give me drugs? My daddy's against drugs. He always talked about drugs at the general meetings."

"He gave the medicine to me, didn't he? And I'm not sick."

"Maybe you did something bad."

"He didn't give you the medicine because you were bad, remember? He gave it to you because you were sick."

The boy didn't respond, and Betty let it go at that. She left the table and began to walk around the room, pacing her cage like any other prisoner. Like all the clients she'd plea-bargained into jail. Choosing a spot at random, she thumped the heel of her hand against the wall and felt it give slightly. It was made of plasterboard. She'd once lived in an apartment with plasterboard walls. It was so thin she could listen to her neighbors making love in the adjoining apartment.

She took the nail file out of her pocket and began to scratch the wall carefully. This was only an experiment and she didn't want her efforts discovered. It was slow going, but she managed to get through the paint and into the layer of thick paper covering the plaster. Satisfied, she put the file back in her pocket and resumed her pacing.

The plasterboard would give way, but it would take time, perhaps days, to get through. She would have to hide the waste. How did they do it in jail? The ones who spent months, even years, digging tunnels? She'd defended prisoners charged with escape, but never one who'd dug a tunnel. Maybe they smuggled the dirt out of the cell and dumped it. That wouldn't help her. She'd have to find a way to hide it within the room. She crossed over to the bureau and pulled it away from the wall. It moved easily. Opening a drawer at random, she found Michael Alamare's wardrobe, a few pairs of underpants, some T-shirts, a gray jacket and a pair of jeans. The rest of the drawers were empty.

She looked across the room at Michael's bare feet. "Where are your shoes, Mikey? Do you have them?"

"My sneakers are under the bed. My daddy keeps the room very warm. I don't need them."

Betty, breathing a sigh of relief, continued to search the room. Yes, she could dig through the wall behind the bureau. She could hide the paint chips and the plaster in the drawers. But what would she find on the other side of the plasterboard? If the house was made of brick or stone, that would be the end of the escape.

Still exploring, she climbed to the top of the bureau and thumped on the ceiling. The hollow echo was louder here, meaning that the space between the ceiling and floor above was greater than between the inner and outer walls. If there was an attic up there, as she suspected, it might be easier to loosen a floor plank than to kick through the outer wall of the house. But there was no way to conceal the hole and there was no way to know what or who was in the attic. There were at least nine other people living in the house. The basement was taken up by the lab and she hadn't noticed any beds on the first floor.

She went back to the table and Michael, who was watching her intently. "I see you have some books, Michael. Can you read?"

"No," he admitted. "Not yet. I look at the pictures and make up stories."

"Really? What kind of stories?"

"I don't know. I look at the pictures and say whatever comes in my head."

"Would you tell me a story?"

"Okay, but let's go on the bed. Let's make it a bedtime story."

The title of the book was *Cooperation*. A group of small animals, rabbits, birds, chipmunks, etc., are menaced by a fox, but instead of hiding in their holes, they confront their enemy and convert him to their philosophy. The final page showed a gentle, toothless fox cavorting with its natural prey.

Simple enough, but the story Michael Alamare told bore no resemblance to the text. He found conflict everywhere. A robin facing away from the center of the action was hiding something. A happy ground hog showing its enlarged front teeth became an angry menace. A lamb appearing on one page, but not on the next, had been eaten by the fox. The animals didn't convert the fox. The fox converted the animals. He took control of their lives. The dancing animals on the final page were slaves and there was no happy ending.

Betty fell asleep without making a decision to sleep. She slept soundly and woke in a fog. Blossom was standing at the foot of the bed, shaking her. The Oriental girl held two syringes and a thin rubber tube in the palm of her hand. She quickly injected the contents of one syringe into Michael's arm, then offered the other to Betty.

"You must inject yourself."

"I don't think I can." Betty noticed Kenneth Scott in the doorway. Somewhere along the line, he'd abandoned his jacket, the better to reveal the large automatic resting on his hip. He was staring intently at the syringe in Blossom's hand. "Do *you* want it, Kenneth? Do you want the medicine?"

He looked up at her, his hatred undiminished by her generous offer. "Eve stands for evil. Eve brings evil into the garden. When the time comes, I will be the one to purge the garden. Davis has promised me this. Blossom, knock on the door when you're ready to leave." He stepped back and closed the door.

"I don't think he likes me. What do you think, Blossom? Does Kenneth Scott like me or not?"

"You must inject yourself."

"I've never done it before."

"I will show you this time, but I am not allowed to show you in the future. Are you right-handed?"

"Yes."

"First you put the tube around your left arm. Just above the elbow. Then you pull it back through the loop until it's tight and fold it under. Make a fist and hold it. There, you see how the vein near your elbow comes to the surface. That is where the needle must be put." She handed the syringe to Betty. "You can do this by yourself."

"Do you mind if I ask you another question?" Betty took the syringe, holding it gently in her palm. "Kenneth said he was going to 'purge the Garden.' He said Davis promised him. What do you think that means? 'Purge the Garden.' How many people does it include? How many until the garden is spanking clean?"

Betty stretched out a hand to rub Michael's head affectionately, wondering if Blossom would go right back to her mentor with the story of how Eve tried to corrupt her. And what the consequences might be. She decided that if Craddock trusted Blossom, he would laugh at the incident, seeing her pitiful attempt to corrupt Blossom as one more proof of his power over her. Power was what all psychopaths sought, power and control. On the other hand, if he didn't trust Blossom, he probably wouldn't allow them to be alone again. Kenneth Scott would remain in the room all the time.

"You must inject yourself. If you don't, Mr. Scott will come back inside."

"All right, Blossom, I'm convinced." Betty put the point against the skin covering her vein and tapped gently. To her surprise, it slid easily into her arm.

"Be careful not to go through the vein. Pull back on the plunger. Gently." A drop of blood appeared in the bottom of the syringe. "Good, now remove the tourniquet and finish injecting yourself."

As before, the rush was overwhelming, but, still, Betty managed to ask another question before Blossom left the room. "Blossom," she asked, "what are you doing here?"

"I'm learning to be free."

*   *   *

Davis Craddock, Blossom Nol and Kenneth Scott in tow, arrived after dark. It was exactly nine o'clock, though Betty had no way to know that. She saw the cellular phone, the two syringes, the absurd, lopsided grin. Suddenly, the sharp, sour taste of bile exploded in her throat. For a moment she thought she was going to vomit.

"What's the matter, Betty? You don't look well. But I'm sure a little medicine will make it all better."

"Fuck you, Craddock."

"Now I *know* you need your medicine." He offered a syringe, the confident smile glued to his face.

Betty struggled to get herself under control. On one level, she wanted the drug badly. The clarity, the energy, the floating safety, the physical comfort—it all reached out to her through the small, blue syringe in Craddock's hand."

"But I'm not sick, Davis," she said. "I haven't been sick at all, have I, Mikey?"

"That's right, Daddy," Michael said. "Betty hasn't been sick even one time."

"Now, now, Betty. You have to take your medicine. Then we'll phone your loved one and let him know that you're recovering nicely."

"Why does she have to take the medicine if she's not sick?" Michael persisted.

Craddock turned to Blossom, his smile transformed to an adolescent pout. "I should've dumped this kid a long time ago," he muttered.

"When will I get better, Daddy? When will I go home?"

"If you think you're all better, Michael, then maybe you shouldn't take your medicine."

The boy's face betrayed his confusion. There were far too many elements for a five-year-old to process—the effect of PURE, the misery of withdrawal, his imprisonment, the disappearance of his mother. "Maybe I should take it," he told Betty. It was closer to a question than a statement.

"Go ahead, Mikey," Betty said. "It's okay." Sooner or later, the child would have to go through the nightmare of withdrawal. If he survived. She looked over at Craddock. He was smiling again, offering the syringe. "No, Davis. You see, Mikey needs his medicine because he gets sick if he doesn't take it. But, as you can see, I'm perfectly fine."

"Kenneth," Craddock held the syringe out to the guard, "would you inject this into Ms. Haluka's shoulder?"

Scott took the syringe and walked over to Betty. He grabbed her by the hair, twisting fiercely, then slammed the syringe into her shoulder.

"In a week, you'll beg for it," Craddock promised.

"Never."

Craddock laughed, then dialed Moodrow's number on the cellular phone. "Stanley," he said, "are we being a good boy?" He listened for a moment, then shook his head. "Such language, Stanley. You should be ashamed. What? Now you're repeating yourself. Why don't you talk to your sweetheart?"

He passed the receiver to Betty. "Stanley," Betty said, "I'm . . ."

Craddock pulled the receiver away. "And that's it, Stanley. See you tomorrow, same time, same station."

Once again Betty found herself on the bed, cradling Michael Alamare while she considered her situation. The hatred she felt for Davis Craddock hadn't receded with the rush of the drug. Instead, it had overwhelmed her, and she was sorely tempted to abandon her escape plan and concentrate on making a weapon. Sooner or later, Craddock's arrogance would lead him into a mistake. Maybe he'd come without a guard. If she could take him out quickly . . . She pictured Craddock, a sharpened toothbrush deep in his chest, staggering backward. The image was comical. She could see the headline in the supermarket tabloids: GURU BRUSHED TO DEATH.

"Are you sick, Betty?"

Michael's voice seemed to come from a great distance and Betty had to force herself to answer. "No, Mikey, I'm not sick." She shifted her position on the bed and the creak of the bed springs awakened her to the obvious. The springs were made of metal, sharp metal. If she could break off a six- or eight-inch piece and fit it to a handle, she'd have a much more formidable weapon than her toothbrush . . .

"I want to go home," Michael said. "I don't wanna stay here anymore."

Betty pulled the child against her. "Do you think your father will give you permission?"

"No." He hesitated momentarily. "Anyway, I don't have a home."

"What do you mean?"

"My daddy's bad," he whispered. "My daddy doesn't wanna take care of me anymore."

"You have a grandmother, Mikey." Somehow, the image of Connie Alamare as loving grandma didn't work. Another problem to be dealt with later. "She has a big apartment and she wants you to live with her. You won't have to worry about anything."

Michael let his head fall back on the pillow. "It doesn't make a difference. My daddy won't let us go anyway."

THIRTY-ONE

Stanley Moodrow's decision, to sit still while Leonora Higgins probed for a paper trail, lasted almost thirty-six hours. He made it through Saturday and, to his surprise, fell asleep right after Craddock's phone call. He slept soundly, without dreaming, and woke, as many New Yorkers do, to the scream of fire engines racing past his window. It was eight-thirty. Still covered by an habitual morning fog, he showered and shaved before remembering that he wasn't going anywhere. He pulled on an old terry cloth robe, its fabric worn as smooth as linen, and headed for the kitchen and the coffee.

The percolator was sitting, unwashed, in the sink. He began to scrub it with a Brillo pad, then recalled Betty's reaction the first time she'd seen him cleaning it.

"Stanley," she'd said, "do you have any idea what the coffee's going to taste like? You have to use as little soap as possible."

"Brillo gives the coffee character," he'd protested, though he had no idea what she was talking about. Most of the time, he made one pot after another without doing more than emptying the percolator into the sink. By the time he got around to cleaning up, it took the better part of a new pad to cut through the crust.

Still operating on automatic pilot, Moodrow filled the percolator with tap water and spooned in the coffee, adding an extra measure as he always did, then watched as the water started to boil. Satisfied, he began to rummage through the refrigerator, looking for the eggs. He found an empty carton and remembered that Betty, on her way to Hanover House, had told him they were out of eggs and volunteered to buy some on her way back. He was about to settle for the instant waffles in the freezer when he made his first mistake. He wondered what Betty was doing and his stomach muscles contracted sharply. He could barely breathe.

After a moment, he retrieved the waffles, then returned to the refrigerator and a jug of Vermont maple syrup that Betty had found in a Union Square farmer's market. "This is the *real* thing, Stanley. You try this and you'll never go back to flavored corn sweetener."

He'd taken a taste and made the proper response, "Yeah, it's great," though he couldn't tell the difference between the *real* thing and Log Cabin.

The phone rang before the coffee was ready and Moodrow, suddenly alert, picked it up and grunted into the receiver. "Yeah?"

"Stanley? You all right?" It was Jim Tilley.

"Me? Why shouldn't I be? I'm sitting in my goddamned kitchen waiting for the coffee to boil."

And what was Betty doing?

"I'm sorry I asked."

"What's up, Jim?" Moodrow couldn't control his impatience.

"You want me to call you back later?"

"No, go ahead."

"Well, I had an idea last night. You familiar with Caller ID?"

"What?"

"Caller ID."

"Never heard of it."

"Why am I not surprised?"

"Gimme a break."

"Stanley, you sure you're all right?"

"This is gonna be a very short phone call if you don't get to the point."

"Okay. Caller ID is a system designed to let you know the phone number of the caller before you pick up the phone. The whole thing consists of a display unit that plugs into any phone jack."

"What's the difference between Caller ID and an ordinary trace?"

"The first difference is that Caller ID doesn't involve the cops or the phone company. The second is it displays the caller's phone number instantly, before you even pick up the receiver. There's no way anyone could get off the line before the person on the other end has the number. That's the good news."

"What's the bad news?"

"Well, aside from the fact that Craddock might be using a pay phone, Caller ID only works on calls originating within a given area code. If Craddock's calling from outside the 212 area, we won't get his number."

"Christ, Jim, that only covers Manhattan and the Bronx. He could be five miles away in Brooklyn and we'd have nothing."

"That's why I decided to call first. Most likely all we'd know is that she's not in Hanover House."

"We know that already."

"We'd know for sure."

Moodrow hesitated, trying to concentrate, trying not to think about Betty. "How easy would it be to get one of these things? What is it? Caller IDs?"

"The city's in the process of installing them in the precincts. And 911 already has them."

"Jesus," Moodrow interrupted, "you mean to tell me that everyone who calls 911 is gonna have their phone numbers recorded?"

"That's it."

"When the word gets out, people are gonna stop calling."

"It wasn't my idea, Stanley."

"Okay, Jim. Can you get the unit out of the precinct without attracting attention?"

"The city's waiting for NYNEX to make the installation. Meanwhile, the display units are in storage."

"I thought you said the system plugs into the phone jack. Why do the cops need NYNEX?"

"Ya know, Stanley, for a guy who wanted to get off the phone, you ask a lot of questions. How would I know why we need NYNEX? The fact is that the property clerk at the Seven owes me a favor. I'm gonna tell him that Rose's been getting obscene calls and promise to return the unit in the morning."

"Then there's no reason why we shouldn't do it. Craddock calls at nine o'clock. Can you come over at eight?"

"Sure. By the way, you said Craddock calls at nine. Did he call last night?"

Moodrow groaned. "Yeah, right on time."

"How did Betty sound?"

"Jesus." Moodrow looked desperately at the coffee pot. "She was only on the phone for a minute. Craddock's probably worried about a trace." He hesitated briefly. "She's alive. That's all I can say for sure."

"Stanley, you want me to come over this afternoon?"

"No, there's no sense in it. Get the Caller ID thing and come over at eight."

"I can hear your mind working, Stanley. Don't do anything stupid. Stay home."

The percolator shut off as Moodrow hung up the phone. He poured himself a cup and drank it down as if it was liquid Valium. Somehow, he expected it to calm him, but the sudden rush of caffeine jerked his fear into the present. Craddock might do anything. The problem with his, Moodrow's, rational analysis of Craddock's options was that it was rational. And Craddock wasn't.

It was nine-thirty when Moodrow finished breakfast. With nothing to do, he decided to go out for a newspaper. He glanced at the window and was surprised by the rain bouncing off the glass.

Betty's inside. She won't get wet.

The thoughts continued to rise, carrying their emotional burden, as he pulled on the same rumpled trousers he'd thrown onto the seat of a chair the night before. The white shirt he chose had spent the night underneath the pants. Oblivious, he shrugged into a tan raincoat. Was it warm out? Cold? He had no idea. He pulled a hat down over his ears, tossed a glance at the silent telephone and left.

He poured himself a second cup of coffee as soon as he got back, sipping at it quickly before hanging his wet raincoat over the tub in the bathroom. Returning to the kitchen, he opened the refrigerator door, took out the empty egg carton and threw it in the garbage. The refrigerator stunk. The whole house stunk.

He sat down at the kitchen table and opened the newspaper. He'd been reading the *Daily News* for as long as he could remember. Before the *Tribune* and the *Journal-American* and the *Mirror* went under. Before the newsprint cranked out by the ancient presses turned your fingers black. When nobody longed for cheap labor in New Jersey and lifetime job guarantees and shutting the goddamned paper down.

What was Betty doing? Right now, this very minute. Had she eaten? Where was Craddock?

The Sunday edition of the *News* was divided into about twenty sections and fifteen of them were bullshit. Moodrow went through the paper before he started reading it, tossing out the store coupons, the advertising circulars, the special section on weddings, *Parade* Magazine, City Lights, TV Week. He glanced at the comics, then added them to the pile; he hadn't read the comics in years, had no idea who most of the characters were. When he finally began to read, he started, as always, with the sports section. The Yankees were in fifth place and rumor had it that the manager was about to be fired. Phil Pepe's column was all about the persistence of the Steinbrenner syndrome in the thinking of Yankee management, even after Steinbrenner's departure.

Already bored, Moodrow continued to work backward through the paper. Tyson was in training again. Sugar Ray Leonard, still box office, was about to set up a third fight with Tommy Hearns. He, Moodrow, had once entertained boxing ambitions, had wanted to be the Heavyweight Champion of the World, the baddest of the bad. Unfortunately, he hadn't had the talent. His body was all right—his strength, stamina and especially his chin—but quicker, lighter heavyweights would stick and move, staying away until the final bell. Then, after the decision was announced, they'd embrace him quickly before raising their hands in victory.

Moodrow recalled a fighter named George Chuvalo, a heavyweight. If every fight had been to a finish, no bells and no rounds, Chuvalo would have been champion forever. As it was, he'd managed to work himself into the national rankings where the better fighters used him for a punching bag, though nobody ever managed to put him on his back.

The hard news in the front of the paper was depressingly familiar. Crime, venal politicians, a teacher turned crack junkie, waste in the Human Resources Administration, taxi drivers taking the long way in from Kennedy Airport. How long had he been reading this bullshit? Twenty years? Thirty? Betty had seen it all, too.

Did Betty have a newspaper? A television? She loved the Sunday morning interview shows. Meet the Press. Face the Nation. *What was she doing right now?*

Moodrow tossed the main body of the paper onto the pile of rejects. He was nothing, if not persistent. Persistence had characterized his career and his life. You did what you had to do without demanding results. He turned to the *Daily News Magazine*. The feature article on city housing ballyhooed the fact that despite a general economic down-turn affecting the Northeast, middle income rents in New York had continued to rise.

Big, fucking surprise, Moodrow thought. If it wasn't for New York City and the goddamn rents, he would have made the Sign of the Cross in Connie Alamare's face and run like hell the first time he'd met her. She was a lunatic, just like Davis Craddock. Moodrow had once threatened to lock Craddock in a room with Connie Alamare. He could picture it. An eight-by-five prison cell with a sink and a toilet. No showers. No books. No television. Deliver food twice a day and push it through the slot. Take the cocksuckers out in bodybags.

He pushed the *Daily News* aside and looked around the room. It was dirty. The whole apartment was dirty. Betty was always after him to clean it. Well, he *would* clean it. He had nothing else to do. Might as well get out the vacuum, the mop and the dust rags. Stay busy, keep his mind off Betty and what she was doing.

It took him three hours to complete the job and while his apartment wasn't exactly spotless when he finished, it was as clean as it was going to get. The area rug in the living room, a cheap Belgian import, was fifteen years old and the scarred maple furniture had never been polished.

What Betty gave you was a real life. A life in the world. What you gave her was death. You let her go into Hanover House, because you were afraid that she'd call you names. You should have phoned Craddock, in Betty's presence, and told him the truth about his new client. She would have had to stay home, like it or not. Michael Alamare or not. But you were afraid she'd call you names.

It was nearly two o'clock when Moodrow finally stuffed the vacuum cleaner back into the closet. Hungry, as always, he made himself a ham sandwich, opened a can of beer and sat down in front of the television. Somehow, the cable revolution had missed him and the images on the screen, no matter which way he turned the rabbit ears, carried definite ghosts. But he'd been watching it that way for years and he didn't mind seeing two baseballs hurled by two pitchers at two batters. What he minded was baseball in general.

He flicked the selector from channel to channel. Baseball, golf, swimming, golf, baseball. An old movie on channel five. *Sesame Street* on PBS.

Betty is the only thing in your life besides the idiot flatfoot game you've been playing for the last thirty-five years. What is she doing now? Right now? Why did all this have to begin on a weekend? How am I going to sit still for the next day and a half?

The recriminations continued to flow, along with his fear. The problem was that he had no answers, not even bad ones. He shouldn't have allowed her to go into Hanover House. It was as simple as that.

By four o'clock, he knew he had to get out. If he didn't expend the energy physically, his mind would spin out of control. He didn't need that. He needed clarity. The endgame would be harrowing enough, even if he managed to remain calm.

He was on the street before he noticed that it had stopped raining. New York City, usually protected by prevailing offshore winds, was covered by a rare, dense fog. Not that the streets were empty. The sun had already dropped behind the taller buildings, but people had come out as soon as the rain stopped. They were gathered on the stoops of the tenements, sipping at cans of beer or soda, passing the Sunday afternoon in the manner of poor people everywhere.

Driven by apprehension, Moodrow walked briskly. This was *his* neighborhood. He'd grown up in it, protected it, loved it deeply. He was recognized and greeted from time to time, but he merely grunted a reply and kept on moving. He went north, up Avenue B and away from Hanover House. The dealers on 2nd and 3rd streets were out in force, trying to make up for the business lost in the rain. Sunday afternoon business was usually brisk as the weekend junkies made their last purchases before resigning themselves to the work week. The dealers saw Moodrow coming, of course, and the pack took a collective breath as he passed by, then resumed their activities. Many of them knew Moodrow, though nobody had the balls to actually greet him. Being streetwise, they also knew he was retired.

Moodrow paused in front of a fenced lot that had been transformed into an impromptu sculpture garden. The art scene on the Lower East Side, though not as well known (or as rich) as that in Soho, had been around since the 1950s. Most of the sculptures had been constructed by welding pieces of heavy steel together. Many were decorated with the detritus of civilization—old sneakers, plastic jugs, varnished newspaper, empty bottles. It was repulsive and beautiful at the same time, an ambiguity emphasized by the heavy fog. Betty had come here often. She knew a few of the artists personally.

He moved on, walking all the way to 14th Street without stopping. On the far side of the street, the red brick buildings of Stuyvesant Town rose 120 feet into the air. Moodrow noted the security booths set up to guard the roads leading into the complex. Stuyvesant Town, owned by Metropolitan Life, was middle-income, mostly white, and a long step up from the tenements of the Lower East Side.

It never changes. Just like you never change. Without Betty, you don't have a life. Why didn't you stop her? You don't even have a plan to get her out.

He walked west along 14th Street to Avenue A, then turned south. By the time he reached Houston Street, a half block from his apartment, he was almost running. He crossed Houston, dodging the light traffic, and continued down Essex Street, past Delancey with its busy shops, past Broome and Grand streets. At Hester Street, once the heart of the Jewish Lower East Side, he turned west again, his pace gradually slowing. At the corner of Ludlow and Hester, he stopped altogether.

It was six o'clock, nearly dark, though the sun wouldn't set for another hour, and the harsh realities of tenement life, sooty stone, broken stoops and doors, abandoned buildings, had been softened by the dense fog. Families were home, enjoying the last bit of their weekend, and the lighted windows glowed invitingly in the fog. Except for the three buildings in the center of the block. Hanover House was entirely dark and clearly deserted.

Moodrow stood on the corner for more than half an hour. He felt Hanover House beckoning to him like a prostitute in a whorehouse window. An invitation, obviously, but to what? Old telephone bills with itemized long-distance records stuffed into a forgotten file cabinet? A checkbook left in a desk drawer? Craddock and his minions had abandoned Hanover House in record time. Had they cleaned it out? It didn't seem possible.

He crossed to the east side of Ludlow Street and began to walk north, toward Grand Street, checking Hanover House as he went. There was no sign of a burglar alarm, no sign of any security. Craddock only needed a few weeks. Maybe the commune's abrupt closing had been an act of desperation. Maybe it hadn't been planned out. Maybe Craddock was stitching it together a piece at a time.

Moodrow paused in front of the main entrance to Hanover House, then, with no real expectations, walked to the door, turned the knob and, much to his surprise, pushed it open.

THIRTY-TWO

When Davis Craddock showed up early Sunday morning, PURE in hand and Blossom following two steps behind, Betty Haluka was not surprised to find her hatred for him undiminished. What surprised her was that she was no longer angry. Her anger had been replaced with a sense of purpose. And she no longer blamed herself for her imprisonment. She'd been right all along. Michael Alamare, five years old and desperate for affection, had slept in her arms. Her fears for his safety had been entirely justified. A child in danger? An innocent five-year-old, his mother nearly dead and his father insane? Abused beyond reason? She decided that one way or another, Davis Craddock was going to pay. If she couldn't find a way to escape, she could certainly get close enough to hurt him. To, for instance, push a nail file into his left eyeball.

She looked closely at Craddock. He was dressed in a sweat-stained T-shirt and black trousers. There was no place to conceal a weapon— even his pockets were flat. Could his belief in his own personal power be so great that he couldn't entertain the possibility that his slaves might decide to rebel? Perhaps he believed that PURE, his wonder drug, would enslave anyone who tried it, that addiction was entirely physical. But, whatever his motivation, he'd come into the room without Kenneth Scott and without a weapon.

"Let me apologize for Mr. Scott's behavior last night," Craddock said. "He was unnecessarily rough and I want you to know that I had a long talk with him. He's promised to behave more civilly in the future."

"Is that why you promised him that he could personally 'purge the garden'?"

Craddock sighed, shaking his head. "Kenneth is a very enthusiastic individual when properly motivated. A bit unpredictable, it's true, but I see it as a trade-off. I also see it as a challenge. Can I control him? Will he rip your head off one day when I'm not around? It's an interesting situation when you think about it. Now, please, it's time for your medication. Doctor knows best, right?"

Betty took the syringe from Craddock, took it eagerly, as if she'd been longing for it all night. In fact, she had no real desire for it, just as she'd never felt any real desire for alcohol. An occasional drink was a social necessity, but the few times she'd gotten drunk had left her with nothing more than a headache, an upset stomach and a desire to never repeat the experience. PURE was pleasurable, but Stanley had been right. She wasn't an addict. It was that simple.

"Well, well." Craddock's grin was both triumphant and condescending. "Are we beginning to appreciate the benefits of PURE? You know what, Betty? The next time I come up, I may have to ask you to do something to earn your fix. What do you think? Is she ready?"

Blossom, busy with Craddock's son, didn't answer.

"Blossom?"

"Yes, Davis?"

"Do you think Betty is ready? Oh, dear, I made a rhyme. I'm a poet and I know it. Well, Blossom, what do you think? Is the fruit ripe for plucking?"

"I don't know what you mean."

"S-E-X, Blossom. With you. Is that clear enough?"

"Michael is here, Davis," Blossom said quietly. "The child would see."

Craddock, his leer firmly in place, stared at her through dead eyes. "Somehow, I can't understand why that matters." He turned back to Betty. "Anyway, I'm happy to report that my work is going well. My helpers labor like ants in a hive. They're *so* anxious to earn their PURE. I've set productivity standards and I reward those who exceed their quotas with an extra ration of . . . Guess what? Do you know about rats and cocaine? If you give rats an unlimited supply of cocaine, they eat it until they die. They ignore *everything*—food, water, sex. They eat it and eat it until their little hearts explode. And, of course, cocaine is nothing compared to PURE. PURE is heroin and cocaine multiplied by ten."

"Then it's drugs," Michael Alamare's angry voice surprised everyone. "And I'm *not* sick. I want to go home."

Craddock's smile vanished abruptly. "A reasonable request. I have to admit it. And a reasonable request calls for a serious response. Here it is: if you don't shut the fuck up, Michael, I'm gonna beat your fucking brains out."

He got what he wanted. Michael Alamare allowed Blossom to finish, then fell back on the bed and turned his face to the wall.

"That was the thing I hated most," Craddock announced, turning toward the door. "The rug rats. I've never liked kids, but, as Hanoverian therapy is dedicated to the production of properly socialized children, I couldn't very well refuse to work with them. It was quite a learning experience for me. They'll believe anything, if you start when they're babies. In the early days, I even dreamed of hanging around the guru scene long enough to produce a little army of fully programmed adolescents. But things didn't work out. Or did they?"

Once Craddock was gone, Michael turned away from the wall to face Betty. The misery in his eyes didn't come from his father's harsh words or the knowledge that his father had deliberately addicted him. It was the look of a child with nothing to believe in and Betty recognized it immediately. His mother had disappeared and he'd been taken from the only home he'd ever known. No surprise that he'd clung to his father's lie: he was sick, but if he took his medicine, he'd go home as soon as he got better. Now there was nothing left. Michael was adrift and he knew it.

Betty took the child by the hand and drew him close to her. She wondered if he would ever be able to deal with what had happened to him. And if Connie Alamare was the one to help him deal with it. But, of course, in order to have a chance, he would have to survive. She thought of Moodrow and hoped he'd managed to stay calm and that he wasn't sitting by the phone and that he'd come after her.

"We've got to get out of here," she said quietly. "You understand that, don't you, Michael?"

"Yes." His voice was angry. "My daddy's a dope dealer."

"I want you to go over and put your ear against the door. If you hear someone coming, let me know. But don't shout. We've got to be very, very quiet."

"What are you gonna do?"

"I'm going to look inside the bed and see if there's something in there I can use to make a . . . a tool."

"From the bed?"

"Maybe from the springs. I don't know, Michael. That's why I want to look inside. But I don't want your father to find out."

"Okay. That makes sense." He went over to the door and put his ear to the wood. "Nobody coming," he whispered.

Betty, turning to her work, was grateful for the drug, PURE. Despite her distaste, PURE had done its job. She felt energetic and peaceful at the same time. She knew what she had to do, and she was going to approach it step by step. Craddock's confidence was a weapon she could use. But only so long as he thought of her as helpless. Even his threat—to make her perform—was simply another part of the equation. She might have to deal with it, but she wouldn't let it interfere with her plans.

She pulled the mattress away from the wall and turned it until the leading edge was facing her. Punching a hole in the fabric, she worked the tip of the nail file back and forth. The hole slowly enlarged, but the metal tore at her skin. She took a handkerchief from her purse, wrapped one end of the file and went back to work. It was slow going—the file had no edge and she had to use the point to gouge a long tear in the fabric—but she got through it. Unfortunately, there were no springs in the mattress, just a single, thick piece of styrofoam.

"Somebody's coming," Michael whispered.

Betty pushed the mattress against the wall and sat on the edge of the bed. She felt no urgency, no sudden acceleration of her heart. Once again, she pictured a convict digging a tunnel. The tunnel might take months, even years to complete.

"Okay. They're gone."

The box spring was resting on a metal frame. It would have to be lifted before she could turn it toward her. And the mattress would have to come off altogether. She tested the mattress and found it to be extremely light. She could stand it against the wall while she worked. The problem was the blanket and single sheet. It would take several minutes to remake the bed and she wouldn't have that much time if Craddock showed up unexpectedly.

"How come you're not doing nothing?" Michael asked, his ear still tight against the door.

"I have a little problem. Come over here and I'll tell you about it."

She explained it quickly, the useless mattress, why she couldn't take it off and what she wanted to do with the box spring. Michael, his face so serious Betty couldn't help but smile, listened closely.

"Maybe," he said, after due consideration, "you could work on the other end and cover the hole with the blanket."

"We'd be taking a big chance. What if the blanket comes off?"

"That's true." He circled the bed, his hands clasped behind his back. "Let's try to slide it backwards."

Michael tugged at the foot of the bed, and the frame, obligingly set on castors, moved several inches. Betty pushed from the top, and together they moved the bed, box spring, mattress and frame several feet away from the wall.

"Why didn't I think of that?" Betty asked.

Michael's proud grin earned him a quick hug. "Now," Betty said, "you go back to the door and I'll get to work."

The box spring was so close to the floor that Betty had to lie on her side in order to work. With much of her weight supported by her left arm, she lost most of her leverage. Nevertheless, she persevered, hacking at the fabric until she opened a foot-long strip in the material. She looked inside, but except for a gleam of metal, she couldn't see anything. The only light in the room came from the fixture in the ceiling. The blackened windows added to the gloom. She reached into the darkness and felt the individual springs. They seemed to be tied down with some kind of twine. She tugged at one of the coils and it moved a little. Not much, but at least they weren't welded onto some kind of a frame.

"I have to get my reading glasses." She pushed herself to her feet and went to get her purse. "I can't see a thing."

"Get the lamp," Michael advised, still whispering as if his father was on the other side of the door. "From the bathroom."

"From the bathroom?"

"Yes. The lamp."

Then Betty remembered that the fixture in the bathroom didn't work. Someone had put a small lamp on the toilet's water tank. "Why didn't I think of that?"

They went into the bathroom together, Michael giggling all the way. Betty unplugged the lamp, then abruptly plugged it back into the socket. "Hold the lamp, Mikey. I want to look at something." She lifted the tank cover and examined the plumbing inside. The toilet's handle was connected to a short length of wire which was, in turn, connected to the rubber stopper at the bottom of the tank. Pushing on the handle lifted the stopper and allowed the water to run into the toilet. As the water ran down, the stopper dropped back to cover the opening. A valve in the left-hand corner of the tank opened as the water level went down, then closed when the tank was full again. The valve was connected to an empty plastic float with a six-inch metal rod. The rod was threaded at both ends. Easy enough to remove, but without the float, the water would run continuously. Still, there must be some way to shut the water off in order to do repairs. She looked behind the toilet and found a valve attached to the pipe running into the bottom of the tank. She twisted it closed, unscrewed the rod and held it up for Michael's inspection.

"It needs a little work, but I think it'll do."

"How can we go to the bathroom?" Michael wrinkled his nose in distaste. "It's sure gonna smell in here."

Smiling, Betty flushed the toilet, allowing the water to run out before opening the valve in the pipe. She waited until the tank filled, then closed the valve. "Does anyone ever use this bathroom besides you?"

"No."

"Then I guess we're in business. You go back to the door. Listen carefully, because it's almost time for lunch. I'm going to rub this rod against the bed frame until it's nice and sharp."

The rod Betty removed from the water tank was not made of steel. It was brass, a far softer metal. If it had been steel, sharpening it to a point would have taken the better part of a week. As it was, she didn't finish until an hour after dark. The fingertips of both her hands were blistered from the constant rubbing. Even as she held the finished work aloft, Betty knew that she had a problem. The seven-inch rod, threaded at one end and sharp enough to pierce the hardwood floor, would make a formidable weapon. But only if she could find a way to hold it, to make a handle.

In any event, Craddock would be along soon. Time to get ready. The bed rail farthest from the door (and, thus, farthest from the eyes of Davis Craddock) was deeply and obviously scratched.

"Mikey," Betty said, "would you bring me two crayons? Gray and black."

Michael, thoroughly bored with his sentry duty, obeyed eagerly. "What're you gonna do?"

"I want to cover these scratches." She pointed to the scarred bed rail. "But I'm also very tired. Maybe you could do it for me."

Michael, grinning his proudest grin, bent to the task. Betty watched him examine the rail carefully. "The black is no good," he announced. "We need light blue and gray."

Suddenly tired, Betty lay back on the bed. She examined her fingers once again. Craddock was coming soon and his threat was becoming more immediate. Betty was not about to participate in Davis Craddock's perversions. If he insisted, she would take her weapon and use it as best she could. Consequences be damned.

She slid the sharpened rod underneath her belt, then tightened the belt until the rod was held firmly. Her blouse, pulled out, would cover the weapon. Now she could concentrate on making a handle. The problem with the naked metal was that it was too slippery to hold in her fist the way she'd hold a knife. And if she tried to put it against the palm of her hand, it would cut her almost as badly as its intended target.

The obvious solution was a piece of wood, perhaps a bed slat. But how would she fasten the metal to the wood? She had no tools. Even if she managed to gouge a hole in the wood, the rod would fall out when she tried to swing it. Wrapping one end in cloth, her handkerchief, for instance, would produce the same unhappy result.

The door opened half an hour later, and Betty, still without a solution, sat up quickly. She tapped the sharpened rod in her belt, looking for some reassurance, but Craddock's face didn't appear in the doorway. Blossom came in, bearing a tray of food and the inevitable PURE, followed by Kenneth Scott carrying a newspaper and a telephone.

"Davis says to tell you he's busy fixing a machine and he can't come personally," Scott announced, tossing the paper onto the table. "He says to tell you the paper's a wedding present, and he's real happy to see that your face isn't on the front page. He says to tell you he'll see you tomorrow. In the meantime, you call the serpent. You say, 'I'm okay,' then you hang up. No bullshit."

Instead of handing the phone to Betty, he put it down on the table, then backed into the doorway. Betty did as she was told, reciting her one sentence in a strong, clear voice, before dropping the receiver onto the cradle.

"Are you a dope dealer, too?" Michael suddenly asked.

Scott lifted his rifle until the barrel was pointed, not at Michael, but at Betty. "You've destroyed everything. Now you're trying to turn the kid against us." His eyes narrowed to slits and the muscles on his neck stood out sharply. For a moment, Betty thought she was dead, then Blossom stepped directly between them.

"You must take this," she said, holding out the obligatory dose of PURE. "We are very busy and we can't stay here all night. Kenneth, you know Davis told you not to stay in the room after the phone call was completed. You mustn't disobey him."

Scott's mouth opened in amazement. How could Blossom Nol, Craddock's latest sexual toy, dare to order him about? But the threat, to tell the boss about his employee's failure to follow instructions, was sharp enough to jar him back to his senses. He tossed Blossom a look that clearly equated her with the evil afoot in the garden, then spun on his heel and exited.

"Why did you do that, Blossom?" Betty asked. "Why did you step in to help us?"

"I was following instructions."

"I don't believe you, Blossom. You know what he wanted to do, and you put yourself between us. Davis Craddock didn't tell you to do that." Betty felt no great surge of hope. Blossom was, without doubt, the proverbial weak link, but her intervention didn't necessarily mean the link was actually broken. Blossom was just another piece of the escape tunnel. "Tell me something, Blossom, do you really think that Davis Craddock is going to let me go? Do you really think he'll let Michael go? What did you accomplish by risking your life? And what's going to happen to you when he's finished with you? You said you wanted freedom, but . . ."

"You must take this," Blossom interrupted. "Before he comes back in to check on you. Please."

Betty took the syringe from Blossom and injected herself quickly. The rush of PURE threatened to overwhelm her and she sat down on the edge of the bed. Satisfied, Blossom knocked once on the door. Scott opened immediately, allowed her to leave, then slammed the door and locked it behind him.

Michael and Betty moved slowly toward the tray of food, canned chili on a bed of white rice. There were no utensils and they had to eat with their fingers. Neither had an appetite. Caught up in the effect of the drug, eating was closer to an obligation than a pleasure. Nevertheless, they picked at the single plate of food and Betty, looking at the bits of rice clinging to her blistered fingertips, suddenly and without warning, had the answer to the problem of a handle for her weapon.

She left the table, Michael trailing behind, and went back into the bathroom. Opening the top of the water tank, she retrieved the plastic float and examined it closely. The round ball was much too large to make a handle, but a small nipple, two inches or so, projected from one end of the ball and was threaded to accept the rod. Working on the other end of the ball, Betty began to break off small pieces of the plastic.

She worked carefully, forgetting that Michael wasn't at his listening post, ignoring the sharp pain in her fingertips. Ten minutes later, she was left with two inches of threaded plastic with a small flare at one end. She twisted it onto the rod as far as she could, until an inch of the thread projected from the back end. Then she filled the sink with hot water and methodically softened the bar of soap. Once the outer surface was pliable, she squeezed it in her fist to create finger grips, then pushed it onto the dull end of the rod until it was tight against the plastic nipple.

"C'mon, Michael, we're almost done." Without waiting for an answer, she walked swiftly to the bureau in the other room and took Michael's extra pair of jeans out of the drawer. The denim was tough, the cuff tightly stitched, but she managed to separate a long strip of material from one leg. She wrapped the fabric tightly around the softened bar of soap and tied it down over the plastic nipple. It was a weapon, now, an icepick. Solid and deadly.

"Are you going to hurt my daddy?"

THIRTY-THREE

Wendell Bogard was a happy man. The first phase of his plan to become the Emperor of PURE was almost complete. After weeks of frustration, he'd managed to get an appointment with a Los Angeles wholesaler named Dinky Thomas—the plane tickets were in his pocket. Dinky's Los Angeles–based posse was dealing all up and down the West Coast, from San Diego to Seattle. If Dinky Thomas decided to buy (and he would, just like the rest of them), Wendell would have orders for every last gram of Craddock's run before the manufacturing was completed. Life was good. Damn, but it was good. And getting better all the time.

Unfortunately, the sample Dinky was demanding, a thousand packaged doses, was larger than Wendell's reserves, but Davis Craddock had come through, right on schedule. The man had sent one of his slaves to Hanover House with a small package and instructions to leave it in a place Wendell Bogard remembered well. The delivery had been scheduled for early afternoon and Wendell, with no wish to be seen by the messenger (eyeball witnesses make prosecutors drool), had arrived in the early evening. He'd gone directly to Craddock's living quarters, to a familiar closet, lifting several floorboards to reveal three large Ziploc bags resting on a pile of video tapes. He removed the bags, casually stuffing them between the silk underwear and T-shirts in the suitcase he'd brought for his trip to the coast.

Wendell glanced at his Rolex (all the big players wore Rolexes; it was almost an ID card) and frowned. It was five-thirty-five and his plane was scheduled to leave at nine-fifteen. Well, better to see the bright side, maintain that positive attitude. Now, there was time to play. He reached back into the hole and took up the video tapes, remembering Craddock's documentary on the demise of Deeny Washington. Unfortunately, Davis had removed *that* little gem. The man wasn't entirely crazy, after all. But the triple-X porno tapes in Wendell's hand would serve to pass the time.

Wendell thought of Marcy Evans and little Blossom Nol and Davis Craddock's personal style. The dope business was so grim. Brothers walking around in thousand-dollar suits, wearing diamonds on their fingers, and still looking like they wanted to kill every motherfucker in the room. But Davis Craddock was *always* ready to play. Not that there was any soft to the man. The man did what he had to do, bad as any brother, but he played even when he had to be hard.

His own life had always been hard, hard and unforgiving. The street didn't allow for slack. It demanded unrelenting vigilance. The street would take anything you had, even if it was a pair of raggedy sneakers and a Yankee baseball cap. That had happened to him. He was eight years old and trying to stay away from his alcoholic auntie when a crew he didn't know dragged him into an alley and stripped him down. The sneakers and jeans they snatched were old and worn (though his auntie would still put a whipping on his butt for losing them), but the cap was brand-new. A sympathetic social worker had bought it for him at the only baseball game he'd ever seen.

Crying didn't help. It didn't make him feel better. What made him feel better was catching some other street kid and taking *his* baseball cap. And his goddamn sneakers which were only ten times better than Wendell's. And then smuggling an eight-inch carving knife past his drunken aunt in case some other crew decided to renew the cycle. He was eight years old and ready.

Well, there was no doubt about it, the streets were hard. Even the basketball games were like wars. Play meant prey. That's what really made the little street rats happy. *All* the little street rats and, Lord knows, there were plenty of them. Hungry kids everywhere. Looking to grab a piece of the nothing they shared.

Wendell flipped on the TV and the VCR, pushed in one of the tapes and sat back in an overstuffed chair. The label on the tape said *Lickety Split*, but the tape was homemade. It began with Davis Craddock lecturing four women.

"You can never be free," he proclaimed, "if you've never been a slave. Freedom isn't natural. You're not born with it. It's not like eyesight or hearing. It's a higher state and can only be achieved through personal effort. You have to dump every vestige of the conditioning that imprisons you. It doesn't happen overnight. There's no sudden flash of insight to lift you into higher consciousness. Freedom flows directly from years of grueling work. Do you understand what I'm saying?" The women nodded gravely. "All right, you may begin."

Wendell shook his head in wonder. The bitches didn't waste any time getting into it. Ordinary women stripping out of their clothes. Hugging, then kissing, then moving on. Not even attractive. See them on the street, he wouldn't turn his head if they were strutting down Avenue B with a finger up their ass. But, somehow, Craddock's video was incredibly erotic. It was hotter than any porno film he'd ever seen. That was because they *wanted* to do it, because their cries of pleasure were genuine, as were their gyrating hips. They were saving their souls, putting their hearts, minds, fingers and tongues into the effort.

Sometimes you gotta do what you gotta do. It doesn't matter how many bitches are begging for a chance to sit on your cock if you're alone watching four women gobbling away on the goddamn TV. Wendell did what he had to do, then, his objectivity (and his equilibrium) restored, sat back to enjoy the rest of the show.

Ten minutes later, the women finished the exercise, dressed and returned to their seats. Craddock's face reappeared on the screen and he began to lecture once again.

"Children, up until the age of five, should be understood as sponges, soaking up the world around them. This is not to say that heredity plays no part in human development, only that environment flows into heredity like a river flowing into the sea. Using the analogy, it's easy to see that, while the sea remains fixed, while an individual's genetic inheritance cannot be altered, the more rivers flowing into the sea, the greater the mix of cultural nutrients. The nuclear family overlooks this simple truth altogether. During those crucial five years in an individual's development, the influences come almost entirely from the mother, father and siblings."

Wendell laughed out loud. Crazy white fucker making sugar out of shit. The four women staring at him through worshipful eyes. And the man didn't believe a *word* of what he was saying.

Wendell shook his head and, out of the corner of one eye, saw Stanley Moodrow come into the room. "Damn," he said, his hand streaking toward the .45 tucked into his trousers.

An ordinary citizen confronted by a very large man reaching for a very large gun will freeze, at least momentarily. Long enough, certainly, to make a perfect target. Moodrow, on the other hand, was well trained. A seasoned veteran. Which is not to say that he reacted calmly. His heart rate shot up with the suddenness of a jazz drummer beginning a solo. A voice in his head began an unrelenting scream: *oh no no no oh oh no no oh no oh no oh no no no no no gun gun gun gun gun*. It played a violent counterpoint to a second voice whispering calm instructions: *He's got a gun. A .45. He's faster than you. Reach for your weapon. Don't make a mistake. He's got the first shot. It's an automatic. He's right-handed. He doesn't practice. The gun will pull. High and to the right. Step to his left. Don't touch the trigger. Clear the holster. Watch the hammer. Watch your jacket. Come straight up. Sight the target. Before you shoot. Sight the target. Don't jerk. Squeeze, squeeze, squeeze.*

Moodrow watched Bogard's .45 sail through the air, watched Bogard fall backward to the floor. He turned away and saw the neat row of holes in the wall behind him. The first hole was two inches from his head, but each succeeding hole was farther to the right and a little higher on the wall. Funny, he hadn't heard the roar of Wendell's .45 while the report of his own well-worn .38 still echoed in his ears.

Wendell couldn't move. Kept asking his body to get moving, go after the .45. *Do* something. But the only part of him that moved was his head.

The blood was running, though. He could feel the blood running down his belly. Hear it dripping onto the carpet. He could see the white man with the revolver coming toward him. Could hear him draw back the hammer. Could understand the words he spoke: "Where's Craddock? Where's he hiding?"

But he couldn't concentrate on the questions. Abou was crowding into his mind. Abou and his warning not to trust a white man, not even a *crazy* white man. Craddock was sitting out there somewhere. Sitting on a pile of white powder that would turn into more money than Wendell had ever seen. Meanwhile, he, Wendell Bogard, was listening to his life drip onto the carpet. He tried to say "Motherfucker," but the only sound that came from his mouth was the liquid gush of dark arterial blood flowing over his lips.

Moodrow's heart began to slow as he stood over Wendell Bogard and realized that the man would never tell him anything. If someone outside had heard the shots and was even now dialing the police, he, Moodrow, was going to be in a lot of trouble. He was tempted to leave immediately, but he knew that gunfire was common on the Lower East Side and the Chinese living in the surrounding tenements as clannish as any ethnic group in New York City. No one had come to investigate the gunfire, which meant that Hanover House was empty. He wouldn't get this opportunity again.

He took off his coat and jacket, then rolled up his shirtsleeves. The blood would come off his skin with the application of a little soap and water, but once it sunk into fabric, it would be almost impossible to remove. He dropped to his knees and began to go through Wendell's pockets, retrieving the bags of PURE as well as the plane ticket to Los Angeles. He noted the departure time, then glanced at his watch. It was just possible that Wendell was making the trip alone, that he wouldn't be missed for a few days.

The PURE went into Moodrow's pocket. He had his sample, now. The lab would be able to prove that Davis Craddock's dope had reduced Flo Alamare to a vegetable and poisoned at least three other people. The case was made. He rolled Wendell Bogard over and dug into the carpet with a small pocket knife, retrieving the single slug he'd fired. Cushioned by the carpeting, it was, as expected, in excellent condition. He put it in his pocket. The cops would find Bogard eventually, but they wouldn't be able to trace the shot that killed him to Moodrow's .38.

Craddock's private quarters, thoroughly searched, revealed nothing. Moodrow was looking for business records, filing cabinets, office desks. He went from room to room, flicking lights on briefly, glancing at dormitories, meeting rooms, kitchens, dining rooms. He crossed to the center building and worked from the bottom up, finding more of the same until he got to the top floor, the combined offices of the Hanover Foundation, which ran the commune, and Hanover House-keeping, Inc. A row of gray filing cabinets lined the wall beneath the windows. They were still full, proof of the haste with which Craddock had abandoned the commune.

Moodrow pored through the drawers, looking for accounts payable, thumbing folder after folder until he found the ones he wanted: Citibank, Chase Manhattan, New York Telephone, The Long Island Lighting Company. He stuffed them into a large manila envelope lying on one of the desks. There might be more, but he couldn't afford to wait around. He turned the light out behind him as he left.

It was only seven o'clock when he got back to his apartment, but he wasn't surprised to find Jim Tilley waiting for him. Nor was he surprised when Tilley took one look at him and asked, "What happened, Stanley? What'd you do?"

Moodrow unlocked the door and walked inside before answering. Then he recited the details of his adventure as if it had taken place years before. The future was pulling him along, all the things he had to do before Betty was free and Craddock where he belonged. He couldn't afford to dwell on the past, even if the past involved bullets screaming by his skull.

"You mean to tell me," Tilley said, "that you went into that room without your weapon in your hand? You're even crazier than I thought."

"I'm not a cop," Moodrow explained. "At the very least, I was trespassing. And I knew Craddock wasn't there. If I walked in with a gun in my hand and someone recognized me, the boys at the Seven would have me tied up for days."

"Stanley, you almost got shot."

Moodrow giggled. "Well, it was a judgment call."

"It was almost judgment fucking *day*."

Moodrow responded by tossing the envelope on the table. "Let's cut the bullshit and get to work, all right?"

Fifteen minutes later they had what they wanted. Someone had made dozens of calls to the same number in the 516 area code which covered two-thirds of Long Island, including Shelter Island. Tilley called a special number, 555-4355, and reached a NYNEX supervisor. He gave her his badge number and she forwarded his request to a 516 operator. It took less than a minute to convert the number to an address. Eleven Bucks Creek Road. Moodrow thumbed quickly through the Long Island Lighting Company bills and found what he wanted. Despite the bills having been addressed to The Hanover Foundation, the address of the actual consumer was printed clearly on each bill: Eleven Bucks Creek Road.

The urge to get moving, to jump in the car and drive a hundred miles an hour all the way to Shelter Island was so powerful that Moodrow felt like he was being sucked out of the chair. Of course, he wouldn't be going anywhere until after Craddock's nine o'clock call. If he wasn't there to answer the phone, Craddock was liable to do anything.

It was just eight o'clock. An hour to wait, assuming Craddock phoned on time. Moodrow dialed Leonora Higgins' number, waiting impatiently for her to pick up, then explaining what he'd gotten and how he'd gotten it.

"I'm going with you," she announced when he finished.

"No way."

"I'm a lawyer, Stanley, and you may need a lawyer before you're finished. Besides, it could be necessary to bring in the local cops. An assistant district attorney is a long way up from a retired cop and a young detective. The locals are more likely to cooperate with me than with you."

"You can't represent me," Moodrow countered. "An ADA isn't allowed to practice law outside the district attorney's office."

"Then I'll be an ex-ADA. Stanley, I'm coming with you."

"All right, Leonora. The truth is we can use your help. But remember, you invited yourself."

After hanging up, Moodrow went to his bedroom closet and retrieved a small, stuffed suitcase. It was filled with maps, maps of every county surrounding the five boroughs of New York. Moodrow, after spending the better part of six hours running in dispatcher-directed circles, had bought them directly from Hagstrom, a company specializing in detailed street maps. He tossed the suitcase on the kitchen table, rummaging through the maps until he found the one he needed. "You want coffee, Jim?" he asked, already filling the pot.

THIRTY-FOUR

By ten-thirty, Betty's arm felt like it was about to fall off. She'd been working steadily for more than an hour, but the hole in the sheetrock was minuscule. With the bureau pulled away from the wall (but not so far away that she wouldn't be able to get it back if someone came down the hall), she had almost no leverage, no room in which to work. Originally, she'd planned to punch through the sheetrock, then lever her improvised weapon back and forth like a screwdriver, but the metal was far too soft. She would have to pick at the wall like a woodpecker chipping at a tree. And the handle she'd constructed so carefully was beginning to loosen. If her ice pick fell apart, if the metal snapped or the handle split, she would have nothing.

"Damn," she whispered, peering into the small hole, "I can't see anything back here."

"I'll get the light," Mikey offered.

"No, you stay where you are." She pushed herself to her feet, retrieved the lamp and plugged it into an outlet alongside the bureau. The hole in the sheetrock was so small that she had trouble seeing, even with the extra light. Still, the dull red color of the outer wall was clear enough. The house was made of brick.

She stood up and pushed the bureau against the wall, determined not to show her disappointment. "Let's take a rest, Mikey."

The boy, his ear glued to the door, nodded gravely, then joined her on the bed. "Is it working?" he asked.

"It's slow, very slow. And I'm afraid I'm going to break the tool."

"If it breaks, we won't have anything."

"That's just what I was thinking. That's why I have to be very careful."

"Because it's a knife, too. Right?"

Betty smiled, giving Michael a little shove. "How come you're so smart?" She looked at his serious face and sighed. "Yes," she said, "it *is* a weapon. More like an ice pick than a knife. But it's a tool first and a weapon only if there's no other way for us to get out."

The boy took a moment to absorb the information. "Do you think my daddy's gonna hurt us?" he asked.

"He might, Mikey. I think he might."

"*I* think he *will*." He moved closer to Betty. "Why does he want to hurt me? I'm his child. He's supposed to care about me."

"It's hard to explain that."

"Try," the boy insisted.

"You know, you're a pretty tough guy."

"Please *try*," he repeated.

"Mikey, have you ever hurt anyone?"

"I once hurt Brian. I got mad at him and I hit him with a baseball."

"How did you feel about it?"

"I said I was sorry, but he didn't talk to me for three whole days."

"Were you really sorry?"

"Of course."

"All right, Mikey. The simplest way to understand your father is that, when he hurts someone, he *isn't* sorry. He's not like ordinary people. If he wants something, he takes it. It doesn't matter who gets hurt. He just doesn't care. It's a kind of sickness."

They sat in silence for a few minutes while Michael tried to put it all together. He had no illusions about the purpose of Betty's ice pick. It was going to be used on his father. As a child, however, he'd never been asked to approve decisions made by an adult. Betty, if she had to, would stab Davis Craddock. But only if he, Michael, said it was okay.

"Maybe we could make another tool. A real tool. For digging," the boy said quietly.

Michael's reluctance to deal with his father came as no surprise. It would take time before the boy would be ready to accept what they might have to do. But Michael was clearly aware of the stakes. He wasn't running away from his father's savagery.

"Okay, Mikey," Betty said, "let's see if we can find a way out of here. We need something that we can use to dig through the wall. Something we don't care about breaking." Something, she didn't add, strong enough to scrape away the mortar that held the bricks together.

"Should we look in the bed again?"

"Yeah. You get the lamp and I'll pull the bed away from the wall."

The boy, his relief at not having to make a decision evident, ran over to the bureau, ran back to Betty with the lamp, then ran to the door and put his ear against the wood. Betty, smiling, bent to her work.

The interior of the box spring was a maze of metal, wood and twine. Betty stared at it, trying to make sense of what she was seeing, and after several minutes the simple construction began to come clear. The outer springs were attached to a metal rail with clips. The rail was attached to the wooden frame with nails. The nails had been driven into the frame alongside the rail, then bent over the rail and driven into the wood on the other side. The rail appeared to be a single piece of metal. It was thick, but she suspected that it was hollow inside, a tube. In any event, the nails, only a few inches apart, had been driven in tightly. If she had a screwdriver, she'd probably be able to dig the nails out, but she didn't have a screwdriver. She had a nail file.

The bed springs were more promising. They were probably designed to move a little bit. That's why they were tied down with twine instead of being nailed to the frame. If she cut through the twine, she might be able to twist one of the springs back and forth until the clips worked loose. The springs, if straightened, would be eight or nine inches long. Betty, propped on one arm, began to saw at the twine with the nail file.

"Someone's coming."

Michael's stage whisper had Betty jumping despite her aching back. She switched off the lamp, shoved it under the bed, then pushed the bed against the wall. She was barely erect when the door opened and Blossom Nol, apparently alone, walked quietly into the room.

"You must leave now," she announced. "Quickly."

"Leave to go where?" Betty, despite her efforts to subvert Blossom Nol, was instantly suspicious.

"I'll show you how to get out, but we must do it before Davis misses me. We only have a few minutes."

Betty glanced at Michael. Like her, he seemed confused. "Why are you doing this?" she asked.

"If you stay, he'll kill you."

Betty willed herself to be calm, to sort out her thoughts. The message was simple, but the girl had delivered it with her eyes fixed to the floor. On one level, Blossom seemed little more than a robot. A robot controlled by Davis Craddock. What if she'd gone back to Craddock and told him what Betty was trying to do? What if Craddock was simply enjoying a little joke, a moment of high drama before he did what he was going to do anyway? On the other hand, Craddock had no reason to kill them before he'd finished his project. Betty's kidnapping had taken place two days ago. If forty-eight hours had been enough, Craddock would never have gone to the trouble of snatching her. Still, the man was utterly unpredictable.

"Michael, look in the hallway. Very carefully. See if anyone's out there."

Michael stuck his head out the door. "I don't see anybody," he announced.

"All right, Blossom. Tell us what you want us to do." Betty's voice was unyielding.

"You must come quickly."

"We're not going anywhere until you tell us what your plan is." Betty took Michael's hand and pulled him close to her.

"The next room," Blossom explained. "It's empty. You can go out the window."

"We're on the second floor, Blossom. If I twist my ankle jumping, we're both dead."

"There's a porch attached to the back of the house. You can crawl along the porch roof and jump down behind a tree where it's dark. But you must come now. I can't stay here. Davis will find out what I'm doing."

"Are you coming with us?"

"I can't."

"Why, Blossom? Davis is going to blame you anyway."

Blossom backed into the doorway. "You must decide now. I can't wait any longer. I won't come back again."

The room Blossom had chosen, a bedroom, was deserted. Betty slid the window up and looked outside. The porch roof, only a few feet below the window sill, sloped to within six feet of the ground. A tall fir standing alongside the roof cast a deep shadow. The scene was exactly as Blossom had described it.

"Are you ready for this, Mikey?" Betty asked.

"Yes," he replied without hesitation.

"Then let's go." Betty unconsciously touched the improvised weapon thrust into her belt before stepping through the window and onto the porch roof. Michael followed and they crawled to the edge together. The ground seemed more like six miles than six feet below. Betty, not wanting to think about it now that she'd made an irrevocable decision, tried to lower herself down, but her hands slipped and she fell heavily.

"Are you okay?" Michael whispered.

"Yeah. Fortunately I've got a big butt and I managed to land on it."

Michael hung his legs over the edge and Betty was able to help lower him to the ground. "I'm glad I didn't fall," he said seriously. "My butt is very tiny."

For the moment, they were safe. The tree they stood under cast a deep shadow, but the twenty feet of lawn they had to cross was brightly lit.

"Mikey, see those trees over there?" She pointed to a stand of birch, eight or nine trees clustered together. "That's where we're going to go. We can't hesitate or stop no matter what happens. Do you understand that?"

"Yes."

"I'm going to carry you, okay? We'll move a lot faster that way. Once we're safe in the trees, I'll put you down."

He answered by climbing into her arms. His small body was shaking with fear, and Betty, her hatred for Davis Craddock rising into her throat, took off at a dead run. For a moment, she thought she was safe, but then she heard the sound of breaking glass, the rapid-fire pop of a semi-automatic weapon, the sharp whine of bullets passing close to her body, the slap of those bullets cutting into the trees surrounding the house.

A setup. Blossom had set them up. Without asking why, Betty continued to run until she felt the sharp tear of the briars at the edge of the woods. She ignored the pain, pushing through until they were lost in the darkness of the 2,000-acre Mashomack Nature Preserve.

Moodrow, Tilley and Higgins left Moodrow's apartment right after Betty's phone call. They drove fast enough to attract the attention of three state police cruisers, but, in each case, Tilley flashed his badge, announcing, "We've got a witness to a homicide. A *reluctant* witness. The bastard's liable to take off any minute." Leonora Higgins' identification removed any doubt the troopers might have had and they were allowed to continue. Tilley was driving Moodrow's big Mercury. He had no trouble maintaining a steady 75 mph, weaving through the traffic all the way to Riverhead, where the Long Island Expressway ended. Then they were forced onto Route 25, a narrow, two-lane road that passed through every resort town between Riverhead and Green-port. Still, by eleven-fifteen, they were lined up for the Shelter Island Ferry.

They discussed the purpose of their trip as they drove, Higgins and Tilley arguing that it should be reconnaissance only. The temptation, once they were sure they'd found Craddock, was to rush in, to get it over with. A temptation that could have deadly consequences.

"What I'd like to do is get my hands on Davis Craddock," Moodrow announced. He could see the ferry moving slowly through the fog. Fog was more common than moonlight on the eastern end of Long Island, a hundred miles out into the Atlantic Ocean.

"We know that, Stanley," Leonora replied evenly. "You've said it ten times already." She was beginning to doubt Moodrow's stability. If nothing came of the first day's surveillance, he would have to get back to Manhattan before the next phone call. She wasn't sure he'd be able to leave.

"I know what I said, Leonora. But I've been thinking about Crad-dock's setup. Assuming that somebody has to go for supplies, food or whatever, it's probably not gonna be Craddock. Maybe we should grab the first person to come out of there."

"What for?" Tilley asked. "What do we hope to gain by revealing ourselves?"

"If Craddock sends one of his workers on an errand and the worker doesn't come back, why would he blame it on me? Maybe the worker just decided to take off. Maybe he got sick of Craddock's lunacy."

"I still don't see what we have to gain."

"C'mon, Jim. It's obvious. Even if we find Craddock's lab, how do we know Betty's in there? Or how many sentries he's got posted? Or where they're posted? Craddock thinks I'm at home, pissing my pants. That's to our advantage. But if we're gonna get inside—if we *have* to get inside—we've gotta have more information."

"That's all very fine, Stanley," Leonora said. "But what will you do after you get the information? Let him—or her—go? Drag him around with you? There's no reason to presume the individual you grab has committed a crime. That makes what you want to do a kidnapping."

"There's a third alternative," Moodrow said quietly.

"I'm not going to let you do that," Leonora replied quickly. "That's why I came. To prevent you from destroying yourself."

"Let me ask you something, Leonora. How long will it take Crad-dock to figure out that Wendell Bogard's missing? And what's he gonna do when he does figure it out? Because I'm tellin' you right now that I'm gonna do what I have to do and I don't give a damn for the consequences. You invited yourself along, but if you wanna back out, I'll understand."

They came off the ferry and took an immediate left, following Route 114 which was little more than a country road. The widely interspersed houses were further isolated by the heavy fog. Many of them were shuttered, summer homes that would be in operation after Memorial Day when the season opened.

Route 114 was unlit, and even with the brights on, they had trouble reading the street signs. Nevertheless, they made progress, driving from one intersection to another, ignoring the horns of weekend visitors trying to make the midnight ferry on the southern end of the island. The road took a sudden sharp turn and Moodrow picked out the name of a street running off at an angle: Ram Island Road.

"We're gonna come to another right turn about a mile from here," he announced. "Bucks Creek Road should be right there." But the only road they found was Cartwright Road which ran back to the northeast. "Maybe the map's off a little bit. Keep going."

They drove another half mile, until their lights illuminated a large sign announcing the entrance to the Mashomack Nature Preserve.

"Too far," Moodrow announced. "Bucks Creek Road should come before the preserve."

They came back very slowly, looking off into the darkness of the Mashomack Preserve as if the trees were highways. Just before the intersection of 114 and Cartwright, they found a dirt road leading into the dense forest. It was completely unmarked.

"Let me get out a minute," Tilley said, opening the door. He walked to the front of the car, then signaled Moodrow to shut off the head-lights. Two hundred yards down the road, the lights of a house cast a dim glow through the trees and the fog.

Tilley came back to the car. "It looks good, Stanley," he said, closing the door. "The tire tracks on the road are fresh. It's been used con-tinually."

"He couldn't have chosen a better spot," Leonora said. "If that's his lab, he's got the preserve on one side and more woods on the other. A dirt road. It's completely private."

"It's good for us, too," Moodrow said. "We can stake the place out all day and night without being seen. Too bad we didn't bring the camouflage."

"No problem," Tilley said. "Just grab some mud and wipe it over your face and your coat. The coat'll most likely come out cleaner."

Moodrow ignored the jibe. "There's a boarded-up house fifty yards down the road. We'll leave the car behind it. I don't know what kind of cops they got on this island, but if one of them sees a car parked in the middle of nowhere, he's bound to get suspicious."

Ten minutes later, they were marching along the edge of the dirt road. They got to within twenty yards of the house, close enough to see the front door, when they heard the unmistakable sound of rifle fire back in the forest. It was early May. The leaves on the trees had only begun to sprout and the beams of several flashlights were clearly visible through the mist.

"It's out of control," Tilley muttered. "It's out of control."

Moodrow didn't bother to respond. The situation was obvious enough. "Leonora," he said calmly, "go back to the car. Find the local cops and get them out here. In force. Do whatever you have to do, but get them out here." He looked into the dark forest. "Fucking woods. Gotta be Daniel Boone to get in there."

"Stanley," Leonora asked, "what are you going to do?"

"What do you think we're gonna do? We're going inside."

"Stanley . . ."

"Enough, Leonora. Just do what I told you. We don't have a lot of time here. We don't have any time at all."

As they began to cross the lawn, the front door opened and both men dropped into a crouch, expecting anything from 9mm handguns to fully automatic assault rifles, but the tiny, unmistakably female figure that emerged, carried no weapon at all. She looked directly at them for a moment, then took a right turn, crossed the lawn and disappeared into the woods.

"Forget about her," Moodrow whispered.

"Why don't we take her? Why don't we take her and find out who's inside?"

"Because we don't have time for strategy. We don't have time to plan it out. The only thing we've got going for us is surprise. Craddock's got a problem out there in the woods and it doesn't have to be Betty. It might be some of Wendell Bogard's people. Or maybe one of his workers decided to take off with a suitcase full of merchandise. Whatever way it turns out, we're the last thing Davis Craddock expects or needs."

A minute later, they came through the front door into an empty parlor. The two rooms to the left and the right of the parlor, connected by archways, were also empty. The staircase to the second floor rose from the far side of the parlor. It, too, was empty. They listened for a moment, hoping against hope to hear Betty's voice, to find a single clue to what was happening inside the building. Their hopes were answered with silence.

The house would have to be searched room by room. It would obviously go faster if they separated, but neither considered separating. They held their .38s out in front of their bodies, eyes continually sweeping the open area.

"We'll work from the top down." Without waiting for a response, Moodrow began to climb the staircase, silently cursing his 260 pounds as the steps groaned beneath his weight. But there was nothing to be done about it and he continued up until he had a clear view of the long hallway at the top of the stairs. It was empty.

"There are three doors on each side," he whispered. "You take the right side and I'll do the left. Just listen at the door. Maybe we'll get lucky and hear Betty's voice. Or Craddock's. If it's quiet, we'll start at the back and search the rooms."

Both men were sweating profusely by the time they reached the end of the hall. They looked at each other, but didn't speak. Their safest course was to crash through the doors like narcs on a raid, to make use of their own adrenaline and the element of surprise, but they couldn't afford to make any noise. Tilley stood to the right of the first door and Moodrow to the left.

Carefully, very carefully, Moodrow twisted the knob, pushed the door open, then stepped through the doorway to find Davis Craddock, his back turned to them, stuffing plastic bags filled with brightly colored capsules into a large duffel bag.

"You motherfucker."

The words came unbidden, but they had the desired effect. Craddock froze for a moment, then slowly turned to face Moodrow and Tilley. His eyes, no longer blank, were filled with hate.

"Where's Betty?"

"Dead, I hope."

Moodrow put his .38 back in its holster. "I think you oughta know that I ran into your business partner back at the commune." He spun Craddock around, then slammed him against the wall, frisking him quickly and thoroughly. He was so angry, he could barely control himself. "I killed him. Shot him dead. Now it's your turn. If you don't produce Betty Haluka in the next ten seconds . . ."

"Fuck you. And fuck that fat bitch, too."

"Don't lose it, Stanley." Tilley's voice was actually pleading.

"Don't lose it, Stanley," Craddock mimicked. "Try to control yourself, Stanley. You know what I did before you got here, Stanley? You know what I did ten minutes before you got here? I tied your fat bitch to the bed and fucked her in the ass. She loved it."

Moodrow's open palm cracked against the side of Craddock's face. "You wanna fight back, Davis? I hope you wanna fight back."

Craddock raised his hands to protect his face, but made no effort to defend himself. Looking up at Moodrow was like staring at an avalanche rushing down the side of a mountain. With the other cop standing in the doorway and his guards out in the woods chasing Betty Haluka, he knew he was finished. His best move was to surrender, to cooperate and try to call off his men before they killed Betty, but somehow he couldn't bring himself to follow his own good advice. Life had to have its little consolations or it wasn't worth living. For instance, wouldn't it be pleasant if he held Moodrow's attention until *after* his boys killed Betty? And wouldn't it be even more pleasant if he took care of Moodrow at the same time? The blue syringe, filled with a deadly poison that had once been the ultimate narcotic, lay behind the lamp on the nightstand. He'd prepared it for little Blossom, because only Blossom could have opened that door, but Blossom had disappeared and Moodrow was right in front of him.

"I have to thank you for one thing, Stanley, even though you've caused me a lot of trouble. Betty's ass was sweet and open, so I figure you put some time into loosening it up for me. Thanks, Stanley."

The fist that crashed into his chest sent him sprawling backward. Unfortunately, it took him away from the nightstand and into the wall. The impact took his breath away and he had to force himself back onto his feet.

"Where's Betty?"

Craddock took three steps to his right. He stopped when he stood directly between Moodrow and the nightstand. "I don't know why you're so angry, Stanley. Look at what you've accomplished. First, you've taken care of me, which means that you'll collect the bounty you spoke about in my office. Second, you're going to be rid of that fat, ugly bitch you call a girlfriend. I tell you, Stanley, even on her knees facing away from me, she was so ugly I could barely look at her. In fact, if she hadn't been so eager, I doubt whether I could have maintained my erection long enough to . . ."

This time Moodrow's fist sent him directly into the nightstand which obligingly turned over. The lamp went flying, but the small syringe ended up beneath his body. He palmed it carefully, his thumb on the plunger, then slowly stood up. When he turned around, Moodrow was standing a few feet away, his balled fists at his sides, his face a mask of boiling anger.

"Stanley," Craddock said, "if you could see what your emotions are doing to your face, you'd be horrified. What you need to do is calm down." He jumped at Moodrow without warning, the tip of the syringe flashing in the light before it sunk into the left side of Moodrow's neck. The last thing Moodrow saw, before his legs deserted him and he lost consciousness, was Jim Tilley firing shot after shot into Craddock's body.

The phrase "nature preserve" may evoke images of Bambi and Thumper at play in a verdant meadow, but the Mashomack Preserve, covering a third of Shelter Island, is a typical lowland eastern forest. The water table, only a few feet below the surface, keeps much of it swampy even in summer. Hardwoods predominate: maple, cherry, white and scarlet oak, beech, hickory and chestnut. Decaying leaves beneath the trees provide the fertilizer for a thick ground cover. Northern bayberry, highland blueberry, huckleberry, blackberry, sweet pepperbush, catbriar and a dozen other species offer superb cover to the small animals and birds living in the preserve. It's a wonderful place for a chipmunk.

For human beings in headlong, panicked flight, on the other hand, the lush undergrowth, especially the aptly named catbriar with its long green stems and sharp thorns, is far closer to the visions of Stephen King than Walt Disney. Even protected by PURE's anesthetic properties, Betty had to fight back an urge to cry out in pain. Nevertheless, pushed along by a fear that cut through every consideration, she stumbled over the fallen branches, Michael Alamare clutched to her chest, until her breath deserted her.

"I have to put you down for a minute," she whispered. "And we have to be quiet. Only talk if it's very important." She looked back for signs of pursuit, noting, without surprise, the flashlight beams cutting back and forth through the fog. Well, if the deep, dark forest was a torment, it was also cover. If they could escape the first efforts of their pursuers, even if they didn't find another house, they could hide until daylight.

"Mikey, we have to get moving again. But I can't carry you anymore."

"It's okay, Betty. I can run."

"I know, Mikey, but there's lots of briars and if we get separated, we'll never find each other. I want you to keep your face against my back and hold onto my belt. Hold tight. Do you understand?"

"Yes."

They began to move, more slowly this time. Craddock's men (if not Craddock, himself) weren't more than fifty yards behind them. The briars tore at her bare legs, but she refused to acknowledge the pain, thanking God, instead, for the flat shoes she'd worn to her meeting with Craddock. If she was wearing heels, they wouldn't have gotten this far.

She kept her hands in front of her face, trying to feel the branches hidden by the darkness and fog. The pursuit was noisy. If it didn't seem to be getting closer, it wasn't moving away either. Michael was crying softly. Despite the protection of her back, he was being whipped by the branches.

They were in a thicket of swamp azalea and sumac. The interlaced branches, stiff and woody, pushed back against them, tearing Betty's arms until they bled freely, until she had to cover her eyes and push blindly forward, until she stepped off the edge of a slope and crashed down into a small pond.

The water, though it only rose to her knees, was incredibly cold. Her first thought was for Michael. She reached down for his small body and took him into her arms. Then images of snakes and snapping turtles, salamanders and toads began to crowd her mind.

"They're shooting at us," Michael said.

"What?" She could almost feel the slimy bodies crawling over her legs.

"Shooting, Betty. They're shooting."

Michael's panic jerked her back to reality. Now she could hear the shots. And the bullets cutting through the brush. They'd crashed down the bank and into the water, giving away their small advantage. The steep banks of the pond were protecting them for the moment, but they had to get moving.

"You see the other side of the pond, Mikey?" It was no more than forty feet away.

"I can swim," the boy announced. "I'm a good swimmer."

Betty had planned to work her way around the edge of the pond—she wanted to put the water between them and their pursuers—but cutting across would be much faster.

"Are you sure you can do it?" she asked.

"We've got to hurry. I can hear them coming."

Betty, with Michael still in her arms, began to wade through the water, losing her shoes to the sucking mud in the first steps. She continued to move forward, the water never rising above her waist, until she got to the far side of the pond. Then, as she started to climb the bank, fallen branches and small rocks began to cut into the soles of her feet. The pain was enormous and, for the first time, despair threatened to overwhelm her.

How far could she go like this? With her feet ripped and bloody, her eyes threatened by invisible branches? She could hear their pursuers crashing through the undergrowth. With no need for silence, they could move quickly. Their flashlights, despite the fog, would reveal the easiest way around the dense thickets. She imagined them in lug-soled hiking boots and thick coats. The terrain meant less than nothing to them. Protected by their clothing and the drug they took four times a day, they would advance like robots until their task was completed.

Without speaking, she began to move forward into the brush, trying to feel the earth before she put her feet down. There was no way she could outdistance her pursuers, not without shoes. She was looking for a place to hide when she stumbled out of the woods and onto one of several trails running through the preserve. With no sign of life in either direction, she turned to the left and began to run.

They were moving easily, ignoring the occasional stones and tree roots, when Betty heard shooting behind her and turned to look. The shots had come from the house, not her pursuers. She watched the glow of the flashlights separate into two distinct clusters, one moving away from her, back toward the house. It was their first break and Betty, suddenly hopeful, told Michael to grab hold and began to run again.

She ran for almost a quarter mile, until the trail forked, then turned right. Craddock's men would have to separate again. They were also on the trail, moving quickly, slicing through the brush with their flashlights.

"Betty, I can't run anymore."

"I know, Mikey. I lost my shoes and I can't run either. But we have to go a little further. Then we'll find a place to hide. I promise." She heard voices behind her and turned to see the flashlights separate again. Now they were being hunted by a single man. She touched the weapon in her belt, almost surprised to find it still there. One man could be handled, she decided. If she eliminated this single hunter, the forest would shelter them until daylight. Or until the police came to investigate the gunshots.

She moved more slowly, now, looking left and right until she came to a small opening in the brush. Another small pond, its dark waters barely visible.

"All right, Mikey, we're not going to run anymore. We can't. I'm going to ask you to do something, but if you can't do it or if you're afraid, I want you to tell me. I want you to *promise* to tell me."

"I promise."

"Do you see that log in the water? I want you to get behind it. There's only one man coming after us now. When you see his flashlight get here, where we're standing, I want you to splash the water as loud as you can. Keep down behind the log, but make enough noise to attract his attention."

"What are you gonna do?"

"I'm going to be right here, behind this tree. When he walks past me to see who's making the noise, I'll . . ."

She didn't have to finish. Michael Alamare, five years old, took a deep breath, then slid down the bank into the water. Betty stepped back until she was up against the bark of the tree, watching the light come closer and closer. She had an advantage now. Her pursuer's eyes, accustomed to the flashlight beam, would not penetrate the darkness and the beam itself would give away his exact position. She waited until he was almost upon her before sliding behind the tree.

The slap of Michael's palm on the surface of the water seemed to crash through the forest, as violent and unexpected as a rifle shot. The flashlight beam swung sharply to the left, passing Betty as the man holding it made his way to the pond's bank. Betty, a smile on her lips, circled behind him as he fired blindly into the water, the weapon she'd worked so hard to create clutched in her right hand. His sharp, quick breathing was clearly audible, despite the gunshots. A single word, a hiss between clenched teeth, echoed in her ears: "Eve, Eve, Eve, Eve, Eve." She never once considered the life pulsing through his veins or his youth or what Davis Craddock had done to him, as she raised her arm above her head and drove the ice pick through the side of his skull.

THIRTY-FIVE

Moodrow drifted for the next two days. Downward, into the cold waters of a dark lake, then up again toward a pale circle of moonlight on the surface. He didn't know how he'd gotten into the lake or why he didn't drown, yet he wasn't afraid. Later on, he would describe his condition as "peaceful," but, while he drifted, he felt no desire to name his state. His mind was wholly occupied with a decision he knew he had to make. Should he struggle toward the pale light above him? Or allow himself to float gently downward into the dark waters at the bottom of the lake? He had no one to help him decide, no guardian angel or long-dead relative. His problem was that it didn't seem to matter. Up or down, it was all the same.

Later on, the doctors would claim that he'd never been in danger. They'd describe the efforts they'd made to drag him back to consciousness—the heart monitor, the plastic breathing tube, the dripping IV, the medications, the morphine. Moodrow knew better. If he'd decided to let himself drift down, he would have died. The bottom of the lake didn't frighten him. It beckoned, coyly sexual, promising an infinitely peaceful embrace.

He thought of Betty and Jim and the child he'd never seen, Michael Alamare. They seemed to be drifting, too, but not in his lake. Not anywhere he could name. He was entirely alone in the water and perfectly content. The others were where they had to be.

Still, he had to make a decision, because he knew he couldn't drift forever. He didn't know why he couldn't, but he accepted the reality of choice, just as he didn't question where he was or how he'd gotten there. What he needed was a reason. Either to rise or sink. The pull of human emotion—love, friendship, loyalty—seemed irrelevant. Or, at least, he didn't feel them. But there was one little item that scratched at his peace. He was curious. He wanted to know how it came out.

Perhaps his curiosity came from a lifetime of seeing things through to the end. Cases resolved themselves, eventually, even if resolution meant nothing more than shoving pieces of paper in a folder marked INACTIVE. Moodrow, though he could barely remember to take his keys when he left his apartment, could recite the history of his career like a schoolboy reciting Robert Frost. "Whose woods are these . . ."

Everything was up in the air. Betty, Michael, Craddock, PURE. Even Tilley and Leonora were in trouble. Cops and ADAs, unlike civilians, cannot decide whether or not to report a crime. They're not supposed to play the part of the vigilante.

He tried to put it together, examining small chunks of memory, but too many pieces were missing. He was certain the gunshots in the forest had been aimed at Betty and the child. And that Davis Craddock's career was over. But that's where the facts ended and the questions began. Did Betty find a place to hide? Did Leonora manage to get the local cops involved? How many guards did Jim Tilley have to confront? Was the lab in the house? How much of the drug had already been distributed?

He began to move up toward the surface of the lake. As the pale circle of moonlight became brighter, he realized that the surface waters were not at all calm. Swept by a dozen currents, they boiled with energy. The closer he got to the surface, the more he regretted his decision, but he couldn't seem to slow his progress. In the end, he was rocketing toward the surface and he awoke in pain.

"He opened his eyes. He opened his eyes."

The words chopped at the pain in his skull, exciting nerves in his neck and shoulder which were already on fire. Then there were more voices and a man in a gown leaning over him, giving orders, and a nurse in a bright uniform with a syringe in her hand.

"Morphine," the nurse announced cheerfully. "You'll feel better in a few minutes."

She was right. The morphine didn't put out the fire, just made it bearable enough so he could concentrate on the voices and faces in the room. Betty leaned over him, smiling and crying at the same time. Without warning, all the emotions that had seemed irrelevant came flooding back. He tried to speak, but his mouth was so dry he could barely open it. He motioned for water, and Betty filled a plastic cup, then held it to his lips.

"I should have taken a drink while I was in the lake," he announced.

"What did you say, Stanley?"

Moodrow tried to think of an answer, but couldn't. "What happened to your arms?" he asked.

"Maybe you should rest for now," she answered.

"I have to find out what happened first. I remember Craddock stabbing me with something. It must have been the poison that crippled Flo Alamare. Why am I still alive?"

Jim Tilley's face swam into view. "He hit you so hard the needle broke off. The doctor says that only a fraction of a drop got into your system."

"And Craddock?"

"The bastard's alive, Stanley. He took four rounds in his chest. Tore up his lungs and took out a piece of his spine, but he's alive. They've got him on a respirator."

"And the lab?"

"The lab is the least of it. Craddock was writing an autobiography. Everything he's ever done. *Bragging* about it. We found a video tape of some girl named Marcy Evans poisoning Deeny Washington. The other lab, the one in Queens, Toxilab Incorporated, says that PURE becomes a nerve poison when it's heated. That's what happened to Flo Alamare. Craddock'll never get out of prison, Stanley. Never. And he's never gonna walk again, either."

"What about you, Jim? The job come down on you yet?" Moodrow, as his curiosity grew, became more and more alert. The lake began to recede like a dream after awakening. "Roll up the bed a little."

Leonora's face came into view. "We're heroes, Stanley. For the moment, anyway. The case has been headlines for the last two days. They're calling him 'The Dope Guru.' We even made the national news. Imagine Dan Rather holding a vial of PURE up to the camera, making solemn pronouncements. There were several *million* doses in that house. What's the phrase? 'Captured the American imagination'?"

"I spent an afternoon with the captain," Jim added. "It looks like I'll get a month off without pay. Eventually."

Moodrow took a moment to gather himself. He wanted to rest, but the remaining questions forced his eyes open. "What happened to your arms, Betty?"

Betty's arms were bandaged from the elbow to the tips of her fingers. She held them up like a Masai warrior displaying the head of a slain lion. Then she went over it, from her first glimpse of Davis Craddock to the arrival of the police, reciting the facts slowly and completely. Knowing Moodrow would not be satisfied with anything less. "It turned out," she finished, "that little Blossom was the smartest one of all. She set us up and when the guards left the house to find us, she went out the front door. No one's seen her since."

The neurologist in charge of Moodrow's case arrived a moment later. He shooed the visitors away, then drew the curtain around Moodrow's bed.

"Welcome back to the world, Mister Moodrow. I'm Doctor Murillo." Without waiting for a response, he shined a light into Moodrow's eyes, a light bright enough to cut through the morphine. Moodrow groaned and the doctor snapped the light off. "The nerves in your head and neck are inflamed. My best guess is that it's temporary and you'll recover completely."

"Your best guess?"

The doctor smiled. "You were poisoned by a previously unknown neurotoxin. Another two or three drops and you would have been dead before you hit the ground. We don't know how the compound works, so we can't offer a guaranteed prognosis. But don't worry. You're a celebrity and we don't let anything happen to celebrities. Not when the reporters are camped out in front of the hospital."

Moodrow groaned again. Another PI would have seen the media attention as a chance to attract business. "Is there a back door to this hospital?"

"There is, but you won't be going through it for a week or so." He gave Moodrow a second to absorb the information. "I want you to take it easy with the morphine. We can't be sure how fast the pain recedes, if you take too much morphine."

"Why morphine?" Moodrow asked. "You run out of PURE?"

"A joke. That's good. And it's not as far off as you think. I got a call from a local pharmaceutical house this morning. Asking for a sample. Funny, right? Davis Craddock, the Louis Pasteur of analgesia?" He pulled back the curtain and stepped away from the bed. "Don't let him get up," he said to Betty. "In a couple of days, we'll take him down to physical therapy and check his balance, but, for now, he needs rest. A few more minutes and out you go."

They ignored his patronizing tone, staring at his back until it disappeared down the corridor before turning to Moodrow. "The cops showed up right after we found Craddock," Tilley said. "You would have been amazed, Stanley. The locals moved through those woods like Indians. Tourists keep getting lost in the preserve and, naturally, the cops have to find them. They actually *drill* in the woods. It took them less than an hour to capture Craddock's soldiers. The soldiers, by the way, didn't offer any resistance. It seems they don't mind hunting an unarmed (they *think* unarmed) woman and a child, but they don't care to be shot at. Meanwhile, Craddock's lab workers grabbed as much PURE as they could carry and ran out the back door, only they couldn't get off the island, because the last ferry left at midnight. Don't forget, it's off-season, plus they were dressed in white uniforms. Except for two who OD'd in the woods, they were picked up trying to get on the first ferry out."

"What about Blossom?" Moodrow asked. He was tired now, ready to sleep, but he wanted to hear the rest of it before he closed his eyes. "How did she get away?"

"Blossom stole a boat and rowed across the bay," Leonora said. "At least, that's the most likely scenario. Some of the homes on the water have slips for small boats and one was reported stolen. It turned up on a beach in Greenport."

"Did she take any of the drug with her?"

"That's a good question, Stanley. Here's a better one—did she take the *formula* with her? Maybe Craddock had it written out somewhere. Hell, for all we know, Craddock could have a hundred pounds already distributed."

Moodrow turned to Betty. "What about the boy? Where is he?"

"Mikey's at the Craig Institute on East Seventy-fifth Street. He was so brave. Standing there in the lobby, already sick, telling me about drugs and how bad they are. The doctors say detoxification will be the easiest part, because after he's clean, he won't have access. Dealing with the truth about his mother and father, not to mention Hanover House and the garbage they taught him, is another problem."

"You forgot about Grandma Connie," Moodrow said. "How's he gonna deal with Grandma Connie?"

"I had a long talk with Connie. I told her there was no way I was going to let her beat Mikey down. If she tried to push me out, I'd move to have the boy taken away from her. I thought she'd be angry, but she wasn't. She wants to make up for her daughter. She actually asked me to stay close to Mikey, to help her and him. Connie Alamare's going to be in our lives for a long time."

"What did you say?"

"C'mon, Stanley. It won't be that bad. Remember, you won't be working for her. You can stay as far away as you want."

"*Connie Alamare* is gonna be in our lives for a long time?"

"Yes, Stanley," Betty said firmly. "She's going to be in our lives. I'm not going to desert that boy."

Moodrow's eyes swept the room, searching for Leonora Higgins. He motioned her to come close, to bend over the bed until her ear was close to his lips.

"What?" she asked. "I didn't get that."

"I said, 'I should've died when I had the chance.'"